HER ALMOST PERFECT HUSBAND

Mary Rensten

SCRIPTORA

Published in Great Britain 2021 by
SCRIPTORA
25 Summerhill Road
London N15 4HF
in association with SWWJ
(Society of Women Writers & Journalists)

www.swwj.co.uk

Reprinted 2022

This is a work of fiction. Any resemblance between the fictional characters and actual persons, living or dead, is coincidental.

ISBN: 978-0-9500591-5-0

Printed and bound by Witley Press Hunstanton PE36 6AD
www. witleypress.co.uk

For my lovely and loving family

My thanks to them, and to my Book Group and SWWJ friends, especially Martin, for their helpful comments and encouragement. Thank you also to Jasmine for her patience and Ben, Michael and Chris for their technical help.

Cover design: Jasmine Lapper-Goodrum

Mary Rensten is a novelist, playwright and award-winning journalist. She is a Vice-President and Fellow of SWWJ (Society of Women Writers & Journalists) and a member of the Writers Guild of Great Britain.

Born in Leicestershire, she spent her childhood in Jamaica, returning to England in 1946 to audition for a place at RADA. After drama school she trained as a teacher and wrote plays for her pupils. In the 1970s, having settled in Hertfordshire with her husband Ivor, and brought up their three children, she combined teaching with free-lance journalism. Drama came to the fore again in the 1980s with acclaimed productions of her plays for adults in London's fringe theatres and at the Edinburgh Festival. Her first novel, *Letters from Malta*, published by Corazon Books in 2015, became an international bestseller.

Inspired by the wonderful Diana Athill, who was still being published in her nineties, Mary is now writing her fourth novel, *Still Waters,* a crime story set on a Scottish loch.

www.swwj.co.uk @MaryRensten

ALSO BY MARY RENSTEN

Novels

Letters from Malta

A Handful of Straw

Plays

The Skip

Knowing Constance Spry

Village Day

The Popping of The Grand Balloon

The Eagle of The Ninth (adapted from Rosemary Sutcliffe's book)

My Very First Antique

On A Par

A Common Woman

The Yellow Wallpaper(adapted from Charlotte Perkins Gilman's book)

No Fixed Abode

Mrs. Pepys

Dear Mr. Kennedy

No Problem

Away on Business

The Devil Is A Cat

Non-fiction

Hertfordshire Brasses

CHAPTER ONE

Bernie Silver's mother was a lovely woman. She would have been happy to have Emma as a daughter-in-law, but Emma had married Andrew Raven, Bernie's best friend; clever, ambitious Andrew. It wasn't that Bernie didn't love her; he did. 'It wouldn't be right, though,' her sister Constance had said. Constance was seven years older than Emma; she knew what was right and what was not, and marrying someone brought up in another faith was *not* a good idea.

Emma had been married now to Andrew for twenty-six years; their son, Jacob, was twenty-one. On the whole, she was content. Never ecstatic, never miserable, just … 'I'm beige,' she'd said to Constance one day when she came to lunch. 'Good,' her sister had replied, 'beige doesn't clash with anything.' Emma had smiled gently, and turned away to put the finishing touches to the salad – lettuce, tomato, cucumber, spring onions. Emma had considered adding olives and herbs and chunks of feta cheese, but she knew Constance would be pointedly careful not to put them on *her* plate.

Bernie's mother, in her apricot kitchen in Chigwell, made superb salads, bursting with all manner of exotic ingredients. Emma and Andrew often ate at her house; Emma came home to Pengate her mind filled with exciting culinary ideas. 'Be bold,' Rose Silver had said on one occasion, 'put in anything you like; make it colourful and fun! You should have fun with food.'

Now Bernie's mother was dead, and there would be no more of those lovely, daring meals. Rose Silver had died on a January Tuesday, and she was being buried the next day. Emma and Andrew were going to the funeral.

It was Emma's first Jewish funeral. Although she had been warned – 'You won't be able to sit with Andrew, you know,' Constance told her. 'It's not done for men and women to sit together on these occasions' – Emma was shocked at the bleakness of the ceremony, the sparseness, the lack of colour, of beauty, of … yes, love, it seemed to her. It was a ritual, performed by only the men, which must somehow be 'got through'. It could have been anybody in that coffin, under that unadorned black pall. Anybody, not a vibrant, beautiful, loving woman. The ceremony over – it was all in Hebrew, which, as far as she knew, no one in Bernie's family spoke – everyone trooped out, following the coffin on a trolley, to the graveyard beyond the chapel, and Rose's body was placed in the ground, in a cemetery where not a single flower relieved the ubiquitous greys of the headstones. 'It's their way,' Constance said. 'It goes back to the desert. Flowers wouldn't survive a day, if you could get them, so for goodness sake don't take any!' 'I know,' Emma had said, thinking she could do with some desert warmth as the chill January wind attacked her ears, 'but

Rose did so love flowers.' 'It's not how it's done, and it's not your place to rock the boat.'

Emma stood, her hand in Andrew's – they were not segregated here – some way back from the chief mourners, and looked across at Bernie. Tears streamed down his cheeks.

'Oh, Andrew, look at him.' She wanted to go to him, put her arms around him.

'He'll be all right. Get through this and I'll take him for a beer.'

'But …?'

'I don't mean now. Come on, we must go to the house.'

The drive to Chigwell, winding up through the bare woodland of Epping Forest, took less than half an hour. Emma wished it was longer; now warm again, she stared out at the stark beauty of the leafless birches, their silvery bark catching the last of the afternoon sun.

Hesitantly she asked, 'What do we do, when we get there?'

'I don't know, I've never been to a Jewish … thing after a funeral.'

'You must have some idea; hasn't Bernie told you?'

'No. Why would he?' He paused. 'We eat, we drink, we talk.'

'Oh, is that it? Just like any sort of …'

'They sit on stools.'

'What?'

'The family.'

'There is no family. No brother, no sister.'

'Cousins, maybe! I don't know. You know what funerals are like, everybody comes, only this is … Jewish families sit on low stools.'

'Why? Why low stools?'

'*I don't know why!* Oh Emma, for goodness sake! They sit on stools, or sometimes they're chairs … and don't ask me why they're low; it probably goes back hundreds of years … and you shake hands and speak to them.'

'Offer condolences, you mean?'

'Yes! And you also say "Long life".'

'See. You do know.'

'Yes, but not from Bernie.'

'Andrew, what's wrong?' Emma reached out her hand, put it gently on Andrew's arm. He shook it off. 'Why are you so grumpy?'

'D'you want me to be laughing?' Flicking his head round he glared at her. His eyes back on the road, he said, gently now, 'We've just buried Bernie's mother. I've known her all my life. Well, best part of.'

'Yes, of course. Sorry.'

They had met, Andrew and Bernie, in 1981, at the start of Andrew's first year at Cambridge. Intent on joining as many of the university societies as he could, Andrew had briefly considered signing up for the opera group. Orchestral music yes, he liked some of that … but opera? Sung in Italian and German. He didn't want to look a fool. He'd think about it; maybe next year when he'd got the hang of this place, this very different sort of life. For now, there were other music societies he could join. Jazz. His dad had liked jazz; it was one of the few good things he remembered about him. Jazz was smart, but not difficult to appreciate. You could listen to jazz, tap your foot, and look as if you understood it; you couldn't, he thought, do that with opera. Then, passing an open window in his college, he heard a voice bellowing a tune he recognised, from a television advertisement; he couldn't make out the words, it didn't sound like English; they weren't, he felt sure, advertising anything. It was just a beautiful melody, even sung in this raucous way, against an orchestral background; without the irritating slogan he found it strangely moving. Noel Coward had said something about the power of cheap music; this wasn't cheap, this was … he didn't know what it was, but it was affecting him, in a very odd sort of way. As he explained to Emma later, it felt significant, important, worthwhile … something he had to make his own. On an impulse Andrew had tracked down the source of the sound, two floors up. The solo singing had stopped, but he could still hear the orchestra, now with a chorus of female voices. Gingerly he knocked on the door. There was no response. The singing started again, tuneful, resonating, powerful, not the rough voice he'd heard before. Something was happening to the hairs on the back of Andrew's neck; he shook the feeling away, banged hard on the knocker of the door. Abruptly the music stopped; the door opened, and a heavily-built young man with curly red hair filled the doorway. Beside him Andrew, dark-haired, tall and spare, looked under-nourished.

'Yes?'

'The music,' Andrew said, as suavely as he could. 'Know the tune, can't think what it is.'

'*Nessun dorma*. Puccini.'

'Ah. Yes. Of course,' Andrew said, none the wiser. 'It's … it's lovely.'

'Lovely? It's magnificent! Stupendous! Everything an aria ought to be!'

'Yes. Quite so.'

The redhead stared at him hard, then shook his head.

'You don't know what I'm talking about, do you?'

Andrew hesitated. He'd been wrong-footed here, no doubt about it. Normally he would bluff it out; he was good at that, and it nearly always worked. This time, for some reason he couldn't fathom, he knew it wouldn't. Besides it was the music that had drawn him here … and he *did* want to know more about it. *Nessun dorma.* He could go to the library, maybe get a record or a tape, but …

'No, I don't.' A slight pause; he had to say more. 'I know I should, but …'

'Why should you? Come on in, listen to the whole thing.'

'The whole thing?'

'The opera, man, the opera! *Turandot*, surely you … No, you don't, do you? Oh, this is glorious; I have a convert! Come in, sit yourself down. Beer? Tea? Whisky? Wine?'

'Er …' What went with opera? 'Wine … if you have a bottle open.'

'Good man. If I haven't I'll open one. Red or white? Best be red, I haven't got a fridge in here.'

Thirty-four years ago, and, now in their early fifties, they were still the closest of friends. And business partners, too.

Emma didn't know what to call the function they were going to – a wake, a reception, a bun fight? No not *that;* heavens, no! – and she didn't want to ask Andrew, he was in such a funny mood. She hoped it wouldn't last long. In all the years she had known Bernie and his mother she had only ever met one other member of the family, Jackie Thomas, Bernie's cousin, and the only reason she and Andrew had met her was because she had married 'out'. 'I'm the black sheep of the family,' she had said when they were introduced. 'I'm welcome in Aunty Rose's house but nowhere else.' Emma was pleased to see that Jackie was here today.

'Emma, it's lovely to see you.'

As they hugged one another, Emma saw over her shoulder the disapproving looks they were getting; with her free hand she smoothed down her russet-brown hair and drew back. Jackie followed her gaze. 'Oh, don't mind them; it's not you they're looking at it, it's me.' Emma smiled weakly. 'You've not heard?'

'No. What?'

'Philip and I have split up; we're divorcing. And I'm ditching his name; going back to Shapiro.'

'Oh no, I'm sorry; I didn't know.'

'Don't be, I'm not. For once my family were right. And now I'm allowed back in,' she added sourly. 'There's no need to look like that, Emma, it was good while it lasted. Well, part of the time. You are so lucky, you know, finding the perfect man.'

'I wouldn't say he's perfect.' Emma laughed gently. 'He's ...'

'He's everything you could want a husband to be. He's kindly, thoughtful, looks after you … and he's still so very good-looking!' Emma smiled. 'Those gorgeous cheek-bones!'

'You sound like my sister; she's forever telling me how fortunate I am to have such a wonderful man.'

'Well, you are. And what's more, you can trust him, which you couldn't say for …'

'Oh, Jackie, was that why you …?'

'Yes, and it had happened more than once. Oh God, yes.' She sighed. 'Maybe it's us, a family thing, you know? Bernie, that didn't last; his parents, my parents. You make the most of your Andrew, he's a gem. I expect he'll miss Rose.'

'Oh, he will. So will I.'

'Look after Bernie, you two, won't you.'

'Of course. We always have. And he's looked after us.' And if it wasn't for my sister, I might have been Bernie's wife; and these people regarding me so fiercely could have been my in-laws.

'Time to go, I think.' Andrew tapped Emma on the shoulder.

'Oh, but … I've not spoken to anyone, not really, just Jackie. I've not offered my condolences …'

'I have, for both of us.' Andrew took her arm. 'Come on, Emma, it's for the best.'

'Andrew's right. The aunts have seen you with me; they won't appreciate anything you say.'

'And you'll probably say the wrong thing, too.' Andrew said, huffily. 'Let's go.'

'All right, I'm coming. Don't drag me! Andrew, please.'

'Sorry.' He let go her arm. 'We're a … we're a bit of an embarrassment.' He whispered the word.

'Yes, I can see that.' Andrew did not like to be embarrassed. 'But I'm not going without speaking to Bernie!'

'All right. Do that, and then we're leaving.'

'Jackie, I'll call you. It's been good seeing you, and I'd like us to get together again. You, me, and my perfect husband!' She felt relaxed with Jackie; she brought out Emma's seldom seen flippant side.

Jackie smiled. 'I'd like that. Find one for me, will you?'

'Oh, I doubt I'll find another one like him.' Emma, smiling, looked round at Andrew. 'A quick word with Bernie … and I'll join you.' Sharply she turned away; Andrew had not been amused. She threaded herself through the tightly-packed gathering until she found Bernie, leaning over an armchair, deep in conversation with a very old man. Not wanting to interrupt, but determined to speak to Bernie, she pulled gently at his sleeve.

He turned round. 'Emma.' That lovely smile in his eyes, even now, today.

'We're going.'

'I know. Thank you so much for being here. Come here.' His arms enfolded her. She laid her head against his chest. What did it matter if they were all looking; she was his partner's wife, for goodness sake; *and* Rose had loved her.

'How could I not come,' she whispered. 'Dear Bernie.' She drew herself out of his embrace. 'Take care.' Her eyes full of tears, she stretched out her hand, squeezed Bernie's fingers in hers. 'See you soon.' Quickly she let go of his hand, turned away, made for the open door into the hallway.

All the way along the road from *The Wake Arms* and down through the forest Emma was silent. A glance at Andrew's face as they pulled out of the drive of Rose's house had told Emma that her husband was not in a mood for conversation. There'd been a lot of these moods lately, too many of them. Andrew – how well the name Raven suited him: glossy blue-black hair, dark eyes and brooding Mr. Darcy looks – had always been the 'strong, silent type'; it was something Emma loved about him, but these moods were different, worrying; it was as if Andrew's mind – soul, maybe? – was not there, with her. She had tried getting him to talk about whatever it was that was troubling him. 'There is nothing troubling me. So shut up, will you. Please,' and he'd gone out and banged the door. Five minutes later he was back, taking her in his arms, apologising. 'It's a headache, that's all.' 'You need new specs.' 'I don't. There's nothing wrong with my eyes!' 'I didn't say there was anything wrong, I just thought it would be a good idea if you had them checked, that's all. Because sometimes …' 'Yes, yes, all right, I'll do it.' 'Promise?' 'Yes, I promise!' but of course he didn't see the optician, and the headaches went away … or did they? This new, strange Andrew wasn't going to tell her, and she had felt she couldn't ask.

But now, she would. 'Have you got another of those headaches?'

'What?'

'I just wondered if …'

'No, I haven't got a headache!' he barked.

'Oh. Well, something has upset you. Was it something Bernie said to you?' She rushed on. 'You looked so serious, so worried, just now, waiting by the car …'

'For God's sake, Emma, what *is* the matter with you! Bernie's lovely mother has died and …'

'Yes, I know, but …' Common sense told her not to pursue it, but some other sense, one that would not be quieted, drove her on. She knew it was foolish, she knew Andrew would not like it – he never liked her asking questions about the business – but she would say it, all the same. If the business was giving her husband these dreadful headaches – oh yes, he still had them, but unobtrusively; 'I'm busy, got a lot of paperwork.', and he'd looked ashen when finally he came out of his study – then she had to know.

'Is it the business? There's something wrong, isn't there?'

'No, there is nothing wrong with the business! Just stop this, please. Or I *will* have a headache!' He sighed. 'All right, if you must know … it is to do with the business, but it's nothing serious, nothing that can't be fixed. I'm not going to talk about it, so don't ask, don't say any more.'

'All right, I won't. I just knew someth…'

'Emma! No more. Please.'

'Yes. All right, darling, no more.' Tenderly she patted Andrew's arm. 'Sorry, but I felt I had to …'

'Yes, well you've asked, and now you've been told.' And that was that, she knew only too well. No more questions, no more probing.

A week later Andrew was in hospital: he had had a stroke.

CHAPTER TWO

'Oh, Bernie, it's my fault. I kept pestering him, I kept on pushing ...'

'Emma! It is not your fault. It's no one's fault. These things happen.'

'He didn't like being pushed, being questioned; he never did. I was there to give him the answers, the right answers, not question him.'

'Emma, stop this.' He put his arm round her. 'Come on, we're not doing any good here.' Gently he steered her out of the stroke unit. 'Let's go and get some coffee.'

In the hospital café Emma sat herself down on a yellow moulded plastic chair at a blue table. All around her there were people laughing and chattering, and although Bernie was just behind her ordering coffee at the counter, she thought she had never felt so alone in her life. She and Andrew were rarely apart; unlike most of her school friends who had gone on to have flourishing careers after they married - she seldom saw any of them now - she had given up work, revelling, at the time, in her role as wife, home-maker, and then mother; feeling safe and protected, happy that Andrew wanted to be the sole breadwinner. She couldn't remember a night in her married life when they had not slept in the same room; separate beds yes, occasionally, on holidays in hot countries, but always he had been there for their silly night-time ritual: stroking one another's noses. Ridiculous, she said to herself; I never really liked it, but now … She held her face in her hands, felt the tears streaming down her cheeks. It was the first time she had cried, really cried, since it had happened. Maybe it was the artificial cheerfulness of her surroundings: they seemed to mock her. Or maybe it was having Bernie there that was allowing her to let go. He'd not been there the day of the stroke; that's what she called it: *The Day of The Stroke,* unlike the day before, unlike the one after. The day before … well, she knew something was wrong, very wrong, when Andrew came out of his study ashen-faced and sweating, his hands cold and clammy. 'I don't feel right,' he said, 'Something's happening to me … and I don't know how to deal with it.' Which is when she knew it was serious. 'Have you any pains, darling? In your arms or …' 'Pains? Yes, of course I've got pains! No, not in my arms! I've got a bloody headache!' Not a heart attack then; well, it didn't sound like one. She knew about heart attacks, her father had had two.

'Coffee.' Bernie put the mugs, both bright red, on the table.

'Thank you.' She lifted her mug, took a sip, put the mug down. 'Oh, Bernie.'

'We'll get through this. Don't worry; he'll be all right.' He pulled his chair close to her, took her hands in his.

'Will he? You don't know that.'

'Well no, I don't, but I do know that your agonising is not going to make him better.'

'Please don't get cross with me.'

'I'm not cross with you.'

Tenderly he kissed her forehead; it felt good, warm, reassuring. She wiped the tears away, looked up at him.

'People get over strokes; they do,' he said.

'Yes.' Not always, but that was not the thought she should foster, certainly not just now. For Andrew, and for Bernie, *she* would have to be strong. What a strange sensation this was, being strong for someone else, when all her life others had been strong for her, poor little timid Emma, never quite having the courage, never 'stepping up to the plate' unless someone was holding her hand: Andrew or Bernie; or Constance, who had more or less brought her up ever since their mother had died when Emma was only eight. That has to change, she thought; it's the only way I'm going to get through this. I mustn't rely upon Bernie; it's only a week since his mother died.

What was it Eleanor Roosevelt had said? She had pinned up the quotation, given to her by Constance, on her bedroom wall. "You must do the thing you think you cannot do." So she'd dyed her hair purple. 'Not that sort of thing!' Constance had said. Which of course Emma knew. It had felt so good though, flouting her sister's authority, just that once. Rose, dear Rose, had said, "Be bold". Could she be?

'Where've you been?'

'Nowhere.' A lift of his eyebrows. 'Yes, all right, I have been away. Nowhere bad, I promise. I'm back now, and whatever is coming … we *will* get through it. There.' Was that enough? No, not quite. She had to say more, she had to commit. 'This is the new, positive Emma,' she said. 'It's about time, isn't it?' Time to think for myself, not just follow Andrew's bidding.

'Yes.' Bernie nodded; he knew.

'I don't expect it will last, but … Well, I've said it, so …'

Bernie smiled, that beautiful smile that seemed to fill his whole being and spill over onto whoever was on the receiving end. She smiled back. For a brief moment she bathed in the glow, felt calm, empowered ... for herself. And for Jacob.

'Oh God, Bernie.' Her smile faded. 'I must try Jacob again.' She began to scrabble in her bag for her phone.

'It's all right, I've spoken to him.' He closed his hand over hers, over the phone.

'Oh Bernie, thank you.' She let go of the phone. 'Is he ... is he coming?'

Bernie shook his head. 'No. He can't, not just at the moment.'

'I know things were difficult between him and ...'

'It's nothing to do with that: he was cleaning a gun – you know there are guns on the farm – and somehow he's managed to shoot himself in the foot.'

'Oh, Bernie, no! Oh my God, is he all right?'

'Yes, he's fine; he's not badly hurt and he'll come as soon as he can.'

'Oh, thank God for that. I suppose, really, it's best if he's not here. I doubt whether seeing him would help Andrew get better. Oh Bernie, was it the right thing to do, send him there, to South Africa?'

'He wasn't happy at school, he wasn't getting on.'

'No, he wasn't.' He might just as well have gone to an ordinary school, a grammar turned comprehensive, like Theobalds, the one she and Andrew had been to, not a posh boarding school for which you paid a lot - well, Andrew did - for the privilege. Andrew liked that word; he liked to feel *his* son was privileged, liked telling people he was at a public school. 'He seems to be happy now, though. Settled. For now, anyway.' Jacob never stuck at anything for long; that had been the trouble at school: lack of concentration unless it was something he really wanted to do, the teachers had said. 'I do wonder sometimes if he'd have been happier if he'd not boarded.'

Bernie smiled at her. 'Yes, maybe. Andrew was happy, wasn't he, at Theobalds?'

'Yes, I think so; he doesn't talk about it much. You know, not like he talks about Cambridge.' Emma looked into her coffee mug. 'I wouldn't be sitting here now if you hadn't both gone there, would I?'

'No, probably not. And if he'd gone to a different school you wouldn't have met him.'

'Well, no, I wouldn't.' They had met first at the school gate, waiting for the buses to take them home, and then later, soon after Andrew came down from Cambridge, at the pharmacy where Emma had been working since leaving school. 'I remember you from school,' he'd said. 'From the buses.' Then, to Emma's surprise, he'd asked her out.

'Unless, of course, you didn't meet there,' Bernie said.

'What?'

'I just wondered which was the right story.'

'Story? What d'you mean?'

'It isn't easy to say this, Emma, but … well, lately, Andrew's had another version of a couple of things. And one of them is your meeting.'

'Our meeting?'

Bernie nodded. 'I wondered if … if the stroke and this … changing the story-line … were connected in any way.'

Emma felt her mouth go dry. She reached for her coffee, now cold, took a sip, put the mug down. 'So … how does Andrew now say we met?'

'At some local function you were both attending, some sort of … cocktail do.'

Emma laughed. '*Cocktails*? That's ridiculous! He might have gone to a cocktail party, but I wouldn't have done. Certainly not back then. Oh, Bernie, he was having you on. And you fell for it, by the sound of it.'

'Yes, you're probably right.'

'I mean … why would he do that?'

'I don't know.'

'The other instance, of Andrew's story-telling … what was that?' she asked, trying to make her words sound casual.

'Oh. Nothing. Doesn't matter.'

'Go on. Tell me.'

'No, it's …'

'*Tell* me.'

Bernie sighed, deeply.

'Bernie,' Emma said quietly, her hands reaching out to him. 'I do need to know. If the thing you're talking about *is* connected to his stroke, the doctors ought to know, too.'

'Yes, of course.'

'Well?'

'It's to do with money.'

'What money?'

'The money he put into the business.'

'When you started up, or recently?'

'When we started up. The money from the aunt in Australia.'

'Oh, that.' Emma laughed. 'Yes; raised quite a few eyebrows, that did. Well, it does sound unbelievable, doesn't it, a great-aunt in Australia leaving him money! Just the sort of thing Andrew would invent: you know how he likes grand gestures. But it was true.'

'Mm.'

Emma drank the last of her coffee. 'I could do with some more,' she said.

'I'll get some.' Bernie picked up her mug.

Emma watched him as he walked across to the counter. Mm, Bernie'd said. What did it mean, that Mm? She couldn't think about that now. Not with Andrew lying *somewhere* in this hospital – they kept taking him for tests – not able to speak, his left side useless; as if all the stuffing had been knocked out of him. She was back in her mother's kitchen, four years old, watching horrified as Sally Moo, her rag doll comfort blanket, whirled round and round in the washing machine. Sally Moo had never been the same after that; she had looked the same; her black pigtails were still shiny and her flowered dress was still bright, but the dolly herself could no longer sit up unaided; she had always to be propped up, otherwise she fell over.

Emma held her face in her hands, opened her eyes to the blackness. Was this what it was like, now, for Andrew? A sort of black nothingness. Was he in pain? Maybe if he was he didn't know that he was. Oh God.

'Here. Drink it.'

Emma lifted her head, took hold of the mug. 'Thank you.' The coffee was too hot; she put it down.

'And then I'm taking you home.'

'No! I can't. I can't *leave*.'

'Emma … you can and you will.' He sat down and took Emma's free hand in his big warm bear-like paw.

His touch was comforting. She had always loved Bernie's hands, his chubby fingers – sausages he called them: 'kosher ones, mind' – so different from Andrew's delicate, tapering 'pianist's' fingers: he wasn't a pianist but his fingers were as she imagined a musician's would be. She lifted her coffee, sipped gently; it was still too hot.

'I know you want to stay,' Bernie said, 'and so do I … but there's nothing we can do here.'

'Yes, but …'

'The best thing we can do for Andrew is get some rest. For God's sake, Emma, we've been here nearly all day! Right now Andrew doesn't need us; the only people he needs are the ones who are attending to him. Doing whatever it is they're doing; things they know how to do and we don't.'

'Doctors.'

'Yes.'

Emma sat very still, as if she had stopped like a clock does sometimes, suddenly.

'Emma?'

She jerked. 'Yes, you're right. We can't do anything here.' She smiled brightly, put down the coffee, stood up, picked up her bag, pulled on her coat.

'We've got our phones. They'll call us.'

'Yes. Let's go.' She was out of the café and into the hospital foyer before Bernie could catch up with her.

'Jesus, Emm! You do go to extremes, don't you?'

She halted. 'Do I?' She was starting to cry. 'I wish I did. I wish I *could*. Extremes! Huh. Beige, that's me.'

Bernie grabbed her arm. 'Emm. Stop it.'

She marched on, pulling Bernie after her, not looking at him. 'You've had a shock,' he said. 'There's bound to be a reaction.'

She stopped, turned to him. 'Is that what this is?'

'Of course.'

'Oh. Well then …'

* * *

At home, Constance was waiting.

'Connie! How did you …?'

'Your neighbour let me in. The one who has your keys.'

'Oh.' She couldn't think straight. She looked, unseeing, at her sister. Maybe she was hallucinating; it could happen when you were exhausted. She had got out of the car, staggered to the door, opened it, stepped into her spacious hallway - perfect for meeting and greeting guests, Andrew had said when they'd first seen the house - so dizzy with fatigue she could almost have flopped down there and then, curled up on the deep Chinese rug and …

'A nice warm drink, that's what you need.'

She wasn't hallucinating, it was the real Constance, tall, spare, greying hair pulled back away from her unmade-up face, taking her arm - if she hadn't Emma could well have fallen over - and propelling her into the kitchen. 'Now, sit down.'

'No!' Emma struggled out of her sister's grasp. 'I don't want anything. I need to sleep.'

'All right. I'll take you up to bed.'

Emma let Constance take her upstairs, help her to get undressed and into bed.

'Just go away now, please,' she said.

'I'm going to bring you up something …'

'No …'

'It's just a very mild natural sedative. It will help you to have a really good sleep.'

'I don't want it!' Emma had a horror of sleeping pills; she had seen men and women come into the pharmacy in Cheshunt desperate for their pills, afraid they'd be denied them, so relieved when she handed over the sealed paper bag containing their drugs. I'll never, ever, get like that, she'd said to herself - she had learned about drug addiction as part of her training to be a dispenser - I'd rather spend the night awake. The only pill she ever took willingly was a paracetamol for a headache.

'Very well,' Constance said, and left her.

‘Thanks, Connie,’ she said. She turned on her side, shut her eyes. Sleep evaded her; her thoughts churned: Andrew, on the kitchen floor, moaning; holding his hand in the ambulance, siren blaring, lights flashing; Bernie with her in A and E, holding her; Jacob, hurt. Oh God; she must call him. She opened her eyes wide, sat up, reached for the phone on the bedside table, swayed with fatigue.

‘Connie,’ she called faintly. The bedroom door was all but shut, and she hadn’t the energy to get up. Not for a minute anyway; she would lie down, try to relax, then pick up the phone and call her son. Her son; yes, in the early years, but when it came to schooling, more Andrew’s than hers. He couldn’t bear to think Jacob might become a ‘Mummy’s boy’. ‘I want the best for my son,’ he'd said. ‘I want him to have the full public school experience.’ Like Bernie, who had been to Repton. Andrew had chosen the equally smart Aldenham School, far enough from home for Jacob to board, but near enough for his proud father to attend all the sporting and social events. And now his son was farming … well, learning to be a farmer … in South Africa. Very colonial, Bernie had said. Nothing wrong with that, Andrew had retorted. Emma had said nothing. She hadn’t wanted him to leave England, but if he was to make something of himself, it was better he did it away from his father. And, sadly, from her. ‘I don’t want you mollycoddling him with lots of enquiring emails and phone calls,’ Andrew had said. ‘He’s got to stand on his own two feet, grow up, be a proper man … and he won’t do that if he’s still tied to your apron strings.’

Emma had, for the most part, kept her distance: antagonising Andrew over this might only have made things worse for Jacob. They exchanged occasional emails and she had sent birthday and Christmas presents. Phoning had been difficult; the farm was remote, apparently, and the signal, until recently, had been poor.

She sat up again, slowly, reached out for the phone. 'Connie!' she called, scrolling down to Jacob's saved number. About to press it, she remembered … it was two hours later there, he might be asleep.

'Connie!'

The bedroom door opened. 'I heard you the first time.'

'Jacob's hurt; he can't come.'

'Yes, I know. Bernard Silver told me.' She held out a mug. Emma shook her head. 'It's only camomile tea; it's not a *drug*.'

Emma put down the phone and took the mug; she drank the herbal tea. 'That was nice and sweet,' she said, sleepily. 'Honey?'

'Yes.' Constance took the mug from Emma's floppy, outstretched hand. 'Now, get some sleep.'

CHAPTER THREE

Bernie watched Emma go into the house, then close the door behind her. He didn't want to speak to Constance; knowing she was there was enough. Of course she'd come, she'd said on the phone. 'I'm her sister; I've always looked after her and I always will, as long as there's breath in my body.' Constance didn't like him, he knew that; in her mind, he did not measure up to Andrew, not in any way at all. It hadn't been easy speaking to her, but it had to be done, and now she was here: she had sent him a text, with the exact time of her arrival. He took the car out of Park and drove away.

He was tempted to return to the hospital, but no, the doctors were not expecting any change in Andrew's condition for some hours; better if he were to go home, get some kip, refresh himself, then in the morning … He couldn't, daren't, think any further; it would all depend now upon … He hoped to God – which god? He didn't have much time for any of them; he loved the music, the art, but as for the beliefs … all *they* did was bring misery, as far as he could see. Well, he hoped the medics – they could be his gods right now – would pull Andrew through.

He couldn't imagine life without Andrew.

Thirty years and more of the closest comradeship two men, two straight men, could have. University, from that first ridiculous encounter at the window of his room, operatic in itself, as they were aware, through family, marriages, business. Business. *That Music Place*, the business they had set up, in a modest way, a few years after leaving Cambridge. It was, to begin with, very modest: a shed at the end of Bernie's Chigwell garden. No computer, no mobile phone, just a very long, thin, plastic-coated extension lead from the phone in Bernie's bedroom, disconnected out of 'office' hours. They did have, though, an answerphone with a chirpy message, doing its best to sound as if it was winging its way to the caller from across the Atlantic, rather than the garden. "Hi there. You're through to *That Music Place*. Yeah, that's the name. *That Music Place*. Tapes, LPs, EPs, horns and drum kits, guitars (pronounced gee-tars) from all over. You want something from the music scene, we got it. And … you got something to sell? Yeah, we buy, too. Just give us a call on this number … and one of us, Bernie or Andy or Jo … we'll get right back to you." There was no Jo, male or female, but Andrew has thought that offering a third contact name made their business sound more professional.

All these years later Bernie still knew that message word for word. He'd been the one to record it. Andrew had tried – the name had been his idea – and although his transatlantic accent was good, it sounded too posh, too East Coast, for their image, so it was Bernie, who *was* posh, public school and all that … whose voice was on the message. Funny that, Andrew sounding too posh, which he loved, when Rose had been asked to decide between their recordings: Andrew, the boy who'd been brought up in a part of north London which, for the most part, didn't do posh; but of course, being Andrew he had worked on his voice, until it was the one he wanted the world to hear. Did he ever drop it, Bernie wondered now. He'd come off the country roads near Emma's house, hit the A414 that would take him to the M25 and then home. Home. An empty house; no Rose. He baulked at the idea of returning to that; he'd go to Jackie's. No, he couldn't take on her problems, not just at the moment. Sleep, that's what he needed, a good sleep, then back to Emma. Another memory lane to wander down. Oh God, he was getting maudlin; best not to go there, not today. Maybe not at all.

Bugger it, he'd done it now, he'd opened the box: Emma in a punt at Grantchester, that day when they had taken her to see where they had both been, to see their staircases. 'Couldn't they have done better than this for you?' she'd asked, not a mite impressed that it was one of the oldest, most prestigious colleges in the university. Her cousin, Barbara, was at a university in the Midlands and she had all mod.cons. including her own *en suite* bathroom. 'You'll learn,' Andrew had said, taking her arm to help her, in her stiletto heels, down the winding stone staircase and into the quad. 'This is nice,' she said. 'It could do with some flowers, though.' She'd walked away, disappointed, they could both see. Andrew caught up with her, took her arm. She smiled up at him, puckered her lips, touched them to his cheek. 'Not here,' he'd whispered urgently. Bernie had grinned; did this man ever step out of line? 'I'll take you in a punt; you'll like that,' Andrew said. And she did, so much. Shoes off, summer dress wet from splashing, soft fabric clinging to her legs – 'Let me, let me do that pole thing,' she'd said, standing up, overbalancing into the river. 'Oh, my God, I'm going to drown!' Andrew, cursing, struggled to rescue the abandoned pole. 'Bernie, help me out!' Expecting to be floundering in deep water, Emma, laughing, found she could stand up, reached up her arms to him; laughing, too, he'd lifted her out and up into the punt - Andrew standing, keeping the punt away from the overhanging willows on the bank - his arms now around her; her body wet, her hair - it had been blonde then - with curls flattened, flicking in his face, her breath coming fast, her face on his chest. 'We'd best get you dry,' he'd said, hoarsely, gently easing her away from him, turning away so neither of them would see the change in his bodily contour. Enough. That was too long ago; no point in going there, being led to other thoughts. I'm on the M25, I must concentrate.

* * *

Bernie slept. Awoke refreshed, lay, for a very brief moment, content. 'Oh God.' He groaned: yesterday was back. He sat up, ran his fingers through his tousled hair, peed, had a shower, wrapped himself in a towel, ran downstairs, put on the kettle; all the time keeping the thoughts at bay. His phone rang. 'Hello.' He'd grabbed the phone, not looking at the number on the screen. 'Emma! Hi. What? No, no news. You?' No, she'd had no news either.

'Listen, love, we must just assume he's had a good night. See you soon.'

Coffee first. He hadn't given her a time, so a few minutes more wouldn't hurt, a few minutes in which he could think about Andrew, hoping, believing, things were no worse. Remembering. Against all odds – lack of premises, expertise, contacts in the music business – they'd made a success of *That Music Place.* Bernie's father was furious: a law degree wasted, the possibility of a career as an eminent barrister, judge maybe, thrown out of the window. 'Not necessarily,' Rose had said, quite openly taking Bernie's side, 'a good businessman needs to know about the law.' 'And what are they going to do for money?' Bernie's father asked. 'That's easy,' Rose had said, 'I'll give it to them.' 'Give?' 'Well, lend, anyway. They'll soon be making money, you'll see.' And they did, but not soon; they were in the shed at the bottom of the garden, with another pre-fab building tacked on – not really the sort of thing you expected to see in a Chigwell garden – to house their stock, for a couple of years. Their move to a modest shop in Crouch End was a gamble; it hadn't yet become a Mecca for foodies and property prices were moderate. Even so it stretched their resources, and Rose, though she still had faith in them, hesitated to put more money into what might never become a serious enterprise. 'Don't let Bernie be reckless,' she'd said to Andrew. 'Keep a hold on the spending, won't you.'

So how fortuitous it had been, when, a few weeks later, Great-Aunt Anna's cheque arrived. The shop, which in its first few months had announced its identity with a streakilypainted cotton banner, could now sport a proper sign, *That Music Place,* in bright day-glo lettering, above the door. And there was a phone number too. And flyers, and an ad in the local paper.

Bernie never did discover how much dear Aunt Anna had given Andrew. It wasn't his business to enquire; whatever it was, Andrew was putting all of it into their enterprise, and he was the one keeping the books. 'When we're going into the red I'll tell you,' he'd said. 'In the meantime, let's both stick to what we do best.' Bernie, with real music knowledge, the front man; Andrew, meticulous with the accounts, in the backroom, and occasionally sounding out prospective backers. It worked. A couple of years later there was a *That Music Place* in Islington, off Upper Street, not far from the *Kings Head*, a pub which was also a thriving fringe theatre. Flyers on their old wrought iron tables brought many a potential punter to their door. This venue didn't have day-glo, just a sandwich board outside, but being off Upper Street that was enough. Soon it was doing better than the Crouch End shop, and unable to cope financially and practically with two outlets at this stage, they let the Crouch End shop go. If only, Andrew had often said since, we'd hung on to the old place as well: it would be worth millions today!

That's enough looking back, Bernie said to himself as he drew up outside Emma's house in Pengate. High brick walls surrounded it; there was a small orchard and a pond and a circular gravelled drive; the house itself had gables and a studded front door; it was, apart from the old manor house, the most impressive house in the village. Oh, how proud

Andrew had been when he and Emma first took Bernie to see it. 'You'll be quite the country squire here,' he had said, then wished he hadn't. He saw, too late, the look on Andrew's face and the small smile of amusement on Emma's: that's why Andrew had bought it!

No need to turn off the engine, no need to see Constance; Emma was out of the front door and into the car within seconds.

'Let's go,' she said, fastening her seat belt.

'Did you sleep?'

'Not really. A bit - Connie gave me a drink with something in it; she swore she hadn't - but then I woke and …

'And you couldn't get back.'

'No.'

'Yeah. Me, too. Come on, let's see what's been happening.' Bernie put the car into Drive and pulled away.

Emma gave a tiny wave to her sister, watching from an upstairs window.

'She's like Mrs. Danvers,' she said. 'Oh God, that was so unkind.'

'She cares about you.'

'Yes. Sorry, Connie.'

'So let her look after you now. I know you don't think you need it.'

'I *don't* need to be looked after. I've told you, Bernie, from now on I am going to be both positive and independent! I have to be, for Andrew, so that … whatever happens … when he comes out of hospital he can rely upon me.'

Bernie turned his head; Emma was looking straight ahead. Though her jaw was set, her hands, clasped together on her lap, were trembling. Would she be able to cope with whatever was coming her way: life without Andrew … or with Andrew paralysed, unable to walk? Or work? No, he must be positive, too: Andrew could make a complete recovery, become once again the man who had made all the decisions in their life, had done ever since he'd chosen Emma to be his wife, his perfect wife. Which she was - beautiful, intelligent, funny … and most importantly, she admired him.

* * *

The doctor was young; well, he looked young to Bernie - floppy hair and pink cheeks - but he was, in fact, a senior registrar, so he should know what he was talking about.

'There's good news and bad, Mrs. Raven,' he said, giving Emma a half-smile. 'Your husband is over the worst, for now …'

'Oh, that's good,' Emma said. She's not taken in the 'for now' Bernie thought.

' … but there is paralysis in his left side.' He paused. 'Quite severe paralysis.'

'How severe?' Yes, I know you're not supposed to tell me, I'm not a relative. 'I'm Andrew's business partner and a very close, long-time personal friend.' The doctor gave another half-smile. What was there to smile about, even partially? Bernie felt himself becoming intensely irritated. 'We need to know.'

‘Yes, of course.’ No more smiles. ‘There is no movement in the left side and … and no speech either.’

‘Oh God.’ Emma lifted her hands to her face. ‘Oh Bernie.’ She turned to him; he put an arm around her shoulder.

‘It’s all right. We’ll get through this. Andrew’s tough … you know?’

‘Yes.’ She took her hands from her face. ‘Yes, I know. He *is,*’ she said to the doctor.

‘So … what now?’ Bernie asked.

‘I can’t give you a time-table, Mr. Silver. We have to take a day at a time, sometimes even an hour at a time.’ He turned to Emma. ‘We’ll keep you fully informed.’

‘Yes. Thank you. Can I see him?’ Emma pushed her chair back, stood up.

‘Well, no,’ the doctor said, rising from his chair. He’s going to bar the door, Bernie thought. ‘Not just now.’

‘Why not? He’s conscious, isn’t he?’

‘Yes, he is conscious, but we’ve given him a sedative and …’

‘I want to see him!’

‘If you will let me finish, Mrs. Raven: your husband is attached to various pieces of machinery at the moment.’

‘Machinery?’

‘You know what the doctor means, Emma; heart rate, blood pressure, all that sort of thing. You don’t want to see him like that.’

‘I don’t care what he’s got attached to him, I want to see him!’ She turned to the doctor. ‘I have a right, don’t I?’

‘Yes, of course.’

It could have been anybody under the maze of wires and the oxygen mask. Emma held Bernie's hand tightly as they stared through the glass panel at the figure they had been assured was Andrew.

'Come on,' Bernie said softly, turning her away from the window, 'you've seen him now. There's nothing else you can do; let me take you home.'

Emma allowed herself to be steered down the corridor, into the lift, through the foyer and into Bernie's car. He leant over her, fastened her seat belt.

'Oh Bernie, Bernie.' Sobbing, she threw her arms around his shoulders, crushing him to her, his hands still on the seat belt, his lower body outside the car.

'Emma, let go!' Bernie released himself from her arms and stood up. 'God, you are strong. Oh, you really hurt then.' He stretched, eased his neck muscles.

'Sorry. It's just that ... If only there was something I could do for him. I feel … helpless.'

'Yes, I feel the same.' He started the car. 'There is something we can do, though.'

'What?'

'Keep everything going, so that when he does come home …'

'I don't know if I can.'

'Yes, you can. Come on. Where's that new positive Emma? I want to see her.'

She turned her tear-stained face to Bernie. 'It's one thing to say that, it's quite another to be her.'

'I know, but …' He smiled at her. 'You're not alone. We'll do this together.'

Constance, alerted by the crunching gravel in the Pengate drive, was opening the front door as Bernie's car drew to a halt.

'Do let her help you,' Bernie said. 'You're allowed a few days of not being strong.'

'Yes, all right.' Emma smiled gently. 'I will.'

CHAPTER FOUR

There was a heaviness in Emma's legs as she walked the short distance from Bernie's car to her front door.

'You poor thing, you must be exhausted,' Constance said, taking her arm.

'I am.' It felt good to agree with her sister; she would start being strong tomorrow.

'Right. In you go. Food, a nice warm bath, then a sleep.' Tenderly Constance led Emma into the house, across the Chinese rug and down the three shallow steps into the exquisitely-furnished sunken lounge – Regency stripes, rich plum and silver, with 21st. century comfort, all chosen by Andrew – which stretched right across the back of the house and looked out, through full-length windows, onto immaculate lawns and flowerbeds.

'No,' Emma said, struggling out of Constance's hold. 'Not in here. I'm sure to drop crumbs or spill something.' Holding onto the long Georgian pedestal table for support, she made her way through the adjoining dining room into the kitchen.

Here, at a modern, stain-proof pine table, she let Constance feed her: leek and potato soup, with homemade herb rolls, one of Emma's favourites. Comfort food, she thought; Connie's so good at doing this. It took her back to her childhood: coming in from school on a winter day, the mingling smells of soup and freshly-baked bread. The other girls in her class came home to shop-bought biscuits. 'Why can't I have them?' 'Biscuits fill you up but don't feed you.' 'Yes, but they're nice.' 'I'm not here to give you *nice* ... or any other sort of biscuit, come to that,' Constance had said, leaving Emma to ponder her meaning.

Now, finishing her soup, she smiled at her sister. 'Thank you, Connie. That was lovely. Better than biscuits.'

'A lot better.' Constance smiled. 'Come on now, bath, and then to bed.'

'Not bed, no. Not yet. I've got to look at some papers, accounts, things for Bernie.'

'Oh no. Anything for Bernard Silver, or anyone else, can wait until later, or even tomorrow.'

'Yes, but ...'

'No! Absolutely not.' Constance shook her head, then, responding to Emma's wide-eyed pleading look, a standard accompaniment to the childhood soup and biscuits routine, she said, 'If you really don't want to go to bed, I suppose I'd better give you this.' She fished in her cardigan pocket, pulled out a folded piece of lined paper torn from a ring-pad. 'Here. It's from your gardener.'

Emma took the note. 'Adam?' She unfolded it. 'Oh.'

'He made himself sound as if he was your private property.'

Emma laughed. 'Well, he is ... sort of. We have another gardener for the heavy work.'

Constance raised her eyebrows. 'Two gardeners?' She took away Emma's soup bowl, put it in the sink.

Much as Constance liked Andrew and approved of her sister's marriage, she sometimes had harsh things to say about their lifestyle and the way they spent their money. Emma waited for such a comment now, but thankfully it didn't come.

She opened the note. *Sorry to hear about your husband. Don't worry about the allotment, I've plenty there to keep me going. Cheers. Adam.*

To begin with Adam had been *their* gardener, hers and Andrew's. Then came the day, just over a year ago, when Emma had brought him out a cup of tea and a cake, and because it was a sunny day, and warm for the time of year, she'd brought a cup out for herself. She sat down on the newly distressed old wooden bench under the Bramley apple tree. 'Come and join me,' she said.

'I will,' Adam said. 'Let's enjoy the sun while we can, eh?'

'Yes.' She knew Adam still couldn't work for long at a time; he had been in a serious car accident two years before, and it had changed his whole life. Prior to this he'd worked in the office at the Waitrose in Hertford, as did his girlfriend, Sara. Once Adam was on the mend he went back to work and their dream of buying, rather than renting, a flat in the town, looked like coming true. After a fortnight back in the office, a fortnight in which Adam became more and more agitated, he quit.

'I just couldn't take it,' he told Emma, when he came looking for work. 'I couldn't cope with being closed in all day, not after what happened.' He had been trapped in the damaged, squashed car for several hours before the firefighters got him out. Determined to find a job that allowed him to be outdoors at least part of every day, he tried his hand at gardening, liked it, found he could do it, even with the limp he now had. There was no shortage of people wanting a gardener in the villages around Hertford; fortunately he could still drive. If this was going to be his life – he could earn a decent wage if he put in the hours – he needed to know more than how to turn over the soil and cut lawns; a nearby horticultural college ran just the sort of part-time courses he wanted.

'I wish I had a garden,' he'd said, 'a real garden, you know, where I could grow interesting things, different kinds of veg, you know … ones you can't buy in the shops, old varieties … Sorry, I'm going on, aren't I?'

'No, you're not, I think it's a brilliant idea.'

'You do?'

'You could take over part of this garden. There's that patch at the bottom, by the field. You know, where it dips down.'

'That would be ideal.'

'I'll have a word with Andrew.'

But when she did …

'No, absolutely not. We're just getting this garden the way we like it and you want to let someone …'

'Not someone. Adam …'

'Yes, all right, Adam. You want to let Adam grow weird vegetables? In our garden?'

'Well ... more or less, yes.' Don't waver, Emma, she said to herself. Stick with it. 'They'll be things we can eat and ...'

'And what if these experiments don't work? Um?'

'Then we'll try something else.'

'We?'

'Well, no. I mean him ... he.'

'You said *we*. Emma?'

This was such a small thing; she could give way, as she usually did. On the other hand, because it was such a small thing to ask, maybe she could just 'push it a bit'.

'I don't see why you should mind, Andrew,' she ventured. 'It's not as if we use that bit of the garden; it's just grass, and we have plenty of that.'

'Grass?' The scorn in Andrew's voice was palpable.

'That bit is; it isn't a lawn. You said yourself we had sufficient lawn area now. Our lawns are lovely, of course they are,' she said hurriedly, 'and Adam looks after them so well, couldn't you just let him ...?'

'No! We've got the garden the way we want it and ...'

'The way you want it.'

'Do you not like it?' As she expected his voice was cold.

'Yes. It's lovely, it's ...'

'Well then, let's keep it that way.' His voice was still cold.

'All right, I'll tell him. No weird plants, no triffids. Not here.'

Andrew picked up his newspaper and began to walk away; for him the subject was closed.

'Triffids?' His back was to her. Slowly he turned round.

'A book by John Wyndham. Sort of science fiction; you won't have read it.'

'Science fiction, no. Definitely not.'

Then, seeing her wan, troubled face, he smiled. Gone was the stern, authoritarian look; back had come the Andrew she loved so much. 'Oh, Emma, you are such a dreamer, darling. Come here.' He enfolded her in his arms. 'I do know what triffids are. I haven't read the book, but I did see the film, years ago.'

Despite the comforting cuddle that was it: there would be no experiment with plants. Not here, anyway, not at the bottom of *The Rectory* garden.

Emma had wanted to change the name; it puzzled her. How could their house, at one end of the village, ever have been the rectory for the fifteenth century church, with its little steeple built into a corner of the tower? It was almost half a mile away by road, at the other end of the village. Maybe this road hadn't been there when the church was built; maybe this had never been a rectory? Oh, what did it matter. She had simply said, 'We don't go to church.'

'Perhaps we should, if we want to become part of this community. Besides, it's a good name, *The Rectory*; it carries a sense of history.'

Emma had smiled, and agreed. What her Andrew was really saying was … it has class, that name. Status. It is where an up-and-coming English businessman could feel at home. A house with no number, just a name, like Howard's End or Brideshead, the sort of house his idol, Mrs. Thatcher, might have aspired to if she hadn't set her sights on Downing Street, an address which, strangely enough, was best known for its number, 10. For Andrew, brought up in a small house joined on to other small houses on both sides, in a narrow north London street, having *The Rectory*, Pengate, nr. Hertford, Herts. as his address gave him enormous satisfaction. It was better, even, than an address in a smart road in Chigwell. To Emma it didn't matter two hoots, but if it gave her Andrew pleasure, so be it.

'Sorry, Adam,' she'd said, 'but Andrew has plans for that part of the garden.'

'Oh. What?'

'I don't know yet, but it certainly won't be experimental vegetables.'

They laughed, together.

'What we need,' Adam said, 'is an allotment!'

'That would be fun. Hang on … there *are* some, on the other side of the village.'

'Oh, wow! If we could get one of those. God, that would be fantastic!'

'You and Adam want to rent an allotment?' Andrew couldn't have sounded more horrified, Emma thought, if she had said they were planning to run away together, which in itself was such a crazy idea – he a sweet, scarred and scared young man with a limp, she the middle-aged chatelaine of *The Rectory*.

'Don't smile about it, Emma, it's not funny.'

'No, of course it's not funny, darling, but …' She had prepared the speech; she had known it would be necessary. Now she was going to use it; she cleared her throat. 'It's a perfectly workable idea, and it won't interfere in any way with our beautiful garden or our lives.'

‘I don’t see how you can say that.’

‘Let me finish, darling. Please.’ She put a gentle, restraining hand on his arm.

‘Go on then.’

‘Adam will work there in his spare time; he’s not charging anything.’

‘I should think not.’

‘And I will just go down there from time to time to see how things are getting on.’

‘Mm. And the cost of this adventure? There are bound to be *some* costs.’

‘Twenty pounds a year. We rent it.’

‘We?’

‘Yes. I am going to rent the plot. It measures four poles.’

‘Poles? Good Lord.’ Andrew laughed.

‘Poles, yes. A tiny bit of old England.’ That will appeal, Emma thought.

Andrew sighed wearily, but Emma knew she’d won him over. ‘Oh, go on then, if it’s really what you want to do. I suppose you will be wearing your *jeans* when you go there.’

‘Mm, probably,’ she said; he didn't like her wearing jeans.

Once he was assured that it wouldn’t interfere with their life, Andrew took it wholeheartedly on board, told his friends, made a joke of it at the golf club. He’s turned yet another thing to his advantage, Emma thought wryly. This time, though, it works in my favour, too.

Emma put Adam’s note into her pocket.

‘I think I shall have to leave the allotment entirely to Adam at the moment,’ she said.

‘Nonsense,’ Constance said, vigorously rinsing Emma’s soup bowl under the tap, ‘it’s exactly what you need, something energetic to take your mind off what’s happening to Andrew.’

‘I don’t want to take my mind off it!’

‘Yes you do. Leave Andrew to the doctors for now. He will need *you* when he comes home. And believe me, that’s not going to be easy; he’ll need you full-time then. So while he’s in hospital, you refresh yourself.’

Constance had been there full-time when their mother had been so ill; she knew what she was talking about. ‘You’re right, Connie. I will.’ Emma leant across and kissed her.

‘There’s no need for that. Just do it.’

‘I will. I promise you. I just have to look at something to do with the business, though … first.’

‘The business? No, absolutely not, that’s Bernard Silver’s affair, nothing to do with you at all. Come on, out of here,’ Constance said, steering Emma out of the kitchen.

‘It’s to do with … buying new stock, for the shops,’ Emma said, hesitantly. She didn’t want to get into a discussion about it with Constance, who had always thought, and said so, that Andrew had wasted a good degree going into the music business with Bernie. He should have his own accountancy firm by now, not just be handling the accounts of Bernie’s friends, and their friends, even though this had proved very lucrative.

‘I thought they had a business manager now for that sort of thing?’

'They have, but he doesn't oversee everything. There's some accounts, small ones, that Andrew still looks after himself.'

There was no point in explaining to Constance that Andrew, as well as being the firm's accountant, was one of the people who did the 'field work', going up and down the country to junk shops and antique fairs, even to jumble sales occasionally, in search of musical items – old LPs, sheet music, instruments, photographs; anything that might have some connection with music – to sell on in their shops. 'You're hoping to find a Stradivarius, aren't you?' Bernie had said, 'or a score by Mozart.' 'And why not?' Andrew was not finding his comments amusing. 'It is possible, you know, Bernie,' Emma said. She knew how much Andrew hated being ridiculed. Besides, he enjoyed himself on these days out; now and then, when Andrew had heard a whisper of something of special interest coming up at a sale, Emma went with him and they'd have lunch in a country pub. Up till now they had never come across a valuable old instrument or a piece of lost music. 'Pity,' Bernie said once, when they'd returned from a foraging trip and taken the day's disappointing finds straight to the Islington shop. 'The sale of a Strad at Sotheby's would boost our funds no end.' 'I am looking!' Andrew had said, crossly, and Emma had, unusually, felt annoyed with Bernie: he knew how much it mattered to Andrew that he pulled his weight financially, how he took every opportunity he could to add to his stake in the business, determined not to be thought of as the lesser partner because he had less capital to invest.

For these jaunts Andrew had a red notebook, in which he wrote down the contact details of people he had met in the shops and at the antique fairs, people who would keep an eye out for the sort of items Andrew required. A world away from their website and Facebook pages, which Bernie enjoyed supervising, this low-key side of the business worked very well. It was this notebook that Bernie had asked Emma to find; if stocks began to get low while Andrew was in hospital, Bernie wanted to know who to contact. Andrew had also kept a separate account for expenses incurred on these trips.

'Just as well, if Bernard Silver is as casual with money as you say he is,' Constance said scornfully.

'I've never said he was *casual,* and I do wish you'd stop calling him Bernard Silver all the time!'

'It's his name, isn't it?'

'Yes, it's his name.' Emma sighed. There was no point in arguing with Constance; she seldom won. Besides she was much too tired. 'I am going to bed,' she said. 'Thanks again for the soup; it was delicious.'

CHAPTER FIVE

Garry's head felt hot; he was sweating, but his fingers were icy cold. Jesus, this was freaking him out! Freak anybody out, this would, finding a whole load of twenties in a battered old biscuit tin in the loft over your Grandad's shop.

Grandad had died, and he'd left Garry what the lawyer had called his 'disposable assets', which turned out to be all the stuff in the flat – furniture and curtains and books and medals. Garry didn't want none of that old junk, thank you. Well, maybe the medals; he'd played with them as a kid, and they could be worth a bit. As for Grandad's clothes … they were so old they'd do well as retro, if they didn't stink so much. Funny that, when Grandad kept the aprons he wore in the shop so white it hurt your eyes to look at them – boiled them, he said, once a week. The shop, too, that was clean, spotless; the floor, as they say, you could eat your dinner off of it. But upstairs … Jesus! … it didn't look like it had seen a duster or a hoover since Garry's Nan died four years ago.

It hadn't taken long to clear the flat: charity shop, jumble sale, the dump; all gone in a couple of days. 'Cept what big sister Paula had decided she'd keep.

She had inherited the premises, including the shop. Trust her, Garry thought, when the lawyer read out the will. Always was Grandad's favourite – smarmy little cow. She was good to look at, he'd give her that; big brown eyes, thick wavy black hair, not like him, pasty white, hair a sort of rusty brown. 'Well, you didn't have the same father, did you?' Grandad had once said to him. He'd not understood, but it didn't bother him none: Dean was his dad, always had been. To be fair though, Grandad never took it out on the grandkids, his daughter marrying Dean, having a kid with another man, then going back to her husband. Don't matter now, nobody thinks anything of it, but back then, forty plus years ago, it was different, maybe not in London, but out here in a Hertfordshire village where you almost never saw a black face, so when your daughter turns up with this guy from a place called St. Kitts, says she's marrying him and she's pregnant … Well, people can't help noticing, can they? Especially when the girl's so proud of him, and herself. And in a funny way, Grandad was, too. Maybe Grandad would have left him more if his skin had been the same colour as Paula's.

'You did look in the loft?' Paula had asked him when they were filling the skip.

'No. What for?'

'What for! There could be some stuff up there; *possessions*, you know.'

'Well, if there are they can stay there.'

'No, they can't! Everything's got to be cleared! So go up and check, while we've got the skip.' She sighed. 'Honestly, Garry …'

It didn't take much for Paula to become exasperated with her brother. Never done a proper day's work in his life, she reckoned; she'd told him, more than once. 'You drop out of this, you drop out of that. Plastering: too messy; packing in a warehouse: boring; driving a van: good for a while, but then … You couldn't resist it, could you? A mate has a mate who needs someone to drive a van in the early hours and the money's good; more than you're getting in your day job, I know. You don't ask why, who, what for, you just say "Yeah, yeah, I'll do it." Idiot!' and she'd shake her head. 'Six months in prison. God, you're so lucky it wasn't more; a different judge and you would have.' 'The judge could see I was innocent,' Garry had said. 'Oh yeah,' and Paula had laughed, 'but only in the sense that … what was it he'd said? Let's see if I can get it right. Oh yes …' and she'd put on a voice like *she* was the judge. ' "The young man does not appear to have been entirely aware of the purpose of his driving. However, the vehicle has been employed in the execution of a crime." '

And when he came out of gaol, his girlfriend had moved on and he had no job. So, no surprise – 'cos no one wanted to give him work, real work – that he embarked upon a life of petty crime, with several more short spells inside.

'You may as well look through the things, might be something you can flog.' If anything would get Garry up in the loft quickly it was the thought of money coming his way.

'Oh, all right.'

Paula smiled. 'Go on then. Chop-chop.'

'How'd you get up there?'

'There's a ladder. Oh, and there's bound to be spiders.'

'Oh, well, in that case …' He felt his stomach knotting; he just could not abide them.

'Don't be such a wimp, Garry!' She grinned at him. 'There could be toys up there.'

'Toys? What do I want with toys?'

'*Old* ones. Collectables … you know? Don't you remember? Grandad used to sell toys.'

'Oh yeah.' His eyes lit up. 'You're not talking Thunderbirds, are you?' They were very collectable now, the old ones.

'Could be. And cars, you know, them little cars in boxes?'

'Dinky toys? Worth a packet, some of them, 'specially still in their boxes.'

'I'm not saying there will be, but …'

'No, you're right, Big Sis, worth having a look, even if there is spiders.' He grimaced.

'Oh, all right, I'll come with you.' It always worked, the Big Sis routine.

Using a broom handle, Paula pressed on the square loft cover; it swung open, revealing a counter-balanced metal ladder. Deftly Paula pulled it down, secured its hinges and climbed up.

Garry watched her disappearing into the darkness above. 'How you going to see anything?' he called up to her.

She laughed and switched on the loft light.

'Oh. Right.' Garry climbed into the loft. The weak bulb pierced part of the gloom, but in the corners, where the sloping rafters met the floor, there was still intense darkness. If he wanted to investigate anything there, he'd have to use the torch on his mobile. He looked around at what he *could* see: a couple of old-fashioned, fake leather suitcases, some battered cardboard boxes and a wooden tea chest, all of them empty. No old Thunderbird toys, no Action Men, nothing that looked to be of any value. Well, this lot'd not bring him any money, that was for sure.

'Thank you, Grandad … for nothing.'

'Not nothing. Garry. You got all his furniture and …'

'Oh yeah, and I had to pay someone to take it away!'

'Excuse me, I paid for that, not you.'

'All right, all right!'

A quick sweep in the shadows with his torch revealed a set of shelves and some more boxes.

'You'd better have a look at them,' Paula said, making her way to the ladder.

The torch flicked off and the shelves disappeared into the darkness. Garry shuddered: he didn't like the dark. All the same … it wouldn't be more than a few minutes, and he'd keep pressing the torch. 'I'll just have a quick shufty,' he said.

'If you find anything, bring it out into the light to look at it,' Paula said; she knew his fear. 'You'll be okay.'

'Yeah. Ta.' He grinned at her.

'Good boy.'

'Eh, you! I'm not a kid any more, you know.'

'Well, don't act like one then!' She blew him a kiss.

Garry panned the torch along the shelves: just a few small cardboard boxes with peeling labels. He pulled them down; his torch went off. He flicked it on again quickly and took the boxes out into the centre of the loft. Thick with dust they looked as if they'd been there for years; probably had, Garry thought, from when he used to come here as a kid and Grandad sometimes let him have a toy to take home. Never anything special, never one of them cars he really wanted, though he did get one on his birthday once; pity he'd lost it, it might fetch something now. He opened the boxes: nothing worth keeping, cheap plastic stuff mostly … although, hang on, might as well let his mate, Baz, who had a stall in Camden Passage, have a look. Yeah, he'd do that, put them in one of them old suitcases; that might sell and all …

'Find anything?'

Wrapped in his thoughts, Garry hadn't heard Paula coming up the ladder. He jumped, dropped his armful of boxes. 'What d'you do that for?'

'Sorry,' Paula said, stepping into the loft. 'Oh …' She picked up a blue furry elephant that had fallen out of its box. 'I had one of them; I was about four. I remember Mum bought it for me; Grandad made her pay.'

'No.'

'He did. Not much, but it wasn't long after decimal came in, in the Seventies, and Mum got muddled with the new money, thought Grandad was charging her a lot, but it was only a few pennies. "To keep the books straight," he said. I remember, 'cause I couldn't understand what it had to do with books.' She laughed. 'He kept the books straight, but he'd leave cash all over the place.'

'What d'you mean?'

'Oh, you know … odd bits here and there, in drawers and sometimes between the pages of books. He didn't like banks; he said he'd rather keep his money where he could see it. You did check, didn't you, before you put the furniture on the lorry?'

'Well, no …'

'Not to worry. I did.'

'And?'

'There wasn't any. He must have had a good clear out when he knew, you know … that he was dying.'

'Yeah. I guess so.' It had been hard for Paula, helping to look after Grandad and knowing he was on his way out. He wished he could think of something cheering to take her mind off that time. 'He knew every penny what came in and out, didn't he, Grandad?' was the best he could manage.

'Yeah, you could learn from him!'

'All right. I know! Anyway … there's no money here; just things. I'll see if Baz can flog them.'

Together they loaded most of the toys into a tattered brown suitcase. 'I'll just make sure there's nothing else; might as well.'

'There's no might about it, Garry; this loft's got to be cleared. So go on, get on with it, and don't be too long. I've done all I need to do in the shop and I want to get out of here.'

'Spooking you too, is it?'

'No! I just got things to do, places to go. Not like you, lazy layabout! I do have a job!'

'Get you!' Garry stuck out his tongue.

'Oh, grow up.'

Paula picked up the now filled suitcase and climbed down the ladder.

Garry shone the beam of his torch on to the shelves.

It was then that he'd seen the old biscuit tin.

Handling the banknotes his legs felt like jelly, but it was the message, in Grandad's careful handwriting, under all the envelopes, that floored him … literally. His knees buckled, his hands shook. "This time, Garry, do the right thing." What the fuck did that mean?

'You coming?' Paula called up to him.

'Yeah. I'm coming.' Garry's voice was hoarse.

'Good. You best get out of there; all that dust's not good for your chest.'

For once Garry was glad he had a weak chest. 'I'll be okay,' he croaked. He bundled the rest of the toys and the tin, hidden under them, into a small leather case with a strap that he'd missed before – that could sell, too; he'd seen them in Camden market. He secured the strap, switched off the loft light, and grasping the handle tightly in his sweaty hand, he eased himself and the suitcase through the opening in the loft and down the ladder.

CHAPTER SIX

Up in her room Emma couldn't settle to sleep; it was ridiculous to go to bed at half-past eight, even if she was tired; she would look at Andrew's papers now, however much Constance remonstrated with her.

'Oh, all right. If you must. While you're doing that I'll just pop to the shop. I could do with some decaffeinated tea.'

'I don't know if they have it; it's only a small shop.'

'I suppose you're lucky to have a shop at all, especially one that stays open in the evening; so many of them have closed down.'

'I don't think this one will; a young couple have just taken it over, and they're doing all they can to make a go of it.'

'That's good. Perhaps they will have decaffeinated then.'

'Yes, perhaps they will.' Emma wished Constance would go.

'Right then, I'm off.' Constance opened the front door. 'Are you sure you'll be all right on your own?'

'Of course I will!'

'I've got my phone, so if you …'

'Oh Connie, I'm fine. Go!'

'I won't be long,' Constance said; she walked out on to the porch.

Emma closed the door after her. It felt good to be alone, not needing to be careful with her words. That was what she so liked about the day each week that she spent with Adam; he never minded what she said or how she said it. Unlike Andrew or Constance. For a brief few moments she hadn't thought of Andrew, wired up in that hospital. She shivered; the house felt cold. That would be Connie, in her two sweaters, turning the heating down, saving pennies. She went into the kitchen and turned up the thermostat; she closed the kitchen door, walked across the hall again and into Andrew's study.

Study, den, office; the name varied according to Andrew's occupation when he was in there. He never locked the door, but it was an unwritten rule that Emma did not enter, either when he was in there or when he was not. She recalled a day when Andrew, sounding agitated, had phoned from the Islington shop and asked her to look in his office for a specific document. 'Don't touch anything else … and when you have read out the address I need you to put that sheet of paper back in exactly the place you took it from. Have you got that?' 'Yes, Andrew,' she had said, and obeyed him to the letter.

It must have cost him a lot to ask that favour of her, relinquishing his authority, letting her into a part of his life that, aside from those occasional stock-hunting trips, he always kept separate. Well, all that had now changed. Goodness knows when Andrew would be able to work in his study again; maybe not ever. Emma sighed deeply. The room was in darkness. She switched on the ceiling light and surveyed the little room: closed curtains at the long window, almost every bit of wall space lined with shelves, except for an area behind Andrew's sturdy oak desk. This held a huge cork board, filled with notes, cuttings, photographs; it was the only haphazard-looking item in the room. On the desk, which she now lit up with the black angle-poise lamp, were computer and telephone; on a table at right angles, a printer; between them a luxurious black leather-covered office chair on which Andrew could swing from computer to printer with ease. Emma had been astounded when it was delivered. 'It must have cost a fortune,' she had said, then wished she had bitten her tongue; Andrew looked so hurt. 'Every successful businessman has an office toy,' he'd said. 'This is mine. And it's more than a toy; it's good for my back and it will last for years.' 'Of course, darling,' she'd said, kissing him gently on the cheek, 'it's worth every penny.'

Emma stood for a moment, uncertain where to begin looking for the notebook Bernie had requested. The desk drawers seemed to be the most likely place, but which one? There were two on each side of the kneehole, a shallow one at the one, a deep one below. Left or right? I must start somewhere, she thought desperately, I want to be out of here before Connie comes back. The top right-hand drawer held stationery, the lower one a collection of coloured cardboard folders, folders Emma recognised from when the business had been in its infancy and paper records had not been completely superseded by computer spreadsheets. The folders looked promising. She opened a blue one: no notebooks there; then a buff one; not there either. It was in the third folder, a red one, the other contents secured by a stout rubber band, that she found what she was looking for. She recognised it immediately – the little faded, red notebook that Andrew carried in an inner jacket pocket on his music-hunting expeditions; it contained the names and contact details of his regular suppliers and the type of stock he bought from them. 'There's priceless information in here,' he'd said once, patting the pocket. 'I can't have it going missing.' Carefully she lifted it out. Beside it was a dark green notebook, one that Emma did not recognise; maybe this one had stock information in it as well. She would take it, just in case. Should she look for other notebooks? No time, Constance was opening the front door. The notebooks in her hand, quickly she pushed the drawer shut, switched off the light, stepped into the hall.

'Did you get what you wanted?' Emma asked.

'Yes,' said Constance. She eyed the notebooks. 'Did you?'

'Yes, thank you.' She hurried on. 'I'll give them to Bernie tomorrow. He'll know what to do with them.'

'No doubt,' Constance said, raising her eyebrows. 'Now that you've done that, you'll probably be able to sleep. Shall I make you a warm drink?'

'Yes please,' said Emma, meekly. 'I'll just pop these in my bag, ready for tomorrow.' Swiftly she crossed her sister's path and ran up the wide staircase. She felt herself trembling; her quick glance at the second notebook had revealed lists of initials, and by the side of each set a sum of money. She had no idea what any of this meant, but whatever it was, she did not wish to discuss it with Constance.

* * *

Overnight there was no change in Andrew's condition.

'Let's go and have some coffee,' Bernie said. 'We can't do anything here.'

Reluctantly Emma turned away from the viewing window. She looked up at Bernie. 'I still had to come though,' she said.

'Of course you did.' Bernie smiled down at her. 'So did I.'

In the hospital café, coffee in front of them, they sat opposite one another. Emma took the notebooks out of her bag. 'I think these are what you want,' she said, pushing them across the table. Bernie picked them up; he opened the red one.

'Oh yes,' he said, 'this is the one. Andrew's little red book. I used to tease him about this.'

Emma looked puzzled. 'Why?'

'Chairman Mao? Little red book?'

'Oh. Yes. Hardly Andrew's way of looking at things.'

'No. He could never understand how, with my background, I voted Labour.' He picked up the other book, flicked through the pages. 'What's this?' he asked.

'I don't know,' Emma said.

'Figures and initials.' He turned the book around so that Emma could read them.

'It could be the money he spent on the stock; I've no idea what the initials are.'

Bernie opened the red notebook again, looked from one to the other. He closed the green notebook. 'I don't think this is anything to do with our stock. You can take it home. In fact, you can take both of them for now.'

Emma picked up the notebooks, held them for a moment, then, very carefully, she put them into her bag. If those figures and initials in the green book were not connected with *That Music Place*, then what *were* they connected with? Her curiosity must have shown on her face.

'Maybe he was paying a private detective to keep an eye on somebody, and those are the payments he was making,' Bernie said, laughing.

Emma looked up. 'Oh, don't be so ridiculous, Bernie! Private detective, Andrew?'

'Well ... you know, in old films, everything written down, and in a little book, usually. And you know Andrew liked old films.'

'This is *not* a film!'

Bernie shrugged. 'Maybe he's the private detective.'

'Bernie, will you stop this please!' She glared at him. 'If you are trying to keep me from worrying about what is happening to Andrew at the moment you are not succeeding!' She spoke loudly, stood up, scraped back her chair: metal on a hard floor, it made a harsh sound. People at the other tables looked round, eagerly; any diversion from their own problems was welcome.

Bernie reached up, took Emma's hand. 'Sit down,' he said, gently. 'Sorry.' Emma sat down, pulled in her chair, quietly. 'You're right, I was trying to distract you. Bad move. Sorry.' Emma did not respond. 'All the same …'

'No, Bernie, please …'

'No, listen … you must admit, it's a bit odd.'

Emma nodded. 'Yes, it is.' Which is why she had got so upset, as Bernie, who knew her so well, was aware.

'Let's have another look at it. It may be something we need to deal with.'

Emma took the green notebook out of her bag, handed it to Bernie.

For a few moments they were silent. Emma sipped her coffee, Bernie slowly turned the pages, a perplexed expression growing on his face. Finally he looked up.

'Well?' She put down her mug.

'I can't make sense of it. Groups of letters and figures; 200, 300. And the occasional date, too; months, but no indication of what year it is, not that I can see. It's like a sort of code. Maybe he's not a detective; maybe he's a spy.'

'Oh, for goodness sake! Here, give it to me.' Emma tried to snatch the book from Bernie's hand.

'Don't worry; it's probably nothing. Just Andrew hanging on to an outdated way of doing things. Keeping stuff in a tatty old notebook rather than on his iPhone.'

'And always using a fountain pen.' She pointed to the book. 'As here.'

'Yes. And not liking internet banking.' He smiled at her. Emma smiled back. He handed her the green notebook: whatever the figures and letters meant, they couldn't possibly be of importance, their smiles said; their eyes, meeting, did not show the same confidence.

'You should see Jackie,' Bernie said. 'Have a day out together, go shopping.'

'Oh Bernie, I hate shopping. Besides I don't want a day out, I want to be here … for when Andrew is ready to see me.'

'Yes. Thoughtless of me … again.' He looked at his coffee, pushed it away; he'd let it go cold. 'You could come to the Islington shop with me one day; you like it round there. In fact,' Bernie said, 'we could come here in the morning, see how things are, pop into the shop, then I'll take you out to lunch. Yes? Do you good.'

'All right. You win.' Emma smiled. 'When you do want to do this?'

'Tomorrow? If … you know, there's no change.'

'Yes, okay. Tomorrow. Good idea.'

CHAPTER SEVEN

There was no change.

It was quiet at *That Music Place* - it was rarely busy on a weekday morning - but the shortage of vintage items was worrying Bernie; he needed to make a stock check. The long lunch he had planned to have with Emma would have to be put off.

'Sorry, it'll have to be a quick bite at the *Kings Head.*'

'You like that place, don't you?' Emma said, as they began to walk back down Almeida Street.

'I s'pose I do. It reminds me of …' His voice trailed off.

'Your acting career?' Emma said, cheekily.

'Huh. More non-acting, as you well know.' Living at home in the vacation after university Bernie had briefly toyed with the idea of 'going into the theatre' rather than the law, and a friend from the Cambridge Footlights had taken him along to a few fringe venues, one of them being the *Kings Head*, then known for its Lunchtime Theatre shows under the direction of Syd Golder, an extraordinary man whose fanciful-sounding stories of his past life turned out to be true. Bernie tried his hand at acting and stage management but, to his chagrin, found he wasn't very good at either. If there'd been some money in it he might have persevered, but as there was rarely more than a free pint at the bar, which still used pre-decimal currency, he decided that the theatre was not for him. The upside of this sad tale, which Bernie enjoyed recounting – he did show some acting talent here – was that, 'One dreary winter day, disconsolately trudging the streets around the *Kings Head*, I came across this semi-derelict building - tiles missing from the roof, broken windows, a battered door - which would later become … *That Music Place*! I like to think of the *Kings Head* as my acorn,' he would finish dramatically, waiting for the applause that did not come. 'Oh well, you know what I mean,' which brought him a laugh and a derisory clap, and probably, if he was propping up a bar at the time, another pint of bitter.

'If you had been a good actor, though … Oh look!' They had turned into Upper Street and were approaching the *Kings Head*. 'There's something on.' Emma read from the billboard on the pavement: *Weird Women and Manic Men.*' The words were painted in black, with red paint dripping from them to represent blood. Ghoulish green faces completed the poster, designed to entice an audience to enter the small auditorium at the back of the pub. 'Ugh. Doesn't attract me,' she said, reading on. 'With Sancha Indigo and Trev Michaels.' She paused, her mouth wide open. 'Oh my God! No!'

'What is it?' Bernie, who'd been quite intrigued by the show's title, looked at her anxiously, then at the poster. 'What's the matter?'

‘I know him,’ she said, pointing at the name. ‘Trev. We were at school together. I was his cover; his parents didn’t know he was gay. Oh, this is hilarious.’

Hardly that, Bernie thought, but it had certainly taken her mind off Andrew, and that, in the long run, could only be good.

‘Oh come on,’ she said, tugging at his coat sleeve, ‘let’s go in.’

‘To eat,’ he said, ‘not to see … whatever it is; horror show by the sound of it.’

‘It’s probably meant to be funny, Bernie.’

‘Even so, I haven’t time. I just want a quick snack and then get back to the shop.’

‘Okay, you have the quick snack and I’ll stay to see the play … if there is one.’

‘I don’t think there is. Look.’ Bernie pointed to a poster on the door they were now opening. ‘Seven-thirty it says, your Weird Women thing.’

‘Oh, never mind. It would have been nice to see Trev though, after all these years.’ They pushed open the glass-panelled doors and entered the pub. ‘I vaguely thought about marrying him once.’

‘What? A gay actor?’

‘He wasn’t then.’

‘Gay or an actor?’

‘Neither. It was one of his straight periods and he was a … a sort of salesman.’

‘It gets worse.’

‘Aren’t you a salesman?’

‘Yes, all right.’

Inside, the pub had lost none of the old-world charm that Emma remembered from her visits there in the Eighties - the wooden floor, the theatre posters on the walls, the rickety wooden tables, the smell – a heady mix of beer and greasepaint – a real coal fire … but the seating, in common with other pubs, had become more comfortable: a squashy leather sofa and a bank of red and blue upholstered theatre seats against the wall just inside the door.

'This will do,' Bernie said. 'You sit down and I'll get some food. What do you want?'

'Oh … a ploughman's, please.' Emma plonked herself down on a blue plush seat close to the fire.

'Think I'll join you.'

'And a glass of red, small one.'

The pub was almost empty – it was early, it would fill up later – and Bernie was attended to straight away. As he waited for their drinks his eyes wandered round the room, to the few other drinkers – out-of-work actors or locals? In Islington they looked much the same – to the door beyond the bar, which led into the auditorium. A notice hanging on the handle said 'Rehearsal in progress. Do not enter'. Could Emma really have considered marriage to Trev Michaels? He hadn't let on, but he had come across Trev before, in his brief foray into theatrical circles, and not really taken to him. The guy was nice enough, a bit affected, but that, he'd found, was how some actors were, usually the less successful ones. Bernie could see the attraction he had for women – the sculpted cheek bones, the floppy hair, the warmly smiling eyes, the very tight jeans – but it was the way all this was aimed at men, too, that had puzzled Bernie.

Either you were or you weren't, surely? He didn't like the thought of Emma being with a man of ambiguous sexuality. Emma was all woman, deserving of a man who was … No, stop. He knew where this was going: was Andrew man enough for Emma?

'Your drinks are here, sir,' the bartender said, breaking into Bernie's tortuous thoughts. 'Your food's ready, too; I'll bring it over.'

'Oh. Yes. Thank you.' Bernie paid and took the drinks across to Emma's table.

'Cheers,' she said, lifting her glass. She took a sip, put the glass down. 'I was just wondering if …'

The bartender brought the food to the table, cutting Emma off. 'Cheers, guys,' he said. 'Or, if you prefer, *bon appetit,*' with a flourish of his fingers. Another out-of-work actor, Bernie thought.

'Thank you.' Emma smiled at him and looked down at her plate: three varieties of cheese, a stick of celery, cherry tomatoes, some sort of chutney, a large chunk of granary bread, a tiny pot of butter, all set out on a pine trencher.

'Is that all right?' Bernie asked.

'Yes. Yes, it looks lovely.' She dipped the celery into the chutney, took a bite. 'Ooh, *that's* nice. Oh, it really is. Thank you, Bernie,' she said.

'Hasn't anyone told you that's rude?'

'What?'

'Talking with your mouth full of food.'

'Yes, all right … I was hungry.'

'Good. Glad to hear it.' Bernie took a long swig of his beer, wiped the froth from his face with the back of his hand.

He put down the glass. 'So … what is it you were wondering about?' He buttered his bread, spread it with runny Brie.

'Um?'

'Before we got the food.'

'Oh.' She sighed. 'Trev. I was wondering about Trev, wondering if I want to see him; it's been a long time and ...'

'So ... Did you?' Bernie asked.

'You mean … do you.'

'No, I mean … *Did you?*'

'It's none of your business,' Emma said, breaking off a piece of crumbly Cheshire, 'but … yes, I did … and before you ask, I had no wish to do it again.' She was tempted to cram the cheese into her mouth; instead she put it down on the plate and sipped at her wine. 'It didn't stop us being friends though,' she said. 'I think he just wanted to see … if he could …' She took another sip. It wasn't a very good wine; she wasn't enjoying it. 'Andrew would have sent this back,' she said, 'he'd have asked for a refund.'

'D'you want me to?' He didn't want to spend time complaining, but if it was what Emma wanted he would do it.

'No, no. Hadn't you better be getting back to the shop? You did say you had no time to eat, and here you are …'

'Yes, all right; I'm going.' He wrapped a tomato and a lump of cheese in a paper napkin. 'See you in … what, twenty, twenty-five minutes?' He stood up.

'Let's make it half an hour. You never know, I might bump into someone I know.' She smiled up at him ingenuously.

'Yes, of course.' He stood looking down at her, then bent over, brushed her cheek with his lips. 'See you,' he said, his throat tight; it hurt, the way he felt about Emma. He straightened up, walked quickly away from the table and flung open the door to Upper Street.

The sooner Andrew was home, and life got back to normal, he thought, the better it would be, for all of them. *If* he got home. What with Andrew's stroke and his mother's funeral he hadn't been here for nearly two weeks, and with Andrew's headaches preventing him coming here for some time before the stroke, their vintage stock was running low and … Maybe it was time he put in a full-time manager, stopped coming here at all. No, they couldn't do that! This shop was their baby and they loved coming here. Someone else could search for vintage stock for their other shops, but only Andrew chose the items for *this* one! It had become a passion with him … and the amazing array of old instruments and records and sheet music continued to bring a steady stream of buyers to their door. They seemed, both of them, never to have lost the buzz it gave them buying this place, rubbing down the doors, slapping on the paint, working all hours to get it going, their adolescent dream coming true.

Bernie would never forget that moment when, after a considerable amount of wine – no glasses, each one drinking straight from his own bottle; red for Andrew, white for Bernie – and a long, meandering, drunken conversation in Bernie's rooms at university, Bernie stretched out on the sofa, Andrew on the floor, they began to talk about their dreams for their lives, not the sensible careers that they and others had planned out for them: the law for Bernie, Civil Service or accountancy as a starting point, for Andrew. 'What I'd ree-ally, reee-ally like to do …' Andrew's speech, as he tipped the last of the bottle into his mouth, was very slurred. '... is – to own – a muuu-sic shop. A shop, yeah … a shop that sells every-thing to do … with … ev-er-y sort of muuu-sic. Fuck the uncivil service, *that* is what I want to do.' 'D'you know what...' Bernie, bottle in hand, rolling off the sofa, to lie beside Andrew, speech every bit as slurred, had said, 'that – is – ess-actly... what *I* would like to do. I would, yes …' Andrew had raised his head fractionally from the floor, looked hard at his friend. 'So … let's do it,' he'd said … and they had both fallen asleep. The weird thing was, that, come the morning they both remembered, more or less, what they had said, and although they continued with their studies and gained their degrees, they never quite forgot the confessions of that drunken night. Two years after leaving Cambridge, already bored and frustrated with their careers, they decided - again on an evening when they were not totally sober – to 'go for it, risk it.' … 'Nothing ventured, nothing won' … 'If you will, I will'. This time, though, the thought of what they were proposing brought them to full sobriety fast. Bernie had enough money to get them started, but had no idea how to manage it; Andrew knew how to manage money, but, aside from his salary as a junior member of an accountancy firm, had none of his own to throw into the pot. Then, a couple of months later, he received the windfall from his Australian aunt. Now he could offer their project both expertise and finance; he felt himself to be meeting the criteria required of the upstanding English businessman he aspired to be. Ditching their careers, but not the expertise that went with them, they embarked upon their new enterprise. The one shop became two, then three; now there was a small chain of them, and they had plans to extend into mainland Europe, beginning with northern France, where a friend of Andrew's had set up a thriving business exporting antique French furniture to Britain. No longer just shops that made money, *That Music Place* contributed to the preservation of old instruments and music-making machines such as wind-up gramophones, and upright suburban pianos which had survived the unbelievably destructive 1960s craze for smashing them publicly and replacing them with music centres.

Bernie turned into Almeida Street. On any other day, it would have taken him a good ten minutes to get this far; he would have been peering into shop windows, popping inside some of the shops, maybe even making a purchase or two. Not today, though; all he could think about was Andrew … and Emma, and how much he loved her, wanted her. It was no good telling himself he shouldn't have these thoughts, especially now when Andrew could be at 'death's door'. Which was, of course, part of the problem: they, both he and Emma, sought comfort, and where could be better than … No, no, no. He strode past the theatre, not even glancing to see what was on, see if it was something he might enjoy; he loved that theatre, as did Andrew, and although their tastes were not the same, they would sometimes take in a show there after the shop closed, then argue about it at length afterwards. Would they ever do that again? Of course they would! Bernie shook himself; he must get rid of these awful thoughts. Thank God he'd reached the shop. Although it was a cold day the door stood open and the strains of 'One Fine Day' floated out into the street. Far from annoying the neighbours, they said they loved it … when it was opera or Frank Sinatra; not, though, country and western; there didn't appear to be any fans living at the top of Almeida Street, so when that was playing the door was kept firmly shut.

There was only one customer in the shop, an elderly, well-dressed woman, one of his regulars – she liked the jazz greats, especially Miles Davis and Bix Beiderbecke, and her late husband had been a trumpeter. The woman looked up from the rack of shellac 78s she had been browsing through; she was holding an old HMV record in a brown cardboard sleeve.

'Morning, Millicent,' Bernie said. She did not like being called Millie; she had only just stopped addressing him as Mr. Silver.

'Good morning, Bernard. You're running very low on stock, you know. There's been nothing new in this rack in the past two weeks.'

'Yes, I know,' said Bernie. 'It's … um … it's Andrew … Mr. Raven … he's in hospital.'

'Oh dear; oh, I am sorry to hear that. Nothing serious, I hope?'

'I'm afraid so,' Bernie said, 'he's had a stroke.'

'Oh no! Oh, I am sorry.' She put the record back into the rack. 'I hope you won't mind my saying this, Bernard, but Mr. Raven has not been looking well for some time.'

'Oh?'

'Have you not noticed?'

'I'm sorry, no ... I can't say I have.' The headaches, yes ... but what else?

'Yes. well, I'm afraid that is often the way. When you are with someone every day you don't spot the little changes in their looks and their behaviour, but people like myself, who only see the person in question possibly once a fortnight ... we notice these things.'

'Yes, I suppose you do,' Bernie said slowly. Millicent was making him feel guilty; what had she spotted that he had missed? That Emma had missed?

'What was it you ... um ... noticed specially?' he asked.

'Well ... it's difficult to put my finger on it, it always is in these cases, but I became aware of a far-away look in his eyes, as if ... Oh dear, this is a bit awkward; perhaps I shouldn't be saying this.'

'No, please ... do go on.'

'Well ... it was as if there was something troubling him, something that he couldn't talk about, to you ... or his wife. I'm sorry, Bernard, I shouldn't have said anything, Take no notice of me.' She patted Bernie's hand. 'We get like this, old women ... we think age gives us the right to interfere in other people's business.'

'No, not all. Don't apologise. I'm glad you spoke; it was kind of you.' Time, though, to change the subject. 'So, Millicent, what was it you were looking for? Perhaps I could get it for you?'

'Oh, that is good of you, but no, it was nothing particular. You know how I like to browse, in the hope that you might have in something new that would take my fancy, but on this occasion …'

'Yes, of course. Well, perhaps we shall have something you like the look of next time you come in.' Bernie was gently edging Millicent towards the open door. He had no idea how long Emma would be in the *Kings Head*, but he didn't want to become involved in another barrage of questions and speculations about Andrew, however kindly, if the old lady was here when Emma arrived.

'Well, I'd better be off, I think. Do give my best wishes to Mrs. Raven if you see her … Yes, of course you will, you'll see her at the hospital. Poor lady, so sad. Strokes are such awful …'

'Yes, I shall pass on your best wishes. Have no fear of that. Now, if you will excuse me …'

'Yes, of course; oh dear me, yes, you have so much to do with Mr. Raven away and …'

'I do indeed.' They were at the door. 'I bid you farewell, Millicent.' Bernie made a small bow; Millicent liked that sort of thing, and if it got her out of his way more quickly …

'And I you, Bernard.' She smiled and held out her hand; Bernie shook it briefly.

'Bye,' he said, 'Be seeing you.' He turned away, hurried back into the shop; Millicent was a lovely lady and a good customer, and he liked talking to her, but right now he had things to do.

* * *

Emma finished her lunch. She had looked up every time there was any movement in the pub, in the hope of seeing Trev. Though why she wanted to see him, she wasn't sure. It was a very long time since they had been 'an item'. They'd been teenagers, experimenting with this exciting thing called sex; everybody in her class whispered about it, but it was hard to tell if anyone had actually done it. Their experiment, behind the bushes at the far end of the playing field, was not a success: the ground was cold, uncomfortable … and hard. 'Unlike me,' Trev had said, looking down at himself. Emma was disappointed, but at the same time relieved; however sex was meant to be, she had read enough to know that it should not be like this. 'Perhaps you fancy boys,' she'd said. 'Maybe I do,' Trev had replied, 'but I fancy you, too.' 'Obviously not sufficiently to …' and she had nodded at his flaccid penis. 'You weren't much help,' he'd said crossly, pulling up his trousers. 'We can still be friends, can't we?' Emma had asked. 'Of course.' Emma became Trev's confidant: he brought all his 'love problems', as he called them, to her. Sometimes it was a girl, sometimes a man.

Lost in her reverie of times long past, Emma didn't at first recognise the tall, balding, grey-stubbled man emerging from the theatre.

'Oh my God!' the man said, stopping dramatically, stretching out his arms towards her.

There was no mistaking his voice, silky smooth, with gravelly undertones – it had brought him a lot of profitable voice-overs.

'Trev!'

'Em-ma. Oh, you love-ly girl …' He clasped his hands together. 'This is just so …'

'Oh, come here. Stop acting and give us a hug.' She reached out and he moved towards her; their arms went round each other. They drew apart, looked at one another, quizzically, but also appreciatively.

'It is so good to see you,' Trev said, no longer with his 'actorly' voice, 'but how come you are here; the play's not on till this evening.' He sat down beside her.

'Oh, trust you to think I'm here just to see your play!'

'Dar-ling …' the actor's voice was back, 'why else would you be here?'

'Because my husband is in hospital and …' Briefly and as unemotionally as she could she told Trev about Andrew, and Bernie and the shop up the road.

'Oh Emma … I had no idea. Oh, sweetheart. Oh, you poor love.' He took her hands in his. 'If there's anything I can do …'

Emma shook her head. 'No, but thanks. Now … tell me about you … and this play you're in. Should I see it?'

Trev shook his head vehemently. 'No. Please don't.'

'Bad as that, is it?'

'Worse. Well, my role is. I know I'm getting on, and my lifestyle has taken its toll, but really, darling … an eighty-year-old down-and-out?' He sighed. 'But it's work … and there's money, not a lot but …' He sighed again, more deeply.' … it helps pay the bills. You know?'

'Yes, of course.' She smiled at him tenderly; like a mother, she thought; underneath the actor's bravura he seemed so sad, so lost. 'How about the voice-overs?' She realised it was some time since she had heard his voice extolling the sexiness of a brand of coffee or the benefits of a breakfast cereal.

'Not a lot there, I'm afraid. You know how it is … you're in something, it's a success, you get more work; not in anything … nobody wants you.'

'So … why not do something else for a bit?'

'Such as?'

'Well, you used to be a salesman, didn't you?'

'Yes, but … I can't just turn up at a business and say …' He acted the part, '"Hell-o, do you need a salesman? Because if you do-oo, I'm here!" Life is not like that.' He looked down at Bernie's unfinished lunch. 'Mind if I eat this? I'm starving.' He scooped up some runny Brie, spread it on the remaining piece of bread. 'Ooh, yummy cheese.'

'I presume you don't mean that literally.'

'What?' He began to crunch Bernie's celery.

'That you're starving.' He didn't look underfed; in fact, he had put on weight since the last time she had seen him.

'Well … no,' he followed her glance, ' … not quite, but … this job finishes at the end of the week and … you may as well know … I haven't anything else lined up. Obviously I prefer to get an acting job, a good part in a good production, but if I can't get one … then it doesn't matter what I do, so long as it brings in the moolah.' He picked up the last bit of Cheddar and wiped it around the remains of the chutney. He seemed so downcast, Emma's heart went out to him.

'Oh, poor Trev,' she whispered.

'The trouble is …' he said, looking up at her, 'I daren't sign up long term, not to any other kind of work, in case …' He smiled, assumed his actor's voice again. 'One never knows, darling … the National might call.' He tilted up his chin. '… Or Hollywood.'

'Well, yes … they might.' Emma smiled.

'Oh, they do a very good ploughman's here.' Trev popped the remaining tomato into his mouth.

Emma wasn't sure if the idea beginning to form in her mind was a good one … or something very stupid. 'So …' she spoke slowly, 'If you were to … find a job … in a shop, say …'

'Anything, my darling, anything … just so long as it keeps that big bad wolf from my door. And I do mean door. I have *got* a place and it's quite nice … and I really do want to keep hold of it … and pay for it with work, not, you know … benefits, although sometimes I don't have a choice.' He looked mournfully at Emma.

'Mm, yes. Difficult. So where are you off to now?'

'Oh … Nowhere in particular … meet a few people, see what's going, look at *The Stage*.' He fluttered his eyelids. 'One never knows, darling, one never knows.'

'Oh, Trev … do stop that!'

' Mm? What?'

'Acting.'

'Darling, it's what I do!' He tossed his head, flicked his fingers through what remained of his hair. 'Sorry,' he said, seeing Emma's exasperated face. 'Can't help it. Well, I can, but it … it helps me to hide.'

‘Yes. I understand.’ Emma stood up. ‘You drive?’ Trev nodded. ‘And you’ve got a mobile?’

‘Yes, of course. How else would my agent … ?’

She handed him her phone. ‘Put your number in for me.’ Trev punched in the digits. ‘I can’t be sure … but there just could be a job going.’ Emma took the phone from him, picked up her coat and bag and began moving towards the door.

‘Whoa, hang on … what do you mean, a job?’ Trev rose from his chair. ‘Emma, where are you going?’

Emma lifted both hands, fingers spread, towards him. ‘Just stay where you are … or at least don’t go far away. Give me ten minutes; I’ll call you.’

‘Okay.’ Trev said, sitting down. ‘They’re good exit lines, I’ll give you that, but …’

‘Just do it! Please.’

‘All right. I will.’ He drew back, in mock horror, laughing. Then, seeing Emma’s serious, determined expression, he said, ‘Jesus, what’s happened to you? You never used to be this positive. Emma …?’

‘Bye,’ she called, going out of the door.

* * *

‘You want me to employ Trev Michaels … to buy stock for us?’

‘Yes. You know, like Andrew did … does.’

‘Would he be any good? I mean … does he know anything about music?’

‘Of course he does; he’s been in musicals and things …’

'Mm. I need to think about this, Emma.'

'He needs work, Bernie, he really does. I'd like to help him, if I can.'

'Is he trustworthy?'

'Oh Bernie … that's a horrible thing to ask!'

'Maybe it is, but …'

'You could give him a month's trial. Couldn't you?' Emma looked at him appealingly.

'It's not fair of you to look at me like that, Emm.'

'You need stock; let Trev see what he can find. You could give him some of Andrew's contacts.'

He didn't entirely like the idea of Trev working for him, but the shop did need stock. It seemed ridiculous that he should be in this situation, having to rely upon information in a little red notebook, just because Andrew liked to run this part of their organisation as if they were still at the very beginning of their enterprise, still in the 1980s; on the other hand he knew that Andrew's contacts, maybe because they were handling old ephemera, liked his old-fashioned way of doing things: face to face, never online. 'All right, send him up here; I'll give him a fortnight's trial. No longer.'

'Thank you, Bernie.' She puckered her lips into a kiss. 'If you're worried, I can always go along for the first couple of trips; I know the routine, I've been lots of times with Andrew.'

'Well … mm … I'm not sure about *that.*'

'Oh Bernie, don't be silly! We were only kids then. I'll call him.'

As Emma lifted her phone out of her handbag it rang. She pressed the answer button. 'Hello? Yes, speaking. Oh!'

She turned to Bernie. 'It's the hospital.' She reached out for Bernie's hand.

'Oh God … what?'

'Oh … oh, that's wonderful news! Oh … thank you, thank you *so much*. Yes, yes, we'll be there.' She was breathless with relief and joy. 'Oh Bernie, Bernie!'

'Well, come on, tell me.'

'He still sedated but there's been some movement in his left hand!' She flung her arms around Bernie's neck.

'Okay, okay. Enough,' he said, taking hold of her hands and pulling them down from his neck. 'So … what now?'

'We go to the hospital, of course! What did you think?'

'Have they said we can see him?'

'Well no, but … Of course we can see him! Come on, let's go.'

'I think we should check first.' He took out his phone, keyed in the hospital number.

'Oh Bernie, stop being so reasonable.'

'And what about Trev?' he asked. 'Isn't he waiting for an answer?'

'I can't think of Trev, now!'

'It's going to be a long time before Andrew is back, buying … Hello?' Bernie spoke into his phone. 'I'm enquiring about Mr. Raven …'

'Yes, you're right.' Emma turned away and called Trev; Bernie's calm, practical response to the news had brought her down to earth.

* * *

Less than an hour later they were in Stevenage, Bernie having treated all amber lights as a signal to speed up before they turned red, rather than a warning to slow down.

Emma sat by Andrew's bedside and held his left hand. She trembled, feeling a slight response in his fingers. 'Oh Bernie, he's … Feel, feel.' Bernie touched his friend's hand. 'He's going to be all right. Oh, thank God.' She lifted Andrew's fingers, kissed them one by one. 'Oh, darling! Darling! You'll soon be home,' she whispered. She seemed not to have noticed that although Andrew no longer had a mask over his face, he was still attached to a collection of wires.

'I think that's enough for now, Mrs. Raven.' Emma looked up at the doctor standing by Bernie. 'If you'd come into my office I'd like to have a word with you … and you, Mr. Silver.'

'Yes, of course,' Bernie said. 'Come on, Emma.' He reached over the chair to help her up.

'No,' Emma said, pulling away. 'I want to stay with him. He needs me.'

'Let's see what the doctor has to say, and then maybe you can come back.'

Reluctantly, looking back over her shoulder at Andrew, Emma let herself be drawn out of the ICU room and into the doctor's office. She listened, as if in a trance, as the doctor explained that it would be some time, probably several weeks, before Andrew could go home. It was good that there was some feeling in his hand … but he was still severely paralysed and he had not yet spoken.

'Mrs. Raven, you do understand what I'm saying?'

'Yes. He will get well, though, won't he?' She turned to Bernie, sitting next to her, as if he, rather than the physician, could supply the answer.

'It's early days, Emma.' Bernie looked to the doctor for help.

'If all goes well …' the doctor said, avoiding Bernie's eyes, 'your husband should make a complete recovery.' Bernie nodded; it was, at this moment, what Emma wanted, and needed, to hear. 'I suggest you go home now, Mrs. Raven, get some rest … and then, if you wish to …' He smiled at her reassuringly. '... come back later in the day.'

'Yes, I will. Thank you, doctor.'

* * *

Emma was silent throughout the drive back to Pengate. Mostly she looked straight ahead, occasionally out of the side window or at her hands clasped tightly in her lap … anywhere but at Bernie's face. As they drew up outside the house, Emma, tense, was reaching for the door handle before the car had time to stop.

'You've locked it!' Emma said furiously, turning to Bernie.

'Yes,' he said. 'I knew you'd do that.'

'Oh, Bernie.' Emma relaxed back into her seat; tears streamed down her cheeks. 'What am I going to do? I thought, when I had that call from the hospital … I know it was silly of me, but I thought … Andrew's going to be all right and … and everything will go back to normal.'

'I know, sweetie, I know. It's difficult to think of Andrew, super-confident, self-reliant Andrew, not being self-reliant and …'

'And not able to speak or move … or even … even shit without someone helping him! Oh Bernie!' She buried her head in Bernie's jacket and let the tears flow.

'Good girl, that's it.' Bernie patted her gently. 'Let it all out.' It was only the need to comfort Emma that was keeping Bernie's own tears at bay: the sight of Andrew, so helpless, such a long, long way from being the man he knew, had distressed him deeply. Over Emma's bent head, he saw Constance opening the front door. 'Come, on, Emm.' He shook her. 'You don't want your sister seeing you like this.'

Emma lifted her head, quickly wiped away her tears. 'No, no, I don't. Oh God, no!' If Constance saw her in this state, she'd have Emma in bed in no time, and want to keep her there. She pushed open the door.

Bernie put his hand on her arm. 'If you get a moment,' he said, 'could you have another look at that notebook?'

'This is really not the time, Bernie.'

'No, sorry.'

Emma stepped out of the car and shut the door behind her. She watched Bernie drive away, using the few moments until he was out of sight to regain a little more composure before she faced her sister.

'Hello, Connie,' she said, turning round. 'I've just come from the hospital. Andrew has some movement in his hand.'

'Oh, that is good; and is he able to speak yet?'

'No, he can't *speak* yet; he's still sedated.'

'No, of course not. Have you any idea when he ...?'

'No, Connie, I haven't! And now, if you don't mind, I've got things to do.' She swept into the house before Constance could ask more questions.

'Oh, so ...?' Constance followed her into the house.

'I shall be going back to the hospital later,' Emma managed to say, walking briskly into Andrew's study and shutting the door. She leant against it, shivering.

'Emma? Are you all right in there?'

'Yes, yes, I'm fine.' She didn't mean to sound irritable; Constance deserved her consideration. 'Sorry, Connie,' she called out, her voice now soft. 'Just ... just got some things to do. Won't be long, and then ... maybe we could have some tea together ... and then, perhaps, I'll go and have a lie-down before I go back to the hospital?' There ... that would please Connie. When she felt quite sure that her sister would not be coming back, she moved across the room and sat down in Andrew's swivel chair.

She had only come into Andrew's office because it was the quickest way to evade Constance's questions, kindly though they were meant to be.

It wouldn't take long for Connie to knock up a motherly meal, probably scrambled eggs with cheese, which she knew Emma liked. Meanwhile she would just sit, and try to relax, which wasn't easy; her mind went back and forth, from the hospital to the *Kings Head*, to the shop, to the hospital, to Bernie ... Bernie had asked her to do something: what was it? Oh yes. Have another look at the green notebook. She might as well, while she was sitting here.

She opened the deep drawer which held the folders. Which one had had the notebooks in it? Yes, of course, the red one, next to the buff one. While she was here, though, she might as well look at some of the other folders; maybe they would throw some light on the conundrum of the notebooks! She pulled out the blue folder: adverts for posh cars. Not surprising; Andrew did love having a posh car. Could he be thinking of getting another one? Not just at the moment, that was for sure. Tenderly she closed the folder, replaced it in the drawer. She drew out the buff one: it was stuffed with newspaper cuttings, all from local papers. How odd, she thought; but, on second thoughts, no, it wasn't. Andrew was on the committee of the local community society and the local golf club, so it was natural that he would be collecting local information. She looked at the top cutting: "Local Golfer Vows to Save Village Shop", with Andrew's name in the opening paragraph. "Mr. Andrew Raven, speaking at last Thursday's meeting in Pengate Village Hall, said, 'It is inconceivable that a village which has an excellent golf course, a school and a church, a pub and a village hall, should no longer have a shop!' Mr. Raven's remarks were greeted with cheers and loud applause." Emma smiled; oh, how sweet, she thought; how typically Andrew, to hide the cuttings in his desk. She had felt very proud of the way he had campaigned against the closing of their village shop, and then helped to find the right people to take it over. She knew, of course, that his action enhanced his growing reputation as a good citizen, a pillar of his local community … which mattered very much to him, as did living here in Pengate where people recognised him, spoke to him; most of all, asked his opinion. It was a place where he was not anonymous, as he had felt himself to be on a housing estate in Cheshunt. Andrew had laughed when Bernie had called him the 'Squire of Pengate', but Emma could see how much he liked the idea; she had told Constance, who had not laughed. 'He deserves it,' she had said, 'Andrew is very community-minded, and his actions are to be applauded.' 'Of course they are,' Emma said, 'it was only a bit of fun, calling him the squire.'

Emma closed the folder, put it back in the drawer. There was no time now, but she would look at more of the cuttings another day: it had given her a good feeling, a feeling of being close to Andrew, reading about what he had done. She pushed the drawer shut with her knee. The green notebook could wait: it was time for warm scrambled eggs.

CHAPTER EIGHT

Garry peered into the back of Paula's Fiesta; it was full of boxes from the shop: he'd have to sit next to her. Clutching the suitcase he had brought from the loft, he clambered awkwardly into the front seat.

'Belt up,' Paula said.

Keeping hold of the case with one hand, Garry struggled with the safety belt.

'Oh, give it here.' Paula reached out for the case.

'No!' Garry said, letting go of the belt. He clamped his hand over Paula's.

'For Christ's sake, Garry! Anyone'd think you got the Crown Jewels in there. Put it in the back.'

She glared at him; he glared back, and she pulled her hand out from under his. 'Don't get your hopes up; they're not vintage, you know, not real vintage.'

'I know,' Garry said gruffly. 'They might fetch something though. You *said* ...'

'I know. I know.' Paula put both hands on the steering wheel. 'You have it on your lap then, if you want to. But put your belt on.'

Reluctantly Garry took his hands off his treasures and secured the belt. Paula put the car into gear and pulled away from the kerb. Garry settled into his seat, his arms hooked protectively over the case. He looked straight ahead as they drove down the narrow village street; the sooner he was back in his flat in Waltham Cross the better; the country was all right for a bit, bank holidays and that, but everyone in a place like this knew your business; or if they didn't they soon found out. Grandad had liked that, people coming into the shop, buying things – pint of milk, chocolate buttons, bacon he'd slice with that machine on the counter; wouldn't ever let Garry touch *that* – then stopping for a chat: how the new baby was, and the son in the army, and the grandkids. And then of course he'd talk about *his* grandkids: Paula doing well in the hair salon in Tottenham, and Garry … well, 'He's been away for a bit, haven't seen him much lately.' But down The Cross you could talk to people if you wanted to, but if you didn't no one gave a fuck. He looked down at the case. Never mind the toys; yeah, they'd bring in a few quid, hardly life-changing though. Still, it was a good cover. If one of them cars brought in a pony it'd keep Paula quiet. But the money, all them notes … How much was there? He hadn't had time to count it. Jesus, it was scary. Okay, it was his, right? Grandad had left it to him, so why not say? Tell Paula; she'd not want it, she had the shop; even in the state it was in – tiles off the roof, mould on the walls, windows that didn't fit – it would still fetch … well, who knew, but it would be enough for Paula to buy into the Tottenham hairdresser's. Garry wasn't getting none of *that* money; she had made it quite clear. 'If Grandad had wanted me to share it with you, he'd have said so, put it in the will.'

It wasn't fair … well, not fair shares anyway, but he wasn't going to argue with Grandad's will; you mustn't do that, go against someone's last wishes. He'd seen a film once, really spooked him, where this guy forced his brother to give him a load of money that wasn't rightly his. It had brought the guy nothing but trouble; he ended up with a very nasty, painful death. No way was Garry chancing that, no thank you. Besides, that kind of dosh brought responsibility, which was something Garry did not do, not if he could help it. No, things were best left as they were.

It wasn't as if Grandad hadn't left him *any* money. She'd be pleased, Paula would, if he did tell her. He knew what she'd say, though: 'honest money,' then she'd spoil it by adding 'at last.' No, he wasn't going to do that. And if he did tell her and she saw the money, she'd want to take it out and count it, bound to, and then she'd see that paper, with the writing: "This time, Garry, do the right thing." Give it to a charity? Which one, though. Put it in a bank? No sense in that, you got nothing for it. Buy a car, maybe? Wheels of his own; yeah, he liked that – but there was no way he was going to talk to Paula about it.

'You all right?' Paula gave him a quick glance; they had left the country road and were now on the A10, heading south.

'Yeah, fine.'

'You're very quiet.'

'Yeah, well …' He didn't mean to, but he looked down at the case on his lap. 'It's just …'

'I know. Grandad's things; bound to be … well, upsetting.'

'Yeah. It was.' It was a good line to follow. 'Yeah.' He sighed, turned and smiled at his sister. 'Sorry, if I …'

'It's okay, I understand.' Paula took her left hand off the steering wheel, patted her brother's arm.

Instinctively Garry drew away. Immediately regretting his move, he said. 'Sorry, Sis. I know you're trying to help, but … it's not easy. You know?'

'I know.' Paula slowed down as they approached a set of temporary traffic lights showing red. She looked at Garry hard; he felt her eyes on him: he mustn't play the bereaved grandson too much. 'Course he missed Grandad, but not that much; he'd hardly ever seen him in the past few years, what with one thing and another … and 'being away'. Grandad had never asked, when they'd spoken on the phone, exactly where Garry had been. Sometimes he really had been away, out of the country, like that time he went to Ibiza. Didn't remember much of it, the holiday, but he had gone on a plane from Luton, and because Grandad had been in the RAF in the war, it was something they could talk about. Garry'd made the flights there and back last him for several 'holidays'. He didn't feel good about it, but it was better, kinder, than letting the old man know where he had been some of those times.

The lights changed; Paula put the car into gear and moved forward.

'You know …' she said, hesitantly.

'What?' Garry turned to look at her.

'Whatever you've got in that case …'

'Toys! I got *toys*! You saw them … old toys.'

'All right, all right! Keep your hair on.'

'Well, stop going on about it then.' The sooner he was out of here the better; thank God they'd soon be at the roundabout with the turn off to the Cross.

'What I was going to say …' Garry sighed heavily. '... Let me finish! I was going to say … You won't like this, Garry, but it needs to be said.'

'Oh, for fuck's sake! Will you stop going on at me! I've half a mind to get out of the car now, and get myself a lift from someone else!' He looked straight ahead.

'Calm down, will you. What's the matter with you? You're not on something again, are you?'

'No, I am not! Jesus! I'm clean, you know I am …' If only she would shut up; if she went on like this, he would need to take something. He still wouldn't look at her.

'I'm sorry, Gaz.' She hadn't called him that in a long while; funny, it gave him a warm, being-a-child-again feeling. He turned his head and smiled at her; she worried about him and he was grateful. No one else did, not any more.

'What was it you wanted to say?'

'It doesn't matter.'

'Okay.' He shrugged his shoulders, looked straight ahead again. Best if they didn't talk; he knew what she wanted to say: 'Time for you to get a proper job.' Nearly there; they'd just passed the big Tesco and Marks's on the right. The silence between them became oppressive. Did Paula know their grandfather had all that cash? How could she? *He* had found it, yeah, but maybe Grandad had written something about it, somewhere; in a notebook: Grandad liked writing things down in notebooks, nearly always kept one in his brown overall top pocket. Maybe Paula had seen that notebook; maybe that solicitor, the one who'd told them about who got what in the will, maybe he'd … This was killing him.

'You hold that case any tighter, you'll break it. It's only cardboard, you know.'

Garry looked down at his hands; his knuckles were white. He lifted his hands one by one, stretched his fingers. 'Yeah.' He laughed faintly. 'Don' like being a passenger.'

'Since when? You was all right going there.' Paula shook her head. 'I don't know … Time you had some wheels of your own.'

'With what?' He hoped he sounded angry.

'Well, that's just it, isn't it?' He had played right into her hands. 'If you got yourself a proper job …'

'I will! Just get out of my face, will you!' Now he was angry.

'There's no need to be offensive. You're forty years old, Garry, it's high time you supported yourself, stopped relying on benefits in between the manky jobs you do get.'

'I know! I will!!' He took the hardness out of his voice. 'I promise you, Sis, I will. I owe it to Grandad.'

'Grandad?'

'Yeah. I've not told you this before …' Garry wished his heart would stop thumping so loud. '... but, not long before Grandad died, he made me promise I'd …'

'What?'

'... stop farting around.' Paula laughed. 'It's not funny.'

'No, I know. It's just …' Paula said gently, 'I can hear him saying it.'

'Yeah.' Garry was pensive; he'd made it up, but even so, in his mind's eye he could see Grandad, in the shop, turning the Open/Closed sign on the door, pulling down the door blind, saying it.

'And?' Paula broke into his reverie.

'And what?'

'Stop farting around with what?'

'Oh.' He looked away. 'Work. He said I should … I should get some, you know … proper work.'

'And so you should.'

They were slowing down for the junction ahead.

'You can drop me off here if you want.'

The lights changed to green; Paula speeded up. 'No, I'll take you to the Cross.' He'd rather have got out here, avoided the next question.

'So … you got something lined up then, have you?'

'Well, no … not for definite. Oh, don't look like that, Sis.' He thought of the money, the notes in the envelopes in the case lying on his lap. 'I will have. I been asking around and … well, I didn't want to say till, you know … till I knew for sure, but there might be a job at the … at a garage.'

Paula – trust her – had noticed his stumble. 'Oh, which one?'

'Oh, it's … down past the Abbey.'

'Oh. Right.' Paula signalled left and they turned off.

'Anywhere here'll do,' Garry said.

'What, you not asking me in for tea?'

'You want to come in … ?' Paula had only ever been once to his third-floor, one-bedroom council flat; she had hated the dirty stairwell – litter in the corners and a stink of pee. He certainly didn't want his sister coming in now; she'd probably want to see what he had brought down from the loft, and he would have no way of stopping her.

'No, 'course I don't. You don't need to look so alarmed; I don't want to have tea in your pit.'

'It's not a pit. I keep it clean, and most of the time it's tidy, too.' She must not come in; he took a deep breath. 'But not at the moment.'

'Oh, okay. Best if I don't come in then, yeah?'

'Yeah. Best not.' A couple more minutes and he'd be out of the car; it couldn't be too soon.

Paula sighed. 'Why do I care about you? Eh?'

'Cos I'm your little bruv?'

'Yeah, must be.' Paula pulled up in front of the church. 'Go on, hop it,' she said. 'I'm not supposed to stop here.'

Garry unbuckled his seatbelt, gave Paula a quick peck on the cheek, and got out of the car. 'Thanks, Sis,' he said, hurriedly. He slammed the door shut; Paula winced, shook her head at him and drove off.

Five minutes later Garry was in his flat, door locked, curtains firmly closed, even the ones that overlooked the scruffy courtyard where kids played on swings. He put down the old suitcase on the battered brown sofa in the living room, wiped his clammy hands down the sides of his jeans, ran them through his hair, rubbed them over his stubble. Jesus, what was the matter with him? He knew what was in the case, so why could he not bring himself to open it? He almost wished he'd told Paula about the money; he could call her, bring her back, here. Oh God, no … then he'd have to explain why he'd not shown her those envelopes when they were in the car. He was sweating hard now; he took a deep breath, straightened up, turned away from the sofa and walked into the tiny kitchen. A drink, that's what he needed. A beer. He opened the fridge, took out the solitary can, pulled up the ring, shut the fridge door with his foot, walked into his living room, stood in front of the sofa … and looked down at the case. He finished the beer in one, tossed the can onto the pile of free newspapers at one end of the sofa, wiped his hands down his jeans again, crouched down in front of the case, and very, very, slowly – God knows what he thought was going to happen if he just lifted the lid in a normal way – opened it. He let the lid fall back on to the seat cushions. Thank God the toys were on the top, not those envelopes. Jesus, if they had been and Paula had come in and she had … Okay, okay. Enough. She hadn't. So now, look. *See just how much fucking money there is in those envelopes!*

Garry lifted out the cars, the lorries, the soft toys; he threw them down anyhow on to the sofa, not taking his eyes off the suitcase. And there it was, underneath … the biscuit tin. Carefully, almost gingerly, as if it contained a bomb, he lifted the tin out of the case and put it on the sofa; opened it; stared at the bundles of envelopes, all shapes and sizes, most of them held together with elastic bands. Funny that, the dosh being in old envelopes with Grandad's name and address on the front: he'd been sent this money! He'd think about that another time: right now he was interested in what was inside the envelopes. When he'd riffled through the tin before, up in the loft, he had glimpsed enough twenties to know he'd found something worth having; he'd already got up to several hundred counting in his head, so if all the envelopes in the bundles had … He sat back on his heels; he was shaking all over: what the fuck did he think was going to happen? Grandad's ghost going to speak to him from the depths of the tin? Oh Jesus … that note, under the envelopes, that note in Grandad's writing … What exactly had it said? Garry dug deep into the tin, lifted out all the bundles and put them on the floor. Yes, there it was, in plain sight, as if Grandad had known exactly what Garry would do – spot there was money here and greedily pull out the envelopes; the old man had made sure Garry wouldn't miss his note, wouldn't get it muddled up with the envelopes once he emptied out the money: he had stuck it onto the bottom of the tin. Crafty old bugger! You had to laugh. This was serious stuff, though; that note had not been put there casually. *This time, Garry, do the right thing.* It was like some message from the grave. Garry shuddered. Oh Jesus, if Grandad's telling him now to do the *right* thing ... he must have known all along 'bout all them wrong things he'd done. Grandad had never told him off, not once. All the more reason to do the right thing for him now. Okay, so ... this right thing: what was it? Do the right thing with the dosh? Had to be that. He looked again at the envelopes; so many of them. How come Grandad had all this money? Where'd it come from? So many fucking questions; it was doing Garry's head in. If only he had another beer, if he hadn't given up his fags. He'd start again; needed to, with all this kicking off. Right … I'm going to count it, he said out loud. He took hold of one bundle, removed the rubber band, opened the first envelope. Twenties, ten of them; nice.

Next envelope: more twenties, another ten. Garry did a quick count of the number of envelopes in the bundle: six of them. If they all held the same amount … Jesus, this was *serious* stuff! Over a grand in just one bundle. Never mind 'the right thing'! What do you do with a load of cash when you live in a shitty council flat where a break-in could happen any time?

CHAPTER NINE

For much of the next day Emma slept. Andrew's condition, though still not good, was stable; there was nothing to be gained from her being continually at his bedside, the doctor had said when she went back to the hospital the evening before. 'Get some rest while you can, Mrs. Raven. If there is any change we will let you know immediately.' Now, in the middle of the afternoon, and with Constance busy in the kitchen, Emma decided to have another look in Andrew's desk before Bernie came to take her to the hospital: there might be something else in there that could be useful for him … or even for Trev. She was having second thoughts about involving Trev in Andrew's business, so the more information she could find to help him make a success, rather than a complete shambles, of taking over the search for new stock, the better.

She sat down at the desk and pulled open the deep right-hand drawer; she looked at the array of coloured folders. Now, which one might have some bearing on *That Music Place*? Not the posh cars one; not the newspaper cuttings one … although, that might have. Maybe there were cuttings about village events as well as shops, events such as antique fairs, at which Andrew could purchase items for the shop, make contact with traders. She lifted the buff folder from the drawer, placed it carefully on the top of the desk and drew out the bundle of tightly-packed cuttings, all held together with two big rubber bands. The top ones were recent, some of them dated only last year. As she went down the pile, simply pulling the tops of the cuttings towards her, not removing the rubber bands in case she got them out of order – which Andrew would notice – she saw that the cuttings went back many years; those at the bottom of the pile, with dates nearly thirty years ago, had become crumbly at the edges. There was nothing about village events. Nothing but articles about village shops. Why collect information about them? It made no sense. The ones about Andrew's part in saving *their* village shop … yes, they did; but the others? One cutting she noticed, near the top of the pile, was advertising a village shop for sale. Emma laughed out loud. No, it couldn't be. Could it? Could Andrew have wanted to have a village shop of his own? Surely not. Carefully, she pulled the cutting out of the bundle. The idea was so ridiculous but at the same time so charming; she laughed again.

'Emma? Is that you?' Constance called from the kitchen.

'Er … yes,' Emma called back. 'I was just on the phone.' It was as good a lie as any. Hurriedly she stuffed the rest of the cuttings into the folder and shoved it back into the drawer. The advert she folded carefully – it already had creases – and put into the pocket of her jeans.

'Don't be long, I'm making you some food. You need something warm inside you before you go to the hospital.'

‘I’m coming.’ Emma locked the desk drawer, put away the key and walked into the kitchen. She sniffed appreciatively at the aroma of coffee, toasted cheese and herbs.

There would be time enough later to consider the implications, if any, of those cuttings. For now, she would eat and please her sister.

* * *

On the way to the hospital Emma told Bernie about the cuttings.

‘Andrew’s always liked little village shops,’ Bernie said. ‘It’s not at all fanciful to think he might want to own one … or several. He loved the ones on the way down from Cambridge; we often stopped and went into one … Barley, Braughing … can’t remember the others. He called them “islands of prosperity”. Most of them have gone now.’

Emma smiled. ‘He likes islands. Sardinia, Malta, Menorca … He says they have a real sense of their own identity. I think that’s why he likes villages; they have defined boundaries.’ Her voice was breaking. ‘We had lots of holidays on islands.’

‘And you will again.’

Emma nodded. ‘Yes.’

‘Nothing more about the stock, though?’

‘No. Well, I didn’t have time for a thorough look. I’ll go through the folders again when I get home tonight.’

* * *

At the hospital Andrew's condition was again unchanged.

'I know you are looking for a major improvement, Mrs. Raven, but I don't think it's helping you to be coming here so much. You should give yourself a break.'

'You said that before, and I did.' Emma was angry. 'What do you want me to do … go out to dinner? Go dancing?' She burst into tears. 'You have no idea what it's like, waiting for …'

'Emma, Emma …' Bernie intervened. 'I think I'd better take her home, doctor.'

'Yes, of course. Mrs. Raven's not on her own at home, is she?'

'No, she's not.'

* * *

Emma did not go home that night. Bernie took her to Chigwell where Jackie had moved in temporarily, to 'look after him,' she said; she knew how much he hated being in the house without Rose.

Forewarned by a call from Bernie, Jackie had a meal ready for them.

'That was delicious,' Emma said, looking down at her now empty plate.

'You know what we Jews are like,' Jackie said, giving Emma a second helping of gedempte chicken in a rich sauce. 'Any problems … we eat.'

Emma smiled. 'You and my sister.'

'This helps, too,' Bernie said, filling Emma's wine glass.

‘Oh yes … but not too much, please.’

‘Go on, do you good.’ Jackie held out her glass. ‘Mine too.’

Bernie opened another bottle, and he and Jackie continued to re-fill their glasses.

‘Oh God,’ Bernie suddenly said, ‘I can’t drive you home, Emma. Sorry.’

‘Nor me, I’m afraid,’ Jackie said. ‘Sorry, honey, you’re going to have to take a cab. I’ll call you one.’ She took out her phone.

‘No, please don’t.’ Emma put her hand on Jackie’s phone. ‘I don’t feel too well … I think I’ve eaten too much. Would it be … could I stay the night?’

‘Of course.’

‘I’ll phone Connie; she’ll be worried.’ She bent over and took her phone from her bag. ‘Oh dear, I feel a bit dizzy.’

‘I’ll do it.’ Jackie took Emma’s phone from her hand. Constance was none too pleased, but had no choice but to accept the situation. Emma, Jackie assured her, would be returned to Pengate, safe and sound, in the morning … and how nice it would be to meet Emma’s loving sister.

* * *

Emma lay awake in the big spare bedroom. The radiator was on, but the crisp clean bedding felt cold; wishing she had asked for a hot water bottle – perhaps they didn’t use such things in Chigwell – Emma thought longingly about her electric blanket at home … and her bedroom, their bedroom, hers and Andrew’s. There, even on her own, she had felt close to Andrew; here, in this spacious, but anonymous room, where the light from a street lamp filtered eerily through the curtains of the one long window, she felt so alone. She had not been sick but she had a headache. She now felt steady enough to reach down to the side of the bed and take two paracetamol from her handbag. Next she would need water; she got up and walked slowly over to the washbasin; there were two upturned tumblers on a glass shelf. She took one down, turned on the cold tap and held the glass under the flowing water. About to lift the glass to her lips she paused. Was this mains water or had it come from a tank in the loft? Did it matter? She recalled that time when she drank water from a bedroom tap and had been very ill. Oh, come on, Emma, that was Spain; this is Essex! Nevertheless, she wouldn't risk it, not with Andrew so ill, and so much, she felt, expected of her.

There was a white fleece dressing gown hanging on the bedroom door. Emma slipped it on over the blue silk shorty nightdress that Jackie had given her. Clutching the headache pills in her hand, she went out onto the landing, found a light switch, and tiptoed down the stairs to the kitchen. By the light coming in from the hall, she made her way to the twin sinks under the window, where more light, slanting through the Venetian blind, illuminated the swan-neck taps. She turned one of them on to cold, let the water run for a few moments and half-filled a mug which stood upturned on the draining board. Thankfully she downed the pills and turned off the tap.

'Emma.' Bernie was standing in the doorway.

'Oh!' Emma spun round, her hand to her mouth.

‘Oh, sweetie, did I scare you?’ Bernie held out his arms and moved towards her. ‘Come here.’ He wrapped his arms around her; she let her head rest against his chest.

‘I’m so sorry,’ she said, the words muffled by Bernie’s towelling robe.

‘What for?’

‘For waking you.’ She lifted her head; Bernie’s face was close to hers.

‘You didn’t.’

‘Good.’ Her heart was beating fast; so was his. His mouth was so near, so very near. ‘Oh, Bernie …’

‘Sh …’ His lips touched hers, lightly. It was warming, caring … and it felt so right. She drew back, looked at him and smiled. ‘I needed that,’ she said, and felt herself trembling, knowing even as the words came from her mouth that she should not have spoken them.

‘We both did.’ Bernie’s voice was hoarse. His lips met hers again, and this time the kiss was not gentle; it was urgent, needy, his tongue deep in her unresisting, open mouth, his hands drawing back her robe, searching.

Emma pulled away. ‘But … Jackie?’ she whispered, ‘won’t she … ?’

‘She’s asleep, she drank a lot.’ Bernie removed his hands from Emma’s body. ‘Come,’ he said, taking hold of her hand and leading her across the hall and into the lounge, where the embers from the evening’s fire were still glowing. Letting go of Emma’s hand, Bernie reached out for the cushions on the sofa; he spread them on the rug in front of the fire, and gently lowered Emma onto them. Tenderly but passionately they made love, and as they held one another afterwards, their cheeks were wet with tears: this had been a long time coming, and now that it had, they didn't know quite what to do with it. They knew they would have to talk about it, sometime … but not now. They restored the cushions to the sofa and straightened the fireside rug; hand in hand they walked upstairs. Bernie kissed Emma lightly on the cheek, let go of her hand. They went back to their rooms. Almost immediately, Emma fell asleep; Bernie, full of guilt, lay awake until dawn.

* * *

A still-drowzy Emma propped herself up in bed and took the proffered mug of tea from Jackie's hand. 'Thank you,' she said. 'Is it late? It feels late.'

'It's ten o'clock.'

'Oh no! You shouldn't have let me sleep so long.' The events of the night before came flooding back to her; she lowered her head, afraid her eyes might betray her, and took a long sip of her tea.

'It did you good; all this to-ing and fro-ing to hospital is exhausting.'

'Yes.' The tea was reviving, the action of drinking it calming. She drained the mug, and handed it back to Jackie. 'Have you seen … is Bernie awake?'

'He's long gone. He left you a message.'

'Oh?' Emma's heart began to pound. She felt her cheeks colouring and it was with difficulty that she looked at Jackie. 'What … what about?'

‘Andrew. What else?’ Jackie studied Emma’s face. ‘Are you all right? You’re very flushed. It’s all too much for you, isn’t it. Oh, come here.’ She leant forward and put her arms around Emma. ‘It’ll all be all right, you’ll see. There’ll be no real harm done.’

Emma pulled herself away. ‘Harm? What d’you mean, harm?’ Oh God, she knows.

‘Andrew. He’ll be all right.’

‘Andrew?’ Emma’s relief quickly turned to panic. ‘What … what’s happened?’ She clutched Jackie’s arms. ‘Tell me.’

‘It seems he may have had another, *very minor,* stroke, but …’

‘Oh God, no. No! Oh please, no. Oh Jackie …’ The tears streamed down Emma’s cheeks. ‘I wasn’t there, I was … Oh God. I must get up, I must go to the hospital …’ She flung back the duvet and swung her legs out of the bed.

‘No, no.’ Jackie grabbed Emma’s arms. ‘If you’d let me finish. Oh, I’ve scared you; I shouldn’t have told you like that. I’m sorry. Listen … he’s okay, he’s not unconscious or anything; the situation has not really changed.’

‘Hasn’t it?’ Emma asked bitterly. ‘I think it has.’ She took the robe from the bottom of the bed, where she had thrown it down carelessly last night. ‘I shouldn’t have come,’ she said, pulling it on. ‘I shouldn’t have drunk so much.’

‘Oh come on, you didn’t drink much. You ate, yes; I suppose you can blame me for that.’

‘I can’t blame you for …’ Emma crossed to the washbasin and began to take off the robe. ‘I must wash,’ she said, ‘and then I must go to … I must go home.’ She couldn’t go to the hospital smelling of … of Chigwell. ‘I need to change my clothes.’

‘I can lend you some.’

‘No. Thanks.’ Emma had not meant to sound abrupt. ‘Sorry, Jackie,’ she said, ‘I just need to go home first.’ There was no reason why she should explain; besides, she couldn’t.

‘Okay. I’ll drive you.’

‘Oh, thank you. That would be really nice.’

* * *

‘Thank you for bringing Emma back,’ Constance said. She made it sound as though Emma was a small child who had strayed from her mother’s side.

‘Not at all.’ Jackie put her arm around Emma’s shoulder. ‘It was a pleasure, Connie, we love …’

‘Constance.’

‘Constance; sure. Yes, well … I’d better be getting off. See you, honey.’ Jackie said to Emma.

Emma saw Jackie to her car and waved her off. She walked slowly back into the house. Constance was still standing in the hall.

‘Did you have to be like that to Jackie?’ Emma asked.

‘What do you mean?’

‘Frosty, stand-offish.’

‘I was not,’ Constance said. ‘I was perfectly polite to her.’

‘Polite, yes; friendly, no.’

'I don't know the woman; I'm not even sure who she is.'

'She's Bernie's cousin. I said, when I introduced her!'

'Oh, did you? I don't remember.'

'It's because she's related to Bernie, isn't it?'

'You're talking nonsense, Emma.' Constance turned away, strode into the kitchen; Emma followed her. 'I just don't like effusive behaviour; all that 'honey' stuff. Your Andrew doesn't like it either. Now, do you want to eat or do you want to have a rest, before you go to the hospital?'

'Neither. I'm going out.'

'Where?'

'I'm going to the allotment; I'm going to see Adam.'

'But … you must be tired after ...?'

'What if I am! I'm tired of doing what other people think is best for me! Excuse me, I need to change my shoes.' Emma pushed past her sister and went into the back porch. She took her old trainers from the rack.

'Emma, come back!'

'No, Connie, I'm not going to come back. In fact, I'm not even going to stop to put my trainers on here; I'll put them on when I get down there.'

Adam wasn't at the allotment – there was almost nothing to do there at this time of year – but just walking among the dug-over beds, most of them covered in damp oak leaves from the tree at the side of her plot, had a calming effect upon Emma. She sat down on the rough-hewn bench that Adam had made for her. 'Why don't you have a couple of deck chairs?' Andrew had asked. 'Or maybe a lounger?' 'I'm not playing, you know,' Emma had said, 'this is proper gardening!' 'Oh, beg your pardon.' Andrew had walked away, grinning; Emma had stuck out her tongue at him. 'You wait,' she called after him. 'Fresh beans and potatoes … and beetroot … and strawberries.' She paused. 'Of course I might not let you eat any of them.' He laughed and kept on walking. 'Sod you then,' she'd said to herself. Oh, why could he never take her seriously? Was she nothing more than a plaything, a child to be humoured? Of course she loved him and the life they had together; what was there not to like? A clever, handsome man, a beautiful house, enough money: all the cliché things were there; there was no reason for her to feel unsatisfied, unfulfilled … and yet she did. Was it sex? She didn't think so; they did it regularly, several times a week, nearly always at Andrew's instigation: that was how he liked it – that was how a wife behaved. A mistress … well, that was different; he'd once told her that – they'd been on holiday somewhere hot and she'd drunk rather a lot of wine at lunchtime; she'd wanted him and said so, and although they did make love, he'd not been totally happy about it; it was as if she had broken some unwritten rule in his code of conduct for a wife.

And now … she had made love to Bernie. How do you measure the broken rules there? she thought. A sudden breeze got up and a handful of brown oak leaves caught in the crook of a branch fluttered down, one of them landing on Emma's knees. 'You are dead,' she said. 'You are dry ... and dead; I am not. And my Andrew is not. Oh, what have I done?' She felt sad, frightened, ashamed. No, she did not feel shame; that was what was frightening her. She knew that she should, that a feeling of shame, and guilt too, was the correct response to what she and Bernie had done. Did he feel like this? If only she had not gone downstairs to get a … No! What was done, was … She stood up; the dry leaf fluttered to the ground. She took a deep breath, held it for a moment, then let it out, slowly. She would make her peace with Connie – 'Constance'; yes, well; Emma allowed herself a tiny smile – and then, later, she and Bernie would have to talk.

* * *

Emma walked away from Andrew's bed disconsolate, and yet relieved to have found him sleeping peacefully. She could not have looked into his eyes, knowing what she had done.

Bernie was waiting for her outside the room. 'Coffee?' he asked,

'No. I need to get home.'

'Emma …' He reached out a hand to her.

She waved it away, strode ahead of him, down the staircase and out into the car park. How could he have been so insensitive as to want to speak to her just outside the room where her husband lay so ill!

Bernie caught up with her and they walked side by side, not speaking, not looking at one another, till they reached Emma's car. Thank goodness we came separately, she thought, clicking the car's remote; the idea of sitting close to Bernie all the way from Stevenage to Pengate filled her with a mixture of dismay … and desire. Oh God, where *do* we go from here?

'Emm …'

'Yes?' She began to open the car door. Bernie put his hand on it to stop her getting in.

'Last night. What happened … I'm sorry. I shouldn't have …'

'Bernie, it happened. Just … just let's try to forget it.' She felt breathless; it was hard to speak. 'Let me get in, please.' She pushed his hand off the door.

'Emma, we can't just pretend it didn't … *we* didn't …'

Emma turned, looked straight at him. 'No, well, that's just it, isn't it? *We ... we* did it!' She was shaking so much she felt she would fall down; she held on to the car door.

'What it is? Emma?'

'Oh God, Bernie …'

'I said I'm sorry.'

'I'm not.' It was little more than a whisper.

'What?'

'I said …' She could feel the words welling up inside her, words she knew she must not say, words that a part of her did not *want* to say. In the hospital, with Andrew there, and the doctors and the nurses, she could not have said them, nor did she want to! But here, alone with Bernie … 'I'm not.'

'You mean …? You want us to … do it again?'

Emma shook her head vehemently. 'No! I didn't say that.' She bent her head, ready to get into her car. '*I don't know!* What I do know is that last night … last night I wanted it, *needed it,* as much as you did.' Swiftly she climbed into the car and reached out to close the door; her hand was shaking. Bernie held onto the door.

'I can't let you go like this, you're not fit to drive.'

'I am. Let go, please.'

Reluctantly Bernie took his hand off. 'Phone me when you're home. I need to know you're back safely.'

'Yes. I will.' She put the car into gear and drove away. She would have to drive carefully, she knew that, but with her mind in a whirl – Bernie, Andrew, Jacob, Bernie – it was not easy. Watch the road, watch the traffic, don't think. If you must, then think about something, someone, else. Think about Constance, think about Trev. Oh God, Trev; she'd forgotten about Trev. She must look out the stuff for him; she would do it as soon as she got in; it would take her mind off Bernie.

Constance was asleep in front of the television. Despite her anguish and inner turmoil Emma smiled. Best not to disturb her; her sister would not like to be seen like that, especially as she appeared to have been watching a comedy programme; maybe she had dozed off during the documentary which Emma knew had preceded it. Very quietly she closed the living room door and crossed into Andrew's study. She lifted the red folder out of the drawer and laid it on the desk; it didn't take many minutes to find what she needed, the names, addresses and phone numbers of Andrew's contacts, the people from whom he bought all manner of musical ephemera. It was astonishing the things people had kept, some of them from the First World War. Even more astonishing was the small amount of money that Andrew had paid for many of them; she'd seen what they had sold for, cleaned up but rarely repaired – that could lower the value, she was told – in *That Music Place*. Oh well, that was business, she'd supposed: everyone had to get their 'cut'. She hoped Trev wouldn't take advantage of Andrew's seemingly casual way of buying and recording these transactions – handwritten entries in a small notebook – charmingly in keeping with his purchases, but hardly twenty-first century bookkeeping.

While she was there she might as well have another look at the buff folder with the village shop cuttings. Bernie had … Oh, God. Concentrate Emma! Bernie hadn't thought it at all far-fetched, the idea of Andrew buying a village shop. So *had* he, was this why the folder was there? Emma lifted it out, and starting at the back this time she began to look more carefully at the cuttings. There were several about a shop in a village Emma had never heard of, one of them dating back to the 1990s, another one from a few years ago … and one from a couple of months back. Could this be the one Andrew wanted to buy? Maybe there were others whose progress or decline he had been following over the years. She started to look through the pile again. Nothing, apart from several cuttings about their own village shop. Oh well, Andrew certainly wouldn't be buying a shop now. It was curious, though, his interest in the one in – where was it? Brockwood. Must be Hertfordshire, or the articles wouldn't have appeared in *The Mercury*. The most recent cutting was dated October last year. The shopkeeper had died, and it was hoped that the village would not lose its shop, and that whoever bought the property would not want to replace it with just a house. Maybe Andrew *was* planning to become a shopkeeper! She suddenly had the most ridiculous thought: was he buying it for Jacob, to lure him home to England? Surely not, *his son* a shopkeeper? Never.

On the other hand, though … *his son* owning a *chain* of village shops … Yes, she could see that.

A sudden sound from the hall broke into her reverie: Constance was awake. Hurriedly Emma put away the folder and shut the drawer.

'Oh, there you are,' Constance said. 'What's going on?'

'Nothing. You were asleep and I didn't want to disturb you.'

'Oh. Yes … mm … yes, I think I did … drop off for a few moments.'

'It's all right, Connie, you're allowed to; it's not a crime.'

Constance smiled stiffly. 'How was Andrew?'

'The same.'

'Oh, my dear …' Constance sighed. 'Let me get you something.'

'Yes, all right.' A bit of Connie's cosseting would be nice. Emma followed her sister out of the office.

'At least you're safely home tonight, not sleeping in a strange bed in Chigwell.'

Emma halted. 'I don't think I will have anything,' she said. It was an effort to keep her voice calm, neutral. 'I think I'll go straight to bed. Goodnight, Connie.'

'Oh. But …'

Emma climbed the stairs swiftly. She didn't look back; she couldn't face the inevitable questions. Sleep, that was what she needed; no more talking, thinking. She fell asleep almost instantly, but only an hour later she was wide awake, and thoughts she didn't want swirled around her brain. There was no way she would risk going down to the kitchen for a warm drink, not with those two creaky stairs, the ones Andrew had begrudgingly promised to look at but never had – 'It's you,' he'd said, 'you will insist upon walking down one side'. Connie, always a light sleeper, was sure to hear her. She could read, she supposed, but her current book was heavy going; it would not distract her. She needed to think about something peaceful, like a walk in the country, or something anodyne, like shopping, but, of course, the thought of shopping inevitably brought her back to village shops, to the shop in Brockwood. Maybe she should go there, see it, tell him about it, maybe put in a bid for it … so that when he came home, and he was well again, he would have a new interest. She'd go there, with a friend … or maybe with Connie. It would be a nice day out for both of them; something different, and yes, something she could share with Connie; she owed her that much. Emma snuggled down under the duvet and closed her eyes.

CHAPTER TEN

The blue van had cost Garry six hundred pounds.

'Where'd you get the money from?' Paula asked. They were outside Garry's block of flats. She had brought him a small folding table that had been in Grandad's flat; it was the only piece of furniture that Garry wanted to keep.

'Sold them toys, din't I?' Garry said, not looking at her, focusing on brushing out the vehicle's interior. It was a shock having Paula turn up like that; he'd have to think up a good story fast.

'You sold them all? Even the Dinky cars?'

'It was them brought in the money.' He dared to look at her now. He'd forgotten about the cars; they would have sold well. 'Like you said, they was worth a bit.'

'How much?'

'I dunno, the guy put everything together and … What? You think I stole the money, is that it? Why would I do that when I got things to sell?!'

'All right, all right, keep your hair on!'

'You said I should get wheels, then I'd get a job. There's no pleasing you, is there?' Garry locked the van and began to walk away. He wished he'd not said he liked that old table. He remembered playing cards with his Grandad, both of them sitting at it; he'd scratched it one time with a pin and Grandad had ticked him off, slapped his hand; he had cried – he was only about six – and Grandad had hugged him. He'd thought it would be nice to have it in his flat; now he wasn't so sure. Having that money, and that note, and now the table; it was getting too much.

'Oh, you've got a job then, have you? Well done, you. Where is it?'

'What?' Garry turned round briefly, then continued his walk down the concrete path to the flats' entrance.

'The job, where is it? What is it?' Paula was right behind him.

Garry prayed she wasn't planning on coming in; she'd see the toys. 'Down the Abbey; I told you before,' he replied quickly. 'It's a garage. I'm going there now; just got to pick something up from the flat. No need for you to come up, I'm only going to be a second.'

'Don't worry, I'm not coming in. No thank you. So what's the job then?'

Best to turn round, look at her, give her a smile, Garry thought. 'I don't know yet; cleaning cars, I think.' Best not to sound too positive, Paula would know he was lying.

'Oh,' she groaned. 'I might have known it; someone offers you a job and you don't ask any questions. It's not a *driving* job again, is it? Because if it is, Garry …'

'Oh, fuck off, will you! No, it is *not* a driving job!'

'Okay, okay. I believe you.'

'Yes, well you better … because it's the truth.'

Garry watched Paula get into her car and drive away. He watched until the car had turned into the road; only then could he breathe normally again. He felt as if he'd been holding his breath from the moment that Paula had appeared in the flats' car park. Just by chance he'd been looking out of his bedroom window at that moment; he was able to race down the stairs and open up the van before she got to the entrance to his block.

There was no job, as yet, but he *had* spoken to a guy at a garage down the Abbey, so there could be work there. Not that he'd actually asked: he was only there to fill up the tank with cheap petrol. When he'd taken possession of the van just two days ago, the gauge, which probably wasn't accurate, was registering under a quarter full: it might be tricky getting up to Brockwood and back on that, especially as he couldn't remember seeing a garage in any of the villages on the way.

Was Paula on her way there? He knew she would be going back sometime, but he didn't think it would be today; she had turned her car in the direction of London, not north Hertfordshire. He'd not wanted to ask, in case she offered to take him there or go in his van. What he had to do in Brockwood, at the shop, was best done alone.

* * *

'So why didn't Constance want to come?' Jackie asked, fastening her seatbelt; Emma had made a detour and picked her up in Chigwell.

'Oh, she said the idea of looking at a shop that Andrew might, or more likely, might *not* want to buy, when he's lying in hospital unable to move or speak, was bizarre …

and "lacking in taste" she said. She's right, it probably is, but … oh God, Jackie, I just felt I had to get out of the house, *do something* … anything … that makes me feel I'm doing something for Andrew. God knows there's little I can do. I said as much to Connie, but she didn't see it that way.'

'Oh well, her loss, my gain. Thanks for thinking of me.'

'Thanks for coming.' It had been an impulse to invite Jackie to come with her, a sort of rebuff to Constance, which she now regretted. 'I was quite rude to Connie. I shouldn't have been, but she does annoy me at times.'

'Normal for siblings, isn't it? Not that I'd know. Tell me, does Constance have a love life?'

Emma laughed. 'I don't think so. If she had she wouldn't tell me. There was someone once, a long time ago; I was in my teens.' She paused, remembering. 'I've got a feeling …' she turned to look at Jackie, 'he was married.'

'Oh yes; makes sense. Someone she worked with, was it?'

'Yes, it was.'

'Oh, poor old Connie. And the wife … as I know only too well. And Bernie, of course …'

'Bernie?' Emma took her eyes off the road, almost swerving into a cyclist.

'For Christ's sake, Emma!'

'Sorry,' Emma said, braking hard. Concentrating on the road ahead, she nevertheless knew that Jackie was looking at her.

'Didn't you know? It's partly why they split up; Eunice had an affair.'

‘Yes, I did know.’ She didn’t want to talk about Bernie’s short-lived marriage to Eunice. It had been a long time ago: Bernie was about to set out on his career as a solicitor and Eunice’s father, a family friend, was the head of an influential commercial law firm.

‘Don’t you think it’s odd that …’

‘That what?’ Emma said, gripping the wheel tightly. That Andrew has never suspected Bernie loves me?

‘That Bernie didn’t know Andrew had a file of cuttings about village shops.’

‘No. Not at all. Why should he? I didn’t know until I found them.’ She took a deep breath; that’s better, let’s talk about the village shop; that’s why we’re here. ‘Look,’ she said, brightly, ‘we’re nearly there; it’s the next village.’

‘Good,’ said Jackie.

They drove in silence, Emma still tense, looking directly ahead, Jackie gazing fixedly out of the window, until they came in sight of the Brockwood village sign, a black and white badger against a background of dark green trees.

‘Oh, how pretty. Look, Emma.’ Jackie’s voice was warm.

‘Yes, it is.’ Emma felt herself relaxing. ‘Look out for the shop, will you, Jackie. Please.’ She slowed the car to a crawl.

‘Can’t be far away, little village like this. Nice-looking pub; we can have lunch there. Oh look! There's the shop.’ Jackie turned her head and smiled at Emma; Emma smiled back. if Jackie *did* know what had taken place between her and Bernie, she wasn’t going to say anything, not today anyway.

'This is fun!' She patted Emma's knee. 'I haven't looked at a property for a long time.'

Emma felt her face going red with embarrassment; 'Oh, Jackie … I didn't ask you to come along because …'

'I'd worked for an estate agent?'

'Oh, Jackie, I'm so sorry.'

'You have nothing to be sorry about; I still love looking at properties, and estimating what they might be worth. In fact, I'm thinking about starting up my own agency soon.'

'Oh,' Emma said. 'Oh, so …'

'So, you see, you're doing me a favour! Come on, let's go and have a look.'

The shop, with a worn fascia in Gothic lettering announcing itself as Brockwood Stores, faced onto the small village green, which was dominated by a larger and more elaborate village sign, this time showing several badgers with woodland behind them. Brockwood Stores was set back from the road with parking space on the gravel area in front. There was one other vehicle there, a blue van. Emma drew up her car beside it.

Through the windscreen the women peered at the shop front, at the faded green door and the small, dusty bow windows on either side. Weeds were poking through the gravel and in the cracks in the concrete path that surrounded the building. There was a battered wooden gate at one side, half-covered in withered brambles which had encroached from the bank alongside.

Emma felt disappointed, and a bit sad: the place had such a forlorn air. 'It looked much better in the newspaper,' she said.

‘The agent will have fished out a picture taken years ago. It’s going to need a helluva lot of work, but it’s very picturesque, and with the right buyer, that could be a real selling point. Let’s have a look round the back; you can often tell a lot about a property from the back.’ Jackie tried opening the old gate but it wouldn’t budge. ‘That’s a pity,’ she said. Emma hadn’t followed her; she was still standing by the car. ‘What’s the matter? Don’t you want to see any more?’

Emma shook her head. ‘No, I don’t think I do.’

‘Why?’

‘I don’t know. It’s just … there’s something about this place I don’t like. Sorry.’

‘No, don’t be. Giving you ‘bad vibes’, is it?’

‘Well, yes.’ Emma laughed weakly. ‘That’s one way of putting it, I suppose. If you don’t mind, Jackie, I’d like to go home.’ Emma walked over to the car and opened the driver’s door. She was impatient to leave. She was puzzled, and disturbed too, to think that Andrew could have been interested in this broken-down building in an out-of-the-way village. It made no sense. And yet he must have been; else why would he have all those cuttings about this one shop?

‘Yes, sure.’ Jackie allowed herself a quick glance through one of the grubby bow windows, then followed Emma to the car. ‘Oh, hang on a minute, though, there’s someone coming.’

A young man in dirty jeans and a grey fleece was sprinting across the road.

'He doesn't look very happy,' Jackie said. 'Hello.' She gave the young man a beaming smile.

'Hi,' he said. 'What are you … ?' Then, as if he realised they might be potential buyers, 'Can I help you, ladies?' he asked, pushing back the hood of his fleece. 'I'm the owner; I can show you around if you like.'

* * *

A rumbling in Garry's insides when he'd pulled up his van outside the shop reminded him that he'd had no breakfast; he'd grab a sandwich at the pub across the road. And while he was doing that he might learn if anyone had been sniffing round. There was always people wanting to get one over on the agent; they'd look up the place online, have a decko, suss out the info they needed, often as not from the local pub … and that was it. Job done; both parties happy, money in the bank. Yeah well, okay, he might not be able to pull that off, but it was always worth a try; no one wanted to pay agents' fees if they didn't have to. He finished his sandwich and went up to the bar. He could murder a beer, but best not; he needed a clear head.

'Any interest in the … mm … ?' He leaned on the bar, jerked his head, casual-like he hoped it looked, towards the shop.

The barman was polishing a wine glass with a tea-towel. 'Why? Are you hoping to get a job there?'

'No! It's *my shop,*' he shouted. Oh fuck, he'd not meant to say that, but Jesus, this guy riled him, the way he looked down his nose, sneering; he'd been happy enough to sell him a sandwich. The few other people in the pub stopped talking. They were looking at him; he knew they were, he could feel their scorn. And he could feel his heart pumping hard. He turned round, glared at them. 'What you staring at? That's my Grandad's shop. He left it to me and my sister. Ask anyone.'

'Your grandfather, eh? So what's his name? Um?'

It was all Garry could do to stop himself reaching across the counter and punching the guy. He wished he never said anything. Okay, he'd do what Paula said he should do when he felt like this: take a deep breath and let it out slowly. In out, in out; a smug smile on the barman's face, the punters silent, waiting.

'Freddie Gesson,' Garry said loudly. They wanted to know: right, he'd tell them. 'He died last year. And my Nan, Myrtle, she died four years ago. That enough *information*' – he meant it to sound sarcastic; he hoped it did – 'for you?'

The barman shrugged, put the glass down on the counter. 'Sorry, mate. You can't be too careful.'

'Yeah, well …' Garry said, thrown off-guard. 'I s'pose not.'

* * *

The owner? This scruffy young man in the dirty jeans offering to show them around?

'No thank you,' Emma said quickly, stepping into the car.

'Hang on,' Jackie whispered, bending down, looking into the car, where Emma was reaching for the ignition.

'I want to go!'

'Just give me five minutes; sit tight, and I'll be with you.'

'Okay. Please don't be long, Jackie!'

'I won't.'

Emma sat, rigid, facing front. What else could anyone want to know about this horrid little shop! Let alone look inside! In the rear view mirror she could see Jackie and the man talking. She watched, astonished, as Jackie took out from her bag what looked like a diary, wrote in it, smiled at the man and shook his hand.

'What was all that about?' Emma asked angrily as Jackie got into the car.

'Oh, nothing. I just took his mobile number, that's all.'

'Whatever for? I'm not interested, Jackie; I don't even want to *see* the place again!' She started up the car. 'It's horrible!'

'Don't you want lunch?'

'No, I do not!' She'd not meant to sound so cross. 'Well, not here anyway. Let's find somewhere on the way home.'

They were well out of the village before either of them spoke again.

'Sorry,' Emma said.

'No, I'm sorry.'

'You didn't say anything about Andrew to that guy, did you?'

'No, of course I didn't!'

Through the villages of Hare Street and Dassells silence hung uncomfortably between them. At last, approaching the junction with the A10 Emma broke it.

'Why did you take his number?' she asked, doing her best to sound light and chatty. There was no point in being at odds with Jackie, nor did she want to be.

'Oh … you know me and property.' Emma could feel Jackie relaxing beside her. 'Well, maybe you don't, but … I just can't resist it, Emma, when I see a property up for sale. I want to know more; I think about possible buyers.'

'Oh. So you don't want it for yourself?'

Jackie laughed. 'No! I don't want it. But if I'm setting up an agency …'

Emma felt a great sense of relief. Now she really could forget about that dull little village, and the shop and everything to do with it. What a crazy idea to think that Andrew would have wanted to buy it!

* * *

Garry watched the two women driving away. He smiled to himself; she'd get in touch, the one who'd taken his number, she'd want to know what he'd take for it, if they could do a deal. He reckoned she fancied him, too, the way she'd looked at him, eyes wide open; women did that when they wanted something from you, he'd found. Maybe this one just wanted him to bring the price down. Wasn't up to him, was it? It wasn't his shop, it was Paula's. Although … if he could cut a deal, save her paying the agent's fee. Oh, forget it, Garry, Paula didn't do things that way. And he could forget the woman. Too old; she was sexy though, in them black jeans.

He took the bunch of keys out of his trouser pocket; he hoped to God one of them fitted the front door, or even the back door, provided he could get through that side gate. There were four keys that looked likely, but he'd brought all of them along just in case. He had found the bunch on a hook in the hallway that led upstairs to the flat. He'd had a feeling Paula wouldn't want him to have a key of his own – yeah, well, it was her shop *and* her flat, now; and she didn't trust him – but he never could resist the look and sound of keys, right from when he was a kid and Dean had given him an old tin full of them and he'd gone round the flat and then down the street trying them in all the doors. He'd got an ear-bashing from his Mum for that, but Dean had just laughed, said it was what kids did, and anyway, wasn't that what keys were for?

The third one Garry tried opened the shop door; he made his way up to the loft. He wanted another look round before the place was finally cleared; that day he'd found the money he had a feeling he'd missed something, that there was something else he was supposed to see. It was a bit like one of them treasure hunts Grandad used to do for them at Christmas when he and Paula was kids. Maybe Grandad had left him a clue in one of them old suitcases; he hadn't had time before to look in all of them.

No, there was nothing, just dust and spiders. The few toys he'd left behind last time were cheap plastic things, some of them with sharp edges, toys that 'Elf and Safety' wouldn't allow today, not even on a market stall. Garry sighed. Waste of time this. Although … maybe not; he'd spoken to that woman – didn't get her name – and she'd taken his number; he should have got hers. Never mind, she might call him – he had given her his real number – and if she didn't? Well … it was the story of his life, wasn't it? Missed the good opportunities, gone for the wrong ones. Today didn't matter, it might only be a small thing, but the money – he still hadn't dared count all of it – that did matter; he couldn't leave it in the envelopes, just spending a bit here and there, like buying the van, and then, in the market, them headphones. Bargain they was, classy, real cheap. Funny how having money changed the way you looked at things; a few weeks back thirty quid for headphones, however good, was too much; now, it felt like small change.

Garry locked up the shop and drove back to Waltham Cross, the envelopes and their contents stored away in a strong metal box under the passenger seat of the van. He didn't like banks - like Grandad he didn't trust them - but there must be some better way of keeping tabs on all this cash than taking it around with him all the time. If only he could work out what Grandad's note meant; maybe that would tell him.

CHAPTER ELEVEN

'Did you have a good day?' Constance asked.

'No, I did not, and I don't want to talk about it.'

'Oh. Well, in that case I won't enquire any further.'

'Connie, I'm sorry. I'm tired, and before you ask, no thank you, I don't want anything to eat.' I'm bothered and upset and I want to see Bernie. And I don't want to see Bernie. Oh, it's all too much.

'You sure? You must keep up your strength, Emma.'

'Yes. I know. And I will, but right now there's something I have to look at in Andrew's office.' Connie raised a questioning eyebrow. 'For Bernie.'

'Oh.'

Emma, feeling the rejection and puzzlement, and also Connie's dislike of Bernie, which she was conveying in that one little word, crossed the hall and put her arms around her sister. 'I won't be long,' she said. 'And then perhaps we could have a cup of tea?'

'And a toasted teacake? I got some lovely spicy ones at the shop this morning. I know you like them.'

'Yes, I do. Thank you.' If she had any sense, she would now go with her sister into the kitchen, help her to butter the teacakes, maybe choose the jam they would like to spread on them, but no … she was going into Andrew's office and she was going to have another look at those cuttings. For what possible reason? She had loathed that shop; why have anything more to do with it? It was like a scab that you couldn't help picking at.

'Don't be long,' Constance said. 'They're best eaten warm.'

Emma pulled out the cuttings connected with the shop in Brockwood; she looked at the dates: they began in the early Nineties, and the latest was October last year. The cuttings about other shops, including the one in Pengate, were all recent, none going back further than three years ago. So what? His interest in the Brockwood shop, which probably started in his years at Cambridge, had sparked off his interest in other village shops … and when the Pengate shop looked to be in danger of closing, Andrew had begun to collect cuttings about all of them. Perhaps he felt sentimental about the Brockwood shop, although sentimental was not a word she would ever associate with Andrew. He despised sentimentality, and said so – he disliked films that had Emma reaching for the tissue box. There must be something more to this. Even if there was, did it matter? Andrew was ill, very ill, in hospital, and here she was fussing over some stupid old newspaper cuttings! Oh, for goodness sake, woman, put them away, go and eat a teacake! She shoved the folder back in the drawer and pushed it shut.

* * *

‘That was lovely; thank you,’ Emma said, wiping away the last tiny bits of cherry jam from the side of her lips. ‘I’d better go and change now, before I go to the hospital.’

‘Must you go? You’ve already done an awful lot today, Emma. Burning the candle at both ends … you know what happens.’

‘I know! But I have to go. I do.’

‘Is … *Bernard* … coming for you?’ It was like an acid drop in her mouth.

‘No, I’m driving there.’ Emma kept her voice deliberately calm.

‘Then I shall come with you.’ Constance at her soothing best.

Emma felt her calmness receding. ‘There’s no need, Connie …’ Yes there was: with Constance at her side there would be no chance of an awkward conversation with Bernie, and she could do without that tonight. ‘... but if you want to …’ she smiled, ‘... that would be lovely. Thank you.’

‘Sensible girl.’ Constance beamed; she had a beautiful smile when she allowed her face to relax. ‘I’ll go and get myself changed, too. I feel sure these clothes must smell of food and cooking. Come on, we’ll go upstairs together.’ She hooked her arm through Emma’s and they walked up the stairs side by side.

It took Emma back forty years, to when she had hurt her ankle playing that stupid hockey at school, and Constance had had to help her up and down the stairs. It felt good to have someone caring for her again; she was suddenly desperately missing Andrew. Yes, he did smother her at times, made decisions for her, always needed to know where she was, who she was with – she felt she sometimes had to fight for privacy; not to have a secret, but just not tell him everything – but he did always care.

* * *

It was a shock for Constance to see Andrew, capable, always-in-control Andrew, like that, attached to wires and with machines beeping around him, registering every signal, or lack of one, that his body was producing; her face had gone white and she had lifted her fingers to her mouth. Emma suggested they have coffee before they drove home: she needed something to keep her awake; it had been a very long, exhausting day, and now, having seen Andrew, and knowing that, at least, he was no worse, she could feel the adrenaline draining out of her. There had been no sign of Bernie for which she was thankful; she was also concerned, and her mind began to race: was he all right? Did he not want to speak to her? Had Jackie told him how she had hated the shop, and had this upset him? All silly thoughts she would not have had if she hadn't been so tired. At the table Emma looked at her phone, which was on silent. A yellow envelope flashed up on her screen; she clicked on it; it was a message from Bernie: *Hi, sorry not with u. Call when u get home. xxx.* Emma clicked on Reply, typed *Will do*; her finger hovered over the letter x.

'Is everything all right?' Constance asked. 'In that message you got.' She nodded at the phone.

'Yes,' Emma said, adding two crosses and sending the message. They were only a formality, they didn't have to mean anything. She felt herself trembling; in this case they did. She closed her phone. 'Let's go home,' she said, abruptly, standing up. 'Will you drive, Connie?'

'Of course,' Constance said, looking up at her, obviously pleased to be asked. 'You just relax and I will do everything.'

'I only want you to drive!' She could read Connie's mind: it is so good to have my little sister needing me again; poor child, she has lost her anchor, with Andrew in peril; all that 'going it alone' is nothing more than bravado. 'I need to send some messages, and with you driving, I can do them on the way.'

'Oh. Oh, I see.' Constance stood up; her disappointment was palpable.

'It will be a great help, Connie, it really will.' She took her sister's arm, hoping to bring back the warmth she knew they had both felt walking up the stairs together in Pengate. 'Then, when we get in, I can go straight to bed.' She smiled at her sister. 'With one of your lovely warm drinks.'

The smile that Constance gave her back made her feel nervous; she had always known when Emma was keeping something from her.

'A problem shared is a problem …' Constance began.

'Well, of course I've got a problem … and we are sharing it! Or do you not think having my husband fighting for his life *is* a problem?'

'There's no need to speak to me like that, Emma.'

'Sorry.'

'I meant … is there something else troubling you?'

'No, there's nothing! What, d'you think that's not enough for me? Oh, let's go home; I'll drive.'

'But you said …'

'I know what I said. The messages can wait.' She couldn't bear the thought of Constance asking who she was texting or emailing, or worse, trying to read what she was typing. The good, close feeling between them had gone and Emma felt too irritated to try to get it back. She wished she *could* tell Connie what else was worrying her; for a start there was the mystery of the village shop – well, it felt like a mystery, not because she hadn't before this week known of Andrew's interest in village shops, but because he seemed to have kept it secret from her – and, of course, there was Bernie. Emma shut *those* thoughts off straight away.

Maybe she should talk to Connie about the shop … and the cuttings.

CHAPTER TWELVE

'Hold on a minute, Jackie. You know someone who might want to buy this shop, but you don't want to tread on Emma's toes? Well, I can't see how you are, if she didn't like it.' Bernie took a sip of his coffee; it had become unpleasantly cold. Jackie had been on the phone to him for a long time.

'Because of Andrew, and his association with it, of course.'

'There was no *association;* it was just a shop he liked to pop into on the way home from Cambridge.'

'There must be more to it than that,' Jackie said. 'Those cuttings he had; he must have had some interest in it.' Silence at Bernie's end. 'Well?'

'All right, if you want. I'll have a look at the cuttings, but I'm not going to make an issue of them; Emma's got more than enough on her plate at the moment. Now, is that it? Because I've really got to go.'

'Yes, that's it, for now. Bye.'

'Bye.' Bernie switched off his phone; he'd been on it most of the morning. If anyone wanted him urgently they could leave a message. He would make himself another coffee, and drink it this time, and then he would have a talk with Trev. Much to his surprise, Trev had settled in well; it hadn't taken him long to become part of the team and the customers liked him; he was probably acting the part of a friendly, helpful shop assistant, but it worked and that was all that mattered. Although Bernie had not yet sent him 'out on the road', he had already brought in a couple of saleable items that he'd spotted in a junk shop near his tube station – a little box shaped like a top hat, holding thorn gramophone needles, and an ancient German shellac record in a cardboard sleeve. Both of them had sold the very next day: it was time for Trev to start hunting in earnest for new stock. He would need a vehicle. Andrew's van; yes, that was it, the van that was kept in Andrew's garage in Pengate, alongside the green Bentley. Bernie smiled to himself. Oh, that Bentley, what a status symbol. It was, for Andrew, the quintessential, well-off, but not wealthy, Englishman's car, classy but not extravagant. Emma's car, reflecting her position as his wife, was a mini Cooper, smaller, as befitted his idea of what a woman should drive, but still very classy, a vehicle that he, too, would be happy to be seen in, and often was. Andrew had been torn between keeping the Bentley safe in the garage and showing it off under the portico of his house; it was Emma who had come up with the obvious solution: outside in the daytime when he was at home, in the garage at night and when he was away. Her mini was housed in a smaller garage at the other side of the house. As for the van … Andrew had at first been reluctant to keep it in Pengate at all, but a break-in at the yard in Islington, before they had security lights installed, had convinced him of the necessity of finding a safer home for it. He did not like being seen driving a commercial vehicle in the village; this all changed when the cricket team's van broke down and Andrew was able to come to the rescue.

Dragging his mind back to the present, and in particular Jackie's request, Bernie phoned Emma, asked her, please, to bring the newspaper cuttings with her later that day when she went to the hospital; it would be easier for both of them, he felt, if they looked at them in a crowded hospital café rather than alone in the close confines of Andrew's office.

* * *

In the café, their coffee mugs pushed to one side, Bernie read the newspaper articles, with Emma watching him as he went through them, slowly and carefully.

'Well?' she said at last. Bernie looked up; his eyes were shining and a small smile played about his lips. 'Will it be any use to Jackie?'

'Never mind Jackie … I have just had the most brilliant idea!' He patted the cuttings with his right hand, put his left hand over Emma's, on the table.

'Idea … for what?'

Bernie took his hand off hers; he lifted up the cuttings and waved them at her. 'For this,' he said, 'the shop! I'm going to buy it and turn it into another *That Music Place*!'

'But …' Emma began.

'No, hear me out.' He knew he shouldn't be doing this; it was none of his business, but he couldn't pass up this opportunity: it would be months, if at all, before Andrew was in a fit state to even consider such a proposition. 'It's the ideal location, close to Cambridge and there's a pub nearby; and it's surrounded by affluent people who store our sort of stuff in their attics and …'

'Oh come on, Bernie, that's not a good reason for wanting to …'

'Yeah, I know … Well, forget that bit, but … Honestly Emma, I have a really good feeling about this.' He was finding it hard to contain his enthusiasm. 'I mean … maybe this was what Andrew wanted; and this is why he had the cuttings!'

'Mm, maybe …'

'Listen, listen … we've just opened a shop in a village outside Oxford and it's going a bomb! So, surely … Cambridge; it has to be. Don't you think?'

'Oh, Bernie …' Emma shook her head. 'I thought you were supposed to be a hard-headed businessman?'

'Me? No, no, not me. Andrew's always been the sensible one.'

'I know, you're the dreamer.'

'Emma, sweetheart …' Bernie leant forward, put his hands on her arms. 'let me run with this a bit, yes? If nothing comes of it, there's no harm done.' He looked at her steadily, his face boyish with excitement. Emma was not responding as he had expected. With a jolt he realised why: the last time he had touched her … 'Sorry,' he said, withdrawing his hands and sitting back in his seat, 'I got carried away there. I didn't mean …'

'It's all right,' Emma said, swallowing hard, not looking directly at him. 'It is an exciting prospect, I can see that, and obviously you …'

'We do have to talk, you know, sometime ...'

'Yes, I know, but not here.'

'No.' She was right; this wasn't the place.

'I'd like to go and see Andrew again before we leave. Perhaps you could tell him about it.'

'Tell him what?' Bernie asked.

'Your idea. For the shop. Maybe that's what he had in mind all along. Who knows?' Emma's voice was hard, brittle. She stood up, picked up the newspaper cuttings, folded them carefully without creasing them, and put them into her bag.

'Emma ... please ...' He leaned forward, half off his seat.

'Let's go, shall we?' Emma turned and walked away from the table.

'I'm sorry,' Bernie whispered, 'I didn't mean to ...' She hadn't heard him, or if she had ... He sighed and reached round for his coat on the back of the chair; he got up and followed her out. Oh God, if only he didn't love her so much; even when he'd been married to Eunice he had loved her.

He didn't go into the ward with Emma; he felt he would be unwelcome at her side and she might have things to say to Andrew that she wouldn't want Bernie to hear. Was Andrew hearing, and understanding, what was being said around him? How dreadful that must be, Bernie thought, to hear, but not be able to respond in any way. And later when he could speak - *if* he could speak - would he remember what had been said? In which case, he hoped to God Emma was not talking to Andrew about the Brockwood shop, in the belief that the prospect of opening another branch of *That Music Place* would cheer him. He looked through the glass panel; Emma was sitting by the bedside, holding Andrew's inert hand. Bernie could see her lips moving. His lip-reading skill was limited, but he didn't think it was the shop she was talking about. Despite a feeling of excitement at the idea of buying the old shop – which might, of course, never come to anything – reading those newspaper cuttings Bernie had had a distinct sense of there being more to Andrew's keeping of them than just an interest in village shops. Unlike Bernie, Andrew was not a dreamer; he was a practical man driven by ambition; he would not have kept those cuttings without good reason. Bernie felt he needed to see the whole folder before he took the idea of a new shop any further.

'Follow me home then, and you can see them tonight. I think those were the only ones about that shop. Oh, and you can't take them away, you know.'

'Why not?'

'You just can't.' She looked away. 'They're Andrew's; they are not mine.'

* * *

Emma took the buff folder out of the drawer.

'Here you are,' she said, 'they're all in here.'

Bernie lifted out the pile of cuttings and put them on the desk. Emma took the folder from him. 'Oh, there's one more,' she said, taking out a small crumpled piece of newspaper from the bottom of the folder. She smoothed it out, but it was still difficult to read the print. She was about to put it aside and turn her attention back to what Bernie was looking at when she noticed the words *Goose and Pheasant*. 'Oh, that's the name of the pub in Brockwood!' She waved the cutting at Bernie. 'Look!'

'What?' Bernie took the cutting from her. 'Good heavens, listen to this. "George Peters, landlord of *The Goose and Pheasant*, said he had been very sorry to hear of the death of Freddie Gesson, owner of the Brockwood Stores, in Addenbrooke's Hospital, Cambridge. Mr. Peters told *The Mercury* that Freddie had never been quite the same since the passing of his wife three years ago. He said he didn't think either of them had ever really got over …" and the rest of the piece has been cut off. How peculiar. What was he keeping that for?'

'I don't know!' Emma snatched the cutting from Bernie's hand. 'He seems to have been obsessed with the place. I suppose I'd better put it back.' She re-crumpled it and pushed it into the crease at the bottom of the folder. 'I think you've seen them all now, the ones about that shop. I hope you don't want to look at any of the other cuttings; I've had enough.'

'Don't let it upset you.' Bernie began to reach out for her.

'No, please.' Emma drew away.

'We can't go on like this.' He sighed. 'Look … can't we at least have the door shut?'

'No, we can't! As it is, Connie will be …' It was Emma's turn to sigh. 'Go out to the car, Bernie,' she said softly. 'I'll say I've left something in there and I'll come out and speak to you.' Then brightly, her voice clear and loud, 'Well, I think we're done for tonight, Bernie. Time for you to go home.'

As if by magic Constance appeared at the door. 'Would either of you like a drink of some kind?'

'Er … no thank you,' Bernie said.

'Thanks, Connie, no. Bernie's got to get home.'

'Oh, I see. Yes. Did you find what you were looking for, Bernard?'

'No, unfortunately.'

'Oh dear, that's a pity. It must be very difficult for you, running your company without Andrew; he has such a good head for business.'

'Connie! Bernie has a head for business too, you know! And he knows a lot more about music than Andrew!'

'Well, yes, of course.' Constance looked taken aback at Emma's vehemence. 'All I meant was …'

'Come on, Bernie, I'll come out with you.' Emma pushed past her sister. 'I think I left something in your car.'

Constance moved out into the hall; Emma was already opening the front door.

'But you didn't come home in Bernard's car ... Oh dear, have I upset her?'

'No, I'm sure you've not,' Bernie said. 'Although, I suppose any mention of Andrew is going to upset her at the moment.'

'Yes, of course. Oh dear, how very thoughtless of me.'

'Are you coming?' Emma shouted from the drive; she was standing by the front passenger door. 'I'm getting cold out here!'

'Coming,' Bernie called. He crossed the hall. 'Goodnight,' he said to Constance. Then, feeling that was not quite enough, he turned back to her. 'Don't worry, I'll look after her, too.' At the door he clicked on the car's remote. Emma opened the front passenger's door and leant in, as if looking for something. 'You know we're being watched,' Bernie said. He turned round and waved to Constance, standing in the doorway. She nodded and raised her hand; she gave Bernie a warm-looking smile, but she didn't move. 'We can't talk with your sister there.'

'I'll come into town. I'll meet you at the shop.'

'There's no need; I'll come for you tomorrow evening and we can talk on the way to the …'

'No we can't! Not *in* the hospital, nor on the way there, and not on the way back either. I can't do it, Bernie, please don't ask me to! It's really best if we don't travel together at the moment.'

'I don't see why, but … All right then, you come to the shop.' He wanted to say, Come tomorrow, but he knew he must leave it to her. 'Soon.'

'Yes,' Emma said. 'Soon.'

* * *

Bernie drove home on auto-pilot, his tangled thoughts anywhere but on the road: Emma, the Brockwood shop, Emma, Trev, Emma … For now he must put aside thoughts of Emma; when she was ready she would talk to him, but until then there was nothing he could do; just love her from afar, and hope that somehow, without either of them hurting

Andrew, they could find a solution. It was the shop in Brockwood he needed to consider now: was it a stupid idea … or not? And why was he even thinking about it? For himself, to enlarge his 'empire'; or for Andrew, a project for him to take on board once he was out of hospital? He could see it: the old, abandoned shop that they had liked so much in their student days coming alive again, with Andrew at the helm. They might even turn part of the building into a café – every business had a café now. He could see it: punters from nearby Cambridge browsing among the instruments and musical ephemera, trawling the racks of LPs and the old sheet music, having a coffee and a pastry, then going back to browse some more and finally buy whatever had taken their fancy. Bernie smiled to himself. Oh yes, this idea definitely had legs. 'But before it can walk anywhere,' he said aloud, as if to tell himself that this was not a fantasy, that this *could* happen, '... someone needs to visit the shop.' He just didn't have the time, not at the moment, with hospital visits and … He'd send Trev! Trev, pretending to be a buyer! He already had a good grasp of the business; he could talk to the guy Jackie had met. 'Yes!' he said aloud, grinning. Ridiculous it might be, but it had raised his low spirits. He would get onto it straight away: a call to Jackie, another one to Trev. And not a word to Emma, not yet anyway.

CHAPTER THIRTEEN

Emma watched Bernie drive away, then turned to go into the house. Constance was still standing by the door; slowly Emma walked towards her.

'What you need is a nice …' Constance began. 'Emma, you're crying. What is it?'

'Oh, Connie, I'm so confused. I just don't know …'

'Come on inside.' Constance held out her hand. 'Let's get a hot drink into you.'

Emma shook her head. 'I don't want anything,' she said.

'But …?'

'I just want to talk.'

'To me?'

'Yes.'

'Oh. Well, we'd better go and sit down.'

Emma smiled; she sensed, even in those few words, her sister's confusion: should she be pleased or concerned?

'Where would you like to …?'

'In the kitchen,' Emma said.

They sat down opposite one another at the big pine table.

'Are you sure you don't want anything to …?'

'No.' Emma shook her head. 'Later. I just need to … clear my thoughts, I suppose, is what I really need to do. Oh

Connie, there's so much going on and I don't know what …'

'Is it Andrew? Or that shop you went to see? You really shouldn't be bothering with something like that, certainly not at the moment.'

'Don't lecture me, Connie. Just listen, please.'

'I will, but I do think it would help if …'

'Oh, go on then … make us a drink!' Emma waved her fingers, shushing her sister away. 'I'll talk to you while you're doing it.' It might actually be easier this way, Emma thought, not having Connie staring intently at her. 'It's … it's everything,' she said.

'If you want me to help you, you will have to be more specific,' Constance said, filling the kettle.

'I'll try.' Emma smiled; already it was easier. 'It is the shop, Connie.'

Constance spooned drinking chocolate into two china mugs. 'I'm listening. Go on.'

'It's weird; Bernie's got this idea that Andrew may have been wanting to buy it …'

'Oh! Surely not …'

'... and that's why Andrew has all these newspaper cuttings, and that buying the shop in Brockwood is something he's had in his mind for years, ever since they were at Cambridge. I mean … It's ridiculous! Andrew wouldn't want to be a village shopkeeper … would he? And yet … he has taken a lot of interest in our village shop, so maybe … maybe Bernie is right.'

Constance took milk out of the fridge and switched off the kettle, poured the hot water into the mugs, added the milk and stirred the drinks. She brought the mugs of chocolate to the table.

'I wish I'd never opened that stupid folder!'

'Why did you?'

'Because it was there!' Emma put her hands around the mug and drew it towards her. 'Wouldn't you have done? Out of curiosity?' If you had never been allowed to poke around in your husband's desk before: she hadn't even known where the key was till the day he needed that document from the drawer. 'You would, wouldn't you? Oh, come on, Connie, please say you would, even if it's only to make me feel better.'

'Yes, I expect I would. Curiosity is a powerful motive; a dangerous one, too, Emma.'

'Yes, I know, it kills cats!'

'I was *not* going to say that. Yes, I know I have a fund of sayings, *and* I know that they irritate you, but there's a lot of truth in them. They are, if you like, a succinct way of putting an unpalatable truth.' The sisters glared at one another; this is no good, Emma thought, picking up her mug and rising from the table. 'I'm sorry, dear. That was not helpful of me. Sit down again, please.'

Emma sighed. Reluctantly she sat down. It *was* helping, just getting things into the open a bit. She had never been able to confide in Connie; she had always felt her sister was judging her. Maybe she was, maybe she wasn't, but she was the only person Emma had to confide in at the moment; she did so need to talk and Connie's no-nonsense, practical approach might serve her well just now.

'I'm frightened, Connie, I'm frightened that Andrew is going to die … and all this … buying a shop nonsense … it's all so … so pointless. And … I don't even know if I should say this … but I feel there could be something … something deeper, darker … at the bottom of all this.' Oh God, I should not have said that! 'No, No, that's just me being paranoid.' She knew her laugh sounded false. 'I'm tired, well, over-tired really. *You* know how I get when I'm over-tired, Connie. My imagination takes a bit of a hold, doesn't it? I'm probably finding things that aren't there at all.' Emma laughed again; she could see her sister wasn't fooled. 'I'm just worried, about the future.' She began to shake with sobs.

Constance got up and walked round to the other side of the table; she put her arms around Emma and rocked her. She felt comforted, as she had when Bernie had held her – no, she mustn't go there. She felt herself tensing up; there was no way she could or would speak about that to Constance. She eased herself out of her sister's embrace.

'Thank you,' she said, giving Constance a quick kiss on her cheek. 'It has helped, all of it, especially the hug.'

'Well, you know what they say, a trouble shared …' Grinning was not Constance's forte, but there was definitely a grin on her face.

Emma laughed, a real laugh this time. 'Yes I do!'

'We may not have halved it, my dear, but …'

'A quarter perhaps, even a third maybe.'

'I'll settle for that.' Constance picked up the mugs, took them over to the sink. 'You can always talk to me, you know,' she said, her back turned to Emma. 'I do understand things, things you might not think I would.'

'Such as?' Emma said warily.

Constance turned round, a mug and a tea-towel in her hand. 'Love,' she said.

'Oh.' Emma's heart began to beat fast.

'And what it can do to you.' She put down the dry mug, began wiping the wet one.

'Yes.' Please, please don't start talking about Bernie.

'Having the man you love so very ill, and fearing you may lose him; it's bound to … well, sort of unbalance you.' Constance turned away, placed the tea-towel on the handle of the Aga's oven and the mugs back in the cupboard.

'Yes, of course.' Was Connie probing or did she really not suspect anything? Best to end this conversation now; those few moments when Constance was busy with the mugs had given Emma time to take control of herself again. 'I think I'll go and have a shower,' she said brightly, 'and then I'll go to bed.'

* * *

She shouldn't have had that shower; she was wide awake, and had been for the past hour and more. She looked at her mobile phone, which served as her bedside clock: 1.30 am. She switched on the light, tried reading, but she couldn't concentrate on the book. She knew why, and why she couldn't sleep: her mind kept straying to the contents of those folders. She lifted her red fleecy dressing gown from the end of the bed, pushed her feet into the accompanying red slippers – both a Christmas present from Connie two years ago – and went out onto the landing. Would Connie still be awake? What if she was? Emma needed answers, and whether her sister was awake or asleep she was going to stay in the room downstairs until she found them! Well, at least until she had made an effort to find them. She paused outside Connie's room, listening; yes, there it was, the soft, purring sound that Emma had known since childhood, when waking in the night and unable to get back to sleep, she had climbed into Connie's bed and snuggled down beside her.

It was chilly in the office – the central heating was off for the night. There was an ancient brown cardigan hanging behind the door: it had been there for years and no one knew why, or whose it was – or claimed they didn't, but Emma had a suspicion that it may have belonged to Andrew's grandfather, who had been a labourer of some kind, and it was a pleasing reminder to Andrew of how far he had risen in the world he had been determined to inhabit. Emma draped the old garment around her shoulders and sat down at the desk.

She lifted out the folder of cuttings, then the one that held the notebooks. She placed them side by side on the desk. She had had a feeling ever since she first searched the drawer for the information Bernie required, that everything in here was connected in some way, but how she couldn't see: a folder of cuttings about village shops and two little notebooks. Her practical sister would say she had been watching too many old Miss Marples; Connie loved the Joan Hickson ones, thought she was the best of the Miss Marples, maybe because she had met her once on a train going up to the Edinburgh Festival. Connie had actually confessed to being excited, sitting almost next to a famous actress.

Pulling herself back to the present, Emma took out the cuttings relating to Brockwood, placed them on the closed folder, took out the green notebook, put it down beside the cuttings.

Carefully she turned the pages, determined not to miss any clues to the possible significance of the words and figures. There were no sentences or phrases, just groups of letters: ORT, BSV, BFG. Then there was RAF. Well, she knew what that stood for; maybe there were other acronyms here. She looked again at the letters BFG … and, as if by magic, she saw Jacob, eight years old, lying on his tummy on the sunlit living room floor, feet up behind him, ankles crossed, head down, laughing as he read again a book he loved – Roald Dahl's BFG. The Big Friendly Giant. She had even bought him wooden stilts; dressed in a pair of Andrew's old cut-down trousers he had staggered up and down the lawn, occasionally falling down, but not hurting himself. They had laughed themselves silly, Emma and Jacob; it was so lovely to have fun with him when his father wasn't there. But then Andrew, arriving home early from work and hearing the laughter from the back garden, had caught them. Briefly, to Emma's joy, he had joined in the merriment – it was a very boyish thing his son was doing – then suddenly his face had darkened. Oh God, Emma thought, he's recognised the trousers; he can't have wanted to keep those, they were almost threadbare. No, it wasn't the trousers, it was the grass. The stilts had dug into his precious lawn. 'It's good for it,' Emma had said, 'it aerates it.' 'Not making bloody great holes like that it doesn't!' Jacob stood, swaying on the stilts; he'd never seen his father so angry. 'And you … get down off that thing and don't let me ever see you on it again.' Although that was the end of the stilts, Jacob still loved the book, continuing to read it, Emma recalled, in full view of his father, as if he was taunting him. Had this been an early sign of Jacob's rebellion? Could a child of eight exhibit such subtlety? Oh yes, Jacob could. Emma, starting to delve into other memories of Jacob as a child, suddenly became aware that she was feeling very cold; she pulled the cardigan more tightly around her, rubbed her chilled fingers together, and brought herself back to the letters and numbers in the notebook. Having decided she couldn't decipher the letters code, she looked at the numbers – 75, 200, 300, then occasionally an odd amount, for instance 110.50. Well, that surely, must mean one hundred and ten pounds and fifty pence. Were the others money or quantities? Two hundred … what? Old LPs? Back copies of New Musical Express or The Gramophone? Unlikely, Emma thought. She sighed deeply. Her brain felt clogged; she would get no further tonight. Best to put everything away, probably best to give up trying to solve this seeming mystery. Maybe it wasn't, maybe she was just making it into one. Maybe Bernie could explain it; he had only taken a cursory look at the book the other day. Yes, she would take it to the Islington shop when she went there for their promised talk; it would make things easier, having this to focus on when they met, before they spoke about their 'relationship'. For a few moments Emma allowed herself to think about this. Her dilemma was, that what she wanted and what she should do, were very different. Of course she wanted him; she could feel her body stirring at the thought of him. Quickly she closed the folders, put them away, pulled off the old cardigan, turned off the light, ran up the stairs.

In bed she tossed and turned, her brain still too active for sleep. She wished she had one of Connie's potions to ease her into slumber, not that she totally believed in them. Much as she disliked the idea of them, she knew that the mild sleeping pills her G.P. had prescribed when Andrew had his stroke, did work. Emma hadn't even wanted to take the prescription from him, but the doctor had insisted. 'It's very important that you sleep,' he had said. Scared that she might become addicted – she had seen it happen – she had only ever taken one. She had slept well that night, with no apparent after-effects. Above all else it was sleep that she needed now; she would take one tonight.

* * *

'Wake up, Emma! Emma! Wake up!'

'Um? What?' Emma looked blearily at her sister; she was waving something in her hand.

'It's the hospital, on the phone. They wouldn't speak to me.'

Immediately awake, Emma sat up, grabbed the phone from Constance's hand. 'Hello? … Yes. … Yes, I'm Emma Raven. … Yes. … Oh, that's wonderful! Oh. Thank you. Thank you so much. … Yes, of course I'll come in. …

When? Oh, right away, as soon as I can get there.' Shaking and tearful, Emma threw her arms around Constance. 'Oh Connie, he's speaking!' She leapt out of bed. 'Oh, God, where did I put my clothes? Oh, yes.' From the armchair, Emma grabbed last night's garments; she had been too exhausted to put them away in her usual well-trained way.

'That's very good news,' Connie said, guardedly, 'but it doesn't mean …'

'Could you … would you make me a cup of tea? Please? And some toast?' She knew Connie would insist she had some food inside her before she drove to the hospital; it also diverted her sister from the 'Now, don't get too excited, Emma,' speech she knew Connie was about to make. 'I'll have a quick wash and come down. Oh, and I'd better let Bernie know.'

'I expect Bernard knows already,' Constance said, picking up one of Emma's socks.

'What d'you mean?' Emma paused at the bathroom door.

Well … wouldn't the hospital have phoned him as well? Isn't that what was arranged? In case there was bad news; so that he could break it gently to you?'

'This is *good* news, Connie! *I'm* the first one to be told. You always have to be so …' Emma grabbed the sock from Constance. 'Oh, go and make me some toast!' She stormed into the bathroom and banged the door. 'I love you, Connie,' she shouted, 'but there are times when your "Do be reasonable" is not what I want to hear! And this is one of them!'

CHAPTER FOURTEEN

Garry twisted round on his seat by the window; he was getting nervous. Twelve thirty, the guy had said on the phone. It was almost one, and he wasn't here.

'Stop looking,' the barman said. 'He'll come when he comes, and if he doesn't, there'll be someone else.'

Garry turned from the window. 'Yeah, you're right,' he said. He'd had the call only the day before. Friend of Jackie, the guy said he was; interested in seeing over the shop. Jackie'd said it had possibilities and could be just what he was looking for. Said his name was Trevor, and he knew the way to Brockwood; he'd lived round that way as a kid. He sounded posh, but at the same time as if he was trying not to be; a bit like Michael Caine, Garry thought. He'd loved *The Italian Job*, seen it more times than he could remember.

There was a car drawing up outside, a Jag by the look of it. Someone coming to *The Goose* for lunch most likely. No, he was pulling onto the gravel in front of the shop. Garry felt his stomach knotting. He'd never seriously thought it would come to anything, letting that Jackie have his number; he wished now he'd given her a false one, then he wouldn't be sitting here, bricking it. Trevor – it might not be him, of course; Garry could be getting all steamed up for nothing – was getting out of the car. Tall guy, with a tache. Bloody hell, he was wearing a cap and a pair of them posh driving gloves with holes cut in the backs. What a ponce! Who cared, though, if he really did want to buy the shop; he looked like he could afford it.

'Your man's there,' the barman called out.

'Yeah, okay. I've seen him.' Garry got up, straightened his jacket – he'd thought he had better look respectable: he'd gone out and bought one in a charity shop, wanted to look as if he normally wore one – smoothed a hand over his hair.

'You'll do.' The barman grinned at him. 'Go for it, Garry.'

'Yeah. I will.' He could hardly get the words out, his mouth felt so dry.

'And bring him in here afterwards. Do that, and I'll stand you a pint.'

'Cheers,' Garry said. He glanced out of the window again. Yes, the guy was definitely there for him. Christ, if he delayed any longer, the guy might go. He sprinted across the road.

'Hi,' he said, surprised to hear that his voice actually worked. 'I think you're looking for me.' He recalled something he had seen in a film – that had been Michael Caine, too. He stuck out his hand. 'Garry Wade,' he said, surprised how good it sounded.

'Trevor Mitchell,' the man said, shaking Garry's hand. 'Good to meet you.'

'Me, too …' Garry started to say, quickly changing it to, 'Likewise.' He didn't know how long he could keep this up, but it felt good; it felt the right way to do this. Maybe this was part of Grandad's 'right thing'.

'Interesting property. Could make a jolly decent house. Good bit of land at the back, is there?'

'The back? Oh. Yes. Um … would you like to see that first?'

'Yes, happy to start there. Lead the way!'

Garry pushed hard on the side gate to open it.

'Not been used for a while,' he said, wishing he had checked it earlier. Finally it opened and he took Trevor into the back garden.

'Oh yes, surprisingly spacious. You could turn the house round, of course, focus the whole building on this area, keep the cars at the front, fence it off for security. Add a nice hedge.' He looked at Garry for approval; Garry nodded. 'Not that that's a problem round here, I should imagine; car thieves and all that.' Don't you believe it, Garry thought; you got a posh motor, someone will find it and it'll take more than a bit of fencing to keep them out. 'Oh no,' Garry said, 'quiet as the grave round here.' He wasn't sure why the guy wanted the property – maybe he was planning to hide stolen motors behind that hedge; the guy had his own posh wheels; who'd take notice of a couple more? – but if he really was interested that was all that mattered. Garry had always thought of the place as a shop, but it could just as easily be a house. Nice place to live, pub opposite; wouldn't mind that himself. 'Yeah, Sure. Your motors will be quite safe here.'

‘Oh, jolly good. Right. Now … show me round inside, will you.’

‘Yes, course,’ Garry said. He unlocked the front door and gave Trevor a tour of the shop and the flat.

‘And there?’ Trevor asked, looking up at the loft cover.

‘Oh, just a loft.’ He felt his heart racing. Come on, he said to himself, it’s only an old attic, with spiders and cobwebs.

‘While I’m here, I’d like to see everything. Get the whole picture, you know?’

‘Yes,’ Garry said. ‘No problem; it’s just … well, there’s nothing much to see.’

Trevor’s eyes narrowed. ‘All the same …’

‘Yeah. Sure.’ Useful place, the loft, for a guy with stolen motors to store spare parts. Garry was pretty sure this Trevor wasn’t who he said he was; come to think of it, he hadn’t said who he was, just that he’d spoken to Jackie. Oh shit, he wasn’t police, was he? It was the tache; you didn’t often see one of them these days, well, not like this one, all sort of bristly; this one had taken him right back to an interview room in Tottenham.

Trevor was looking around the loft. ‘With some windows in the roof, it would make a great place for the kids to play. Or, better still, make that opening a bit bigger and I could get my billiard table up here! Put a bar in that corner, where the roof slopes down, a nice long sofa on the other side. Oh yes, this is the business. Thanks, Garry, I wouldn’t have wanted to miss this.’

Garry felt himself relaxing. Crazy where the mind can take you; he’d really been off on one there – copper! – when all the guy wanted was a place to get away from his woman and have a few beers and a laugh with his mates; show them how far he'd come up in the world. Essex boy, that's what he was, this Trevor; that posh voice wasn't his; when he was talking about how he'd use the loft … oh yes, Garry could tell where the guy really belonged.

'If you have any more questions,' he said chirpily, 'perhaps I could answer them for you … over a spot of lunch across the way?' *Spot of lunch* … yeah, he could tell by Trevor's response he'd got the right words there.

'Excellent idea. And it's on me, by the way. You have been most helpful, Garry.'

Any minute now he's going to be calling me old chap, Garry thought. Posh guy is back. I don't mind; I'll talk to either of them, just so long as I can get something out of this. And if he did pull it off, Paula would be well pleased; maybe not at first, but when she realised how much he had saved her, bypassing the agent, she would, *and* she'd be happy for him to take a cut. Only fair; he was doing all the grafting.

CHAPTER FIFTEEN

'So, what do you think? Worth my while going to have a look at the place?' Bernie leant back in his office chair, folded his arms. He was trying not to be irritated with Trev, half-perched on the desk and still wearing his cap and driving gloves. 'What I need to know is …' Bernie sat upright. '… is it the right place for a shop like ours? Or not?'

Trev stood up and moved away from the desk. He took off his coat and his cap, and carefully placed them on a chair; then, as if deep in thought, he took off his gloves, finger by finger.

'Well?' Bernie said, his patience beginning to run out. Oh, come on, man, get on with it!

Trev laid the gloves carefully on top of the folded coat. 'Yes, I think it would.' His Trevor Mitchell costume discarded, he at last stopped acting the part.

'Good.'

'However … There's something not quite right about all this, Bernie.'

'Oh?'

'The guy I met … Garry. Something about him; well, for one thing, I don't think he was supposed to be there, you know, showing me around, as if he owned the place. Turns out it's his sister who's inherited the shop from their grandfather, and Garry's got … well, as far as I could make out … he's just got some old furniture and the stuff that was left in the loft. I got the feeling there was some jealousy there; sibling rivalry, that sort of thing. Anyway, it's what he said about the stuff in the loft that I think you might find interesting.'

'Well, tell me!' Come on, Trev, you're not auditioning for a part in the West End.

'He gave the first hint …' Bernie sighed. '... when we were up there. Showed me where he'd found all the old toys that his grandfather used to sell in the shop, said they were worth a bit, that he could most likely sell them. Then, as if he'd said something he shouldn't, he just shut up. Anyway, by then I'd seen the whole place, the shop area, flat, everything … and really, I could have left it there. You know, shaken hands, said I'd be in touch …'

'But you didn't.' Bernie said, trying to push Trev along, 'because you felt there was something else you should know.'

'Exactly!' Trev's smile was smug. 'So I bought him lunch at the local pub.'

'Oh. And I'm paying for that, am I?' Bernie asked.

'Depends if you think the information is worth it.'

'Oh. Well, go on, then. What *is* this gem of information I may be paying for?'

'He'd had two pints …' Trev began; he liked to tell a good story, 'and he started talking about his grandfather and what the shop had been like when he was a kid. It took another half, and a good bit of wheedling on my part, to get to the nub of it.'

'Trev, Trev. I know you're enjoying this, but please, I'm not down the road in the Almeida! I'm in my office, it's quite late in the afternoon and I want to go to the hospital. There is a slight improvement in Andrew's condition and …'

'Oh, that is good news.' Trev leant forward, enthusiastically, 'you must be so …'

'Yes, it is.' Bernie broke in quickly 'and I am. *And* ... I'd like to see him *today*, so please, just tell me what you've learnt that might be important.'

'It may not be important …'

'Just the words! Never mind the interpretation, I'll do that bit.'

'Yeah, sorry, I do get carried away, I …'

'Well bloody well come back! Now!' Bernie shook his head. 'It's the final scene, Trev, and the theatre's closing in …' he looked at his watch. ' … ten minutes. Tops!'

'Okay. Third drink inside him, Garry tells me, leaning over, all confidential … You know?'

'Yes, go on!'

'He says it's not just toys he found in the loft.' Trev paused, dramatically. 'There's cash … in envelopes; white ones, brown ones; two or three hundred in each, going back years.' Another dramatic pause.

'Just get to the end.'

'Okay. So … we have a laugh about that. *Cash in the Attic.* You know?'

‘Yes, I know.’ Bernie didn’t even try to keep the weariness out of his voice. At the same time, though, there was something nagging at him … ‘Did you say there were two hundred, or three, was it? In each envelope?’

‘Yes.’

‘And nothing to indicate who or where they were from?’

‘No, nothing. Well, he didn’t say there was. I could see from his face, though, and the way he kept moving his beer glass around on the mat, that he wished he’d not told me about it. “It is mine, that money,” he said, “Grandad left it to me, not Paula; she don’t know about it.” He really was *very* nervous; he said it several times, about his sister not knowing. As if I might want to find Paula and tell her! So, there you are. Something … or nothing? You’re the boss, you decide.’

‘Yes, well … Thanks, Trev, it’s worth the price of a lunch, anyway.’

‘Thank *you*. Oh, and if I could keep the bill … Expenses, you know? I have to submit them to the tax people.’

‘So do I. You’ll get your money and that’s it!’

‘Sorr-eee,’ Trev said, his face like a penitent clown.

‘You can put the performance down on your CV though,’ Bernie said, getting up from his chair; the debriefing was over. ‘If you want to.’ He just wanted to get out of the shop … and think.

‘Oh, cheers, Bernie. Thanks. Will do.’

* * *

All the way to the hospital it nagged: cash in envelopes, two or three hundred at a time. He pulled into the hospital car park. Oh my God … That notebook in Andrew's office, the little green one. The lists of figures – two hundred, three hundred – with initials beside them.

Bernie locked the car and walked into the hospital.

CHAPTER SIXTEEN

Emma, sitting as near as she could to the bed, was holding Andrew's hand as if she would never let it go.

'Iss, iss... hurss, hurss …'

'What, darling? What did you say?' Emma leant in close. Although Andrew could now speak it was very difficult to make out the words. She looked up at the nurse who was standing by the door.

'I think your husband is saying that it hurts.' She nodded towards Andrew's hand. 'You're probably holding it a bit too tightly.'

'Oh.' Emma looked down at her fingers, locked around Andrew's. 'Oh. Yes.' She released Andrew's squashed-together fingers from her grasp. 'Oh, my darling, I'm so sorry.' Gently she lifted his hand to her lips. 'I wouldn't hurt you for the world.'

'Ssanks …'

'I think that might be enough for now, Mrs. Raven,' the nurse said.

'Yes, of course.' Poor Andrew, he looked exhausted; his head lay on the pillow and his eyes were barely open. It was going to be a long time before he was back to full health. Instinctively she turned to the glass panel that separated the room from the corridor outside; yes, Bernie was there. She smiled weakly. She felt drained; it had been a deeply emotional experience speaking to Andrew. Bernie smiled back. Emma was glad he was there; she didn't feel she could hear what the doctor had to say on her own.

'His slurred speech?' the doctor said. They were in his office; the doctor behind his desk, Emma and Bernie side by side, facing him. 'Yes, well that's partly because of the medication he is on. Think of it as a medical hangover if you like.'

'Oh, I see.' Emma managed the beginning of a faint laugh, but within seconds she stopped it; Andrew's speech was not her main concern. 'But he's still …' It was hard to say the word. '... paralysed, isn't he?'

'Yes, he is,' the doctor said, 'but it's a really positive response, the fact that your husband is trying to speak. He is doing well, Mrs. Raven, and there is a good chance that he will make an almost full recovery …'

'Almost?'

'Hear me out, Mr. Silver, please.'

Bernie lifted both hands, palms upwards and spread. 'Carry on,' he said.

'I say *almost* because there is likely to be some residual weakness – we can't say yet what form it will take, mental or physical – but there is no reason why, eventually, your partner should not be able to lead a totally normal life and resume his career. But not for some considerable time and, of course, there must be *no pressure* put on him, either to return to work or not.' The doctor paused, cleared his throat. 'I'm sorry to sound so prescriptive,' he said, then seeing

Emma's smile, he relaxed, sat back in his chair. 'Yes, I suppose it is an appropriate word for a doctor to use … although … I cannot, nor can any medical man … person …' He made quotation marks with his fingers, '"write the future", and every stroke patient's recovery is different.'

What a difficult job this man has, Emma thought, annoyed with herself for being irritated by him earlier. He knows that people like me, like Bernie, want only good news.

'We understand,' she said. 'We know it won't be easy, but …' She looked at Bernie. '... we both love him – Bernie is a life-long friend as well as a business partner – and we want the best for him.'

'And that you shall have.' The doctor stood up; the consultation was over. They shook hands and left the room.

Standing just outside the door, not caring if the doctor could see them, Emma put her head on Bernie's chest. 'We'll get through this,' he whispered. She drew back. Oh, my God, what am I doing, she thought.

* * *

Emma pulled into the gravelled Pengate drive ahead of Bernie. They locked their cars and walked side by side to the front door. Emma put her key into the lock.

'Before you go in,' Bernie said, putting his hand over Emma's. 'I meant what I said: we *will* get through this.' He took his hand away.

'Yes. We will.' Emma's voice was flat; she was tired and there had been enough emotion floating around for one day. She wished Bernie had not driven home with her, but he had muttered something about the green notebook and how he needed to look at it, now. Emma had felt too weary to argue.

The house was quiet and Constance had obviously gone to bed. She wouldn't be asleep; she'd be reading, waiting to hear the sound of the key in the lock.

'That you, Emma?'

'Yes, and I've got Bernie with me. He's just getting some papers from Andrew's office. I'll be up in a minute.'

'Do you want me to make a hot …?'

'No, Connie, thank you. Go back to sleep.'

'Oh, I wasn't asleep.'

'Yes, well, whatever you were doing go back to it,' Emma said, trying not to sound cross.

Bernie had already gone into the office.

'Come and sit down,' he said, pulling out Andrew's swivel chair.

Emma shook her head. 'No,' she said, 'just take what you want and go.'

'Emma?'

'I'm tired, Bernie. I want to sleep. I just want to stop thinking, wondering, worrying.'

'Come here.' Bernie held out his arms to her.

'No. No. Please.' The way she was feeling, if she went to him now … 'No, Bernie.' It would be so lovely, so easy. It was a good thing Connie was awake. 'Take the book and go. Please.'

Bernie dropped his arms. 'Bottom drawer?'

‘Yes. Red folder.’ A whisper was all Emma could manage; she suddenly felt faint. While Bernie opened the drawer and took out the folder, she put her hand on the back of the swivel chair, steadying herself until the faint feeling passed.

‘Got it,’ Bernie said, turning round.

‘Good. Well, I hope it gives you the information you need.’

‘Don’t you want to know what …?’

‘No! If it’s anything to do with that horrible shop, I certainly don’t! Not now, anyway.’ She waved Bernie and the book towards the door. ‘Maybe tomorrow, when I’m not feeling so …’

‘I know.’ His voice was full of warmth and tenderness. ‘You can’t think straight when you’re tired.’ Please, Bernie, just go. ‘I’ll see myself out. Call you tomorrow. Sleep well.’

CHAPTER SEVENTEEN

The Chigwell house was warm. Bernie took a glass and a bottle of malt whisky into the living room. He put them on a small table beside his favourite chair; it had been his mother's and now it had become his. Although the sight of it, empty, made him sad, it was strangely comforting to be sitting in it.

For a while he just sat there, sipping his drink and thinking. Emma, Andrew, their future, their past. There was something in their past, his and Andrew's, that troubled him. Andrew hadn't always told the truth; Bernie knew that, but it had never bothered him. On the contrary, he had found it amusing. If he had had what Andrew called, in an unguarded wine-fuelled moment, his 'humble beginnings', maybe he would have wanted to invent different ones, starting himself off higher up the social register. Had Andrew's father owned a small hardware shop, but become too ill to run it, and subsequently died? Or had he lost money, gambling on a business venture, then left his wife and child? Or was neither of those stories true? As far as Bernie was concerned it didn't matter two hoots, but then it was easy for him not to care; he had an assured, well-documented background: successful lawyer turned businessman father, mother from a prosperous Jewish family almost as well established as the Rothschilds.

He drained the glass and reached for the bottle; one more dram and he would look at that notebook. Dutch courage; he felt he needed it. He downed the whisky quickly and took the notebook out of his jacket pocket. He stared at it for a few moments. For God's sake, what was he expecting? That something horrific from Andrew's past was going to jump off the pages and hit him? Oh, pull yourself together, Bernie, it's only a notebook with numbers and letters in it; it's just Andrew doing what he liked to do, giving the appearance of being mysterious, a schoolboy playing with codes. If Andrew had had a different background, one like his, Bernie reckoned he might have become a spy; he had told him so once, and Andrew had taken him seriously. 'Oh yes,' he had said, 'I could have done that very well.'

Figures and initials. That was all the information, if you could call it that, the notebook contained, and to Bernie's eyes it seemed very random. The figures could mean anything: pounds sterling, dollars, euros … or not money at all; units of merchandise maybe? And the sets of initials … well, they were anybody's guess. Places, people, map references. It was no good; the more he stared at the pages the less he understood. Besides, it was late; time he went to bed. He glanced at his watch: 10.45. Probably not too late to phone Trev; get the number of that guy he had met at the shop. That would seem the only way, Bernie thought, of making sense of all this: talk to … Garry, that was his name. See if the two and three hundred pounds in envelopes had any connection with 200 and 300 in the notebook.

'Oh, hi Trev. I need some info from you.'

* * *

Bernie pulled into the car park of *The Goose and Pheasant*. The pub didn't appear to have changed in the thirty years since Bernie had been here: mock-Tudor frontage, pebble-glass windows, the same two birds on the swinging sign. Inside, too, it was as he remembered it: dark oak beams and furniture, an ingle-nook with a real wood fire and faded hunting prints on the dun-coloured walls; it was almost exactly how an American tourist would expect an English pub to look, with the exception of the wide-screen TV, not on just now, at the far end.

Trev had advised against talking to Garry: 'I think the guy said more than he meant to. You might do better with the landlord; his name's George. If you get there around twelve he'll be there, and he'll have time to talk.'

'A half of your best bitter,' Bernie said, walking purposefully up to the bar, where a large, imposing-looking man was polishing glasses.

'Certainly, sir.' The man pulled the beer and placed the over-flowing glass on the towelling mat.

'And one for yourself, of course.' Bernie put a ten pound note on the counter.

'Oh, thank you, sir.' The man took the money, gave Bernie his change. 'And will you be having lunch too, sir?'

'Oh. Yes … I may as well,' Bernie replied, as if he wouldn't have thought of it if the landlord, as the man obviously was, hadn't put the idea into his head. 'It is about lunchtime. Yes, good idea, landlord.' His acting skills were not so rusty after all.

'George.'

'George,' Bernie said, smiling, lifting the glass of foaming beer.

Bernie drank deeply; he would need to eat after this. He smacked his lips. 'That is a very good ale, George. Mmm. Very good.' Fortunately it was.

'Local brewery, sir.'

'Really?' Up to now Bernie hadn't decided quite how he would 'play this part'. He began to see a way. 'Yes, yes … I do seem to remember … let me think … Mm … Chilbey? Charlbey, something like that ...'

George laughed. 'You're nearly right, sir. Chorley's.'

'Chorley's! Yes, of course. Oh, it's there on the pump! I must need specs! Right,' he put the glass on the counter. 'let's have a look at your menu.'

'On the board, sir, above you.'

'Ah, yes.' Bernie stepped back and looked up at the chalked board above the bar. 'I think I'll have the … um … yes, I'll have the steak and kidney pie.' He was tempted to ask if it was home-made, but thought better of it, in case it wasn't. He was doing all right with George; he didn't want to put a foot wrong now.

'If you like to sit down, sir, I'll bring it over.'

Bernie had already noticed that there was a free table by the window that looked across the road. He walked over to it, sat down and peered out of the window. 'Brockwood Stores,' he said aloud, as if reading the faded sign. He paused, dramatically he hoped, and turned to the landlord.

'D'you know, I thought I recognised this pub the moment I walked in here.' He pointed out of the window. 'And that shop opposite. Good lord. Yes, it's all coming back.' Oh, Trev, eat your heart out. 'Must be … oh, let me see … thirty years ago, at least.' He looked up at George. 'You weren't here then, were you, George?' By his reckoning the landlord would have been about ten when he and Andrew used to come into the pub for a pint – and then go into the shop to buy sweets to hide the smell of the beer.

'No no, I've been here fifteen years. I think. Dotty,' he called into the kitchen, 'is it fifteen years we've been here?'

'Sixteen,' Dotty answered.

'Sixteen,' George said.

'And how long has the shop been closed? Lovely little shop; sold just about everything, I seem to remember.' George was looking puzzled. 'Student,' he said, 'on my way from Cambridge, snatching a quick pint before I went home to my mother!'

'Oh yes, we still get some of those.'

Bernie continued to look out of the window, as if entranced by the view, until George brought his food to the table. It hadn't taken long – five minutes in the microwave, probably.

'Enjoy your meal, sir.'

'Thank you; that looks good,' and before George could turn away, 'Tell me, George, why is the shop closed?'

'Oh well …' George slung the tea-towel that had held the hot pie dish over his shoulder, 'the old man died.'

'Oh, sorry to hear that. He was a nice old chap … well, he wasn't old when we … when *I* knew him. What happened?'

'He was just old. He was about eighty, I think.'

'Yes, of course. And his wife?'

'Oh, she died some years ago. I don't think she ever got over the problems they had.'

'Oh?'

'They had a break-in.'

'Oh, that's nasty. Yes, very.' Bernie paused. 'So … what's going to happen to the shop now?'

'Well … someone'll buy it, we hope.'

'Oh. Yes.' Bernie hoped he wasn't sounding too ingenuous. Thank God he'd not given George his name, just in case Trev had mentioned it in his conversation with Garry. 'Yes. Pity to see these village shops closing.' Another look across the road, appearing to be sad to see this once-lively shop forsaken; in truth Bernie had no idea what he was going to say or do next. He would take a flier: 'Who's the agent, d'you know?' he asked casually.

'Estate agent, you mean?'

'Yes.' What other kind of agent would be selling a village shop?

'You thinking of buying it, sir?'

'Me? Oh no, but I do know someone who might be interested.'

'Hm … that's two in a week. Garry's going to be very pleased.'

'I'm sorry …?' Bernie was now either getting somewhere or the landlord had smelt a rat; he would have to be careful.

'Garry Wade. He's old Freddie's grandson; he's selling it.'

'Of course. Freddie, yes …' Bernie rubbed his chin, as if thinking hard, 'and his surname was …' Oh God, what was it? Somewhere, in the back of his mind, he did know it.

'His surname was …'

'No, let me see if I can remember!' A dramatic pause. 'It was … it began with a 'G', I know that. Um ... Goossen ... no, that's a family of musicians.' George was giving him a very odd look. Time to come clean; well, half-clean. 'It's what I'm in; classical music.'

'Oh.' George seems reassured, but unimpressed.

'No, definitely not Goossen. Hm ... something very like it.' Come on, George is waiting. 'Got it! Gesson. Yes?'

'Yes, that's right.' George nodded and smiled. Bernie felt he was undergoing some kind of test.

'And his wife … his wife was … Oh, I can see her now, small round lady doling out sweets from a big jar.'

'Freddie had some of them right to the end; kids loved them,' George said, not supplying the name that was eluding Bernie.

'Probably not allowed now.' A glance out of the window, as if seeking inspiration from the shop itself. He had known the woman's name; he just couldn't quite bring it to mind; and then it came: 'Myrtle, that was her name.'

'Yes, that was her.' He'd passed the test. 'Anything else for you, sir?'

'Yes, a coffee would be nice in a minute or two; thank you.' Bernie wasn't ready to leave yet; he wanted as much information as he could get. With George behind the bar counter – a group of five laughing women, who obviously knew him well, were in need of 'his service' they said – Bernie finished his steak and kidney pie. Home-made or not, it was very good. He placed his knife and fork tidily together on the plate and sat back in his chair. Now what? He knew the name of the shop owner, Freddie Gesson – well, he sort of knew that before, really – and the name of his wife, but how was having that confirmed by George going to help him? And how did it connect with what Trev had told him, or with Andrew, or Andrew's green notebook? He took the notebook out of his pocket, opened it at a page with the mysterious letters and numbers. He began to run his finger down the column of figures, the two hundreds and the three hundreds, and next to them the initials B.F.G. He felt his hand turning clammy, his mouth dry. He reached for the beer and drained the last drop; he put the empty glass down on the beer mat; his fingers were shaking. B.F.G. Brockwood, Freddie Gesson. It had to be. Andrew had been giving money to Freddie Gesson. Bernie's stomach churned.

'You all right, sir?' George had brought his coffee.

'Yes. Yes, thank you.' He reached for the coffee, trying hard to keep his hand from trembling. 'Thank you,' he said again, wondering why the landlord had not moved away. He lifted the cup to his lips. As he drank, he felt his nerves steadying. 'Good coffee.' He put the cup down on the saucer, spotted the tiny caramel biscuit. 'Ah,' he said, unwrapping it, 'I like these. Never see them for sale, though, do you?'

'They're specially for the catering trade, sir; I can let you have a few if you'd like.'

'Oh, that would be nice; thank you.'

'You live in this area now, do you, sir?'

The question threw Bernie; oh God, think quickly, man. 'Er... no. I live in Essex. I have a friend who … who wants to move into this area and …' a sudden semi-truthful inspiration ' … Well, I quite often go to Cambridge, you see and … I thought, well … go back the way I used to, when I was a student … through all the lovely old villages, so many of them beginning with a B.' He gave a faint laugh. 'Barley, Barkway, Braughing … Brockwood. Yes … mmm … and I don't think any one of them has a village shop now. Do they?'

'Braughing does.'

'Oh, really? Oh, that is good.'

'The others, no. Sadly, they've gone.' George smiled and went behind the bar. Quickly Bernie gathered up his coat and gloves and paid his bill: he'd been here long enough.

'Don't forget your biscuits, sir.' George held them out over the counter.

'Oh no. Thank you.'

'If you come this way again, do please drop in.'

'I'll do that, George, I will definitely do that. 'He took the biscuits from George's hand. 'Thank you. My wife will enjoy these.'

'Good. Bring her next time you come, sir.'

‘Ah yes. I’ll do that.’ Bernie waved his hand in salute, and without turning round walked quickly to the door. Once outside the pub he let out his held breath, gulped in some fresh air. This acting lark was not for him.

Making sure that he was not seen from inside the pub, he took out his mobile. ‘Trev? I need Garry’s number. Now.’

CHAPTER EIGHTEEN

'There's no parking in the road, but you can bring your van into the yard behind the shop,' the guy – Bernie, he called himself – had said on the phone. 'Call me when you get here, and I'll open the gates for you.'

He'd not liked the sound of that, but if this guy really was interested in buying Grandad's shop and wanted Garry to see if he thought it could become some sort of music place like this one in Islington … well, he wasn't going to pass up the chance of a good deal, even if it did mean a couple of minutes of panic when the gate shut behind him. If he had to, he could always go out the front door of the shop, leave the van.

'Ah, Garry … hello.' The guy, looking much as Garry had thought he would – tweed jacket, some sort of posh school tie – was waiting in the yard. He thrust his large hand through the van's open window.

'Hi,' Garry said, shaking Bernie's hand.

'Glad you could make it.'

'Yeah. Me too.' He was finding it hard to get even the shortest words out. He wished he knew why he felt so nervous; all he was doing was meeting a guy who wanted something: it was what Garry had done all his life. Trouble was, meetings like this often ended in just that … trouble. This time, though, if the deal came off, he could make a packet, whereas the other times … chicken feed, not worth the hassle. He'd had no savvy then, either. Now he had: he'd learnt a lot inside.

'No need to lock it; it'll be quite safe here.' Bernie held up a zapper, and the yard gates closed. 'This way,' he said, ushering Garry into the back of the building. 'Coffee before we look round … or d'you want to see the shop first?'

'Er … well. Just a quick shufty first; give me an idea, you know … what we're talking about?' See where that bleeding front door is.

'Good man. Just what I'd have said. Oh, before you go ... how d'you like your coffee?'

'Oh, white with one sugar. Please.' Not that he cared.

Having located the front door, Garry began to feel he could relax. Back in the office, Bernie handed him the coffee; he could have done with a fag.

'Well, what do you think?' Bernie perched on the edge of his desk. 'D'you think your grandfather's stores would make a good music shop?'

'I dunno really.' I haven't a clue, mate; what do I know about music shops? A lot of tat in there I wouldn't give a shit for. 'I mean … well … you know your business.'

'Quite right. Wrong question. Or, at least, wrong way of putting it. What I mean is … is Brockwood, d'you think … you know the village … would it be a good place to have a shop like that? I imagine Brockwood Stores in its heyday attracted a lot of custom, both passing trade and regulars. Yes?'

‘Oh yeah, plenty.’

‘And you’d be happy with that, would you?’

‘Sorry, happy with what?’ Christ, had he missed something the guy’d said?

‘With Brockwood Stores being turned into a music shop?’

‘Yeah, sure.’ I’ll be happy with anything, just so long as it brings in the dosh.

‘Good, good. Now … I haven’t had the opportunity to see over the property yet, but, as I told you on the blower, a friend of mine has, and I’ve asked him here to …’ The door from the shop opened. ‘... Ah. Here he is, right on cue. Come in, Trev … Trevor.’

Oh Jesus, it was the guy he drank those beers with. The door to the shop was still open; he could make a dash for it.

‘Hi,’ Garry said nervously, standing up.

‘Well, hello …’ Trevor’s voice was quite different from the other day. ‘Good to meet you again, Garry. Oh, do sit down.’ Trevor was giving him a big smile.

‘No, I’m all right. You … you have the chair.’ Garry moved away, nearer to the door. As if in slow motion he watched as the two guys looked at one another, said something he couldn’t hear, and then looked at him.

‘Right, Garry,’ Bernie said. ‘We all want what’s best, don’t we? We’re all after a good deal. Yes?’ Garry nodded. ‘Come on, sit down, let’s talk this thing through.’

Reluctantly Garry went back to the chair: he’d rather have stayed on his feet.

‘Good man. Now … did you have any figure in mind? Something we could start from, perhaps?’

‘Wha … what d’you mean?’

‘What are you asking for the property?’ Bernie was looking directly at him, eye to eye.

‘Well, I … I hadn’t got to that.’ He was starting to sweat. He glanced at the doorway; he hadn’t meant to, but …

‘Listen.’ Bernie leant forward. ‘You want to sell, I’m interested in buying, and we both want to get the very best deal we can. Right?’

‘Yes. Yes, of course, only …’ He’d have to tell them; he couldn’t go through with this on his own. He’d thought he could, but now, when it came to talking real money, he was going to bottle it, he knew he was. He was sweating hard now; it was like that time Pokey and Sam had him up against the alley wall – ‘Yeah, sure I’ll drive, any time,’ he’d told them – never thinking the actual time would come, and now it had, and there was no way of backing out, not even backing out down the alley, with Pokey’s nails digging into his left arm, ‘just friendly-like, mate,’ Pokey’d said … and Sam’s steel-capped boots stamping on his trainers.

‘Well …’ Garry cleared his throat, ‘I can’t …’ he croaked, ‘I need to …’

‘Like some water?’ Bernie asked.

‘No. Ta. I’m fine.’ Another clearing of his throat. God, he was making a noise; no wonder Trevor was wincing. ‘Yeah, I have a … a chest thing.’ He fluttered his fingers in front of his anorak, ‘you know.’ Bernie and Trevor nodded, sympathetically; well, it looked that way. Garry took a deep breath. ‘Money … yeah. That’s fine, only … well, the shop’s ... the shop’s really my sister’s. My grandfather left it to her. He left stuff to me, of course; things in the house.’

'And the loft. Don't forget the loft, Garry,' Trevor said. 'You found some really good stuff up there, didn't you?' He turned to Bernie. 'I didn't tell you that, did I?'

'Tell me what?'

'About all the wonderful things Garry found in the loft. Old toys, some of them really quite valuable.'

'Oh yes?'

'Dinky toys, that sort of thing, you know? *Very* saleable. Isn't that right, Garry?'

'Yeah.' Garry gulped. What was going on with these guys; did they not want to buy the shop then? Was it something in the loft they wanted? Nah, couldn't be. It was just him; he was all but bricking it.

'Oh … and tell Bernie about the money.' Trevor sat back, all expansive, like the loft was his.

'The money?'

'In those envelopes.'

'Oh, that. Yeah.' Garry ran his tongue around his teeth. 'Oh, that was just a bit of cash Grandad left in a box.' He couldn't remember all of what he'd said to Trevor in the pub.

'No no,' Trevor said, leaning forward again, 'it was more than a *bit* of cash; a couple of hundred in each envelope you said. Do you not remember, Garry?'

'Yeah, course I remember.' Garry could feel himself getting really angry now. What did they take him for, some kind of fool who couldn't remember what he'd said. Bugger of it was, he didn't remember. Had he really said that … about the envelopes? 'Envelopes. Sure. Wha' 'bout them?'

The guys were staring at him now, real hard, eyes wide open, both of them; he felt trapped and the silence was becoming oppressive. It was beginning to feel like he was down the nick, in one of them interview rooms. Jesus! Maybe that's who they really were, these guys, the fuzz, the plain clothes lot. Oh shit, what had he got himself into?

'Listen ... we *are* interested in buying the shop, we really are, make no mistake about that, but I – not Trevor – I am also very interested in the money in these envelopes.'

'That's *my* money!' Fuck them.

'Of course it's your money. I don't *want* it, Garry.' Bernie was laughing. 'I just want to ask you a couple of questions about it, how it came to be there and ... It's just one of those coincidences that life throws up sometimes.'

'I don't know what you're talking about.' He really didn't, but whatever it was, the sooner he was out of here the better.

'Okay,' Bernie said, 'I will explain. First though, would you like some more coffee?'

'No. Thanks. No.' Whatever this is, let's get it over. 'So go on then, what's this 'bout. Is it all right if I smoke?' He looked at Trevor; his guess was the other guy was the boss.

Trevor looked enquiringly at Bernie. 'Go ahead,' Bernie said.

'Ta.' While Garry lit up and took his first drag, the two men looked at the walls, the floor, anywhere but directly at Garry. He smiled inwardly; they'd not done anything like this before, he could tell; it was like they was acting, the pair of them. One more drag and he'd be ready. 'Yeah, okay,' he said, blowing out the smoke through his nostrils, 'What d'you want to know?'

'Well, Garry, it's like this.' Bernie paused, as if he didn't know quite what to say next. 'You have found some money, notes, in envelopes, each time two, or three, hundred pounds … and I have found a notebook, with two hundred and three hundred pounds listed in it, many times, and beside the figures the letters B.F.G.'

'Okay. So ...?'

'Well … I'm pretty sure that those initials stand for Brockwood and Freddie Gesson.'

'What?' Grandad's name in some guy's notebook? He didn't like the sound of that. 'I can't see why; they could mean anything.'

'You're right, they could, and I wouldn't have given them a second thought but for the fact that the person who had these figures and initials in his notebook *also* had a lot of newspaper cuttings about the Brockwood Stores, including one about the break-in there.'

'Oh?' Christ, where was this going?

'Why do you think your grandfather had kept that money?' It was Trevor leaning forward this time. 'Why had he not spent it?'

'I dunno.' They were waiting, the pair of them; he'd have to give them some sort of answer. 'Well, I got the feeling, when I found them, you know, the envelopes, hidden away like that … that Grandad … felt he *couldn't* spend it, like it wasn't his money … you know?' The two guys nodded; he had their full attention.

'Are you saying that money had something to do with the break-in?' Bernie asked.

'Well, yeah. I know it sounds crazy, but … well, somebody sent my Grandad that money, posted it to him and … I did kind of wonder if … if he knew who'd taken it. Some kids he knew, maybe, in the village, and he knew their family and he didn't want to get them into any more trouble – he was like that – and if they paid it back he'd not tell the police, or their parents. You know?'

'Sort of blackmailing them, you mean?' Bernie asked.

'Well, yeah. Sort of …' Garry didn't like hearing that word in connection with Grandad. '... but he wished he'd not done that; then when he got the money he couldn't spend it.'

'And he couldn't tell the people in the village,' Trev said excitedly, 'or they'd want to know who he was shielding.'

'Yeah.' Garry nodded.

'In one of your TV dramas, perhaps,' Bernie said. 'No, this money, if it *is* linked to the burglary, has, I think, come from somewhere outside the village. Did he need extra money for anything, your grandfather?'

'Well, my Nan was quite ill one time; maybe it was for her.'

'He didn't spend it, though, so it can't have been that,' Trevor said.

'He spent some,' Garry said, and told them about the empty envelopes which had 'For Myrtle' written on them.

Garry reached in his jeans pocket for his fags; this whole thing was getting too much. 'Sorry.' he said, pushing the packet back in.

‘No no, you smoke if you want to,’ Bernie said. ‘I don’t know about you, Trev, I could do with a drink.’ He stood up, opened a drawer in the desk and took out a bottle of whisky. ‘Glasses in the cupboard behind you.’

‘Oh, right.’ Trevor put the glasses on the desk.

Bernie poured out two good measures. ‘You’re very welcome, Garry, but I know you’re driving.’ He lifted his glass. ‘Cheers,’ he said.

Garry nodded. He was glad he had the fag; he didn’t know what was coming next, but he had a feeling it wasn’t going to be good.

‘Your grandmother … was it cancer?’ Bernie asked, gently.

He'd not expected that.

‘Yeah, it was, but … well, she’d never been really right since the break-in; made her nervous, you know, being tied up like that.’

‘What? Tied up? Oh my God.’ Bernie’s face had gone white; he downed the rest of his whisky.

‘Yeah. The guys who broke in … they tied her up, and Grandad.’

‘When was this break-in?’ Trev asked.

‘December, I think. I know it wasn't long before Christmas. It was in the paper, *The Mercury.’* There was an odd look on Bernie’s face. ‘You know, the local rag?’

‘Yes, I know the name of the paper.’ The look was still there; it wasn’t to do with the newspaper. ‘If he did know who the thieves were – maybe he recognised one of them – perhaps he thought this was a better way to punish them;

make them keep on paying for what they'd done. What do you think, Trevor?'

Trevor nodded. 'Yes, that sounds very likely.'

'What money was it they stole, do you know?' Bernie asked. 'Was it the week's takings or …?'

'I think most of it was Christmas Club.' Bernie and Trevor were looking blank. 'You know, people in the village, paying in a pound or two a week, saving up for Christmas, then spending it in the shop.' Grandad had always made sure he stocked the things people would want most – so Paula had said – and that there was enough for everyone, so no one was disappointed, and then they'd save with him next year.

'Ah, yes, of course,' Bernie said. 'And with possibly the whole village depositing their savings, there could have been a lot of cash there in early December.' He finished off his whisky, lifted the bottle to pour another drink, changed his mind, and put the bottle away in the drawer. 'So …' he said, 'what have we got? A break-in at the shop, money in envelopes in the loft, and figures and initials in a notebook.' He was sounding calm and matter-of-fact now, and the colour was coming back into his face. Something had shaken him, though, Garry was sure of that; he wished he knew what it was.

'And the newspaper cuttings,' Trevor said.

'Yes, of course; the cuttings. Thank you, Trevor.' Christ, the guy was acting now like he was some sort of lawyer in a court room. 'I think what I have to do next is go back and have another, thorough, look at those cuttings. What d'you think, Trevor?' It's as if I'm not here, Garry said to himself; he cleared his throat loudly.

'I *am* interested in the shop, Garry,' Bernie said, 'I really am, I promise you, but first I want to find out, if I can, what the figures in the notebook mean, and how they match up with the money in those envelopes.'

'That's important, is it?' Whether it was or not, Garry could see that these guys weren't going to budge on this: if he wanted to sell the shop he'd have to play along with them.

'It is.' No arguing; that was Bernie's bottom line. 'So, what I'd like you to do … is make a note of how much money there was in each envelope and the date it was posted, and then text it to us.'

Garry shrugged his shoulders. 'Yeah, sure, if that's what you want.' He couldn't see the point: the guy wanted the shop, and by the look of him he had the dosh, but he was more bothered about a pile of old envelopes and a notebook. 'So, is that it?' he asked. He wanted out of this place.

'Yes, I think we're done for now.'

CHAPTER NINETEEN

Bernie stood up, stretched his back. He had been poring over the newspaper cuttings for nearly an hour. He was ready for the mug of tea Emma was holding out to him.

'Have you found anything?' she asked.

'Yes. I have.' He gulped down the tea and put the mug on the desk.

'Well … ? Come on, tell me …'

'I don't know, it doesn't quite add up. But at the same time, it does.' Bernie's findings, coming on top of what Garry had said, had made him profoundly disturbed.

'Oh, that's very helpful!'

'Emma, sit down,' he said gently. This was going to be difficult but it had to be done.

'Okay,' Emma said, sitting down on the edge of the desk.

She was already looking worried; how was she going to look when he'd said his piece. There was no acting now. He wished Trev was here; he'd do this so much better. And if Andrew was here … No doubt there would be some act he could put on, too. Oh yes, Andrew, it would appear, was a better actor than either of them.

'Emma …' He took her hand in his. She looked down at it, then slowly lifted her eyes to Bernie's face.

'What is it?' It was little more than a whisper.

'I may be wrong, I hope to God I am, but …' Bernie took a deep breath, 'I think that Andrew … a long time ago … may have stolen some money from the Brockwood shop.' That the money was the village's Christmas Club fund, and that to get it Andrew had tied up the shopkeeper and his wife … that would have to wait. Upright citizen Andrew Raven a thief, was a shock in itself.

Emma was laughing. 'Oh, don't be so silly,' she said. 'it's gone to your head, this obsession with that shop. Honestly! Andrew? He's the most scrupulously law-abiding person you could wish to meet.'

'Yes, he is now, but was he always? When he was hard up, when he really needed money?'

'No. I'm sorry, Bernie, but that is just … well, apart from being quite ridiculous … that's a terrible thing to say.' Emma got up from the desk, walked over to the window and looked out at the winter night. Bernie could see her distraught and angry face reflected in the glass. 'I think you'd better go home.'

'Emma, love, you have to let me tell you …'

'No!' She turned round and glared at him. 'I don't! You've just accused my husband … your best friend! … of being a criminal. I don't want to hear any more.'

'All right, I'll go …' Bernie raised his hands as if fending off Emma's words. '… but you've got to hear it some time.'

'It's that money from Australia, isn't it? You've never believed … well, never fully believed … that he had a great-aunt in Australia. Oh, I know! I've seen the look on your face when you've mentioned this before. And if I tell you that her name was Maud and that she had a parrot, you'll still not believe me, will you?' Bernie shrugged. 'She did, and it sat on her shoulder!'

'Emma, stop. Stop!'

'I've seen photographs of her. Mad as a hatter she was, by all accounts, but she was real, and *she did leave money to Andrew!'* She was shouting now; it was a good thing Constance was not in the house; she had gone home for a few days, 'to see to her affairs,' she'd said. Bernie had choked with laughter when Emma told him. 'I want you to go home! Now!' She scooped up the buff folder and the notebook . 'And here, take these with you, too.'

Bernie pulled the front door shut and walked across to his car. He felt sure Emma would be watching him through Andrew's office window. He wasn't surprised when suddenly the front door flew open and she was there, not rushing into his arms as he hoped, but grabbing the folder and notebook from him.

'No. You can't take those. They belong here, they're Andrew's; he'll be home soon, and he'll miss them! You mustn't take them, Bernie.'

'All right, I won't … but please let me come back inside. I need you to understand why … why I am having these *bad thoughts* … because they are bad thoughts … about Andrew.' Emma's head was down, her arms wrapped around the folder, as if she was protecting it from him. 'Will you let me do that? Please, Emm.' He waited. 'Don't cry.'

'I'm not,' she said, lifting her head, but still not looking at him. 'It's the wind; it's cold out here.' She sniffed, then, reluctantly, turned her head and looked at him. 'Oh, come on then, best get it over and done with; I probably won't sleep when you've told me, whatever it is, but then I wouldn't sleep anyway, worrying about what it might be that *you* think you know about Andrew … and *I* don't!' She flung her final words at him and marched back into the house. Bernie locked the car and followed her.

'We've got two things here, Emma,' Bernie said, placing one hand on the open notebook, and the other on the pile of newspaper cuttings which he had taken out of the folder. 'Two things that are connected.'

'You don't know that,' Emma said. She had pulled up the only other chair in the room and they were sitting side by side at Andrew's desk, their shoulders touching.

'Well no, not for certain …' Bernie said. He would have to do this very carefully if he were to convince Emma. '… but look at what we've got.'

'I'm looking!' She moved her shoulder away. He couldn't blame her, but he would have to find a way to break through her hostility.

'Emma, sweetie, I don't like doing this, you know, not one little bit …'

'No.' Her voice softened. 'I don't suppose you do. Go on, show me.'

'Okay. The cuttings. Everything that seems to have been reported in *The Mercury* about the shop in Brockwood over the past twenty years or so. You've read them, I've read them.' He paused. 'I have a feeling, though, that some reports aren't there.'

'What reports?'

'I'll come to that. Let's look at this green book.' Bernie ran his finger down the page. 'BFG, a hundred pounds, BFG two hundred pounds; over and over again, the same amounts. And now look at this.' He turned the page. 'RAF fifty pounds … that's Royston, Arthur Freers. And this one … BPS seventy-five pounds, that's Buntingford, Peter Simming. These are the initials of Andrew's regular suppliers of stock. I know some of these guys, I've met them. Remember, *I've* been with Andrew a couple of times on his hunting trips. TTE, that's Tim Exton from Throcking.' He could feel Emma tensing beside him, her clasped hands pressed tightly against her mouth.

'Freddie Gesson was not one of our agents,' Bernie said gently.

Emma took her hands away from her mouth.

'Yes,' she said.

'Yes … what?' Did she know? Had she known all along?

'It's how Andrew would do it.'

'Do what?! Oh, for Christ's sake, Emma, what are you saying?' Bernie's throat was tight; she did know.

'Keep a record … like this.' Bernie felt his throat muscles relaxing. 'Sort of hiding things and yet, if he was challenged, he would say, "It's all there, see for yourself.". You know, like the way he hid the van?'

'Hiding in plain sight.'

'Yes.'

'Yes, that fits.' Bernie sighed and sat back. Gently he swung the chair from side to side. He was acutely aware that he was waiting for Emma's next words.

‘So … you think that …’ The words were coming out painfully. ‘ … that Andrew was paying money to the shopkeeper … and that *he* was … what? Blackmailing Andrew? Because he knew … ?’

‘Yes. Something like that.’

Emma waved her hands at the papers on the desk. ‘It doesn’t make sense, Bernie.’

‘It does, sweetie, it does.’ As unemotionally as he could, and leaving out some of the more disturbing details he had learnt from Garry, he told her about the break-in at the shop, the stealing of the Christmas Club money, the envelopes that had been found in the loft, the amounts tying in with the figures in the notebook. He felt her trembling beside him as he recounted the details. ‘I have no doubt in my mind that Andrew broke into Brockwood Stores and stole that money,’ he said, taking hold of her hands. They were cold and he began to chafe them: it was the only comfort he felt he could give her at this moment.

‘Oh Bernie …’ He hated what this was doing to her. ‘Why did he do it?’

‘Because … well …’

‘If you know, *tell* me.’

‘Because … because I had money and he didn’t and … well, you know … Andrew couldn’t bear to feel that he might be thought lacking in something; in this case, money. And it didn’t matter how much I told him that money wasn’t important, the fact that I had enough, more than enough, thanks to my mother … to start up the business, and run it … well, for a while anyhow … it galled him.’

‘It would.’ Emma put her head in her hands. ‘What a horrible way to get …’ Her body began to shake with sobs. ‘Hold me, Bernie, hold me.’

He put his arms around her and she buried her face in his shoulder. He felt a stiffening in his groin; it was so inappropriate, but he couldn’t help it.

‘Emma,’ he said softly, beginning to take his hands off her. ‘I think I should go home.’

‘No! Don’t go, please.’ She pressed closer to him.

‘But …’

She sat upright. ‘Stay with me.’

‘Is that what you really want?’

‘I can’t face a night on my own after … what you’ve …’ She stood up and stretched out her hand to him. ‘Come,’ she said. There was a fierce determination in her voice and the tears had stopped. Still holding Bernie’s hand she switched off the office light, turned the key in the mortice lock of the front door and walked him up the stairs.

Halfway up, where the stairs turned, Emma stopped.

‘What I don’t understand,’ she said, ‘is how this has been kept secret for so long.’

‘I don’t think this is quite the right time to start asking ourselves that.’ Please God she wasn’t going to suggest they go through all those cuttings and figures again. ‘I think we’ve had quite enough for one day, don’t you?’

‘Yes. We have.’

CHAPTER TWENTY

'Cup of tea?'

Emma opened her eyes. Bernie was standing by the bed, her favourite 'owl' mug in his hand. He was fully dressed.

'What time is it?' As she sat up the duvet fell away.

'Don't do that,' Bernie said, looking down at her.

'Sorry.' Emma pulled the duvet up, hugged it to her. 'Put it on the side,' she said, nodding at the mug; she couldn't keep herself covered up and take the mug from him. 'Why are you up so early?'

'It's late, not early, and I have a business to run. Besides, isn't your sister coming back today?'

'Oh God, she is! I must get the house straight … Oh God, if Connie knew you had spent the night here …'

'And brought tea up to you in the morning! What would she think of that?'

'Oh, Bernie …' She reached out to him. 'I could ring and put her off.' Shamelessly she knelt up in the bed; she put her arms around Bernie's neck and drew him to her.

He took her hands from around his neck, held them in his, and kissed her gently on the lips. 'Drink your tea,' he said.

'I don't want to drink tea, I want to …'

'Emma, sweetheart, there's something else you have to do today.' His voice was sad and concerned.

'I know.' Today she had to begin making arrangements for Andrew to come home. 'Pass me that wrap, please.' She stretched out her hand; Bernie took the silk gown from the back of the door and held it out to her. She put her arms into the sleeves and drew the gown closely around her. 'I had not *forgotten*,' she said, 'but last night … I know it was wrong, but … it felt so right.' Tenderly she stroked his face. 'If Connie doesn't come back today … I don't want to be alone.'

'I'll come back.' He smiled, then sighed. 'I have to go, I have a meeting I really can't get out of.' He opened the door and began to back out of the bedroom.

'Oh, Bernie, what is it going to be like when he's home?' Emma clambered out of bed and followed him out of the room. 'They said he could be in a wheelchair, and that he might be grumpy and …'

'Let's deal with that when we come to it; it might not be like that at all.' He started down the stairs.

'And what about us?'

Bernie turned round and looked up at her; she was leaning over the banisters, her robe slipping from her shoulders. 'Emm, sweetheart, one thing at a time. Please.' She did so want him to run up the stairs and take her back to bed. 'I'll come to the hospital if I can get away in time,' he said.

'Yes. Please do.' Emma put her fingers to her lips, blew him a kiss. Not wanting Bernie to see the tears welling up in her eyes, she turned away and walked quickly into the bedroom.

Sitting on the bed, Emma listened to the sounds of Bernie's departure. Then suddenly filled with guilt, she let the tears flow: who did she think she was, cavorting in bed with her lover while her husband was fighting for his life in hospital? The heroine of a Mills and Boon novel? Well, if she was she would give up her lover and stay true to her husband; that would be the correct ending, but they weren't anywhere near the ending yet. All those question marks hanging over Andrew. *Had* he done all these awful things that Bernie had told her? If so, who was he, Andrew? A thief, a liar … and if those, what else? Emma had thought she knew her husband.

She shivered; the wrap was thin and the bedroom heating was low. They had slept in the big guest room overlooking the back lawn. She looked around her at the lavish fittings, there to impress, as was the silk robe she was wearing, should a guest considered worthy of impressing stay the night. 'I must not let Bernie stay again,' she said aloud. She jumped up from the bed and flung off the wrap. She ran across the landing and into her own shower room; suspending all thoughts, good and bad, she stood under the needles of hot water.

* * *

'Yes, your husband could come home, Mrs. Raven, but it would be much better if he went to a rehabilitation facility for a week or so first. The final decision is, of course, yours.'

‘Thank you, doctor. I’ll think about it,’ Emma said. It was a big decision to make, either way.

In the hospital café she stirred the froth on her cappuccino. If Andrew came home now, right now, how would she cope? In practical terms it would not be difficult: they had the space and the money to engage a private nurse and a physiotherapist, if that was what was required. Could she cope emotionally though, being in the same house with him, knowing what he had done? Knowing what she and Bernie had done? She looked down at her coffee; she had all but stirred the froth away. There was no point in drinking it now, it was the frothy bit she liked best.

In the car she texted Bernie. ‘He could be coming home. I don’t know what to do.’

* * *

‘It’s a good thing *I* had a set of keys,’ Constance said, opening the front door to Emma. ‘Where’ve you been?’ Her tone was accusing.

‘To the hospital, to see my husband.’

‘Oh. I thought you might be …’

‘Whatever you thought, I don’t want to know. Now, would you let me get into my house, please.’ Emma pushed past her sister, strode across the hall and into the kitchen. Noisily she filled the kettle and banged it down on its base; she had enough worries without Connie adding to them.

‘I did wonder if …’

Emma swung round. ‘If what?’

‘It doesn’t matter.’

'It obviously does.'

'No. I only wondered if you had had breakfast somewhere before you went to see Andrew. There was no sign of your having eaten …'

'No, I didn't. I had a cup of tea here, and then, at the hospital I had a coffee which I didn't drink. Is there anything else, any other minutiae of my life since you went away, that you want to know?'

'Oh, Emma. My dear, what is wrong?'

'What is wrong? Everything is wrong! Just … oh, just leave me alone, Connie, please. I'm very tired; I'm going to take this cup of tea and I'm going to bed. Please don't come and ask me questions, and don't me bring any food either.' In silence Emma made her tea and took a stale roll from the fridge.

'What …?'

'I'll dunk it!' Emma said and left the kitchen. Thank God she and Bernie had not slept in her room; Connie was sure to have looked in there. She was halfway up the stairs when her phone rang: it was Bernie. Conscious of Constance standing in the hall watching her, she said brusquely, 'No thank you, I do not need any solar panels.' Without switching it off, Emma put the phone back in her pocket. 'Don't let me sleep too long, Connie,' she said. She went into her room, shut the door and took the phone out of her pocket. 'Oh God, Bernie,' she said, 'what a tangled web we are weaving.'

CHAPTER TWENTY-ONE

We are indeed, Bernie thought … and you don't know the half of it, Emma. Did she really need to be told that Freddie and Myrtle had been tied up? He could see in his mind the ordeal they must have endured at Andrew's hands, the meticulous way he would have drawn the rope – he assumed it was a rope – around them, knotting it neatly, ensuring it would hold until he was well away from the shop. And then there were the gags. What had he used? Freddie's tie, Myrtle's scarf? Or had he taken the gags with him? Knowing Andrew he felt sure that he would have planned everything with great care, so the chances were that he had gone there – on his motor-bike? – with all the equipment required for this operation. It could, of course, have been a spur-of-the moment thing. No, that was not Andrew's way. Climbing the stairs to Bernie's college rooms to listen to Puccini was probably one of the very few spontaneous things he had ever done. He wondered now whether Andrew's apparently sudden invitation to Emma to go out with him, that day in the pharmacy, had been as unpremeditated as it appeared.

First, though, if he was going to tell Emma about the attack on the shopkeeper and his wife, Bernie had to check the newspaper accounts of the break-in at the Hertfordshire Archives office in Hertford. In the cuttings he had seen in Pengate there had been no mention of Freddie and Myrtle being tied up and gagged: this was just the sort of thing that a newspaper would make much of, and yet, there, there was nothing. Admittedly he had not read every word of every cutting, but he doubted whether he would have missed something so salient.

On microfilm in the Archives office Bernie found the information he was seeking, complete with lurid headline: 'Couple Held in Vicious Smash and Grab' and a photograph of Brockwood Stores taken on the morning after the event. As he read the account of the break-in Bernie realised that he had seen this before, but without the picture or the heading, or any mention of binding and gagging: these were the missing parts of the cutting that had puzzled him. He had been right; even for Andrew, keeping a full hard copy account of his conduct that day had been too much. The calculation of it chilled Bernie; the break-in itself was bad enough, as was Andrew's treatment of Freddie and Myrtle, but his hiding this part of it, even from himself, for some reason felt worse. Not only was Bernie chilled, he now felt physically sick. He sat back in the chair and closed his eyes. When he felt sure that he was not actually going to vomit he rewound the film, returned it to its correct place in a tall set of drawers and thanked the librarian for her assistance. He glanced at the drinks-vending machine in the adjoining room, but seeing nothing there that would lift his mood or ease his stomach, he pushed open the swing doors into the foyer. He stood there for a moment, uncertain what to do next.

Outside the building a wedding party was being photographed, the bridal couple covered in a shower of glittering gold and silver confetti. Bernie nodded to them briefly, ran down the steps and into the car park. Would these young people have fifty golden years of married bliss? Or silver even? Andrew and Emma had just the year before celebrated their twenty-fifth anniversary with a dinner at the golf club; would they get to the next milestone?

Bernie flicked off the confetti and got into the car. He took out his phone and scrolled through his address book till he got to T. No, there was no point in talking to Trev; he wouldn't know anything. He couldn't trust himself to call Emma, not just now; he was too angry and upset, and besides, he needed to have *all* the facts before he did speak to her. How could he tell her what he had just learnt?

There was only one person he could think of who could help him at this moment. Reluctantly, he scrolled up to G. He would need to be careful how he phrased this: a wrong word and he'd scare the guy off. His thumb hovered over the options key; he took a deep breath and clicked on Call.

'Hello. Garry? It's Bernie. Those envelopes: any chance you could bring them here? Rather than just text me the info?'

CHAPTER TWENTY-TWO

The gates to the yard in Almeida Street swung open as Garry approached them. He wished he knew what these guys wanted. 'Just the envelopes,' Bernie had said on the phone, 'it's the postmarks we want to look at.' Not a word about buying the shop. Oh fuck … what if them gates open *only* by remote? He felt himself beginning to sweat. In the wing mirror he saw Bernie emerging from the back door of the shop. Garry opened the van door; he wasn't going to stay trapped in the vehicle. Who was to say the other one, Trevor, wasn't coming at him from the other side?

'Garry, hi. Good to see you.' Bernie stuck out his hand. Garry was glad he still had his gloves on. It might not be the polite thing to do in Bernie's world but it saved him from having Bernie know how cold and clammy his fingers were.

'Hi,' Garry said.

The doors to the yard swung to. Side by side Garry and Bernie walked to the back door.

'Coffee?' Trev asked.

Garry nodded; he couldn't trust himself to speak just yet. It wasn't that he was afraid of these guys: if only he could work out what they were about.

'You did bring them, didn't you?'

‘Yes. It’s why I’m here, innit?’ They looked at him, startled. He’d not meant to sound that aggressive. ‘I mean … yes, course I have. Like you said, just the envelopes.’ He took the bundle out of his anorak pocket and handed it to Bernie.

‘Thanks,’ Bernie said. He put them on the desk. ‘Quite a mixture, aren’t they?’

Garry nodded; Bernie, hunched over at the desk, began leafing through the bundle, peering at the postmarks. As Garry knew, most of them you couldn’t read. Trev handed Garry his coffee.

‘Ta.’ He took a sip; it was too hot. He went to put the mug down on the floor beside his chair.

‘Here, I’ll take it,’ Trev said, in a whisper.

Garry gave him the mug. ‘Cheers,’ he whispered back, his eyes fixed on Bernie. For Christ’s sake, what was going on here? It was only a bundle of fucking envelopes! How important could that be? And, more to the point, what did it have to do with these guys buying the shop? If he wanted to make this sale he’d no choice but to keep schtum … and wait. It was like that game he’d played as a little kid, where you spun round and round and then you had to stop; you could be on one foot or anything, it didn’t matter; the one who won was the one who could stay still the longest. His coffee might have been too hot before; if this went on much longer it would be fucking cold by the time he drank it. He risked a look at Trev; he was like a statue. Statues, yeah! That’s what that game was called. Trev wasn’t moving a muscle; it was like he was made of stone. He’d seen Harrison Ford and Bruce Willis do that; not a flicker … then they'd suddenly pounce, like a tiger. Jesus, the guy was an actor! Garry'd seen him, way back, on telly, he was sure he had; in *The Sweeney.* No question, playing some kind of copper. No wonder Garry'd thought he was one for real; he felt his taut muscles relaxing.

'Yes, very interesting,' Bernie said, sitting up, straightening his back, 'but I don't think they are going to be much use to us.' Bernie pushed his chair back and swung round to face them. 'So, Garry, what now, eh?' Bernie was smiling.

'Dunno.' He didn't like the smile. 'You tell me.' He took his coffee back from Trev. Whatever they said, the money was his, and nobody was going to make him give it up: it was first time in his life, in nearly forty years, he'd had what you could call *real money* that was his own. Grandad had wanted him to have that money, or he wouldn't have ... Christ, they're waiting for me to tell them! All right then, go for it. 'I can't see how these ...' He waved his hands towards the envelopes which Bernie was carefully restacking into a bundle. '... postmarks and things have anything to do with you wanting to buy the shop.' There, he'd said it. Straight out, no messing. Well, why not? He had to know, otherwise all this was just a waste of his time, time when he might be sussing out a whole load more buyers. Well, maybe a couple. Now what are they doing, looking at one another? Deciding which one of them's going to say, "Sorry, Garry, we don't actually want to buy your Grandad's shop."? Oh Christ, they've not found a rare stamp on one of them envelopes, have they?

Bernie nods at Trev. Trev says, 'Yes?' Bernie nods again. 'The thing is,' Trev begins: posh voice, like he's a judge in a courtroom, and he's looking at me like I'm in the dock or something, 'when you consider buying a property, Garry, you need to know everything about it before you decide to make the purchase.'

'Yes, that figures. So?'

'So …' It's Bernie's turn. 'It's not just a question of wet rot or dry rot.' Jesus, these guys are really getting up my nose now.

'Yeah, I know that!'

'It's the history that a building may have. For instance, although this …' He taps the bundle of envelopes. '... this money does appear to have come into your possession because of a burglary that took place some …'

'You've no right to bring that up. That's money's mine; Grandad left it to me. It's nothing to do with any burglary. Just give me them envelopes and I'm out of here.' Garry stood up.

'No no, Garry, don't go like this, please.' Bernie stretched out both his hands, palms down. 'Do sit down.' Garry remained standing. 'Of course it's your money, I'm not disputing that for a moment.'

Reluctantly Garry sat down.

Bernie sighed. 'Listen … I just feel … I need to know more about that break-in before I can go ahead with … with buying the shop.'

'Why? How does a break-in thirty years ago stops me selling.'

‘It doesn’t, not really. But … Look, you’re going to have to trust me on this, Garry.’ He couldn’t figure these guys out; he wished he knew what they really wanted. ‘I wouldn’t want to take this further without finding out a bit more about that break-in. I’m not saying it *is* relevant, but I do feel I have to look into it.’

‘So ... what d’you want to know?’

‘Your grandparents ... they were tied up, I gather ... but they weren't hurt, were they?’

‘Hurt? What d'you mean? They was tied to their chairs ... *and they had gags stuffed in their mouths!’*

‘Yes, of course. That would have hurt.’

Bleeding right it would! He couldn't for the life of him see what that had to do with selling the shop now. Did these guys know something he didn't.

‘Perhaps we should talk to your sister?’ Bernie said.

‘My sister?’

‘You told Trevor you had a sister, older than you. In the pub, remember?’

‘Oh. Yeah.’ He couldn’t remember half he’d said that day.

‘Paula. Yes?’

‘Yes.’

‘And if I remember rightly …’ Trev said, pointing his index finger at Garry, ‘... your grandfather left the shop to her.’

Was there anything he hadn’t told this guy? He’d never been any good drinking during the day; he’d had to sleep it off in the van for a couple of hours before he dare drive home.

'Yeah, that's right.' He knew, Trevor did, so why pretend. And he'd told Bernie.

'So …' said Bernie, 'it might be helpful if we could talk to her; she may know more … about what happened.'

'Okay, I'll ask her.' Anything, anything, to get out of here.

'Get her to call me, will you?' Bernie said.

'Yeah. Sure.' Not on your life, mate.

'Good man.'

'Another coffee before you go?'

'No, ta. I'll … um … I'll just take those envelopes.'

Bernie put the bundle into Garry's outstretched hand. 'Thanks a lot for coming, Garry. I feel we've cleared up a lot of things today. Been most useful.'

'Yeah. Thanks.' Garry smiled, nodded. God knows why he *was* smiling. Cleared up? *What*? Oh well, if they were happy, he wasn't going to rock the boat.

* * *

Safely out of the yard, and away from Almeida Street, Garry looked for a street without yellow lines. He badly needed to stop – there was so much whirling around in his head – and take stock. There was a garage ahead; that would do. He pulled into the side of the forecourt and switched off the engine. He had a bottle of water on the passenger seat; he took a long swig – that fancy coffee had left a bitter taste in his mouth. The water and the action of drinking it cleared his brain a bit. So … should he speak to Paula? All's said and done, it is her shop. Come to think of it, she might be pleased, she might see what he'd done as a good thing, her little bruv doing something useful – 'Yes, all right, Paula.' – for a change. Okay, he'd speak to her; not just yet, though. Give it a couple of days, think how best to tell her. And what all that was about Grandad and Nan being hurt? No idea. He didn't like thinking about it, he knew that. And most of the time he didn't. Well, never really. It was thirty years ago; he was only a kid when it happened. Besides, he had good memories of Nan and Grandad - Nan in a red cardigan, not nearly as tall as Grandad, and sort of round and cuddly; she loved a hug, Nan did. He wished now he'd let her hug him more, instead of running away when she had held her arms out to him. Grandad didn't hug; he lifted Garry high in the air and swung him round, playing aeroplanes. There were things hanging up in the shop - baskets and wellies, and he had a feeling that around Christmas one year there had even been some hams up there - and he'd loved seeing how many things he could touch as Grandad whizzed him round. He could have stayed up there for ever but after a bit Nan would make Grandad stop. 'You'll make the boy sick,' she would say, and although Grandad would laugh, the game would be over ... till the next time. It was good to have *those* memories, they helped keep away the bad ones. He could do with one of Nan's hugs right this minute.

He hoped to God they'd not been hurt, really hurt, knocked about. Maybe Paula knew, had known, but she'd kept it from him. Best not ask her; let it be.

The days ran into a week, then a second one. He'd not seen Paula, not heard from Bernie. He began to panic:

s'pose he'd gone cold on the deal. *Or* … he'd gone to the police! Oh, Jesus. He had to tell her.

'You've done what?' Paula's voice at the end of the phone was loud and piercing; Garry held it away from his ear.

'Just calm down, Sis, and listen.'

'This better be good, Garry.'

CHAPTER TWENTY-THREE

Bernie put down the office phone. Garry's sister, Paula, was coming to see him, and she was on her way. He wished Trev was here. It would be easier with two of them; he'd found that when they'd spoken to Garry. Reluctantly Bernie had had to let Trev go to an audition: it was, after all, the guy's real day job. He was surprised how well he and Trev were getting along, and how reliable he was; he had become quite a shrewd buyer, too, delighting Bernie with some of his acquisitions, and even more with the prices he had paid for them. Bernie had obviously underestimated him; he would be sorry to let him go when Andrew was fully recovered. That day, however, was some time away. Emma hadn't yet found a convalescent home that she felt was right for him; the ones she had visited so far were too noisy or the food was not good, or the rooms were too small. She was visiting another one today, this time in north London, and if it seemed suitable she wanted him to have a look at it, too.

Although Andrew's speech and movement had now returned in some measure, he seemed disinclined to talk and positively refused to be walked up and down the corridor outside his room. Clearly his state of health would not improve if he remained in hospital, and his bed in the stroke unit was needed for another patient. Neither was he ready to return home, even with a physiotherapist and a carer making daily visits: the obvious answer was some kind of rehab facility. More worrying to Bernie than his physical health was Andrew's attitude, in the past week, to Emma. Encouraged by the doctors to talk to him, even when he was unable to reply, she'd got into the habit of giving him a daily digest of her activities, telling him about Constance – he liked her – and Bernie and the shop, and going out for the day with Jackie: she'd not said where they had been. This change in his response to her spiel seemed to have begun when she told him, thinking he might be worrying about what was happening to the business in his absence, that Bernie had found someone – she didn't say it was Trev – to buy in new items, and had given him Andrew's ever so helpful contact list, so there was no need for him to be concerned that the Almeida Street stock was running low. He had become very agitated and had turned away from her; Emma hadn't known what to do. The nurse, who had come in at that moment, said it was only because he still found any conversation tiring – Emma had been with him a longer time than usual that afternoon – and that he would be fine once he'd had a little sleep. 'He kept his head turned away nearly all the time,' she had told Bernie afterwards, on the phone. 'As if he didn't want to look at me; it was horrible. Was it something I said? Or something in my body language? You don't think he could know, do you, about us?'

'No, I don't think it's that,' Bernie said. He hoped to God it wasn't.

'I need to know, so I don't mention it again, whatever it was.'

'You didn't mention the notebooks, did you?'

Emma nodded. 'Well, yes, I did - the red one - but only because I wanted to reassure him that we were looking after the stock; he cared about that so much. Oh God, Bernie, what have I done?'

It was a good thing Emma was doing something positive this afternoon; he hoped it would stop her worrying, for even just a short time.

Bernie looked up at the security monitor: a car was pulling up just outside the yard gates. It couldn't be Garry's sister, it wasn't afternoon yet. Oh Christ, it was: the numerals 12.57 were showing on the display. He zoomed in on the vehicle; yes, there was a woman in the driving seat, and Garry was beside her.

Bernie pressed the buzzer which allowed the car, a newish-looking Toyota Yaris, to enter the yard. Paula must be doing quite well, or maybe she had gambled on the prospect of buying into the hair-dressing business where she worked, with the money from the sale of the Brockwood shop.

He watched as the driver's door opened and the woman stepped out of the car.

Bernie didn't know what he had been expecting, but having met Garry, it certainly wasn't this: a slender, statuesque, self-confident-looking black woman with lustrous hair piled high on her head; she was wearing tight-fitting leather trousers and a red furry jacket. It was as if Naomi Campbell had by magic appeared in the yard. He went on staring as Paula looked slowly all around the yard, sizing up her surroundings; apparently satisfied with what she was seeing, she turned to her passenger, waiting patiently beside her. He had been so taken up at the sight of Paula that he hadn't noticed Garry, at least a foot shorter than his sister, emerging from the car. With a delicate movement of her hand, silver bangles glinting in the afternoon sunshine, she clicked on the remote and locked the car. Elegantly and purposefully she walked across to the back door. Garry followed meekly behind; he was not looking happy.

Bernie let out the breath he had been holding. So much for lunch.

He opened the office door.

'Good afternoon,' he said. 'Do come in.'

CHAPTER TWENTY-FOUR

Garry wished she'd not dressed like that: it was only the back yard of a shop they'd come to. And the way she was looking at Bernie, he just wanted to crawl away and fold himself up.

It weren't surprising though, after what he'd told her. Once he'd said, 'Sis, there's something I need to tell you' she'd come to the flat and seen the money. 'How much?' she'd said. 'Dunno.' 'You *don't know!* Jesus, Garry!' She'd narrowed her eyes. 'I don't believe you. *You* have money … and you don't know how much? Huh! Come on, little bruv, time to find out!'

Envelope by envelope they pulled out the notes, stacked them up on the little table. Paula looked at them in awe.

'Jesus, Garry.' Her voice was little more than a whisper, 'I don't wonder you was scared.' She ran her tongue round her mouth. 'What?' she said, 'my lips are dry, is all. Right … let's count.' She leant forward, picked up the first pile. 'No. Wait.' She put the notes down, picked up her handbag from the floor, scrabbled around inside it and brought out a pen. 'Pass me one of them white envelopes,' she said.

Pile by pile Paula and Garry counted the notes and Paula wrote down the amounts on the back of the envelope. When all the piles on the table had been counted, she added up the figures she had written down. Garry sat watching her, his mouth now dry, his heart thumping wildly.

Paula threw the pen down on the table and began to laugh.

'What?'

'You jammy bugger!'

'Wha …?'

'Have you any idea how much you've got?'

'I know it's a bit, but …'

'A bit! It's a bleeding lot!' She picked up one of the piles, shook it in front of his face. 'Each one of these is near a grand! … and see how many piles there are! You, little bruv … have come into money.'

'Yeah … I can see that.'

'So,' she'd said then, 'tell me the rest of it.'

'What … rest?' he'd said, swallowing hard; there was no way he would tell her about Grandad's message.

'The shop, ninny! The guys who want to buy it.'

'Oh. Yeah.' So he told her.

'Listen …' Paula put her hand on his arm. 'I know you was trying to do me a favour, making a deal on the side, and I appreciate that, I do really, but now …' she patted his arm, 'now *I* need to see these guys.'

'You?'

'Yes, me. You don't know about business … I know you think you do … but I do. Okay?' Garry nodded. 'So we go and see them and I do the talking.'

* * *

And she did.

'So, Mr. Silver …'

'Oh, Bernie, please.'

'Thank you, but I prefer to keep this formal, if you don't mind.'

'No, of course. Whatever you're comfortable with. So ... what exactly do you want to talk to me about? You said on the phone ...'

Paula looked at Bernie as if he was some kind of moron.

'Do you, or do you not ... want to buy my grandfather's shop? Because, if you do, then please stop farting around, getting Garry to bring you a whole load of envelopes … as if they have anything to do with it!' Nice one, Sis.

'Oh, I think they do …'

'You may think that, but …'

Bernie raised his hands, palms towards Paula. 'Before we go any further, would you like a coffee? Or tea?'.

'No thank you, I just want an answer to my question,' Paula said politely, smiling at him.

'It isn't that simple. Garry, d'you want a …?'

'No, ta.'

'It's very simple, Mr. Silver. You want to buy the shop … or you don't. And if you can make me a good offer, and I accept it, it's good for both of us, isn't it?' That's right, Sis, you tell him.

'Oh, I agree with that, and make no mistake, I am interested in Brockwood Stores, very interested, subject to all the usual searches, and so on; and when my surveyor's given the place a thorough going-over …'

'Of course,' said Paula. 'Doesn't stop us coming to some sort of … arrangement now, does it?'

'Well, yes and no. We both want to save ourselves money, that's just common sense, but … I can't rush into this.'

'I'm not asking you to, just …'

'Are you sure I can't offer you any refreshment?'

'I said *No*! Listen, if you're going to start messing me around …'

'No, Miss Wade, I am not *messing you around*, as you say ... but I can't decide *anything* until I know where that money in your grandfather's loft came from! Goodness knows what criminal proceedings might be involved!'

'Criminal proceedings?' Paula looked at Garry. 'You're not saying that …?'

Oh Christ, if Bernie finds out he'd been in prison. 'He doesn't know I've …' Garry whispered.

Quickly Paula turned her eyes back to Bernie. 'What … you saying that that burglary … all them years ago … could have some effect on me and Garry selling the shop? No. No way. Sorry. You just trying to stall me, aren't you?'

'Of course I'm not. I do want to buy that shop, but I also need to know, for quite a different reason, why the shop was burgled.'

'For money. What else?'

'I don't mean why, I mean when … and how.'

'I don't get this,' she said. 'There's something you're not telling me.' She paused, waiting for a response from Bernie.

He just looked at her, uncomfortable-like. 'I'm sorry, we can't do business if you are hiding something I need to know.'

'Yes, I can see that.' Bernie looked away, got up and walked to the door. He stood there for a few moments, gave a huge sigh and turned round. 'All right,' he said. 'There is something I think you should know, but I can't tell you until I have spoken to someone else.'

'Who?'

'I'm sorry, I can't tell you that, not until I have spoken to her.'

'Her?'

'It's that Jackie, innit?' Garry'd not meant to say anything; he'd promised Paula he wouldn't, but he could see how upset she was getting: she'd started to pull at her hair, and he knew that sign from when they was kids.

'Jackie?' Paula tugged at her hair, turned to Garry. 'Who's Jackie?'

'No, no. It's not Jackie,' Bernie intervened. 'It's nothing to do with Jackie.' In answer to the questioning look in Paula's eyes, he went on, 'Jackie's just someone who went to see the shop.'

'Oh. If you say so.'

'There was …' Garry began.

'What? Christ, Garry … if you know something, then for fuck's sake say it!' She took her hand down from her hair. 'Sorry,' she said, smiling weakly at Bernie. 'Actually … I wouldn't mind having that coffee, if you're still offering.'

'Yes. Sure.' Bernie said. 'Sorry, it'll have to be instant; is that all right? The machine …' he waved it, 'it's my partner's baby; I really don't know how it works.'

As if, Garry thought. He wants this over and done with quick, not be sitting round waiting for Trev's fancy coffee-maker to do its stuff.

'I'll have one, too, if you're making,' he said.

'Of course; yes.'

Paula began to fiddle with her hair again.

'Why don't you have a look in the shop, Sis, while Bernie's making the coffee?' Garry knew it was a bold thing to suggest – this was Paula's party, not his – but he had to get her alone.

'Why? What do I want to …?'

'Yeah, good idea. Go on, Garry, take her through.' Bernie all but pushed them out of the office, Garry leading the way. As he turned round to make sure Paula was following him – knowing her she might well decide not to – he could see that Bernie was reaching for his phone. His heart lurched: if that was the police he was calling … Jesus! As Bernie picked up the phone it rang.

'Oh, hi,' Garry heard him say, 'I was just about to call you.'

Garry let out a sigh of relief.

'Okay, so what is it?' Paula stopped by one of the racks of old LPs. 'You obviously want to tell me something.'

Garry drew his attention away from Bernie. 'No, not tell you; ask you.'

'What?'

'You know that break-in, when Nan and Grandad was tied up?'

'What about it?'

Garry took a deep breath: this wasn't easy. 'D'you think … d'you think Grandad recognised whoever did it, and was …'

'Oh come on, Garry, what you trying to say?'

'Was Grandad … d'you think Grandad was blackmailing him … them … and that's where the money's come from?'

'What?!'

'I know it's sounds crazy, but …'

In the office Garry could hear Bernie saying to whoever was on the phone, 'That's good. I'd love to, but …'

He turned his attention back to Paula. 'Okay, so you tell me how come there was all that dosh, *in envelopes that'd been posted*?'

Bernie, sounding far from happy now, was saying, '*Now?* No!' A pause, then, softly, 'Of course I'm not angry, it's just that I've got someone here about buying the shop …'

Oh Christ, they're talking about Paula.

'Shit,' Paula said. 'Is that what you think?'

'I don't want to, but … yeah.' There didn't seem to be any other explanation for all that cash being there, and if that's what had happened, then *that* could be the criminal thing that Bernie was talking about.

'Oh, Gar-ry. Grandad, blackmailing someone?' She shook her head violently. 'No! You been watching too many heist movies!'

'No, I've not.' He might have known she'd not take him seriously.

'I hope to God he wasn't.'

'Yeah. Me too.'

Paula, her face pained, turned away from him and began fiddling with the old vinyl records in front of her. Garry watched her for a moment, unsure what to do or say next; he'd not wanted to upset her, but she had to know. Best he went back to the office and let her come in when she was ready.

'Coffee's ready,' Bernie called out.

Two steaming coffees awaited them in the office; Bernie had poured himself a generous tot of whisky.

'Thanks,' Paula said, picking up a mug with a picture of David Bowie on it; Garry's had a Union Jack.

For a few moments they drank in silence.

'So,' said Paula, putting down her mug. She appeared to have regained her calm. 'Can we do business, Mr. Silver?'

'I think we can, but as I said, I have to speak to someone else first.'

'Is that who you was on the phone to?' Garry asked.

'Ga-rry … behave yourself!' Paula gave Bernie her best 'favourite customer' smile. 'Yes, that's fine, you talk to her. You did say it was a woman?'

'I did.' Bernie nodded, smiled back at Paula. He took a swig of his whisky, slowly put the glass down on the desk. 'Her name is Mrs. Raven; she's coming here today.' He's saying it like it was a speech in one of them plays, Garry thought, like Trevor had told him how to say it. He had a feeling they were being set up, him and Paula. His stomach was cramping something awful. This woman: not a genuine buyer, he'd bet any money on it. Solicitor, that's what she'll be. Well, someone legal, some smartass woman making out the money isn't his: he'd met her sort before.

'Good. We're making headway, by the sound of it.' Paula said.

'I can't see how.' Garry's whisper was croaky. 'I think we should go.'

'No!' Paula whispered back, 'and listen, you don't say anything, specially not what you told me in there.' She inclined her head towards the shop. 'You let me handle this. Okay?'

'Yeah, okay.' Garry was wishing he'd not said that about Grandad.

'Ah, she's here now,' Bernie was looking at the video screen. 'I'll just let her in.' He picked up the remote and pointed it at the screen; the gates swung open. 'Do drink your coffee; shan't be a minute,' he said, and walked out into the yard.

CHAPTER TWENTY-FIVE

Emma knew, almost as soon as she walked into the high-ceilinged entrance hall of *The Oaks* that she had found the right place for Andrew. She had been impressed with the facilities when she saw them online, and then, this morning: the tall, crested, wrought-iron gates, the fat, cheerful man on duty, and the approach to the building, along a driveway winding gently through secluded grounds, where rhododendrons were interspersed with oak trees and the occasional conifer; even the visitors' car park, nestling among more trees and shrubs, had an ambience of tranquillity. A short walk took her to the front of the main building, white stone with a Georgian portico, and gleaming modern wings on either side. It all added to her feeling of being in the right place; and finally, the welcome she received from the staff, combined with a sense of their genuine personal interest in each of the patients, convinced her that Andrew should come here.

Yes, all right, they wanted her money – and the care here wasn't cheap – but she saw the way the patients responded to their carers, and there was no way that could be faked. She had spoken to several of them; one of the men, Gabriel, loved the place so much he wanted his wife to come and live there, too. 'It's a perfect retirement home,' he told her. 'There's everything here you could wish for.' She had smiled, pleased for him. It was a great testimonial, as was Maisie's: 'Never eaten so well in my life.' Yes, this would suit Andrew – cosseting and good food – until he regained his strength. And then? She must only think about now; *then* had too many question marks hanging over it, the biggest one, her relationship with Bernie. Despite what they had done, she did still love Andrew. Despite what *he* had done. If he *had* done it. At home, looking at the notebooks and the cuttings, talking to Bernie, she'd felt certain he had … and they could never be close again. But here, in this superb convalescent home, with its spacious suites, elegantly furnished lounges and well-kept lawns, all so in tune with their own comfortable lifestyle, the idea seemed ridiculous … and insulting.

Even Emma's clothes today had been right for *The Oaks*. Now, as she waited for Bernie to open the gates to the yard in Almeida Street, she looked down at herself, at the beautiful, top quality camel coat, the Emma Hope boots, with matching gloves, the La Borsa bag that lay on the seat beside her next to the colourful brochure from the home; it was the way Andrew liked her to dress, expensively, but not overtly so: not for him a Gucci bag, of which there were cheap replicas; he chose a lesser-known name, but one with an elite cachet. He had good taste in clothes and he always knew what looked good on her.

The yard gates were opening; she took off the hand brake and drove in. Bernie in faded jeans – *he* never minded what she wore – stood waiting for her, at the back door of the shop.

'Why the long face?' she asked, stepping out of the car. 'It's good, it really is; you wait till you see it.' She waved the brochure at him.

'I'm sure it is, and I'm pleased for you, but …'

She was too excited to let him continue: 'It's going to be so good for his rehabilitation, Bernie; he's even going to be able to come *here* when he wants to!' She reached back into the car for her bag and gloves. 'I know it's not going to be easy,' she said, shutting the door, 'but this place … it's given me the first bit of hope I've had for what lies ahead. Come on, let's go inside, and I'll show you.' She took his arm.

'No,' he said, shaking her off.

'What?'

'I've got someone here, Emm. I told you.'

'So? I'm only just holding your arm!'

'She's on the war-path, pushing the sale of the shop. I'm just warning you; she's quite aggressive. But, on the plus side, she has no idea who you are, just thinks you are someone I need to speak to about the sale, and …'

'And I just happened to turn up? Oh Bernie, why say anything about me?'

'I don't know, I just did. She phoned, and then she came here – that's her car – and … I don't know, she just got me rattled, and then you rang and … I'll just say you might be interested in setting up another music shop.'

'All right,' Emma said gently, although she couldn't understand why Bernie was quite so stressed. She withdrew her arm from his, turned up the collar of her coat and tucked in her silk scarf: the wind funnelling in through the still open gates was bitterly cold. 'Oh, let's get inside.'

'Yes, sorry.' With the remote Bernie closed the gates.

'Don't worry, it'll be fine.'

'Yes, of course it will.' Bernie's smile was nothing more than a stretching of the skin on his face; Emma had seen that smile before, when they'd been at the hospital, waiting for news of Andrew, just after the stroke. He's scared of something, she thought.

Bernie was still smiling as they stepped into the office. 'Miss Wade,' he said, 'may I introduce you to Mrs. Raven.'

The woman stepped forward, took Emma's hand. 'Hi,' she said, then turning to the man behind her, 'This is my brother …'

'Garry?' Emma felt the hairs on her neck standing up. 'It is you, isn't it?' What the hell was he doing here?

'Yes.' Garry's face was ashen, his voice a hoarse whisper. 'Hi.'

'But …?' Emma's composure had gone. Oh how stupid, to be thrown off-balance at the sight of this anxious-looking man. 'I had no idea you had a sist …'

'How come you know Garry?' Paula's tone was abrupt. 'Garry, how come you …?'

'We met at the shop in Brockwood,' Emma said, trying desperately to remember if there was anything significant she was supposed to know about Garry.

'Yeah, 'sright. You was with Jackie.'

‘Ohhh. Yes.’ The woman’s eyes were glinting; why was she enjoying this? ‘Garry said there was another woman. Didn’t you?’

‘Yeah.’ He’s wishing he wasn’t here, Emma thought. She glanced at Bernie; the smile had gone.

‘So … what’s your connection then, Mrs. Raven … with all this?’ Paula asked.

‘Well, I … we, Jackie and I …’ Desperately Emma looked to Bernie for help: she had forgotten what she was supposed to say.

‘Mrs. Raven is one of the people interested in setting up another music place, like this one.’

‘In Brockwood? In Grandad’s old shop? Oh, please …’ Paula’s laugh was hollow, mocking. ‘I’m not a fool, you know, nor is Garry. Don’t you be taken in by the way he looks, lady, he’s very shrewd, is my brother.’

‘I don’t think for a moment Mrs. Raven was suggesting that …’ Bernie took a step towards Emma.

‘It’s all right, Bernie, let me do this.’ Emma lifted a restraining hand to him; it was not the moment for him to be protective. She, Emma, would deal with this. ‘You’re right, Miss Wade, I’m not interested in buying the shop, but Bernie is … and I need to tell you why.’

‘No, don’t. Please.’

‘Why not? Isn’t it time we all came clean about all this? The money that Garry has … and the break-in. And the notebooks.’

‘Notebooks? Don’t know nothing about notebooks.’

‘They’re notebooks in which my husband …’

‘No,’ Bernie jumped in. ‘Don’t worry about notebooks, they’re not important.’

‘Yes they are! Please, Bernie, let me speak. We can’t go on like this, pretending, making out things don’t matter. Andrew’s notebooks are extremely important, and all the cuttings he had. He’ll be coming home soon, and before he does, I need to know the truth, about *everything.* I may be quite wrong … but I think that Miss Wade …’

‘Paula …’ the woman said.

‘Paula … thank you. I think that Paula …’ She looked round behind Paula to Garry. ‘ … and her brother … may know things we don’t, and …’ She turned to Bernie. ‘I can’t stand any more of this not knowing, this wondering if these awful things really did happen.’ She reached into her coat pocket for a tissue to stem the tears beginning to roll down her cheeks. ‘Sorry, but I can’t.’

‘Oh, love.’ Paula sprang up from her chair, put her arms around Emma. ‘Don’t cry.’ She looked up at Bernie, ‘though God knows, I’m not far from it.’

‘Thank you,’ Emma said, blowing her nose.

‘She’s right,’ Paula said. ‘It’s quite obvious to me, and to … to Mrs ... oh, I can’t be doing with this …’

‘You’re the one who wanted formality, Miss Wade,’ Bernie said.

Emma looked up at him; all pretence of a smile had gone.

‘My name’s Emma.’

‘Emma. Ta. I don’t know about you, Emma, but I am not leaving this office until I know exactly what has been going on.’ Paula sat down in her chair and folded her arms.

'Perhaps another cup of coffee would be …' Bernie said, reaching for the empty cups on the desk.

'No,' Emma said.

'Stuff your coffee,' said Paula.

'Yes, let's get on with it, now we've started.' Emma could feel a weariness coming over her. 'You tell her, Bernie. I have a feeling you know more than I do.'

'I doubt it, but …'

'Please.' Whatever it was, she wanted it over. Now.

'All right. Well, not to make too long a story of it, my business partner kept a notebook, in which he wrote down amounts that he paid out to people from whom he bought items to sell in this shop.'

'The business partner is my husband, Andrew.'

'Emma …' Bernie whispered. 'That's not relevant.'

'Of course it's relevant. It's relevant to me. And don't whisper; it's a small room, we can all hear you.' None of this was his fault. 'Sorry,' Emma said, looking up at him, reaching for his hand; Bernie waved it away.

'Is that it, then?' Paula asked. 'Someone wrote down payments in a notebook. What about them?'

Emma and Bernie exchanged looks. 'Go on, tell her,' Emma said.

Bernie stood up and walked to the door; he looked out into the yard.

'You have to do this, Bernie.' Emma's voice was gentle, cajoling.

Bernie turned round. 'Yes. I know.' He walked across to his desk, sat down behind it and drew the bottle of whisky towards him. 'The amounts in the notebook tally with the money in the envelopes that Garry found in the loft.' He unscrewed the bottle and reached for his glass. 'These payments, the ones listed, went to Brockwood, to Freddie Gesson.'

'Oh, fuck.' Paula said softly.

Bernie poured himself a generous tot, downed it in one.

'Looks like I was right, Sis,' Garry said. 'Grandad *was* blackm...'

'No, wait a minute; there's something missing.' She turned to Bernie. 'You've still not told me the whole thing, have you? Why should our Grandad be blackmailing her husband? Mm? 'Cos that's what you're saying, isn't it?'

'Well …'

'Oh, don't piss about! It *is* that, isn't it? Our Grandad was blackmailing your partner because he knew … Or he was the one! … who stole the money from the shop, the Christmas money!'

In slow motion Emma and Bernie look at one another.

'Yes,' Bernie says. Emma nods. 'It's a very long time ago, and it was a terrible thing that he did, but the money was paid back, to your grandfather; so can we not draw a line under it, please?'

'Oh, my God.' Paula's laugh rang out loud and raucous. 'No, man … no.' Her hands went to her hair. 'You don't get round Paula Wade that way. Uh-uh.' She turned to Bernie. 'So you think that makes up for it, do you? It's all right then, is it, to beat up an old man and his wife if you pay them back the money you stole from them? Jesus!'

'Nobody beat anybody up! My husband would never do a thing like that. Never!' Emma began to tremble, her mouth dry, her hands icy cold.

'Okay, okay. So he didn't beat them up. Wrong word. Sorry. But he did *tie* them up and gag them.'

'No! He didn't, he wouldn't.'

'You knew, didn't you?' Paula stared hard at Bernie, disgust all over her face. 'Course you did, I can see it in your eyes.'

'He wouldn't do that, not Andrew.' How could Bernie know something she didn't? No, this woman was making it up. 'Bernie, tell her.' Emma's heart was racing.

'Yes, go on; tell her!'

'Oh, Emm, I wish to God you didn't have to hear this.' He sighed deeply. 'Yes. He did.' His voice was flat, his face like a stone.

'No!'

'He tied them up and put gags in their mouths.' Paula said.

'He *wouldn't*! You've got this all wrong, both of you.'

'You'd be surprised what some people will do for money,' Paula said. 'Tell her, Garry. Go on.'

'It's true. Yeah.'

'How … how do you know this?' Emma looked from Paula to Garry, then to Bernie; this was a conspiracy, they were in it together. 'You're making this up, you're …'

'Emma, Emma.' Bernie took hold of her hands. 'We're not, nobody is. There was a full account of it in *The Mercury*.'

'But ...? We looked at all the cuttings in the …'

'I know we did, but this account, detailing what was done to the shopkeeper and his wife, was *not* in the folder. I found it at County Hall, in the archives.'

'What are you saying? That Andrew didn't dare to keep … ?'

Bernie nodded. 'Either that, or he wanted to block it out of his memory.'

'As if you ever *forget* doing something like that!' Paula's face was contorted with anger.

'Oh God, I feel sick.' Emma stood up, clutched hold of Bernie. 'Bernie, take me home.'

'Oh no, you don't get off that easily.' Paula took her phone out of the pocket of her furry jacket, 'either of you,' she said and flipped the phone open. 'I'm calling the police!' She began pressing the keypad.

'No, don't.' Garry lunged forward, clamped his hand over the phone. 'Don't do that, Sis. Please.'

'I have to.' A look passed between the brother and sister that Emma could not interpret. 'No. All right, I won't.' Paula said. Garry took his hand off the phone and slowly Paula closed it.

'It's not their fault,' Garry said.

Emma looked gratefully at Garry. She had no idea why he had intervened. 'Thank you,' she said, smiling weakly at him; she still felt sick, but Garry had given her a breathing space, perhaps more than that. 'How could he?' she whispered to Bernie.

'Not now, later,' he whispered back fiercely. 'While we're meting out blame, and thinking about calling in the police,' he said loudly, to Paula, 'don't let's forget your grandfather.'

'Grandad? He didn't tie …'

'Maybe not, but ...'

'There's no maybe about it, he was an honest …'

'He was a blackmailer!'

'You don't know that!

'Oh, I do …'

'Bernie …?' Emma began hesitantly. The pressure of Bernie's fingers on Emma's hand was painful. Was there something else she didn't know? If she didn't get out of here very soon she *would* be sick … or faint: Paula's face, looking strangely smug, began to wave from side to side. Take a deep breath, she said to herself, keep calm.

'Our grandfather is dead. There's nothing you can do to hurt him.'

'And my partner has already been punished.'

'Oh really? How d'you make that out?' Paula's laugh was bitter. 'Banned him from one of your posh clubs, did you?'

'He's had a major stroke,' Bernie said. His voice was calm but Emma, still close to him, could feel the tension in his body, 'and he's in hospital; he's very ill.'

'Oh …' For a moment Paula seemed thrown off balance, or maybe that was just how she appeared to Emma's vision, in which not even the room was now staying still. 'He'll get better though, won't he, and then he can go …'

Emma could see two Paulas now, but neither of them was going to get away with that. 'He could die!' she screamed, lunging for both of them.

* * *

When Emma opened her eyes, she was sitting on a chair, with Bernie holding her hand and Paula dabbing her face with a damp tissue.

'What …?' It was little more than a whisper.

'Sh … sh. It's all right.' Bernie's voice was soft, concerned. 'You fainted.'

'I don't faint.' Emma's voice was coming back, but she still felt strange, disorientated. Why was she here, like this, in Bernie's shop, and who was this beautiful black woman? 'Oh God … no.' Everything was coming back to her. She no longer felt faint, but she did feel nauseous and the taste in her mouth was unbearable. 'Water,' she said, grimacing. The woman – Paula, that was her name – held a cup to her lips; gratefully she sipped, then waved the cup away. 'I need to go home.'

'Yes, of course.' Bernie turned to Paula. 'I think we're done for today.'

'Well, not really …'

'I know, but first things first; I have to see to Mrs. Raven.'

'Of course you do.'

Emma didn't like her tone, but she felt too weak to protest.

'I'll be in touch,' Bernie said.

'You'd better,' Paula said.

'Give me your number.'

'You've got it. It's in your phone, from when I called you.'

'Oh, yes.'

Emma was beginning to feel woozy again. In a daze she watched as Bernie began ushering Paula and Garry out of the shop.

'Hope you feel better soon,' Paula said.

'Thank you.' Garry just nodded; she nodded back and shut her eyes, glad they had gone.

Bernie locked up the shop and the office – it was dark now and almost closing time. 'We'll take my car.' He helped her across the yard. 'Yours will be safe here overnight.'

'Yes,' Emma said. There was no way she could have driven home to Pengate, or anywhere for that matter, feeling as she did. She was glad Bernie had put the seat beside him into a reclining position.

'Try to have a sleep.'

Oh, how she would love to sleep. Oblivion. Not having to think, to question, to be angry. So, so angry. It was her anger and her disgust that was keeping her awake. Behind her closed eyelids she watched as Andrew gagged and tied up Freddie Gesson and his wife; over and over again it was played out - first the ropes around their bodies, then the gags stuffed in their mouths and their feeble attempts to cry out - and each time she tried to replace the scene with some less hurtful image it returned, with Andrew's behaviour becoming more violent, more despicable: the rope became coarser and thicker, the gags were pulled tighter; and now he was binding their ankles and tipping back their chairs ... and laughing. She felt a hollow sickness in the pit of her stomach; words from a play the school drama society had put on – she had been working backstage, in charge of the props – came to her: "lower than the bone, deeper than the beating heart, a sickness invades us, disgust, disillusion, disintegration." The words were so apt: intense disgust – she could feel the bile rising again in her throat – and hurtful, oh so hurtful; disillusion: talk about feet of clay, Andrew had his feet in a cesspool. As for disintegration … this could well apply to her marriage. After this, knowing what a – she hesitated even to think the word – what a monster her husband was, how could she ever, ever, live with him again. As for having him make love to her … even this minute, safe in Bernie's car, she shrank from the thought of Andrew's hands, hands that had knotted a rope, pushed in a gag, touching her. She shuddered, opened her eyes.

'Cold?' Bernie asked. 'I'll put the heating up.' He reached forward to a knob on the dashboard.

'I can't *ever* go back to him.' Emma turned her tear-stained face to Bernie. 'I can't live with him. Not now, not after …'

'We could be wrong. He might not have; I mean, he might have stolen the money, but not tied up the …'

'Oh, Bernie, don't humour me. Please. And don't take me to Pengate.' The thought of telling Connie … In her sister's eyes, Andrew could do no wrong. 'I can't stay there tonight.'

'What?'

'Just drive to Chigwell.'

'But … well, of course I'll drive you to Chigwell, if that's what you want, but … Do you not even want to get some … night clothes … or something?'

'Why would I want *night clothes* if I'm in bed with you? And if Jackie's there, I don't care. I'm sure she knows, anyway.'

'All right, we'll go to Chigwell, but you must call Constance; she'll be …'

'You call her, tell her I've been sick, tell her we're going out on the town, tell her anything you like, I don't care.'

'I will, but ...'

'Just do it. Please!'

'All right, I'll phone her, 'but I'm going to get you to bed first.'

'Oh yes, yes. Do that,' she said, laughing raucously, cutting across his next words. 'Oh God, yes. Yes, please do that!' He'd not meant it that way, she knew, but, oh God, it was what she wanted, needed: with Bernie's arms around her, his body merging into her, she might just be able to stop thinking. Behind her eyelids Andrew was still there, tying up the shopkeeper. I'm going mad, she thought. She opened her eyes, wide, stared at the road ahead; they were out of Islington, going north up the A1. The traffic was still heavy – this was rush hour, although no one was rushing; it should be renamed 'crawl hour' or 'stop and sit' hour. Or 'not going anywhere fast' hour. Any silly thought about London traffic was better than … Oh God, she was back in the shop and Andrew was … She shivered as the road and the traffic began to sway. 'Bernie, stop the car, I'm going to be sick.' And she was, into the road.

Emma slept the rest of the way to Chigwell. If Bernie stopped en route, or phoned anyone, she was unaware of it. When she woke up, she was in the car, drawn up in front of Bernie's house, with a thick fleece tucked around her. It took several minutes for her brain to get into gear: why was she in Bernie's car? And where *was* Bernie? She didn't have long to wait; someone must have been watching from a window; the front door opened and Jackie ran out, with Bernie just behind her. Smiling weakly, Emma pushed aside the fleece.

CHAPTER TWENTY-SIX

'What you got there?' Paula asked, turning her head to look at Garry. They'd not spoken since they drove out of Bernie's yard in pouring rain. Paula didn't like driving in these conditions, but he'd not offered to take the wheel: she was sure to bite his head off. The visit to *That Music Place* had not gone according to her plan, far from it with that silly bitch Emma going all faint on them. They were no further selling the shop than when they walked in the door, and as far as Garry could see there was no way of getting the deal back on track. Well, not if was left up to Paula; she'd not helped any, losing her rag like that. Mind you, it must have been a shock knowing what Grandad had done. So, now what? He wasn't going to give up, no way. Maybe, if he could talk to Trevor … 'Sorry, what did you say?'

'Things in your hand, what are they? You was rustling them.'

'Oh. Was I?' Garry looked down at his hands. 'Oh, they're just some leaflets I picked up from Bernie's desk.'

'I might have known; you and leaflets. You never could resist them.'

'They don't do no harm!' He glared at her. 'You never know, might be just what you're looking for. Remember that time I had the leaflet 'bout the paints for the car?' That would shut her up; Dean had been really pleased with him that day.

'Yes, I do,' Paula said wearily, 'they was exactly what Dean wanted. Just don't leave them in my car, though.'

'I won't!'

'All right, see you don't.'

'Oh! Be like that!' He wound down the window, hoping to aim the bundle at a litter bin as they drove past.

'For Christ's sake, Garry, shut that window!'

'Sorry.'

'Yeah, well I'm sorry too.' Paula sighed, patting Garry's leg. 'It's not been the best of days, has it?'

Far from it, and they still had the shop to sell.

'You gone quiet; you all right?'

'Yeah, just thinking.'

'What about?'

'Nothing. Just … thinking.' If she knew the idea that was forming in Garry's mind, she'd go spare.

'Come on; tell me.'

He'd have to say something. 'The shop. Hope we'll sell it soon. I did try, you know, Sis.'

'I know. My turn now. Yeah?'

'Yeah. Okay.' At least that had been easy, and it was, more or less, what he wanted, leaving him free to get on with the other thing … the plan. Well, he hadn't got a plan, not yet, but he would have, once he could sit down and think it through, this thing he wanted to do, had to do. That man, that partner of Bernie's … something Raven … he had to pay for what he done to Grandad, and most of all to his lovely Nan. He reckoned that's what had made her so ill, being gagged and tied up like that. Garry'd never been one for violence, scared of getting hurt himself, but Jesus, he would like to punch that guy. If he could find him.

'Gar-ry … what the hell are you doing with your hands?'

Garry looked down; both hands were in tight fists. 'Dunno,' he said, relaxing his fingers. 'Just a bit, you know, uptight. I s'pose.'

'Yeah, well, bound to be,' Paula said, sympathetically.

'Stopped raining now,' Garry said, looking out of the window.

'It stopped a while back, soon's we got out of London. Sun's out, too. Did you not notice?'

'Oh. No.' He'd been too busy, thinking.

Paula sighed, shook her head. 'Sometimes, Garry, I despair of you.'

Not for long though, Sis, oh no. You just wait; you'll see.

CHAPTER TWENTY-SEVEN

Bernie and Jackie looked down on Emma, now sleeping peacefully.

Jackie had persuaded her to have a warm drink, into which she had put one of her own over-the-counter sleeping pills – 'It won't hurt her,' she'd said when Bernie protested, 'it'll just switch off her brain and make sure she has a good sleep' – and they had taken her upstairs to bed.

'Poor girl, she was exhausted,' Jackie said. 'Come on, Bernie, let's go downstairs and have some food.'

'I'm not sure I feel like eating.'

'Maybe you don't, but you will.'

Bernie smiled and followed her down the stairs; he could do with a bit of cosseting. Suddenly he missed his mother … and her cooking. Rose had been a brilliant cook, conjuring delicious dishes out of the most unlikely mix of ingredients, seldom using a cookery book. 'You want a bit more, you put in a bit more,' she used to say. 'If I hadn't already been a Jewish mother I would have had to become one.'

They took their bowls of soup and warm rolls into the lounge, and ate from a low table in front of the fire.

'Mm … that was good,' Bernie said, wiping the last of the bread around his bowl, 'the sort of soup my mother used to make.'

'She taught me, you know.'

'To make soup?'

'That, and other things.'

'I didn't know that. When?'

'When I used to come here in the school holidays, when my mum was at work.'

'Where was I, then?'

'Oh, somewhere about, I expect … out with your mates. Seven years between us is nothing now, but when I was nine, in pigtails, and you were sixteen you wouldn't have noticed me.'

'True. Just another pesky kid Rose had taken under her wing.' Bernie raised his hands to protect himself from the bread roll Jackie was threatening to throw at him. 'She was good at that, encouraging people.' He chuckled.

'What?'

'Promise you won't laugh?'

'Try me.'

'I played the trumpet because of Mum.'

'Trumpet! You?'

'All right; it's not that improbable. I am musical, you know.'

'I know, but … the trumpet?'

'I'd wanted to play the sax, very cool I thought that would have been, but then I heard Eddie Calvert …'

'Who?'

'He was a famous British trumpet player. I used to listen to him on Mum's old L.Ps. She bought me the trumpet. Dad said it was a total waste of money, and he was right; I was never any good at it. I sold it, to someone at Repton; I sold quite a few things to people at Repton.' He laughed, remembering that his father was not at all cross with him for that, and later, although he had never been happy about his son giving up his law career to run a music shop, he admitted that he had known from Bernie's schooldays that he would be a good salesman.

'She encouraged Andrew, too.' In his mind's eye he could see Rose walking in her garden, trailing her fingers along the tops of the brightly-coloured perennials in the herbaceous border, in earnest conversation with Andrew, his face very serious as he listened to whatever advice she was giving him. What the advice was, Andrew had never said, and Bernie had never asked.

'Oh? In what way?'

'I can't be sure, but I think, when we were starting up the business … I think she persuaded him, somehow, that he could be part of *this mad enterprise* – his words – and still be a successful accountant.'

Jackie smiled. 'Yes, he'd want to be sure of that, wouldn't he?'

Bernie nodded. 'And she encouraged Emma, helping her to become more confident, get herself out from under Andrew's shadow. You know what she was like; a great feminist my mum, couldn't abide the idea of the little woman stuck in the kitchen.'

'Yet that's where she most liked to be!'

'Oh yes, but only when she chose to be, not because my dad was coming home expecting a meal on the table.'

'Are you saying Andrew did?'

'More or less, yes. He not exactly dominated Emma. but he did make the rules.' Jackie raised her eyebrows. 'Well, not so much rules as ... standards of behaviour, dress. Befitting the standard of living he had chosen for himself.' He laughed. 'As a sort of … well, successful businessman-cum-country gentleman.'

'Was that because of his working-class background?'

'Oh, definitely. Andrew always felt he had to prove he was as good as the next man, even though there was no need; he was. He got a better degree than I did.'

'Must have been difficult for Emma to live up to that.' Jackie stood up. 'D'you want some more soup?'

'Yes, if there is.'

'Give us your bowl then.'

'I'll bring it in,' Bernie said. He followed Jackie into the kitchen and leant against the counter while she reheated the soup.

'More bread?'

'No. Ta.' He moved away from the counter, lifted his spoon and held out the bowl to Jackie. 'What you were saying, about Andrew's background … it does sound pretty ridiculous now, but it wasn't so much then, thirty years ago. We forget how much more uptight people were about that sort of thing.'

'They shouldn't have been, not with Thatcher in power; she never hid her background.' Jackie ladled soup into Bernie's bowl. He walked across to the long deal table and sat down. The soup was very hot; he blew on it, supped it slowly.

'You not having any more?'

'No, we've got more stuff than this, you know. Look.' She pointed to the kitchen table. 'Quiche - broccoli, mushroom and Swiss cheese. And it's a kosher one … from your local deli.'

'I didn't think you bothered.'

'I don't, at home; as you know, I love bacon! But here … I don't know … it didn't feel right, somehow, in Rose's kitchen.'

'She'd eat anything in a restaurant, but she kept a kosher kitchen, even after Dad died.' He'd been the fussy one; not because he believed in it that much – as Bernie had heard him say, the dietary laws belonged to another age – but because it was expected of him as a prominent Jewish businessman; he'd been a bit like Andrew, in that respect, careful to present the required face to the world.

'There's salad, too.' He wasn't keen on salad, and this one lacked his mother's artistic touch, but for Jackie's sake he would eat a bit of it.

' … and we've got new potatoes.'

'Let's eat the rest of the meal in here then.' He took another spoonful of the soup. 'This really is good. Could you make it again?'

'I shouldn't think so,' Jackie said. 'I just bunged in what was in the fridge.' She watched as Bernie finished the soup and pushed the bowl away from him. 'I'll just heat up the potatoes and then you can dive in.' She turned away, opened the microwave door and put in a dish.

He had enjoyed the soup – it was easy to get it down – and the quiche looked delicious, but he wasn't sure that his knotting stomach would accept it. He stared out into the dark garden at the far end of the room; he hadn't switched on the lights his mother had installed; it didn't seem right with her not there to enjoy floodlit trees and shrubs, choisya and vibernums and elaeagnus, the pond she loved so much, and the patio where they had eaten so many happy summer meals, sometimes with Emma there … and Andrew; always his thoughts came back to him. He turned and looked at the food. 'I don't promise to eat it, but … Oh, anything to take my mind off all this stuff with Andrew.' He sighed. 'I wonder …'

'What?' Jackie pushed the dish of olives towards him.

Bernie shook his head. 'He admired Thatcher, you know.'

'Of course he did. She was the perfect role model for someone like Andrew, clever working-class boy with aspirations. When you think about it … he was the archetypal Thatcher's child.'

'Yes, he was.'

'There's nothing you can't achieve,' Jackie said, 'if you set your mind to it, especially if you …' The microwave pinged; she turned away, opened the door.

'Go on.'

'Nothing, that's it.' She took out the potatoes.

'Nothing you can't achieve,' Bernie said, 'if you don't mind treading on other people's toes to realise your dream; although, to be fair to the lady, I doubt it was what she was advocating.' He sighed. 'And for Andrew, brought up on a council estate, that would bring so many things: nice wife, big house, posh friends …' He sighed again and shook his head. 'Oh Jackie.'

'Whereas you and I … we had it all from the beginning.' Jackie put the potatoes, glossy with melted butter and sprinkled with parsley, onto the table. 'Come on, eat,' she said tenderly.

'I'm not sure I can, but … I'll try.'

While Bernie helped himself to potatoes Jackie cut into the quiche. 'I should have heated this up,' she said, sliding a slice onto his plate.

'No, it's fine as it is.' He wasn't going to be able to do justice to it, either way.

He picked out a few salad leaves, then a tomato.

They began to eat, looking steadfastly down at their plates; the tick of the kitchen wall-clock sounded loud. Bernie put down his knife and fork, leant back in his chair. Jackie lifted her head.

'No?' she said.

'No. Sorry, I can't. It's Andrew … and Emma.' Bernie pushed back his chair and walked over to the patio doors; head down, shoulders hunched, he held onto the door handle, steadying himself: his stomach was churning; his mind, too, was reeling, thoughts chasing one another feverishly around his brain. Up to now he'd felt it possible to contain the situation, but now, with Emma knowing everything … He shouldn't be here, scoffing food; he should be with her, for when she woke up. He lifted his head, straightened his shoulders, let go of the door handle.

'You love her, don't you?' he heard Jackie say, her voice seeming to come to him from far away. His heart began to beat fast; he reached for the door handle again.

'Yes. I do.' He took a deep breath and turned round.

'From way back.'

He nodded. If he hadn't, he might have tried harder to hold onto Eunice.

'Come and sit down.' Jackie patted the chair next to her.

'No, I must go and see how she is.'

'No, Bernie, let her be. What she needs now is sleep, not you …' her eyes glinted, ' … however gorgeous and macho you may be!'

'I'm not *macho,* am I?' He disliked the word; he had always associated it with gauchos, envisaging tough men in leather chaps, riding across the pampas, swinging lassos.

'Well, I hope you are, otherwise she's wasting her time, isn't she?'

Bernie laughed; it felt good to laugh, it broke the tension that had been building up in his body. 'Sorry about the food,' he said, 'I'm sure it's lovely, but …'

'Oh, for God's sake!' Jackie stood up, began to clear the table; she'd not eaten much either, Bernie noticed. 'Look … you go into the lounge, I'll bring you some coffee. Get yourself a brandy.'

'Thanks.'

In the lounge Bernie leant back on the sofa, his legs on a stool, stretched out to the fire; he swirled the brandy around the glass, the light from the flames of the fire catching the movement; it was like watching a flamenco dancer; in his head there was music from *Carmen*, the habanera. One day, when all this was over, he would take Emma to Spain; they would go to the Roma caves near Granada, watch the dancers; they would dance, too, a tango, and he would hold her close. The night air would be scented with roses and …

'Wake up … coffee.'

He jerked up. If the brandy glass had not been empty he would have spilled the contents.

'Give me that,' Jackie said. She took the glass from him and put the coffee mug into his hand. 'Got it?' she asked.

Bernie nodded. 'Sorry, I must have …'

'Do you good, have a kip.'

'Yeah.' Bernie sipped his coffee. 'For the moment; then you begin to think again.'

'Which is why …' Jackie pushed Bernie's feet off the stool, drew it closer to the sofa, and sat down, facing him. '... you need to talk to me.'

'Well, all right, but …' What good would it do? What difference could talking to Jackie make: this was a problem, in all its aspects, that only he and Emma could resolve.

' … and I need you to tell me everything, from the beginning. Don't lift your eyebrows at me like that, Bernie Silver. If I'm to help you, I need to know everything.'

'Wet rot, dry rot? Unstable foundations?'

'Yep, all that, especially the foundations. So … from the beginning. And no leaving anything out, however trivial you may think it is.'

'Are you sure you're not a detective as well as an estate agent?'

'Stop prevaricating. Come on, talk.'

He told her everything, about the notebooks and the newspaper cuttings, the burglary, the assault on the shopkeeper and his wife, the money in the loft, the possible blackmailing, his visits to the pub in Brockwood and to the newspaper archives. Though not completely in sequence – he was no longer sure exactly what had happened when – he hoped he had related the events without omitting anything vital, and with enough cohesion for Jackie to understand their concern, his and Emma's … which was what really mattered.

'Well, there you are, that's it,' he said, finally. He sat still, staring at the fire. He had felt no need to say more of his love for Emma, nor what the future might hold for them; that they would have to sort out between them once Andrew was home. For now, it would just be good if Jackie could bring some fresh, clear thinking to everything else.

'Another brandy?' Jackie asked, not looking at him.

'Yes please,' he said.

Jackie walked across to the small table that held the decanters. Bernie watched as she poured out two measures, then replaced the decanter on the table. She brought the glasses to the sofa, handed one to Bernie, sat down on the stool and lifted her glass.

'L'chaim,' she said.

'L'chaim,' Their glasses clinked; they drank deeply.

'Well,' she said, 'I can't provide you with any immediate solution …'

'I didn't think you could, but …'

'No, listen to me. There *is* one thing that bothers me.'

‘Oh, what?’ He took another swig of the brandy; Jackie’s tone was not reassuring.

‘The blackmailing.’

‘What about it?’

‘How sure are you that it was blackmail?’

‘Pretty sure. Why?’

‘Based on what?’

For a moment Bernie felt unsure; had he not made it clear? ‘Well, the money, in those envelopes that Garry found in the loft.’

‘Yes, I know all that, but it doesn’t tell me why the money was there. When you think about it … it wasn’t the shopkeeper’s money. It belonged to his customers, it was *their* Christmas Club; why hadn’t he given it back to them?’

‘Well … I don’t know really. Remember, this money appeared some years after the break-in - at least that’s what we think - and anyway, how would he distribute it? Bit by bit, a few pounds here and there?’

‘Maybe he was insured, and had already paid back his customers from the insurance money.’

‘He *would* have been insured; well, he should have been. And then, yes, he may well have paid them.’

‘It doesn’t answer the question as to why there was all that money in the loft. Why hadn’t the shopkeeper spent it?’

‘He spent some of it, on his wife, Myrtle – lovely lady – for her treatment, for the cancer, but …’ The rest of it …? This was something he had not considered; maybe another swig of the brandy would help; he upended the glass, emptying it. ‘I don’t know, maybe he regretted blackmailing Andrew, or whoever he thought it was who’d broken in … and he just couldn't bring himself to spend it.' He waved the brandy glass vaguely.

'Tainted money?' Jackie asked, taking the glass from him.

'It has to be that.'

'It doesn't. There could be another explanation.'

'Such as?'

Jackie put both glasses down on the carpet beside the stool, leant forward, took both of Bernie's hands into hers, her eyes never leaving his face. 'It's not Freddie who has regrets, it's Andrew.'

'Andrew?' Instinctively he tried to throw off Jackie's hands, but his own were held fast.

'Yes. He regrets taking that money, doing what he did to that old couple. He has a … crisis of conscience, let's call it … You did say he'd started going to church.'

'Oh, that was only for show.' He threw off Jackie's hands. 'Part of the village squire image. Besides, used notes in brown envelopes? Not Andrew's style at all.'

'Could be, if he was trying to cover his tracks.'

Bernie got up, went over to the fireplace and squatted down; he took a log from the basket and placed it carefully on the glowing embers. He needed to think. Maybe he had got it all wrong, and the numbers and letters in the notebook had nothing to do with the money in the envelopes: someone else had broken into the shop, tied up the old man and his wife. In which case, Andrew was not a criminal … and he and Emma had been engaging in pointless supposition: what a relief that would be. The thought of Andrew being involved in something so sleazy, so underhand; a man like that deserved to be in prison!

Bernie got up, went back to the sofa.

'Maybe we've got this all wrong,' he said, 'and it's nothing to do with Andrew …'

'What, you think he *didn't* steal the money?'

'I don't know! It's like being lost in a maze! Short of confronting Andrew, which I am not about to do, although God knows I have been tempted … I just don't know where to go from here.'

'You could start by looking at the envelopes again; look at the handwriting, the postmarks, anything …'

Bernie began to tap his front teeth with his finger. Seeing Jackie frowning at him he stopped. 'Sorry,' he said. 'Silly habit; Rose hated me doing it; she said I did it when I couldn't remember something.'

'What can't you remember?'

'I don't know. It's something Andrew said, quite recently. It was about a shop being for sale somewhere, and I'm just wondering if it was that one.' He sighed. 'Oh, Jackie, I do so want it not to have been Andrew that took that money.' He began to tap his teeth again; he stopped: it wasn't helping. He needed to understand … and to stop feeling so shocked, discovering that the man you thought you knew so well, you didn't really know at all. And if he felt like that, how must Emma feel? Betrayed, cheated, conned? All of those. And Garry, too, learning that his beloved, kind Grandad was a criminal, too, and that the money he had found in the loft had probably been acquired through blackmailing. And Jacob, of course, out in South

Africa: he'd have to be told, sometime. Oh God, what a mess.

'Have you looked at bank accounts, for the things Andrew bought?'

'It was always cash, which could have come from anywhere, and it certainly wouldn't have been one of our business accounts, they're scrupulously audited every year, have been since we began in the late Eighties, when we had those big injections of capital from Rose and from Andrew's aunt in Australia.'

Bernie had never known exactly how much the Aussie aunt's legacy had been; he had put the cheque straight into his own bank, and then he'd … 'Oh, fuck.'

'What?'

'Just give me a minute. I need to make sense of this in my own head first.' Bernie sat back, eyes shut, eyelids twitching as he processed his thoughts. When he felt they were ready to be aired he sat up. 'Okay,' he said, glancing briefly at Jackie, then away, looking down at the carpet; he needed to give his full attention to what he was about to say. He spoke deliberately, as if addressing a meeting. 'The money, from the cheque, was in his bank, but Andrew said it didn't match Rose's share and he felt that was not right. I said that was okay, but he wasn't having it: he had to put in more he said, if he was going to be an equal partner. Then, a couple of weeks later …' a quick flick of his eyes to Jackie, '... could have been three,' then back to the floor' … he said he'd heard from his aunt's solicitor again and there was to be another payment; something about a parcel of land that had since been sold, and he, Andrew, was entitled to a share of it.' He paused, looked directly at Jackie. 'I know it sounds far-fetched, but I am wondering if …'

'The extra money came from the burglary.' It was a statement, not a question.

'Yes.'

'It's not far-fetched at all,' Jackie said. 'Not in the light of all the other things we know.'

'Think we know.'

'Yes, okay, think. Even so, you have to do something.'

'I know I do,' Bernie said wearily. He felt exhausted, drained; he couldn't take in what Jackie was saying, something about a bank … All he wanted to do was climb into bed beside Emma, wrap his arms around her and go to sleep. He couldn't do that though, not just yet; not while Jackie was helping him to solve his problem … Emma's problem; more than anyone else's it was Emma's: she'd never live with Andrew again, she'd said. And then there was Paula and Garry … *and* the shop. He must concentrate. He sat up straight, shook his head.

'Say that again.'

'No, you're tired.'

'No, say it. We need to do this, now.'

'Okay. Maybe you could somehow get a look at Andrew's old bank statements – you said he always kept everything; people do, twenty, thirty years sometimes – see if, soon after the Aussie cheque went into the bank, there was *another* large payment into the same account; failing that, in another account, perhaps in a different bank.'

'Mm, maybe. You know, the *real* problem with all this, is that we can't *prove* anything. There's nothing, in the stuff we have, that would stand up in a court of law. A good lawyer, even a mediocre one, would pull it to shreds, in minutes.' The mere thought of having to provide some kind of provenance to a solicitor or a barrister, sat like a heavy, damp incubus on his body and his brain.

'Come on, bed for you, or you'll be the one in shreds.' Jackie said.

It was all Bernie could do just to lift himself from the sofa. He couldn't remember a time he had felt so low, so despondent; a small boy in need of his mother's arms around him. He shook himself and stood up.

'Night, Jackie,' he said, patting her shoulder as he went past. 'Thank you. It's helped to talk.'

'Good. Sleep well.'

'Yeah. I will.'

He had to; he'd always needed plenty of sleep. He had never understood how some people, doctors in particular, seemed able to go without sleep for nearly forty-eight hours. Andrew had been like that, studying far into the night when they were at uni, whereas he - okay if he was out partying; he could stay awake then, but put a book or an essay plan in front of him and his eyes began to droop. But then his degree was never vital to him, in the way that Andrew's was.

Emma was turned on her side, leaving the half of the bed next to the bedroom door empty. Bernie lifted a corner of the duvet, felt the scent of Emma's warm, sleeping body stirring him; he did so want to touch her, hold her.

No. Best to sleep in his own bed.

Gently he put the duvet back in place and tiptoed out of the room.

CHAPTER TWENTY-EIGHT

Emma stirred, opened her eyes; a desperate need to go to the loo had awakened her.

'Oh, God …' It was all coming back, in stark detail.

'Tea?' Jackie stood in the doorway, mug in her hand. 'Emma?' She put the mug on the bedside table and leant over Emma. 'Honey, what's wrong?'

'Everything's wrong.' The words came out between great heaving sobs; she sprang out of bed. '... *and* I must go to the loo.' She sped to the adjoining bathroom.

Back in bed, Emma clasped the mug of tea in both hands. The relief of having a pee had lifted her for a few brief moments, but now the darkness of her thoughts was closing in again. She gulped down her tea, hoping that the caffeine would give her a boost.

'Oh, Jackie, it is all so awful.'

'I know.'

Emma shook her head, 'No,' she said, handing her empty mug to Jackie, not looking at her. 'I don't think you do.'

'I do, Emma. Bernie has told me everything.'

'Everything?' Emma looked up.

'Yes. All of it.'

‘What, him and …?’

‘Yes, that too.’

‘Oh Jackie, what a mess …’ Emma lay back on the pillows. ‘... and I have no idea what to do about it.’

‘Just as well I have then, isn’t it?’

‘*You* have?’

‘Yes. First of all you get up, have a shower, get dressed, come downstairs and have a good breakfast.’

‘You sound just like Connie! Oh my God, Connie!’ Emma reached over the bedside for her bag, began to scrabble in for her phone. ‘I must ring her, she’ll be going spare.’

‘No she won’t. I’ve spoken to her and so has Bernie.’

‘Oh. Thank you.’ Emma withdrew her hand but kept a tight hold on the bag, as if it was the only thing she *could* hold on to.

‘I have something else to tell you.’

‘Oh no. Please, Jackie.’ Emma turned her head away. ‘No more.’

‘Jacob’s coming home.’

‘What?’ Emma’s head spun round, her eyes lit up. She let go of the bag and flung her arms around Jackie. ‘Oh, Jackie, that is so wonderful!’ She had so hoped he’d come but hadn’t dared believe that he would.’ She drew back. ‘I must go home and get ready for him. Does Connie know?’

‘No, his call came after we phoned her.’

‘He phoned you?’

‘No, Bernie. He tried you but there was no answer.’

‘Oh.’

'Bernie put yours on silent when we brought you upstairs; he didn't want you disturbed.'

* * *

'I won't come in,' Jackie said, as they pulled up in the Pengate drive, 'unless you want me to.'

'No,' Emma leant across and kissed Jackie. 'I'm truly grateful to you for everything, and I would love you to come in, but it's only putting off the evil moment …'

'She's not that frightening, is she?'

'No, not really. Anyway, the news of Jacob's homecoming will deflect her from any lecture she might be about to give me.'

'Lecture?'

'About staying out again! Bye, Jackie.'

Emma climbed out of the car and walked to the front door. There was no need to get out her key; she had seen Connie, her face stern, peering through Andrew's office window. Sure enough, there she was at the door as Emma, a beaming smile at the ready, stepped onto the porch.

'You'll never guess what's happened,' Emma said, breathlessly. Not waiting for Connie to guess or protest, she went on, 'Jacob's coming home!' She had very nearly said 'Jake'; she didn't like the name, and she knew Connie didn't either, and much as part of her wanted to annoy Connie, Emma also needed her sister on her side.

'Oh, that is so good.' The news had, as Emma hoped, taken Connie so completely by surprise that she could only smile: she was very fond of Jacob. If she had been his mother – she had said so more than once – he would have turned out quite differently.

CHAPTER TWENTY-NINE

It was three weeks since Garry had been in that office in Almeida Street, three weeks in which he'd spent every waking hour on his plan. It was almost ready now – just a few more details to put into place – and then …

Garry grinned; he was going to enjoy this. Oh yes, give the bastard a bit of his own medicine. And not before time, either.

He'd not said a word to Paula. There were moments when he'd wanted to; it was just so fucking good! He knew she would see that, see how clever her little bruv could be when he put his mind to something; watch her face when he told her what he was going to do. No, he mustn't do that: she might turn it down flat, his great idea.

It was them flyers he picked up from Bernie's office table, the ones Paula had heard him rustling in the car, that had started it off. Once back in the flat, Garry'd taken them out of his pocket and chucked them onto the low table by the sofa and driven straight to the pub. Coming out mildly pissed, he'd bought some chips to soak up the alcohol before getting into his van. He couldn't risk being stopped by the police: he'd got the chance of a driving job the next morning, and much as he didn't really want to do it, it would be worth it just to get Paula off his back.

It wasn't till the next day he noticed some of the leaflets had slipped off the table onto the floor. The name of a band he liked caught his eye; maybe he'd round up a few mates, go to the gig; he could afford it, so why not. In case there was anything else that might be of interest Garry riffled through the other leaflets – no, nothing; he put them back on the table. Where there was another one. Not a flyer, this was a sort of brochure; for a holiday, maybe? That was a nice thought; go to a posh place, meet some cool bird. Bird? No. A woman, that's what he wanted now; he was getting too old for just birds. A woman, a real woman … who'd move in with him, maybe even have kids. A boy first would be nice, then a little girl.

Reluctantly dragging his mind back to the present he focused his eyes at the booklet. It took him some minutes to work out that it wasn't advertising a hotel; the building pictured on the cover was some sort of home for oldies. Oh fuck! That woman, Emma, must have dropped it and Bernie'd picked it up and put it on the table. Well, he certainly didn't want to go there. Hang on a mo … Wasn't that the place where her husband, the bastard who beat up Grandad, was going? 'Perfect for him …' He felt sure he'd heard her saying that to Bernie as they came through the door, then something about getting to work from there. Used to have a long name, them places, now they called it Rehab; you went there when you came out of hospital. Baz's Nan had gone to one, up in Norfolk, by the sea. Bleeding cold it had been, but she'd liked it; loads to eat and people waiting on her. Yes, that's what this was, only this one looked real posh, the sort of place you have to lay out a lot of dosh to get in.

Where was it? Worth having a look. He turned to the back cover: Hewers Hill, this one was.

Garry thought again about Grandad's note: "This time, Garry, do the right thing." It was like he'd suddenly been struck by lightning; he knew for certain what he had to do. How, he didn't yet know … but he would find a way. Fuck, yes. He couldn't wait to get started.

Now, three weeks later, he was ready.

CHAPTER THIRTY

Emma had been right about *The Oaks*; it was the perfect place for Andrew. Bernie was pleased, and relieved, to see how well he had settled in there. At the same time he was amused, in a bitter, black humour sort of way, observing how comfortable in himself Andrew appeared to be. Could he be totally unaware that during his time in hospital his wife and his best friend, besides becoming lovers, which they didn't think for one moment Andrew suspected, had unearthed horrendous secrets from his past? Should he be told, yet, what they had found? What would happen if they did tell him? Would he have another stroke?

Not wanting nor daring to risk this outcome, they felt it best to say nothing, do nothing, just go on behaving as if all was well. And later, when Andrew was out of rehab? That would be comparatively easy for him, Bernie - they were unlikely to meet every day until Andrew was well enough to return to work - but could Emma, at home, pretend that nothing out of the ordinary had occurred in these last two months? There was no way he could see her doing that. For now, though, they would carry on with the routine they had slipped into – Emma visiting *The Oaks* every day; Bernie too, but never at the same time, both afraid they might betray their feelings and their shared knowledge, in some way. Maybe they *should* come straight out with it now, tell Andrew they knew what a bastard he had been? In the short term it would feel good to do that; in the long term … he didn't know. What he did know was that if you put things off indefinitely there came a time when you could *not* do anything about them. And if that happened … well, they'd all live the rest of their lives as one great big lie. 'No,' Bernie said out loud, 'we can't do that.'

He had been standing in the Chigwell kitchen, staring out into the early morning garden without seeing anything, unaware that the signs of spring were in front of him – daffodils under the silver birches, and crocuses at the edges of the shrub beds. He had no idea how long he had been there; speaking those few words aloud had brought him out of his painful musing. It was a good thing he was alone in the house, he thought; Jackie had already suggested he was 'losing it'; she had caught him tapping his teeth again. If she heard him talking to himself …

More for something to do than because he wanted a second cup of tea, he moved across to the counter, switched on the kettle, reached for a teabag.

No date had yet been fixed for Andrew to return to Pengate. He seemed quite content to stay where he was, enjoying the meals, the company, the games of bridge – 'Good exercise for my brain,' he said – and on a different level television programmes, sitcoms and reality shows he would never have watched at home. He had been pleased to see Bernie, always greeting him affably, more often in one of the lounges than in his room, but beyond an early vague enquiry, 'Business doing all right?' he had expressed no interest in it; when Bernie had said, 'Yes, it's doing fine, but of course we miss having you …' he had simply nodded and looked away. Emma seemed to think this a good approach – stimulating but not in any way stressful – and urged him to try again, but the following day, in the garden lounge, when Bernie began to tell him about Millicent and her enquiries as to Andrew's health – he'd always enjoyed chatting to her - he merely said. 'Oh, good. Now … you will stay for tea, won't you? They do the most splendid pastries here.' He never asked about their business again, nor responded to anything Bernie said about it. 'Almost as if it had never been part of his life at all,' Bernie told Emma later.

With Constance returned to her own house until Andrew came home, there was now nothing, in practical terms, to stop Bernie spending every night in Emma's bed, either at Chigwell or at Pengate. At Chigwell there had been no problem – Emma had been assigned a room by Jackie, 'for whenever you want to stay over' – and Bernie had felt very comfortable, even with Jackie in the house, going across the landing to Emma's room, a couple of times spending the whole night there, at other times going back to his own room to sleep. Only twice though, since Andrew had gone into *The Oaks*, had Bernie slept at *The Rectory*. It had not felt right, being there. It should have done: having a bedtime drink together, checking that the house was locked, brushing their teeth side by side in the bathroom, the sort of things that any married couple might do. Maybe that was the problem: they were not a married couple, they were lovers. In bed, Bernie recalled, pouring the now boiled water over the tea bag and stirring it round, it had been fine. More than just fine, it had been beautiful, passionate, complete. It was the next morning that was difficult. He sighed, added milk to his tea and went back to his station by the patio doors. They'd not said anything to one another, but they both felt it, the awkwardness, that shouldn't have been there – Bernie shaving, even using some of Andrew's shaving cream; they both liked a wet shave – and Emma calling up the stairs, asking him what he wanted for breakfast; him replying 'Toast, loads of it' and Emma not remembering whether that was white bread or brown, or if he liked black or milky coffee in the morning. They should have been making the most of this time they had to themselves; they knew it would come to an end, this feeling of being in a place where guilt did not intrude. All this would change when Andrew came home. Maybe *that* was the problem, not knowing what would happen then.

He looked down at the mug; he'd let most of the tea go cold. He tipped it into the sink, swirled cold water around the mug, upended it on the draining board, looked up at the kitchen clock; it was six o'clock. No point in going back to bed now. He was on his own in the house; he'd get into work early – the roads would be fairly clear at this time – and then later in the morning when he knew Emma would not be there – she visited at the same time every afternoon; it was what Andrew liked – he'd go to *The Oaks*, see if he could, gently and diplomatically, prize something out of Andrew. What that something would be, he didn't know, but he felt he had to try: this situation, this stalemate, could not be allowed to continue indefinitely.

Approaching the Islington yard Bernie's attention was diverted from the road by the sight of a tall black woman coming towards him along the pavement in front of the shop: oh God, he thought, it's Paula. No, it wasn't her, but the sight of the woman had pulled him up sharply; he had barely given Paula and her brother a thought in the past few weeks. He ought to make it clear to Paula that he was no longer interested in buying Brockwood Stores. No, why should he? He'd signed nothing, made no promises; best to leave things as they were. If she had wanted to follow up the conversation they had had in the office, the day that Emma had fainted, she would have done. Maybe she had also thought it best to let it go; she wouldn't want her beloved grandfather exposed as a blackmailer.

Bernie breathed a sigh of relief and drove into the yard.

* * *

It was the sort of mild day you sometimes got in late February, as if the weather was saying, I'll give you a taste of spring but don't get too excited; I've not quite done with winter yet. At *The Oaks,* the lounge doors that led onto the terrace had been thrown open and the early afternoon sunshine was streaming in. Andrew, his eyes closed and face lifted to the sun, leaned back in his armchair; Emma sat beside him on an upright one. It was easier meeting him here, where there were other people around, rather than in his second floor room, spacious though that was; there their conversation had been stilted, and Emma had felt uneasy, unable to look directly at Andrew. Here she could gaze at him, then look away, smile and nod at the other guests and patients; there didn't seem the need for non-stop talking. He looks a lot older, she thought, but more relaxed than I can ever remember seeing him, as if he hadn't a care in the world. Was it possible that he didn't remember what he had done to that couple, to Freddie and Myrtle? Could the stroke have done that do him, blanked out a time he didn't want to remember, without affecting his everyday memory? Does not remembering the sin wash it out? *No! It can't!* He did that dreadful thing, and even if it's not in *his* mind, it is in mine! I will never, ever, get into his bed again!

She felt her hand being touched; she jerked away. Andrew was looking at her strangely, his lips smiling, his eyes filled with an emotion she couldn't interpret: fear, anger? Love? No, she had seen his eyes full of love; this was not a look of love. Perhaps her face had revealed *her* thoughts. She shivered. 'It's getting a bit chilly, don't you think?' she said.

'Not for me.' Andrew's voice was silky smooth. Emma stared at him; she was aware that she was staring. She didn't care. He knows, she thought.

'I think I should go now,' she said. She looked down at her watch; thankfully it was nearly five o'clock. 'I don't want to get caught in the rush hour.'

'No, you don't want that. Besides, Bernie will be here soon.' He paused, smiled. 'I don't expect you'll want to bump into him.'

'Why not?' He'd taken her off-guard.

'Well … because of the way he is at the moment. The peculiar way he's behaving.'

'Peculiar?' Emma's mouth felt dry. 'I've not noticed anything peculiar,' she said. Oh no; she could have bitten her tongue.

'So you have seen him?'

'Well, yes.' Should she go for it? Why not, he had given her opening. 'He … um … he wanted some information about …'

'Information?' Silky smooth still … 'About what, Emma?'

'Oh … He was … mm … asking about places we'd been to, you and I … you know, when we used to go out … looking for stock for the shop. Those lovely days we had, tootling round the villages, going to all those funny little sales, you know … looking for things that might sell.' Stop. Stop.

'And did you give it to him?' Oh God.

'Well … no. I … I just told him about the people we used to meet, you know, the ones you bought things from, the ones who …' She felt herself on the verge of saying: whose names are in that little red book you always carried with you.

'The ones who what?'

'The ones who...' Think, think! 'The ones you hoped might one day have a Stradivarius for sale.'

Andrew laughed; not a nice laugh, Emma thought. 'Oh, he's not still on about that, is he? Such dreams some men have, don't they?' Maybe she was reading something into it that wasn't there, but Emma did not like, not one little bit, the look Andrew was giving her.

'Yes; silly, wasn't it?' she said, her breathy laugh sounding unreal. 'Well, I'd better be off.' She stood up, bent over, kissed Andrew fleetingly on the cheek.

He grabbed hold of her hand. 'I love you; you know?' he said.

'Yes. I know.' She released her hand. 'I'll see you tomorrow. Bye, darling.' She blew him a kiss: her husband and she's blowing him a kiss? That won't do. She leant over him again. 'You know I'd love to stay, but …'

'I know, the traffic.' He sounded resigned.

'Yes. Sorry.'

'You could stay the night.'

'Oh, but …?'

'There are guest rooms.'

'Oh, yes. I do know, but …'

'No, you're right, I'm not ready for that; not yet.'

'No.' She smiled. 'Soon though,' her voice light. I must get out of here before I say anything more. Oh God, is he going to put Bernie through the same thing? I'd better warn him. She felt sick at what she was doing, thinking. 'Bye,' she said, waving, turning away, walking through the lounge, smiling at some of the other residents, getting at last to the door, then into the hall, trying hard not to run – Andrew would be watching her – and out through the front doors, turn right, into the car park; her legs weak, her heart going like the proverbial clappers: she'd never understood before what that meant; she did now, she could hear it, banging away inside her chest. She sat in the car, took her phone from her bag.

'Bernie,' she said. 'Be careful. Andrew …' She couldn't bring herself to say it. Did she not still have some shred of loyalty to her husband?

'What? Emma?'

'Just be careful what you say to him, later, when you see him.'

'Oh? Why, what's happened?'

'Nothing. He was just a bit … probing. Wondering if you and I had met; you know, because we don't visit him together …' Should she say that she'd almost told Andrew what they'd found in his office drawer? Just to make sure that he didn't jump to the wrong conclusion; which was, of course, also the right conclusion. She wasn't sure which aspect of her relationship with Bernie she minded more about Andrew finding out.

'Oh, okay, I won't rock the boat, don't worry,' Bernie said before Emma could put her thoughts into words. 'Not today, anyway.'

'Good.' If he did, Andrew was sure to be suspicious; certainly the Andrew she'd seen today would be.

'We have to do it sometime.'

'I know.' Unless we go on living this lie. 'See you soon,' she said, lightly, switching off her phone.

* * *

'That's great,' Garry said. 'Well done you.' Paula had had what seemed a good offer for the shop. 'So you think I should go for it?' she had asked him. She'd no need to ask Garry's opinion, but he was made up that she had. He put the phone down on the passenger seat of his van, checked his rear mirror, and drove off. He was on his way to work.

'Work?' Paula had said. 'Yeah, work. Got some driving.' 'Oh …?' 'And before you ask … it's totally legit.' 'Then well done, you, too.'

No need for her to know it was only temporary. Or where it was.

Definitely not where it was.

CHAPTER THIRTY-ONE

Garry didn't normally believe in luck – he'd never had any – but this time, he had to admit it, Lady Luck had played a part. Not that she would have been any use to him if he hadn't been ready for her, he said to himself, as he turned into the driveway of *The Oaks.* Fucking clever planning, that's what this was.

First thing he'd done was look online; masses of info there, all about the Premier Rooms – they were on the first floor – and the Suites, 'with magnificent views over the gardens and the ancient oaks in the woodland' on the second floor. Next thing: make sure that the guy was here; fucking waste of time doing all this if he wasn't. That bit hadn't taken long: a phone call in a posh voice – he hadn't half had to practise that – enquiring if Mr. Raven had received the wine safely. "Er … yes, I think so." The woman answering hadn't wanted to sound like she didn't know. "Got to his suite all right, did it?" Garry had asked; then came the tricky bit. "Number six." "No, four," the woman said. "Yes, of course, four. We have another customer in number six. Thank you. Goodbye." With fingers trembling and sweaty, he had ended the call, which of course he had made untraceable … unless it was the coppers who wanted to know; they'd find it. And the woman wasn't going to tell anyone; she'd realise, too late, that she'd been conned, and she wouldn't want to risk losing her job for one tiny mistake. Garry'd got the idea for the numbers bit from an ad on telly warning people about phone scams where they got hold of your PIN number; clever, that was … and very useful.

A thorough recce of the place was the next thing: who went in, who went out, how they got in, what checks were made. Easy-peasy, that had been; he'd parked the van in a side street, stood on the other side of the road from *The Oaks* ... and watched. A blue van going in, regular-like, that's what he needed. Fat chance of that happening; there was a white one brought in fish twice a week, an old red one with fruit and veg, again two days, Tuesday and Friday; a Sainsbury's van and a dark green one from some posh shop up west. The way in, and out, was past high, wide, wrought-iron gates, with spikes on top – a bit like the nick – with a big fat guy, sat in a little sort of kiosk thing, minding them. Okay, so he'd have to get past him – Wally, he'd heard the driver of the white van call him – even to get into the grounds; there was no other entry for vehicles; he'd checked. Now all he needed was *his* reason for getting inside those gates. So … back to who went in; how could *he* become one of them? Check out the nearby streets and the businesses there. Garry reckoned he'd never done this much thinking in his life, not even when he'd been inside. Well, he'd had no reason to think in there … 'cept about how to get out before the end of his stretch … which never happened.

This was going to, though; oh yes. He'd made sure of that, as much as he could; done all his homework - the place, the streets, everything. All he needed now was a bit of luck. Meeting Jamie – you could call it luck, but it wouldn't have happened if he'd not been looking for someone like Jamie – then finding him, with his van - the red one that delivered the fruit and veg to *The Oaks*; how lucky was that?! - broken down just streets away and full of perishable stuff that needed delivering asap. So of course he offered to help. I mean ... anybody, saw a guy in trouble with his van, would do that. With Jamie's van needing to go in for repairs, and Garry doing a good job that day, helping out and that, doing the delivery to some posh flats nearby ... well, it wasn't surprising Jamie'd been pleased when Garry said he could do that again, if Jamie wanted. Which he did, 'cos his mate, Pete, who did some of Jamie's runs for the greengrocer, including the ones to *The Oaks,* was taking time off because his girlfriend was having a baby, and Jamie'd not found anyone to take Pete's place. Fucking hell, this *was* luck! It was also scary, like it was a set-up. Could it be? Nah, common sense told him it wasn't. All the same ...

Most of the time up till now he'd been able to keep the scary bits of what he was doing out of the way – a few pints and sometimes a wank to get himself off to sleep at night – but now … today, Tuesday … it was going to happen. Tuesdays and Fridays were his days for deliveries at *The Oaks*, but not for long now. The guy he was standing in for was due back in a week; he had one Tuesday and one Friday left, so, if it didn't work out today … No, it had to; there was no way he was having two goes at this. He just hoped to God he wouldn't bottle it. No reason why he should, not really; he knew exactly what he was going to do, and how he was going to do it. And Tuesday morning was the perfect time: they were never here, not in the morning. Afternoon, yes; He'd got that from the brochure thing: "*Family and friends visiting time, from 2pm, unless you have booked into Lunch with us.*" Most times it was the woman first, then Bernie. With roughly fifteen minutes in between; fifteen minutes in which they sat in the car park, usually in his car, sometimes in hers. Then one of them would get out, go into the building and the other one would drive away. Been well worth hanging around, to watch from a safe distance after he'd made his drop: last thing he needed was to bump into one of them, not even on the driveway. He'd seen them there three times now on his Tuesdays and Fridays; never varied, their routine. Made sense; places like this kept to a strict time-table, bit like prison. Half eleven, when he got to *The Oaks,* staff were busy getting lunch ready, so the inmates – guests, they called them here – were on their own, most of them in their rooms, though they could also be having a walk in the gardens or just sitting in one of the lounges – like a bleeding hotel it was – having a drink. Nice for some; mind you, they were paying for it, through the nose, too. A cuppa and a custard cream cost a fiver, Jamie said: he'd got to know one of the old women in there; she'd invited him, couple of times, to have coffee with her and he'd seen the chit she had to sign, for his Guest Refreshment.

So … this was it.

He could feel the adrenaline kicking in. He was smiling, grinning, couldn't stop himself, as he showed his pass to Wally, drove through the gateway, rehearsing in his mind one last time what he had to do: make his delivery, a bit of chat with Dot, the woman who took it in – nearly always on her phone she was when he went in, barely looked at him. She'd sign she'd got it, he'd sign to say he'd seen she'd got it – definitely like the nick, that bit – and then he'd be away. Once the paperwork was done she'd be back on her phone; she couldn't have cared less where he went. Turn left, turn right, she wouldn't know, specially if she was on Facetime, which sometimes she was. Fingers crossed she was on it today.

Christ, what a bit of luck! She was. She even smiled at him today.

'Grandkids,' she said, 'on half term.'

'Oh, right. Good.' Mega-good this was. Nothing was going to take her attention away from them. He smiled at her. 'See you Friday,' he said. Not if he could help it.

She nodded, her eyes on her screen.

Garry moved away, heart beating fast now – there was still time to turn round, go back to his van, leave it till Friday. Deep breath, relax your shoulders; yeah, that's it. He turned left down the corridor, his trainers making no sound on the tiled floor, then on through double doors into another, wider, carpeted passageway and up the stairs, that led, so the classy sign informed him, to the Guest Suites on the second floor.

So far, so good.

Okay, so now you just walk slowly, say Hi to anyone you meet, just keep walking, all gentle like, till you get to Suite No. 4. Shiny gold door knob, name-plate: Mr. Andrew Raven. No bolts, no keys. Quick knock; no answer; turn the knob; walk in; close the door behind you.

* * *

'Why did they want both of us to come?' Emma said irritably, looking across at Bernie, walking stony-faced beside her down the corridor to the manager's office. It was as if Mr. Camper felt that on her own she could not make a decision about Andrew's future; because that's what this was about: was he or was he not ready to go home? Confer with his wife, of course, but also ask his business partner, sensible chap, not like the pretty little woman. Mr. Camper, short and wiry – obviously proud to have such a good figure at his age; he looked to be in his mid-fifties – had been the one fly in *The Oaks* ointment for Emma, whereas the matron, Cecelia Campbell, well-rounded, in her forties, of Nigerian-Scottish descent, was one of the most empathetic people Emma had ever met. Emma had thought it odd at first, calling her the matron, but apparently the title suited the clientele, particularly the men, Cecelia told Emma: the ones with a public school background, and there were always several in residence, knew where they were with a matron; asking for the Floor Manager, the title that was used in a residential home nearby, made them feel uncomfortable, as if they were in a department store. The staff, too, all of them, were superb. It was just this man, this money man, who spoilt it. Still, it wouldn't just be him at this meeting; surely not?

'We'll soon find out,' Bernie said, smiling now. 'Don't worry, you don't need to make any decisions today. As long as he's getting your money, Camper won't want to chuck him out.'

The manager's office, on the ground floor of the central building, overlooking the croquet lawn, was set out ready for the meeting, with chintz-covered armchairs around a low table on which were coffee cups and plates of Duchy Original biscuits.

'Come in, Mrs. Raven, Mr. Silver.' The manager ushered them into the room, and with his hand outstretched indicated where they were to sit. 'Do make yourselves comfortable,' he said. 'Thank you for being punctual; the others should be here at any moment.'

He's timed it this way on purpose, Emma thought; he likes to think he runs this place single-handed. 'I think we are a bit early actually,' she said, smiling. 'What delicious-looking biscuits.' She reached forward to the table and took one off the plate. 'You do look after everyone so well, Mr. Camper.' By her side she heard Bernie subduing a guffaw.

'Oh, thank you,' he said; he didn't often get compliments, but then his work didn't require them: he was here to make sure *The Oaks* ran efficiently, and made a profit, too. 'Ah, here's Matron,' he said, as the door opened. 'We'll be able to have our coffee now.'

Bernie got to his feet as she came in. 'No need for that,' she said, smiling, waving him back into his seat. 'Emma dear, how lovely to see you again.' She bent over and kissed

Emma on the cheek. 'We seem to have missed one another the last few times you've been in.'

'Would you see to the coffee for us, please, Matron?' the manager asked; he did not like Cecelia's informality.

'Of course,' she said, beaming at him. It will take a lot to ruffle your feathers, Emma thought. She felt she had made a real friend in Cecelia; she didn't know if it would be allowed, but she would love to have her visit Pengate one day.

'Thank you. Ah, and now here's the doctor.'

Emma and Bernie turned round, as a stockily-built, handsome man in a dark blue turban entered the room. They had met Dr. Pooni before, when Andrew was admitted to *The Oaks*. He shook hands with Emma and Bernie, and nodded to the matron, busy pouring coffee. The manager, to Emma's satisfaction, he appeared to ignore.

'Good morning, doctor,' Cecelia said cheerily. 'No coffee for you, I know. Don't worry, I've brought your favourite.' From a pocket in her full-skirted dress she brought out a packet of herbal tea bags. 'Lemon and ginger.'

'Oh, I have that sometimes,' Emma said, 'it's refreshing and stimulating at the same time.'

'Indeed it is,' the doctor said, taking the seat next to Emma. 'Very cleansing for the palate too, I find, especially if ...'

'If we could make a start, please, ladies and gentlemen.' The manager shut the door loudly. 'Much as we might like to chatter ... we do not have an unlimited amount of time.'

'Oh, this won't take long, Arnold. Sit down and have some coffee,' Cecelia said. 'We all need to take a break sometime.' She turned to Doctor Pooni. 'What do you have to tell us, doctor?'

Emma felt her stomach knotting. Instinctively she reached out for Bernie's hand.

'Don't look so worried, Mrs. Raven,' Dr. Pooni said gently; he smiled at her. 'I have good news for you: your husband is ready to come home.'

* * *

Garry stood stock-still. He could not believe his luck: the guy was sitting in an armchair, far end of the room by the window, reading, his back to the door. And the radio was on! Jesus, if he'd set this up, it couldn't have been better. He already had the soft, silky scarf in his hand – scarf first so he couldn't call out – and it wouldn't take him a moment to pull out the rope from under his sweater.

Past the bathroom, door ajar, on his left; mirrored wardrobes on his right. Three swift, silent steps across the room and he's there; scarf in both hands now, lift it up and over the guy's head, pull the two ends together tight, tie them. Done. Now, though, comes the tricky bit: quick, before the guy lifts his hands to pull at the gag … 'Nothing to be afraid of, mate,' Garry says, whipping the rope out from under his sweater. 'Not goin' to hurt you. Just making sure you don't move for a while.' Over the man's head it goes, tight across his arms so his hands can't move, round the back of the chair, once more round, bit lower down, tie it tight at the back. The guy's struggling now, twisting from side to side, kicking out with his feet. 'I'd not do that if I was you, mate. You don't want to tip the chair over, do you?' He walks round the front; doesn't matter if the guy sees him, he doesn't know who he is. Asked to describe him, what's he going to say? "Guy in a T-shirt, jeans … trainers, I think."

'Just so's you don't struggle too much,' Garry says, 'we'll give the old feet a bit of a go as well; just wrap them up a bit. Nothing nasty, just another nice scarf, soft like the other one; you know?' He's not sure how long he can go on like this, being polite and gentle, when what he'd really like to do is kick the chair backwards, yell at the guy, 'That's for my Grandad!' Slap him round the face: 'That's for my Nan!' Just 'cos he never actually hurt either of them physically, don't mean he should be spared. The only thing stopping Garry was his own sense of self-preservation: he didn't fancy going inside for GBH … well, no … he'd not go that far, not ever; ABH, more like. He'd never even done that, not really. Couldn't stand being hurt himself, so …

He stood over the guy, looking down at him, feeling tall. Maybe just rock the chair, just a bit. No. Time to get out of here. He'd done what he wanted; he'd given Mr. Smarty-pants Raven a bit of his own medicine. Oh yes, the guy knew what this was all about; Garry could see by the look in his eyes. He'd like to have seen his look when the scarf had gone round his face – he reckoned that would have been fear – but this … this was better: *this* was recognition. Maybe he's been waiting for this, knowing that one day … Nah, not a guy like this. He knew about it now, though. Oh, man, this was sweet. Garry felt his face stretching into a wide grin.

As quietly as he had come in, he let himself out into the corridor; then, having made sure no one was about, he began walking, as planned, slowly, and with outward calm – his heart was still pounding – towards the swing doors that led to the stairs. He had done it! He had fucking done it! He pushed the doors open and went through into the stairwell; he stood for a moment, taking deep breaths, waiting for his heart to slow a bit, his brain whirling with triumph. He almost shouted down the stairwell, he felt so good. 'Shown that bastard, din't I? Tied him up, good and proper; take him some time to get himself out of that lot … if at all.' Jesus. Garry felt himself go icy cold. What if he'd …? Oh God, no. He'd not meant to, not *wanted* to … kill the guy, not even hurt him, but what if he had another one of them strokes, like he had before, that had put him in hospital? If he couldn't get himself loose and … and nobody came to set him free and … Oh Jesus, if the guy died … They'd find him, Garry; they would, they always did. His legs now like jelly, his heart banging painfully, he turned round, flung open the doors, raced back down the corridor, threw open the door to Andrew's room. Thank Christ: the guy had not died. He was still very much alive, thrashing about on the chair, muttering to himself behind the gag. Garry paused, unsure what to do next, angry with himself for not having foreseen this. He thought he'd covered every possibility; this one he had *not* thought of. His heart rate slowing, he began to think logically again: one thing he was not about to do was release the man; that would be stupid. There had to be something between injuring him – he didn't want to think murder – and releasing him: he looked around the room. He let out the breath he'd been holding. Yes, that was it. That orange cord with a ring at the end of it hanging by the bed; he'd seen one of them in a film not long ago: it connected with a bell somewhere. If he could just get across the floor to the bed and pull it … then someone, some nurse or worker or … anyone, didn't matter … would hear it and set the guy free. Can't be just *one* of them things – the one he'd seen in a film had been in a bathroom – in this suite. Sure to be one here. Garry pushed open the bathroom door. There it was, by the bath, and there was another one, just inside the door; he could see it, and himself, reflected in a mirror on the far side of the room. No need to go in; one hard pull from where he stood, then another one just to make sure; a few steps to the suite door … he didn't even shut it this time … and he was out in the corridor, across to the swing doors and down the stairs, not caring if he made a noise. Out of the door at the bottom, along the gravel path, past the flowerbeds, turn the corner, another path, with tall hedging on one side, halfway along an opening; through it and into the car park. Easy, no rush now; there's the van; into it, reverse; out of the car park, left into the driveway; nothing coming either way; gentle, drive slow now, past the beds with them shrubs, all with glossy leaves on, so he wasn't seen from the building; one straight, short stretch to the gate, show his pass … and he'd be out. Come on, open the fucking gate; he'd waved his pass at Wally, sitting in his little lodge – cushy job that was – so what was he waiting for. Garry gripped the steering wheel hard. He felt his hands shaking, sweat pouring off him; it couldn't go wrong now, not now. What was the lazy sod doing? Watching fucking telly, course he was. Any other time Garry would have stuck his head out, sworn at him, had a laugh. Not today. And now there's a bloody white van roaring up behind him: Derek, the guy who delivers fish; like him, Tuesdays and Fridays, always in a hurry. 'You like wet fish hanging round, stinking the place out?' he'd joke, and Garry usually had some answer for him. Not even going to stick his fingers up at him today; just want to get the fuck out of here as fast as he can. Derek hoots, yells, head out the window – Garry can see him in his rear view mirror; Wally looks up from his telly, gets up slowly from his chair, waddles out of the lodge, down the two steps, waves at Garry. Garry waves back. Stay calm; any minute now and he'll be out – never, ever, coming back to this fucking place – and away, down the road, the road that you can't see, 'cause of the high hedges, thank God, from the building itself. Foot on the accelerator, ready to shoot through once the gate is open. A car wanting to come into *The Oaks* ... and Wally's going to open the right-hand gate. Oh Jesus, no … the sweat is pouring off Garry's face, his heart feels like it's pounding in his head, and Derek's car horn at full blast is keeping in time with it. Now what? Wally's stopped moving to the right-hand gate; he's on his phone and looking straight at Garry. Oh, fuck. Garry can feel the hot piss soaking into his jeans.

And now Wally's coming over to him. Oh, Jesus. No. No... They've found the guy … And he's dead. Can't be, not done anything to him, didn't hit him. So ... he's alive and he's told them. How'd he know I had a van? He didn't, they're just stopping everyone. If I hadn't got the van I could have got over the wall … No, I couldn't; there was railings on top. For Christ's sake, Wally, let me outta here.

* * *

The meeting was coming to an end – a date, convenient 'to all parties', as Mr. Camper had expressed it, had been fixed for Andrew's discharge from *The Oaks* – when the matron's phone began beeping.

'Sorry, I must deal with this,' she said, getting up quickly from her chair.

'Surely it can wait five minutes, Matron,' the manager said.

'No, this can't wait. Doctor?'

'I'll follow you, Matron,' Dr. Pooni said.

'Yes, do. It's Suite No.4,' she whispered, turning away from Emma.

Bernie, though, had heard her. 'That's Andrew's.'

Emma, eyes wide open, gasped. 'Oh my God!'

'It's all right, Mrs. Raven,' Dr.Pooni said. 'I'm sure it's nothing to be worried about. As I said to you earlier, your husband is in very good physical health now.'

'Yes, I know, but …' She couldn't tell them, not even lovely Cecelia, that it was Andrew's mental health she was concerned about; only Bernie knew what she was now being asked to face up to, having Andrew back home in Pengate. She didn't dare look at Bernie; instead she turned her eyes on Mr. Camper, giving him a tight smile: he wouldn't be getting any more of their money, but at that moment she would have given him everything she had to delay

Andrew's home-coming: she just wasn't ready. She felt overcome with guilt: Andrew knew she didn't want him home and he'd done something awful to himself.

'I must go to him! Bernie, come with me!'

'I'm not sure that's wise,' Dr. Pooni said, placing a gentle hand on her arm.

'I don't care if it's wise or not, I'm going.' Holding onto Bernie's arm, almost dragging him, she pushed past the doctor, caught up with the matron, already running down the corridor to the lifts.

'Sorry about that,' Bernie called over his shoulder to the doctor.

'No need for an apology. Totally understandable.'

In the brief journey to the second floor no one spoke.

Emma ran out of the lift and along the corridor, calling out as she went, 'Andrew, I'm coming darling!' The door of Suite No. 4 was open and a nurse was removing the scarf from Andrew's face. 'But … I don't understand …' She had expected to find her husband either writhing on the floor from an overdose of pills or leaning over the washbasin with slashed wrists, and here he was, sitting roped to a chair, his face puce with anger.

'I'm all right,' he shouted, 'Just get the bugger who did this! For God's sake! The security in this place …!'

The nurse began to untie the rope.

'Oh, leave it alone, woman! I want the manager to see this.' He turned his head, saw Bernie. 'Bernie, what the hell are you doing here?'

Bernie wasn't listening to Andrew; alerted by the sound of raised voices outside, he had crossed to the window, from which he could see over the gardens to the main gate.

'Oh God! Matron, will you please get on the phone to that guy at the gate. Tell him, under no circumstances is he to let that blue van through.'

'Blue van?' Emma, taking her arms from Andrew's shoulders, crossed to the window.

'Look,' Bernie said quietly, pointing. 'Over there.'

'Oh my God.' She turned to Bernie. 'That's … his. Isn't it?' It was little more than a whisper. 'Darker blue door.'

Bernie nodded. 'Yes.'

'What are you two doing, looking out of the window? Will someone get me out of this ridiculous bondage! Or whatever it's meant to be.'

'I'll do it, I'll do it.' Mr. Camper rushed forward, pushing the nurse aside. He began to untie the ropes.

Emma and Bernie, too stunned to hide the expressions on their faces, turned towards Andrew.

'What is it?' he asked tetchily. 'What's the matter with you?'

With a chilling realisation, looking into Andrew's eyes, Emma knew without a doubt that it was Garry who had tied him and gagged him … and that Andrew had known, if not *who* he was, then certainly why he was there. The corners of his mouth went down and he averted his eyes from her.

After what seemed to Emma like an age, with everything happening in slow motion – the matron talking on her phone, then leaving the room, Mr. Camper finally freeing

Andrew from the ropes, the doctor taking his pulse – her husband spoke.

'Well …' he said, easing his shoulders and rubbing his arms, where the rope had been. 'whoever he was I hope they've got him by now.' He began to rise from the chair.

'Not just yet, Mr. Raven,' Dr. Pooni said, gently pushing Andrew down into the chair.

'Sounds as if Matron is on to him,' Andrew went on, as if there had been no interruption, his voice now firm and strong.

'Oh she is, Mr. Raven; of that you can be sure; and so am I.' The manager's brow was furrowed with anxiety. 'This was the most appalling thing to happen. I can't apologise enough.'

Andrew was not to be mollified however much Mr. Camper grovelled. 'It's a total breakdown of your much-lauded security.'

'Indeed it is, and …'

'The sooner I'm out of here the better.'

'Ah, well … I quite understand, but do let me assure you that something of this nature has never before occurred at *The Oaks*; and, as you would expect, I shall be informing the police.'

'No.' As if with one voice, they said it.

Mr. Camper looked from one to the other. To Andrew, then Emma, then Bernie.

'But …?'

'I said no.' Andrew's voice was shaky, but at the same time, firm.

Bernie shook his head. 'No, don't do that. Hold him, yes, but no police.'

'Mrs. Raven?'

'No, there's no need to bring them into it.'

'Oh. Well …' The manager relaxed visibly. 'That is … that is most kind of you.'

'Kind?' Bernie said. 'There's nothing *kind* about …'

Emma jumped in quickly. 'We just don't want the other residents to be upset by any … disturbance. Do we, Bernie?' Oh, please, Bernie, agree with me.

'No, of course not.'

'Oh, well … Thank you,' Mr. Camper said, smiling. 'If you are sure?'

'Yes,' Bernie said, 'we are, all three of us.' He looked fixedly at Andrew. 'Aren't we?'

'Yes.' Andrew swallowed hard. 'We are. No police.'

'Ah. Right.' This situation is beyond Mr. Camper, Emma was thinking. 'So what would you like me to do with the … the culprit?

'Let him go, 'Andrew said. 'I'm perfectly all right.'

'I think I should be the one deciding that, Mr. Raven.' Dr. Pooni, silent up to now, intervened.

'I *am* perfectly all right. You know I am. Pulse and blood pressure, you've being doing it all just now, haven't you?'

'Your blood pressure is a bit high,' Dr. Pooni said, 'but that is not surprising.'

'You want us to let him go, a guy who would tie someone up … and gag him with a scarf?' Bernie was only just holding on to his temper.

‘Yes! Let him go.’ Andrew looked past Bernie, not meeting his eyes.

Bernie’s voice was still hard. ‘Is there any particular reason for your decision?’

‘No, Bernie, don’t.’ Emma put a hand on his arm; he shook it off.

‘I ask because … well, after all, *you* are the victim, Andrew, the one who was attacked; we agree with you, that the police should not be involved, but it should be you, rather than us, making the final decision.’

Emma could feel his anger charging the air around her. ‘Bernie, stop,’ she said, hoarsely, her throat dry. Another bit of her brain was seeing him in court, in a wig. He would have been a good lawyer, she thought.

‘Have I not made it clear what I want?’ Andrew’s voice was equally cold; he was still not looking at Bernie. ‘Let the man go. As you say, he did no real harm and I am perfectly fine.’ He turned to Emma. ‘Take me home,’ he said. ‘Now.’

‘What?’ The room felt oppressively hot; she hoped she wasn’t going to faint. She stared down at him, trying desperately to mask the agony she was experiencing. ‘Darling, I don’t think I can, I …’ She looked away from him, up into the doctor’s face. ‘Can I?’

‘No.’ Dr. Pooni, standing behind Andrew, shook his head reassuringly. ‘Not just yet.’

Emma felt herself relaxing, the danger of a faint retreating. Andrew twisted his head round, shouted. ‘You can’t keep me here against my will! If I want to go home, that is where I will go! I will discharge myself.’

'Don't do that, Andrew.' Bernie's anger had subsided; a steely determination had taken its place. 'You have had a shock and a very nasty experience. You need to remain here for at least another twenty-four hours. Isn't that right?' Over Andrew's head his eyes sent Dr. Pooni a message.

Oh, thank you, Bernie, thank you.

'Yes, Mr. Silver, you are quite right. I should be failing in my duty to you, Mr. Raven, if I let you leave now.'

CHAPTER THIRTY-TWO

Garry sat rigid, hands clamped to the steering wheel, bile rising in his throat; the seat of the van was hot and damp. Foot on the accelerator, he was poised, ready to drive out the moment the gate was opened.

For Christ's sake, come on, come on. Maybe he could swerve to the right and get through the 'In' gate before Wally had closed it after the Merc had come through. If only he hadn't turned back to press that fucking alarm he'd be well away by now; Wally wouldn't be attending to an incoming car and that stupid clown behind him wouldn't be banging on his horn and yelling at him. If this went on much longer it wouldn't be just piss that he'd have in his … What now? Wally, nodding his big, fat head, was speaking into his phone, again; God, he did like that phone, made him feel so important. 'Phone rings,' he'd said to Garry, his first day at *The Oaks*, 'that's what I have to see to. Any message comes through, from the house, from the doctors' – he so liked saying that bit – 'my duty is to deal with that before anything else. You remember that, lad.' Okay, Garry'd said, but he'd not given it another thought … until now. Shit! Some doctor's heard the alarm, gone into the room, found the guy dead. Stop nodding your head, you arsehole; just move your great fat carcase out of the way, open the fucking gate and let me … He is opening it! He's fucking waving me through! This has to be a mistake. So, who cares if it is? If Wally loses his job … well, tough shit; serves them right for having a moron doing it.

Without even a sideways glance or a thank-you nod, Garry shot through the opening, gave the fleetest of looks to his right, swung left into the road, his mind devoid of any thought, other than he had got away. He drove, for how long and where, he didn't know; he didn't care. When, at last, he stopped sweating and his heart rate began to drop he pulled up at the side of the road. He was somewhere he didn't recognise; it wasn't Hewers Hill, that was for sure: big block of council flats on his left, scruffy grass in front of them. Main thing was, he wasn't in that fucking driveway anymore. Slowly he uncurled his stiff, clammy fingers from the wheel, eased his knotted, aching shoulders. He sat back in the seat, began, slowly, to move his buttocks. Oh no … he screwed up his nose; the oozy feel and the smell was … revolting, unbearable; quickly he wound down the window, gulped in some fresh air. If only he had a spare pair of jeans in the back of the … He did, well, not jeans, but some khaki overalls, from when he'd done that bit of decorating a few weeks back. He wasn't supposed to, but he'd nicked them; well, not really nicked them, just not handed them in when he'd left the job.

He couldn't put them on now; he'd just have to put up with the pong until he could find somewhere he could change. First, though, he needed to know where he was. Grimacing, he eased himself out of the car seat, made his way uncomfortably to the junction of the next street; Lackamay Road, N22 . Wherever that was. He hoped to God it was nowhere near where he'd just come from: he could have been driving round in circles for all he knew of the last – ten minutes? Half hour? He had no idea. He pulled his phone out of his jacket pocket, punched in the name of the street. That was a relief; he was no longer in Hewers Hill; somehow he had driven east and landed near Wood Green. Forty minutes and he'd be home and he could get out of these stinking clothes.

He started the engine, drove, carefully this time, aware of everything around him – the take-aways, the bookies, the mums with buggies, the parked lorries delivering stuff; the traffic lights, *specially* them, hard as it was to wait, not go on the amber. On the move he was more or less okay: he couldn't drive and think. But when he stopped – oh God, the lights were red now – he didn't know which thought to deal with first: The guy in that room? Paula, what she'd do to him? The police, would they find him? What Grandad had said to him?

Oh fuck, he'd not thought of *this* one: CCTV cameras at *The Oaks*, clocking him every time he went in and out of those gates. He had to ditch the van! He'd get a train; bound to be a station somewhere nearby. No, he couldn't do that, not stinking like this. It wasn't far to the Cross; he'd chance it, get into some clean gear, dump the van.

A lorry hooted behind him: the lights were green. Garry took his foot off the brake and the van shot forward.

* * *

Slumped in the passenger seat of Bernie's car Emma began to shake violently and tears rolled down her cheeks.

In Andrew's suite, in the corridor outside, in the manager's office, along the gravelled drive that led to the car park, she had, somehow, kept it all together, barely saying a word, leaving the talking – the thank-yous and farewells, the arrangements for Andrew's security for his extra time at *The Oaks* – to Bernie. She knew that if she allowed herself to speak, she would be opening the floodgates to her whirling emotions, letting out a jumble of ill-formed, terrifying thoughts.

Bernie put his arms around her and pulled her close.

'Emm,' he whispered. 'It's all right. It's over.'

'Over?' She shook her head. 'No.' With the heels of her hands she wiped away her tears, looked down at her mascara-stained palms. 'It's going to get worse,' she said.

'Here. Let me.' Bernie pulled a man-size tissue from a box on the dashboard and gently removed the black streaks from Emma's hands. With a second tissue he dabbed gently at her face. 'There, that's better,' he said, kissing her still-damp cheek.

'Oh, Bernie, what are we going to do?'

'I'm know what I'm going to do,' Bernie said, reaching into a pocket for his phone. 'I'm going to make a call.'

With one swift movement Emma jerked herself upright, reached out for the phone. 'No.' It was a hoarse, urgent plea. 'You mustn't. Please, Bernie. We all said ...'

'I'm not calling the police, sweetheart.'

'Who then ...?'

'I'm calling Garry.'

'Garry?'

'We need to know where he is … and what he's going to do next.'

* * *

The phone rang again. Best look, see who it was. With his left hand Garry picked it up, saw the name on the screen: Bernie. What the fuck did he want? Oh, Jesus … someone had called him, told him, someone at *The Oaks*. Yeah, okay someone there might tell Bernie – the Raven guy being his mate and that – but why should Bernie ring him? There was no way Bernie could know he'd been at *The Oaks* today. Was there? Whatever it was he wasn't going to answer. He put the mobile back on the seat and drove on. Seconds later, it pinged: text … from Bernie. Oh Jesus … Okay, so he'd read it … but not till he got home. He wasn't going to do anything, not even look at a text, until he'd got out of these clothes. Another ping from the mobile; Garry glanced at the screen: Bernie again. Maybe he should call Paula, see if she'd heard from him. No. She'd want to know why he wanted to know. Again his phone pinged; another fucking text from Bernie. Jesus, what was so urgent the guy couldn't wait? Well, he'd have to.

Garry picked up the phone, switched it off.

* * *

'He's not answering,' Bernie said.

‘Of course he’s not. Would you?’ Emma was beginning to get irritated. With all the other problems they had facing them, why was Bernie so anxious to talk to Garry; what he’d done was done … and although he’d been acting in his own interests, his actions had served their purpose well: Andrew’s reaction to the suggestion of calling the police removed, for Emma, any lingering doubts she might have entertained that he *had* tied up those old people.

Bernie tapped out a third text.

‘Oh stop, will you! It doesn’t matter how many texts you send, if he doesn’t want to answer them … he won’t.’

‘All right, I’ll leave it for now.’ Reluctantly Bernie closed his phone, put it in his jacket pocket.

‘Good,’ Emma said. ‘Now can we please go home.’

‘Is that your home … or my home?’

‘Mine. I have a lot to do before … before Andrew returns.’

Bernie started the engine, drove out of the car park.

Emma sighed. Bernie’s calls to Garry had, briefly, diverted her thoughts from the problems ahead, problems exacerbated by the knowledge that they all now shared. She dreaded having Andrew home; just her and Andrew in that big house. No one to turn to …

‘Constance,’ she said, loudly.

‘What about her?’

‘I need her back.’

‘Call her then.’

‘I will.’

‘Do it now, in case she can’t come, and we have to make other arrangements.’

'We?'

'Yes, Emma, *we.* This is as much my responsibility as yours, my darling.' Keeping one hand on the steering wheel, Bernie took hold of Emma's hand, lifted her fingers to his lips, kissed them gently.

'Oh, Bernie.' Emma felt her body responding to his touch. She leant back and closed her eyes, allowing herself for a few brief moments to be taken over by the sensation.

Quickly she sat up, opened her eyes. 'Constance won't be able to get here till tomorrow, at the earliest,' she said, hoping she sounded practical, matter-of-fact.

'No, she won't.'

'I don't think I should be alone tonight. As you said, we don't know what Garry might do next.'

'Quite right; we don't.'

'So … ?'

'First, though, we go to Islington.'

* * *

Need to talk to you, the first text said. Oh Jesus! Second text: *Or should I speak to Paula*? Christ no! *It's about the shop*. Oh. Garry let out a deep breath. He'd put off looking at the messages until he'd had a hot shower, got himself into some clean clothes, taken a beer from the fridge, settled himself on his sofa, switched on the telly. At last he was beginning to feel normal again; slowly the horrific events of the morning began to lose some of their impact, and as they did he even began to wonder if they had really happened. Had he, Garry Wade, done that, *really* done that … tied up that guy, put a gag in his mouth? He had; he'd worked out a plan … and he'd executed it … *and* ... he'd got away with it. Christ knows how … but he had. In his mind he ran through the events of the morning – parking the van, going in, talking to Dot, walking up the stairs, doing what he had to do, getting in the van; then the panic at the gates. Silly that, getting so stressed about it. No one, certainly not that dozy Wally, was going to connect him, the guy delivering fruit and veg, with what had happened in Suite No 4. He let out a deep breath; all that panic … for nothing.

Pity he couldn't tell his mates what he'd done. They'd like it; a lot.

So far, so very good. Then he remembered the texts from Bernie. The good thing about texts was you could pretend you never got them; happened all the time with texts, not going where they was supposed to go; same with voicemails, you could ignore them, too.

If the shop really was all Bernie was bothered about, well … he had Paula's number, he could call her. Still best get rid of the van specially as, for once in his life, he'd done the straight, honest thing … he'd insured it! He'd given his real name and … Oh fuck! … he'd given Paula's address; he'd not thought of that when he gave the false one to Jamie. The van had to go. Pity, he liked having that. Maybe he'd wait, couple of days. No, that was no good; if the boys in blue was after him, they'd be knocking on his sister's door anytime now. Oh Jesus … she would go ballistic!

'Hi, Sis, how you doing? Gimme a bell when you got a minute.' He sat down on the sofa, mobile in his hand. If she wasn't doing someone's hair she'd pick up straight away, get back to him.

'Hi, bruv. How're you doing? Not heard from you in a while.'

'Me? Doing great. Fine.'

'So … why the call? Now. You sure everything's okay?'

'Yeah, course. Why wouldn't it be? No, I was just wonderin' …

if, you know, there was anything more 'bout selling the shop?'

'No, not really. A couple of nibbles, that's all.'

'Nothing more from that guy who made an offer?'

'No, but there's somebody else I might chase up.'

'Yeah, right. Good.'

'You sure that's all you want to know?'

'Yeah. What else would there be?'

'I don't know. Listen, I got to go; got my packing to do.'

'Packing?'

'Yes, you dozy thing. I told you. Me and Lisa are going to Manchester for a hair do.'

'Why you going to Manchester to have your hair done?'

'Not a hair-do, you idiot! A hair do, as in hair-dressing conference, duh?'

'Oh … right. Yeah, yeah. I remember now.'

'See you when I get back, yeah?'

'Yeah. Sure. Have a good time, Sis.'

'Will do. Bye, bruv.'

'Bye.'

So ... Paula'd not heard. Maybe he *had* got away with it. Maybe he should call Bernie. Maybe he should get a can of petrol, set fire to the van. Maybe he should hang on to it till this all blew over: if he got a new van, people would notice, start talking, and - Oh Jesus! - there could be all that malarkey about insurance again. No thank you. Maybe he should call Jamie, tell him he couldn't do the run on Friday: there was no way he was going back *there*. Maybe better if he didn't call him. Maybe he should … stop pacing the floor, switch off his phone, get out of the flat … Go to Epping Forest, have a walk, pick some mushrooms like he'd done once with Dean when he was a kid – no, wrong time of year for mushrooms; that had been in the autumn; he remembered all the dry leaves on the ground, kicking them, throwing them at Dean. If Dean was here, he'd know what to do.

His phone rang. Without thinking, or looking at the screen, he answered.

'Hello.' Idiot! What had he done that for!

'Garry. Hello.' Oh Christ, it was Bernie. Garry swallowed hard.

'Oh, hi Bernie. Good to hear from you. Texts? No, didn't get them. Is it about the shop, because if it is it's still up for sale so you know if you do want it and you talk to Paula I'm sure she'd be happy to …'

'Well, yes … it is about the shop. If you'd read my texts you'd know.'

'Oh. Yeah. Sorry 'bout that.'

'Any chance you could come to Islington? Have a chat about it.'

'Oh. Well …'

'I'd really like to get this thing sorted … and as it was you we saw first, Garry, it seems only right that you should … um … get the benefit, you know … from any sale that we … um …'

'Oh. Yeah. Right. Got you.' Huh, he thinks I'd take less than Paula; well, he's right, I would. Not much, though. I'm not a fool, Bernie, even if you think I am.

'Okay. So when can you come?'

'Well … can't do tomorrow … or the day after. I'm working. I could do this afternoon, actually, if that's any good to you?' The sooner he found out if Bernie did know anything about this morning the better. And tomorrow he definitely wouldn't have the van. Maybe he could even ditch it in Highbury somewhere, get a bus to Bernie's place, come back on the train.

'Yes, this afternoon's fine. Good man. See you … what, about half three?'

'Yeah. Sure. Cheers, Bernie.' Garry ended the call, sat staring at his phone. He looked again at Bernie's texts: *Need to talk to you.* That could mean anything. *Or should I talk to Paula?* About what? The shop, what else? I wouldn't have answered those two anyway. *It's about the shop.* Well, he could have said that in the first one. So … did he go, see Bernie? Better than staying here churning everything over all the time; and if the filth *was* after him … well, they'd not come looking for him in Almeida Street. Oh, fuck; they might, though. If Bernie'd told them what he'd done … No. No! How could Bernie know where he'd been this morning? Oh, Jesus, this was doing his head in. Maybe he should call Bernie, put it off … or just not turn up. If Bernie really did want to make him an offer on the shop … It was true this had all come through him, meeting that Jackie … so yeah, it was right he had first pick … and with Paula going away he could make some money for himself; and he'd please Paula by getting the sale.

He got up from the sofa, walked around the room, looked out of the window … onto the grey garage roofs and the grey car park, the grey sky. Fuck, yes. He'd do it, he'd go to Islington.

* * *

'Don't look so worried, Emma.' Trev put the cappuccino down in front of her. 'At the slightest hint of trouble, I can be in from the shop. Tell her, Bernie.'

'I've told her. Look, sweetie, the man is no danger to you, or to me. He's not going to have a gun or anything.'

'You don't know that.'

'I do. If he'd had one, and had wanted to scare Andrew, he would have used it, then.'

'Yes, okay.'

'And we do need to know if he has anything else planned. I mean … you don't want him turning up at Pengate once Andrew's home.'

'He wouldn't. He doesn't know we live in Pengate … does he?'

'He knew about *The Oaks.* How did he discover that? The man may look a fool, but he's obviously not. And let's face it, Emma, he has every right to be angry with Andrew, and to take revenge for what he did to his grandparents. I know if I was in his shoes, I'd want to …'

'You wouldn't do that, though, would you … tie someone up, put a gag in their mouth?'

'I might, if that had been done to someone I loved. Maybe not to hurt them, not seriously, more to show them that I knew what they'd done, which I think is what Garry was doing. A sort of warning, if you like. So we need to know what the guy is going to do next. Oh, hang on … he's here. Into the shop, Trev.'

With the remote Bernie opened the gate to the yard.

'Yes, boss. On my way.' Trev saluted. He mouthed a kiss at Emma. 'You'll be fine.' He fluttered his eyelids. 'I do wish I had a big, strong man to protect me!'

Emma laughed.

'That's better. See you.' Trev waved, and went into the shop.

* * *

'Come in, Garry,' Bernie said, opening the door.

He'd not expected to see the woman. Why was she here?

'Oh, hi,' he said. She half-smiled at him.

'Coffee?' Bernie asked.

'No, ta.' The sooner this was over, whatever it was, the better. He could see Trevor through the glass panel in the door to the shop. Was he part of this, too?

He'd nearly not come; twice on the way here he'd pulled into a side road, sat, shaking, uncertain, wishing he had a fag – that was it, that's what he needed. Second stop, he'd seen a shop on the corner, got himself a packet and a lighter. A couple of drags, he began to feel calmer. It was still having the van that was doing it, he knew that, but if he'd turned up without it … well, that would have had them asking questions, for sure. And if he didn't turn up at all … then Bernie'd call Paula and she'd call him, and while he could blag it with Bernie, there was no way he could do that with Paula.

He'd driven on, and now he was here.

He perched on the edge of the cane chair, ready for flight. Which way, though? The yard gates would be shut till Bernie chose to open them; through the shop, Trevor'd be ready to nab him or trip him up. He could feel himself beginning to sweat.

'So what did you want ?' He looked up at Bernie, standing by this desk, his phone just a finger away.

'Ah, yes.' Bernie moved in front of his desk, leaned back on it, crossed his ankles, smiled.

Okay, so it's play-acting time again. Garry smiled at both Bernie and the woman; they both smiled back, all very cosy.

'Garry, mate, I expect you're wondering why we've asked you here.'

Well, of course I am, you fucking idiot. 'You said it was about the shop.'

'That's right; it is.' Bernie stood up, folded his arms, walked over to the outside door.

Jesus, he's going to lock it!

Bernie turned around, his back to the door. 'It's all about the shop.' He paused. 'Isn't it?'

'Sorry … what's all about the shop?'

'The outrage committed there, when your grandparents were attacked all those years ago …'

'Oh.' He didn't like the way Bernie was looking at him, like he was in court and Garry was in the dock.

' … and what you did today, at *The Oaks.*'

Jesus, how did *they* know? How could they know? Oh fuck, he was going to start bricking it again, he could feel it.

'I don't know what you're talking …' His voice was coming out all croaky.

'You tied up my husband,' the woman said. 'You put a gag in his mouth.' Calm, like she was that Dr. Foster woman on the telly.

'I … I don't know what …'

The door to the shop was opening.

'Hello there,' Trevor said.

A strangulated 'Hi' was all Garry could manage: Trevor was standing in the doorway. Garry looked across the room at Bernie. Oh Jesus, that's both exits blocked.

'As I am sure you know, Garry,' Bernie said, folding his arms across his chest, his voice all smooth and silky, 'either Mrs. Raven, or myself, or someone else at *The Oaks* ... could have called the police ... and *you* ... would now be in a police station.'

The police didn't know; maybe he could blag it. 'Where'd you get all that from?' he said, hurt-like; he could do a bit of acting, too, when he had to.

'Where did we get it from?' A longish pause; everything and everyone in the room sort of frozen. 'From being there … both of us.' Bernie looked down at Emma, put a hand on her shoulder. 'Seeing your van; you know, your blue van, with the back doors a deeper blue than the rest of the vehicle?'

Garry was sweating hard now. 'You could have seen that anywhere, in the street or …'

'Yes, we could … but I doubt whether we would have seen Mr. Raven gagged and tied up anywhere else. Would we, Garry?'

Garry clenched his buttocks. 'No,' he said, faintly. If he'd thought for one moment that they would have been there: they never came till the afternoon. Never. Oh Jesus, how long would he get? Just when he'd turned his life around, and actually got some money – he still wasn't sure how much it was – and the prospect of some proper work; Jamie had been real grateful to him.

The woman was speaking again. 'We wanted to thank you.'

Thank me? What kind of stupid game are they playing, these people?

'Sorry, what did you say?'

'I said …' The woman looked up at Bernie. 'I can't do this, Bernie. You tell him.'

'Okay, you drink your coffee.' Bernie moved away from the door, perched himself on the corner of his desk, smiled at Trevor. Trevor nodded, went back into the shop, shut the door.

Garry sat, buttocks still clenched, waiting.

'I know it's a weird thing to say, especially as …' Why was the guy finding it so difficult to get the words out? The woman hadn't *really* said thank you, had she? For saving her husband's life, maybe, going back and ringing that bell, so someone would come and the guy wouldn't die.

'… what you did was both criminal and inhumane, tying up a very sick man, a man who was just getting over a major stroke, in that callous and calculating way. You had obviously been planning this for some time.'

Best say nothing.

'We … um …' It seemed like Bernie had run out of words. So, was that it? They'd told him they knew what he'd done; and now he was free to go? No. Life wasn't like that; not Garry's anyway.

'Garry …' The woman reached out her hand to him. 'We understand why you did it, and in an odd sort of way … we are grateful to you. Although your action *was* wrong, totally wrong, it confirmed our suspicions about the break-in at the shop, in Brockwood.'

'Yeah, well. Right.' A case of scratch my back, I'll scratch yours: they say nothing about this to anyone, and I don't say any more about what happened to Grandad … and they can go on pretending it never happened, that their precious Mr. Raven was nowhere near the place. It was still kind of odd, though. Something must have happened in that Suite 4 after he'd left that made them decide to keep the police out of it. Whatever it was, he wasn't going to rock the boat. So, okay, if they'd keep schtum, he would too. What he wanted right now was to get out of here.

Just one last question, though. He didn't plan on seeing these clowns again, didn't want to, but he wasn't going to pass up on a chance to make himself a bit more cash.

'So …' he said. 'The shop. You still interested?'

Bernie looked at the woman, she looked at him, both their faces serious, sad.

'I think not,' said Bernie. 'Best we forget all about it, the shop.'

The woman nodded. 'Yes,' she said. 'That would be the best thing to do.'

'I was prepared to do you a really good deal on it.' For fuck's sake, what was he doing? He needed to get away from these people, not get in deeper! He felt his stomach muscles tense, his breath held tight.

'That's very kind of you, Garry,' Bernie said, smiling now, 'but no, thank you. We won't be taking it forward. Not now.'

'Right. Yeah. Sure.' He breathed out, felt his muscles relax.

Bernie began to tidy a pile of papers on his desk, the woman picked up her posh handbag from beside her chair.

'So … We're done?' Garry asked.

'Yes. We're done.'

* * *

'Poor little sod, he doesn't look very happy,' Trev said, watching on the screen in the office as Garry drove out of the yard.

'He damn well should be.' Bernie poured whisky into three glasses. 'He wouldn't have stood a chance if the police had got their hands on him. It would have served him right, too, if we'd let Camper call them.'

‘I feel quite sorry for him, actually,’ Trev said. ‘In his forties, and still struggling to make something of his life; I know what that’s like.’

‘We did what we did for Andrew’s sake, and for Emma’s. You surely know that, Trev.’ Bernie pushed a whisky towards him. ‘The last thing either of them wants now is the police sniffing round.’

‘Ta,’ Trev said. ‘Yes, of course.’

Bernie held out a glass to Emma.

She shook her head. ‘No, but you have one. I’ll drive.’

‘You sure?’ Bernie asked.

Emma nodded. ‘I’ll drink when I get home,’ she said. ‘And it will be more than one tot.’

‘Poor Garry, he never seemed to get it quite right, did he?’ Trev laughed. ‘Not even as a villain.’

‘I really don’t think he needs your sympathy, Trev.’ Bernie’s voice was hard; he poured himself another drink. ‘He’s got away with a crime, thanks to us.’

‘He has; you’re right.’ Emma said, and so has Andrew, she thought. ‘but I know what Trev means. Not everyone’s life works out the way you want it to.’

‘Lives rarely do.’ Bernie screwed the top back on the whisky bottle and put it in his desk drawer. His action took Emma’s mind back to the drawer in Andrew’s desk.

‘We may have finished with Garry,’ she said, ‘and that shop, too, thank goodness, but I have Andrew coming home in a few days, and what happened at *The Oaks* this morning, *and* what happened at Brockwood, can’t just be swept under the carpet.’ There was pain in Emma’s sigh. ‘I really don’t know how I am going to deal with it all.’

CHAPTER THIRTY-THREE

'Your hair's a mess, Jacob,' Andrew said.

Emma, clearing the table after lunch, braced herself: she was not going to interfere. It was only a little thing, the state of Jacob's hair, and it didn't bother her – in fact, she quite liked it long – so why spend even a fraction of her meagre store of energy becoming involved. For her, any arguments Jacob might have with his father were heavily outweighed by having her lovely boy at home. She wished she'd been able to keep in touch with him more over the past few years; they had exchanged emails, weekly at first, but less regularly as time passed, and the radio signal at the remote farm was too weak for Facetime or even proper conversations. Whether they would ever return to the closeness they had had when Jacob was growing up, was doubtful, but there was still the ease in their relationship they had always enjoyed; she had never had to be wary of saying the wrong thing to Jacob, nor he to her. And with Connie here, too, Emma felt she could let herself begin to relax. Her fear was, that once they had both gone - they wouldn't stay in Pengate for ever - and she was alone with Andrew … No, she would not go there today, not on Jacob's first day at home.

It had been so good to see him at the front door. Emma had been standing by the long landing window that faced onto the drive, looking at the front garden, searching the still bare branches of the three silver birches and the ground beneath them, for signs of spring, when the taxi pulled up at the gates. Without waiting to see who the passenger was – she knew it would be Jacob; he had sent her a text from Heathrow – she had raced down the stairs and opened the door.

'Oh, my darling!' She had flung her arms around his neck.

'Help, you're strangling me!' He'd laughed, picked her up and lifted her off her feet. 'Mum. Hi.' He'd put her down; they'd looked at one another, tears of joy in their eyes.

'Oh, Jacob.'

'I know, I know. It's been too long. But I'm here now.'

'What's going on?' Constance, wiping her hands on a piece of kitchen roll, came to the door.

'Jacob! Oh, how lovely to see you,' she said, stuffing the kitchen roll into her apron pocket, and holding out her arms to her nephew. 'You're looking very … bronzed,' she added, as if suddenly embarrassed by her unaccustomed display of affection.

'Auntie Constance! Wow! Hi there.' Jacob hugged her.

'What's all the noise about?' Andrew, walking slowly, his right hand tightly grasping a walking stick, emerged from his office. 'I saw a taxi draw up just now. Jacob! Oh. You're here.'

Please let this be all right, Emma said to herself, as Jacob, taking in the stick and the limp-looking left hand, moved towards his father.

'Hi, Dad,' he said, putting his arm around Andrew's shoulders.

Yes, that was just the right amount of affection: more, and Andrew would have drawn away; less, and he would have been hurt.

'Hello, son. It's … it's good to have you home.'

'It's good to be here.'

'That's quite enough standing around for you, Andrew. Come on, all of you, let's go into the lounge and I'll bring us some coffee.' Constance led the way into the lounge, opening the double doors, and pausing on the threshold. 'Mind that step, Andrew. Jacob, help your father. Emma, you sit down, too.'

While father and son, seated on the long sofa facing the continuous floor-to-ceiling window that looked out onto the back lawn, had a non-conversation about airports and convalescent homes – 'They're called re-hab now, Dad' – and the quality of the food provided in both of them, Emma sat quietly, observing them, the men in her life – well, two of them; the other one would be here later today.

He had grown, her boy; always tall and lanky, he was now filled out. So like his father to look at, except for the eyes – Andrew's deep brown, Jacob's bluey-grey, flecked with gold. Jacob shrugged off his leather jacket and flung it casually over the back of the sofa. Emma tensed, then relaxed as Andrew, noticing, resisted the temptation to comment. Jacob pushed up the sleeves of his check shirt, revealing well-developed muscles in his sun-tanned arms. He's showing off, and Andrew knows it, she thought; it's good that he's not responding. It won't be long though, unless they have both changed radically, before they start behaving like the two alpha males they fancy themselves to be.

'Coffee,' announced Constance, backing into the room with a tray of mugs.

Already Andrew had begun to ask the sort of questions she sensed Jacob did not want to answer –'What exactly do you do on this farm? You've never explained.' 'Decent pay structure, is it?' – so when Jacob sniffed appreciatively at the smells coming from the kitchen as the door swung open, Emma made use of it to move everyone over to the dining table, already laid for lunch.

'It's nearly lunchtime so we'll have our coffee there,' she said merrily, beaming at them all. To Jacob she said, 'Your father finds it easier on an upright chair, don't you, dear?' She helped Andrew up from the sofa and propelled him over to the table before he had a chance to object.

They got through the meal without any mishap, other than a brief exchange, in which Emma did not participate, about what Jacob should now call his aunt. When Jacob addressed her as Connie, Andrew expressed his disapproval, vehemently; Constance, bless her, immediately reached across the table and patted Jacob's hand. 'I quite like you calling me Auntie,' she said. 'It's special; no one else may call me that.'

'Okay. How about I call you Auntie Con?'

'Yes, that would be nice.'

Andrew grunted and reached for the bottle of wine.

They began to talk about cricket, a passion with Jacob, an adopted interest for Andrew, who had discovered, via the village team, that he was quite a respectable bowler, which had pleased him no end. Emma, watching unobserved from an upstairs window, had seen him practising over-arm movements in between his golf swings on the side lawn; she had always felt very tender towards him on these occasions: this was the Andrew she remembered from their early days, anxious to be seen to be the best, but not wanting to let anyone into the secret of how he had got there. Sighing, she would move away from the window; he would so hate to know he had been observed in the process of reaching the desired high standard.

As now, with the daily physio sessions, he did not want Emma there. 'Just the professional, thank you, dear.' And so she had left him in the care of the physiotherapist, a charming young woman who seemed able to get Andrew to do whatever she required of him, without protest of any kind.

Thank God Connie was there, too. The gentle encouragement she gave Andrew – 'One step at a time.' 'Don't run before you can walk.' – which would have irritated Emma in the same situation, made him smile. Connie's 'It won't be forever; best for now though.' had been such a blessing when Emma had had to tell Andrew, on the day that he came home from *The Oaks,* that he would be sleeping in his office. Swayed by Connie's concern about his use of the stairs – 'What if you fell? You need to have full use of your legs before you go climbing!' – reluctantly he had agreed. Emma was not ready to have him in her bed – would she ever again? – and Connie's simple, practical advice had saved her; for now anyway. 'Thank you,' she'd said, as they crossed the hall to the kitchen, leaving Andrew to rearrange some books and papers in his office. 'Well, I don't expect either of you is ready for the intimacy of the bedroom just yet,' Constance said. Emma laughed, embarrassed. Although sex was something the sisters rarely spoke about, it was Constance's quaint phrase that Emma found embarrassing. 'Why are you laughing?' 'At your choice of language.' 'Oh, all right then; having sex. Is that better?' Without waiting for an answer she marched into the kitchen and put the kettle on. Emma, following her, smiled; there are no flies on Connie, she thought.

With Constance there, Emma had also been able to escape to the allotment. She went there most days, just for an hour, usually during Andrew's physio sessions. Although it was winter and nothing much was growing, it was still a haven, set apart from the world around her, a place where she could find peace, if only temporarily, from the turbulent thoughts that plagued her. Down here, among the remains of the broad beans and the dry, yellowed raspberry leaves, she felt safe, cocooned; and with her phone on silent no one could break, unwanted, into her solitude. Sometimes Adam was there with her; they pottered about, tidying up the plot, sweeping out the shed, putting away the old canes – she knew she should throw them out, get new ones, but she never did, and the plants they supported had always thrived. They spoke little, and any words they did exchange came as a balm to Emma, soothing her with their openness, words that meant just what they said – 'Think I'll turn this bed over.' 'That can go on the compost.' – unburdened with hidden meanings.

She never saw Bernie alone, only during his visits 'to see Andrew', when the three of them sat together, reminiscing. No one mentioned – dared to mention? – what had taken place at *The Oaks* that day. Emma wasn't going to, nor was Bernie. Any conversation about that day had to be instigated by Andrew, but it never was, so there it lay, if not an elephant in the room, certainly a sleeping tiger. Or maybe a sleeping dog. She recalled a play she had once seen, 'Dangerous Corner' it was called, in which one ill-considered remark about a cigarette box had opened a can of very unpleasant worms. It wouldn't take much for their own can of worms to be sprung open. Best it remained tightly shut; but for how long? For the rest of their lives? Surely it would have to be opened sometime.

Now Jacob was home, perhaps?

The comment on Jacob's hair had come at the very end of lunch, as Emma and Jacob were clearing the table, and Constance was helping Andrew out of his chair.

Calm and smiling, Jacob, holding a stack of dirty plates, had replied - 'I know,' he'd said - then followed his mother into the kitchen.

He placed the plates down on the counter above the dishwasher. Emma put food away in the fridge next to it. She glanced at him, pleased to have him there beside her, pleased he'd responded so politely to his father's jibe.

'What's going on with you and Dad?' Jacob asked, opening the dishwasher.

Emma's heart gave a leap. 'Scrape them first,' she said, closing the fridge.

'Mum, I asked you a question.'

'Yes, I heard you. Nothing's going on, he's been very ill and now …'

'That's it. Nothing. There *is* nothing … Well?'

Emma turned away, walked over to the table, picked up the salad bowl, went back to the fridge. What had Jacob seen ? He had always been sensitive, able to pick up on any changes of mood, ready to please or provoke, according to his own needs. It didn't feel like that this time; there had been genuine concern in his voice.

'I know it's been difficult, and I'm sorry I've not been here …'

'Yes, why didn't you come?' Better to have Jacob answering a question than having to look him in the eyes and answer *his* query. She had never been able to lie to him; he'd always known when she was. As *she* knew when *he* was evading the truth; which had been often, too often, in his teenage years. She had become adept at keeping Jacob's misdemeanours from his father; but now the boot was on the other foot: Jacob, she decided in a flash, must not know what his father had done.

'You know why, Mum. I'd broken my foot; it was in plaster … and it hurt! It hurt a lot.'

'Yes, all right. I'm sorry. Is it …' she nodded, gesturing towards his feet: she was unsure which foot had had the bullet in it. 'Is it healed now?'

'Yes, yes, it's fine now.'

'Good.'

'It's aches a bit, you know, if it's cold … or damp.'

'Which it wouldn't be in South Africa.'

'Too right, it wouldn't.'

'So … you'll have to be careful, while you're here, not to let it become cold … or damp.'

'I'll be careful, Mum. Promise you.'

'That's good. Now, let's get this stuff put away; you go on loading the dishwasher and I'll see to the rest of the food, and then we'll go into the lounge. Your dad might fancy a game of chess. You do still play, don't you?'

Jacob hesitated, his hand on the door of the dishwasher, before replying. 'Yes, but not very well; I don't play much now.' He pushed the door shut. 'I don't think Dad would like it if I … if I made a lot of mistakes.'

Emma smiled; she was pleased that Jacob had owned up to a failing – perhaps he *was* growing up – even if she was still doubtful about the condition of his foot. 'No, he wouldn't; you're right.' There was no point in presenting Andrew with an opportunity to berate his son, especially over something as unimportant as a game of chess, and so early in Jacob's visit. 'Let's walk down to the allotment. I'd like you to see it, even though there's not much growing at the moment.'

'I'd like that,' Jacob said, 'but not today, Mum. What I'd really like is to go round the garden with you, see what new stuff you've put in since I was here.'

'Well, there's not a lot to see here, either; but yes, if that's what you'd like.'

'I would.' He looked down at his feet, gently rotated the left one. 'Don't feel I could walk very far, not today.'

‘Then that’s what we’ll do. You grab our coats – mine’s the blue anorak – and I’ll tell your dad.’

Emma had noted that it was Jacob’s left foot that had been broken; would it be the right one next time they spoke about it, she wondered, then hated herself for the thought. She must not begin to doubt everything and everyone because of what Andrew had done.

CHAPTER THIRTY-FOUR

'Bernard, it's Constance. Would you like to join us for dinner this evening?'

'Oh. Well yes, thank you.' Whose idea was that? Whoever it was, he had to accept.

'Good. I haven't started cooking yet. I just wondered … is there anything you can't eat?'

'Er, no. No, I'll eat anything; I mean, I eat everything.'

'We'll see you at seven then.'

Bernie enjoyed every morsel of his lamb cutlets, potato croquettes and glazed carrots, followed by a chocolate mousse that rivalled his mother's. Having praised the food he asked about its source – 'Is the lamb from Herdwick sheep, by any chance? It does have such a special flavour.' – so that talking about the rest of the components of the meal seemed a natural follow-up. How was he to know that most of them had come from the village shop? Or that Constance would then go on to extol the virtues of small independent shops. Realising too late that he had trodden on dangerous ground – Andrew was looking steadfastly at the food on his plate; Emma was pressing everyone to have more carrots – he turned to Jacob, and began asking him in-depth questions about life in present day South Africa, particularly about farming, contrasting it with his own apartheid era visit in the 1980s, when he had stayed, briefly, on a farm. Jacob had little to say on the subject, and Bernie began to hunt around for a new topic of conversation. It was Constance who came to the rescue.

'Do you play cricket, Bernard?' she enquired, her face very serious.

Andrew laughed. 'Play cricket? Him? Never.'

'No, rugby was my game.'

'Too polite for Bernie, cricket. He likes a bit of rough stuff, our Bernie, don't you?'

'Well …' Bernie had no idea where this was going, but he didn't like it. Neither did he like the puzzled look that Jacob was giving him, nor the frantic way Emma suddenly began, very noisily, to clear the table. She was dressed, he had noticed, the way Andrew liked her to look - cashmere sweater, tweed skirt.

'You sit down, I'll do that,' Constance said, getting up and wresting the pile of plates from Emma's hands. 'And you, Andrew …' She wagged a finger at him, 'don't drink any more wine! I'm not sure you should be drinking alcohol at all … not with your medication.'

'Oh, I'll be fine …'

'No, Dad,' Jacob interrupted, 'Auntie Con's right. You should take notice of her. You may not realise it, but she has your best interests at heart.' He turned to her. 'Don't you, Auntie Con?'

'Well, of course. Naturally.' Constance, suddenly – and thankfully – the centre of everyone's attention, blushed.

'And you're going to stay, aren't you, until Dad's better?'

'Well, yes, if I'm wanted.' She was looking at Andrew, but it was Emma who replied.

'Yes, of course you are, Connie.' Bernie saw the desperation in Emma's eyes. 'Isn't she, Andrew?'

'Um?'

'Connie … We both want her to stay, don't we?'

'Yes,' Andrew said, 'by all means.'

'Oh, well, in that case, I'd better bring some more things from home.'

Bernie watched as a triangle of glances shot between the sisters and Andrew, keenly observed by Jacob. Emma's he could interpret easily – 'Thank God I'm not going to be left alone with my husband.' Andrew's: as expected, it gave nothing away. But Constance ...? Why was she looking so flustered, and at the same time so pleased, he wondered? And why was Jacob's smile best described as a smirk?

It was good to have shared a meal with them, but it's time I was out of here, Bernie thought. Best to leave them to it. There was no way he was going to be able to talk to Emma on her own. As for Andrew … what he would say to Andrew if the two of them were left alone, he had no idea. They had not spoken, not properly, not as they used to, since that morning at *The Oaks.* Yes, it was definitely time to say his thank-yous and goodbyes – a friendly hug for Emma, a wave to Jacob, handshakes for Constance and Andrew – the men had never gone in for embraces – and go home.

As his feet scrunched on the gravel drive, Bernie became aware of another set of footsteps behind him. He turned round sharply, hoping against hope it was Emma following him.

'Andrew! What the hell are you doing?'

'Sorry. Did I startle you?'

'No, but … Should you be out here … in the cold?'

'I'm not going to be long. Just need to have a word.'

'About what?' Bernie swallowed hard.

'Well, the business, really. We've not had a chance to talk about it since …'

You've not wanted to, you mean. 'The business? Well, whenever you're ready.'

'Shouldn't be too long, now. I have to take things gently to begin with ...'

'Yes, you have.'

'I've said ... and I will. I shall start, slowly of course, by building up the Islington stock again.'

'The stock?' Bernie's heart was beginning to race; he didn't like the way Andrew's eyes seemed to be fastened on his, like an alien in a sci-fi movie transmitting a harmful beam to his enemy.

'Mm, the stock; you know, the vintage stuff. I imagine it's got very low lately, with no one going out in search of it, as Emma and I used to do. So … I thought that's what we'd do, Emma and I; I still have all my contacts – I expect they've been wondering why I haven't been in touch recently.'

'Er … yes. Good idea.' Did Andrew not realise, *really not know,* what had been happening in his absence? Bernie's next words needed to be chosen very carefully. He could test the waters with what would sound an innocent remark, if Andrew had absolutely no inkling of what he and Emma had discovered in his desk; or, if Andrew had gone through his notebooks since coming out of hospital, a loaded one. 'Although, we're not actually short, at the moment.' There, Bernie thought, that's not giving anything away.

'Well, I am surprised. The shop not doing very well, is it?'

'No, it's doing fine, it's just … well, you know, after the Christmas period, people are not buying very much.'

'You've had someone in, haven't you? Buying stock. Of course you have. I would have done.'

'Well …' He had to find an answer. Andrew was a tenacious bugger; he wouldn't be satisfied until Bernie had given him the answer he required.

'Yes, we have. I didn't want to bother you while you were …'

'I'm not ill now. Tell me, who is it?'

'It doesn't matter, does it? So long as we were able to keep up with the stock. We weren't using your contacts, if that's what you're worried about.' See what you make of that.

'Well, no, I should hope not. It's taken me a long time to build up my network of people I can trust to come up with really good quality stuff. I'd still like to know who it is.' This is becoming uncomfortable, Bernie thought. 'If this person has made some new contacts for us I may as well take them over.'

'Yes, of course. We have found some new contacts' – no way was he going to tell Andrew about Trev – 'but we've also had a few things from elsewhere.'

‘Oh? Where?’

This was not a moment for truth. ‘Someone contacted us; can’t remember where he was from. A village somewhere.’ *Why the hell had he added that!*

Andrew smiled. ‘A village? That’s where most of my suppliers are, in villages.’ His smile faded. ‘Which one?’ he asked abruptly.

‘Oh … It begins with a B, I think.’

‘B? Well, there’s plenty of them. Braughing, Barkway …’

‘That’s it, Barkway!’ This was not how this conversation was meant to go.

‘Oh, well, it’s not one of *my* suppliers then. There’s no one in Barkway. Never has been. You’ll have to do better than that, Bernie.’

‘What do you mean?’

‘Oh come on, stop fobbing me off! If you’ve been getting stock, tell me where you’ve been getting it!’

He’s either being very clever … or very cool. Either way, by making an issue of the stock he’s pushing me into a corner, making it look as though *I’m* the guilty party.

‘Well, to be honest …’

‘I wish you would be. I think you owe it to me to give me some explanation of where you’ve been getting …’

‘Yes, all right, all right. We’ve been getting stock from all over the place … including France. We’ve had quite a lot of good stuff …’

‘France? Oh.’

You didn't expect that, did you? 'Oh yes, from farmhouses and, like you do, from villages. He speaks fluent French, the guy who's been doing it.'

You idiot, Bernie, all you've done by mentioning France is provide a diversion from what Andrew really wants to find out. Being him, though, dogged and persistent, he'll soon get back to it.

Andrew nodded, smiled. 'So ...' he began.

'Andrew! Come inside!' Constance, loudly, appearing in the doorway. 'You should not be out here, in the cold!' Running footsteps on the gravel. 'Shame on you, Bernard, keeping him out here talking!'

'I ...'

With Constance's protective arm around his waist, Andrew was hustled off into the house. Bernie stood beside his car, watching them, his tense muscles beginning to relax. Another few minutes and ... A sudden movement drew his eyes to the long landing window; framed in it, the light behind him, was Jacob. Bernie waved – it was no good pretending he hadn't seen him – got into the car and drove off.

* * *

He slept badly, his mind in a ferment. At three a.m. sleep had still not come, and amid the jumble of thoughts and images besieging him came one of himself and Emma, naked on the rug in front of the fire. He sat bolt upright, reached for his phone; he so wanted to speak to her. He put the phone back on his bedside table, went downstairs, poured himself a large whisky and sat down at the kitchen table. The alcohol, he hoped, would, eventually, help him to sleep; meanwhile, seated on an upright chair, under the harsh kitchen lights, a sensible course of action began to form in his now less-fevered mind. We cannot go on like this, he said to himself, in this mire of deceit, and Andrew cannot just pick up his life where he left off before he had the stroke, as if nothing untoward had ever happened.

Bernie drank the last of his whisky, put the tumbler on the draining-board, switched off the lights and went back to bed. If the idea that he had still felt right in the morning he would act upon it.

CHAPTER THIRTY-FIVE

It was the perfect morning for a walk – sunshine, a light breeze, not at all like February. Emma and Jacob, in anoraks and trainers, walked briskly down to the allotment. They had invited Andrew to join them – 'We'll walk slowly, Dad.' – but much to Emma's relief, at a shake of the head from Constance he had declined.

'Auntie Con's really got him under her thumb, hasn't she?'

'Under her thumb? Why'd you say that?'

'Oh, come on, Mum, haven't you noticed? She's taken charge of him.'

'Well, yes. I've no quarrel with that.' Was this the moment to give Jacob some idea of what had been going on in his absence? Not too much, and not to the detriment of his father – It would be wrong of her to do that – but just enough for him to understand that there were *issues*. 'It relieves me of having to …'

'Spend too much time with Dad on your own?'

Emma turned sharply; Jacob was not looking at her. Just as well; he wouldn't see the consternation in her eyes.

'Well … yes, it is difficult, there's no denying it. And it's better for your dad; he does things for Connie that he wouldn't do for me.'

'Such as?' Jacob turned, stood still, head on one side, eyebrows raised.

'Resting, eating properly, taking his medication.'

'Ah. Right.' He walked on.

Emma caught up with him, took his arm. 'Why? What did you mean?' She knew she shouldn't be asking that; she had to do it, though. It was best to find out just what Jacob thought – guessed? – had been taking place in his absence before she blundered in and told him things he had no need to know.

He smiled. 'Oh, it's probably me being silly, but … well, I did wonder …' He patted Emma's arm. 'I don't want you to be upset by this, Mum … but I did wonder if … if Connie and Dad might be having an affair.'

Emma exploded into laughter. *'Connie and your dad?* Oh Jacob … honestly! She's fond of him, yes, but …' She tugged at his arm. 'Oh, come on, enough of this nonsense; let's get to the allotment.'

They walked the rest of the way – down the village street, past the school and the shop, and into the tree-lined lane at the end – in silence.

Could it be, Emma wondered. No, surely not. Not that she, Emma, would mind. What had Jacob seen, she wondered, to make him think such a thing? Whatever it was it had stopped him from having dangerous thoughts about herself and Bernie.

'We're here,' she said, unlocking the tall metal gates that led into the allotments.

'Good God, why are they kept locked? Peaceful village like this! Who d'you think is going to break in? The dreaded cucumber thieves, or … the creature in that Wallace and Gromit film; you know the one I mean?'

'Oh yes. I do.' Emma laughed; it was so lovely to be talking about something so light, so inconsequential. '*The Curse of the Were-Rabbit.*'

'That's the one!'

Emma's allotment was on the left as they walked down the main path. There were thirty allotments in all, none of them large, although some of the serious allotmenteers, who fed more than their family, had a double plot. Emma's was triangular with an overgrown stream running through it, and having decided that half the plot would be quite enough for her needs, the section with the stream had been fenced off. A low wooden gate led into No. 28.

'The numbering starts from the other end,' Emma said, opening the gate.

Jacob surveyed the raised beds and the garden shed, the tub of winter pansies and the fruit cage. 'Cool,' he said. 'Well done, you.'

'Oh, I don't do it on my own; I have a gardener, Adam. I'm sure I've told you about him. Next month he's going to take over the other half of the plot and grow stuff for himself.' Not something your father is keen on, but there's no need for you to know that. She sighed: there was such a lot Jacob didn't know, and she wanted to keep it that way.

'Mum? You okay?'

'Yes, of course. I just want to have a look at the raspberries.' Emma led the way to the fruit cage and opened the mesh door. She stepped inside; Jacob, dipping his head, followed her. 'Adam will cut them back next week; it's a job I like doing but I haven't the time just now. They're called Autumn Bliss, this variety; the flavour's delicious. I rarely get enough to make any jam, but it doesn't matter, I just like eating them fresh, with perhaps a dollop of cream or ...'

'Why were you sighing, Mum?'

'Was I?' She looked up at him; he was very close.

'Yes, Mum, you were ... and you always sighed when there's something you needed to say to me, but you couldn't quite find the right words; it nearly always involved something that would upset Dad if he found out.' He stooped and picked up a shrivelled berry from the ground. 'Well ... am I right?'

'When you see them like that it's hard to believe how succulent they can be.'

'Mum, stop talking about the raspberries; you've already made a long speech about them.' He dropped the dry berry onto the soil. 'Come on, tell me.'

'Well, there's ... there's nothing, really.' Emma pushed open the door and stepped out of the cage. 'Nothing more to see here, today; another month or two and it'll all be sprouting like mad.' It was a relief to be out; although there was air all around them in the cage she had begun to feel ridiculously trapped by the netting. She turned away from Jacob and let out a deep breath, desperately keeping it from sounding like another sigh.

'Nothing to see, and you have nothing to tell.' Jacob climbed out of the cage, and closed the door. 'In that case,' he said, carefully replacing the wooden peg in the metal hasp, 'you won't mind if I ask *Dad* what the problem is.' He grinned, just as he had when he was ten years old and his latest misdemeanour was about to be revealed. 'Will you?'

Emma sighed, deeply, not hiding it.

'Come and sit down,' she said. On the paved area that surrounded the shed were two yellow metal chairs tucked under a small round metal table. Emma pulled out one of the chairs and sat down, suddenly very weary. She had no idea what she was going to say to Jacob; she would let him start the conversation, see where his questions led, and hope to God she could find answers that would satisfy him.

'I don't need to be Einstein to see that something's wrong.' Jacob pulled out the other chair, sat down, took Emma's hands in his. 'Right, spill the beans,' he said.

This was not how Emma wanted it to be. 'I don't know what beans you want me to spill,' she said, hesitantly, hoping it sounded as if there were no beans at all. 'Your father's been very ill and I'm very tired. What else is there to know? Come on, let's go home,' she said, getting up. 'I'm getting cold and the damp underfoot is not good for your foot.' She began walking across the gravel and out on to the path.

'All right, Mum. I get the message.' Jacob stood up, pushed in the chair. He closed the gate of No.28 and followed Emma along the path. With the outer gate securely locked, they walked side by side up the lane to the village street. Just before they reached the junction Jacob stopped, turned around, his back to the street, facing his mother. 'If you won't tell me what's been going on …' Emma could feel his eyes, the gold flecks glinting in the sudden sunlight, piercing hers; her heart began to race: this was the Jacob who annoyed his father, the Jacob who nearly always got his own way. '... then I shall just have to ask Bernie. He knows, I'm sure of it.'

'No, Jacob, don't do that. Please.' Emma grabbed his arm. 'I will tell you.' What could she tell him, though, that wouldn't bring the whole, already flimsy, house of cards down on their heads? 'But not just now.'

'All right, but don't leave it too long.'

He had manoeuvred her, as he had always done. She'd never minded before; in fact she had quite enjoyed it. Not this time, though.

'I won't,' she said. 'But do let's get home now.' She began walking very quickly up the street, leaving Jacob to follow in her wake; she didn't want to have to stop and talk nor introduce Jacob to anyone.

'Hold on, Mum,' he said. 'I can't walk at your speed with this foot! I didn't know you'd taken up Power-walking.'

'I haven't,' Emma called over her shoulder, 'I just want to get home, I'm getting cold.' She slowed, giving Jacob time to catch up with her. They turned into *The Rectory* drive and Emma led the way over the side lawn to the back of the house. 'Just going to put out some more bird food,' she said, suddenly swerving away from the door and crossing to the cedar summerhouse.

'I thought you were cold.'

'I am, but I must do this; I forgot to do it earlier.' Emma opened the glazed summerhouse door and a blast of sun-warmed air greeted her. 'Oh, that's nice.' She reached up to a high shelf and lifted down a net of fat balls and a box of bird seed. 'You do the seeds,' she said, handing the box to Jacob, 'and I'll do the balls.' They walked across the lawn to the ornate bird station outside the kitchen. A quick glance through the window assured her that no one was in there, watching for their return. Perhaps this would be as good a time as any to tell Jacob what had been going on; no details, just a brief, heavily edited, account. She hoped that what she had to say would satisfy him; the last thing she wanted was Jacob questioning Bernie, especially in Andrew's presence.

With the bird food in place, Emma took the box from her son's hand. 'Let's go and sit in the summerhouse,' she said. With the door closed and the low winter sun streaming directly on to them, it was cosy in there. They watched as a pair of magpies that had been strutting about on the grass launched themselves at the wire cage that held the fat balls; with wings beating rapidly they pecked hungrily at the food.

Emma sat down on the bench, patted the seat beside her. 'So, what is it you want to know?'

'Well, for starters,' said Jacob, sitting down, 'why a stroke? I mean … had he been ill, and you'd not told me or …?'

'No no, he'd not been ill. I think it was the business, too much paperwork, you know, forms and all that; there's so much of it nowadays. Far from cutting down on it, computers just seem to have increased the volume.'

'Okay, so … you're saying you don't know?'

‘No, not really.’

‘Strange … umm. There must have been some reason.’ Jacob looked at her quizzically. Was he waiting for more from her? He stood up, took off his coat. ‘That’s better. It’s getting really hot in here,’ he said and sat down again. ‘Okay. So, next question.’

Emma gave an inward sigh of relief; she was glad Jacob had not pushed her on the reason for the stroke; she had been about to tell him that his father, for some reason that she did not yet fully understand – except that it might be connected to a village shop, and how ridiculous that would sound! – had been under a great of stress lately, and stress could cause a stroke.

‘Fire away,’ she said, confidently.

‘You and Bernie,’ he said, smiling at her.

‘What?’ Emma’s hands went cold, her mouth was dry.

‘I’m not a kid, Mum; I notice things. About people. The signals they give. I need to in my work.’

‘Farming? What signals do you need for that?’ Anything to divert him from Bernie. ‘From the animals maybe; they can’t tell you what’s wrong; but humans … I wouldn’t have thought you’d …’

‘I’m not on a farm.’

‘What d’you mean, you’re not ...?’

‘I haven’t been working on a farm for a couple of years.’ Jacob got up, stood in front of the glazed door, blocking Emma’s sunlight. Involuntarily she shivered. ‘I work in the city now, in a psychiatric clinic.’ He turned round, sat down beside his mother again. ‘I had a breakdown,’ he said, not looking at her.

'Oh, darling.' Emma put a hand on his arm, began to stroke it. 'Why didn't you …?'

'No, please.' Jacob shook his head, waved his hands, palms forward, pushing away his mother's concern. 'I don't want to talk about it; not now.' He stood up, his back to her.

'Yes, all right, if you don't want to, but … How are you now? Darling, I need to know.'

'Mum, I'm fine. I've had counselling and I'm on medication, and yes, I *am* taking it.' He turned round, stretched out his arms to Emma. 'I'm sorry. Come here,' he said.

She stood up, and let herself be encircled by Jacob's arms, her own arms clasped tightly around his waist. After a few moments they instinctively drew apart, Emma not wanting Connie or Andrew, wandering into the garden, to find them like this; Jacob, Emma thought, probably feeling the same.

'I was only farming to get Dad off my back. I never liked it and I was no good at it.'

'Oh, darling.' The sun was now warming Emma's face again, but no amount of sunshine could take away the chill she felt inside. 'Why … why did you keep this from me?'

'I didn't want to, but … I didn't want to worry you … and I didn't want Dad to know. I was already a disappointment to him.'

'No, I wouldn't say …'

'Mum, there's no point in being nice about this; I know I was, but I didn't want to add to it, by telling you …'

'I wouldn't have told him!'

'No, I don't think you would, not intentionally, but I wasn't going to lay that burden onto you. I mean …' A wry smile. '... it's not easy, is it, keeping secrets?'

Emma felt herself blushing. He'd be good, she thought, working with people who had emotional problems. She wished she'd known that was what he was doing. She wouldn't have told Andrew; Jacob's soft, sensitive side, which was coming into its own now, had always annoyed his father; 'unmanly' he had called it. The recollection of Andrew using the word – she couldn't now recall why – prompted another thought: was her son gay? For her it would be no problem, but for his father … There was more than enough going on already without introducing that possibility into the equation.

'So … the gun.' She nodded towards his foot. 'Did you get shot, or was it just an excuse not to come home; I wouldn't blame you, I know how difficult …'

'No, I wouldn't have done that. I really did get shot. There are plenty of guns in South Africa. A patient shot me; he was high on … well, never mind what it was. It was an accident, he wasn't trying to harm me; it just went off and my foot was in the way.' He smiled, pulled Emma back onto the bench. 'Anyway, that's enough about me; let's get back to you and Bernie.'

'Oh, Jacob, let's not.'

'You can tell me, can't you? I'm not judging you, Mum.'

Although Emma had no intention of revealing the details – nor even an outline – of their relationship to her son, his stillness soothed her, and she said, quite calmly, 'It's not an affair. We've been through a bad time, both of us, and we felt in need of … of comfort.' That, for now, is all he needs to know.

The sound of a car coming at speed into the drive, then braking hard, broke into her thoughts.

'That sounds like Bernie's car,' Jacob said.

'It is,' Emma said, getting up. 'We'd best get inside.' She pushed open the summerhouse door and walked, almost ran, across the lawn.

'Mu-m,' Jacob called after her. 'I won't say anything, you know.'

'I know you won't; it's just … Bernie only drives like that when he's upset.'

CHAPTER THIRTY-SIX

He slammed the car door and crunched his way noisily across the gravel to the front door, banged hard on the knocker.

'What is the matter?' Emma, with Jacob close behind her, appeared from the side of the house. 'Bernie?'

'Sorry,' Bernie said. 'I didn't mean to hit it so hard, I just …' Suddenly all the wind had gone out of his sails.

'There has to be something wrong, the way you drove in!'

'Bernard!' Constance, at the door. Then, seeing her sister, 'Emma? What's going on?'

'Nothing is *going on.*'

'Sorry, Constance, it was just me, being noisy.'

'Yes, well … you might have a little more consideration for Andrew.'

'Why? Is he not feeling well?'

'He could have been sleeping.'

'Oh. Was he?'

'No … but he might …'

'Oh, Connie, for goodness sake, move out of the way and let's all go inside.' Emma pushed past her sister into the hall. 'Come on, Bernie,' she said, turning round to him.

'And you, Jacob. I don't know what you're laughing at. It's not funny, it's just silly, the three of us standing around getting cold for no good reason!'

'Hey, cool it, Mum!' Jacob looked enquiringly at Bernie.

I wonder how much he knows, Bernie thought. Not that it matters; very soon he'll know it all. Well, maybe not *all.* Not about Emma; that must come from her. But the rest of it …

'What?' he asked.

'I said,' Emma began, 'you look awful, as if you haven't slept.'

'I haven't.'

'Why not?'

'Because …' Blearily he looked around the hall. Constance and Jacob had disappeared somewhere; he and Emma were alone. 'Can you sleep?' he whispered.

'Not very well, but … Oh Bernie, please don't do anything stupid. What if he were to have a gun?'

'A gun? Oh, come on, Emm.' She couldn't really think that. Could she? If he had frightened her … 'Andrew? No. Never.' He realised he was shouting. He looked quickly around the hall; there was no one else there. He took her hands.

'He won't have,' he said, his voice quiet again. He smiled at her. 'You know he won't.' Emma nodded. 'Don't worry, I'm not going to do anything stupid, or dangerous. Just one more thing though before we go in … How much does Jacob know?'

'Nothing. I haven't said a word to him.'

‘I know that you and Mum have been having a … sort of affair.’ Jacob stood in the cloakroom doorway.

‘Jesus!’ Bernie turned to Emma, his already pallid face now completely white. ‘Did you tell him?!’

‘She didn’t need to; I read the signs.’

‘No, Jacob, don’t. Please.’

‘It’s all right, Mum. I’m not saying any more.’

‘I’d best go home,’ Bernie said.

‘Yes, I think you should,’ Emma said, hurriedly; she, too, had gone pale.

‘Don’t go. Come on, man, come inside. I’ll get you a drink; you look as if you could do with one.’

‘No thanks, Jacob, I don’t want …’

The lounge doors opened and Andrew stepped up into the hall. ‘Bernie. Hello! I thought I heard your voice.’ It only needs Constance back here, Bernie thought, and then we have the full cast.

‘Hi,’ Bernie said. He so wanted not to be here, but could he leave … now? Willing Jacob not to say anything, he walked across the Chinese rug, stretched out his hand to Andrew. ‘You’re looking good.’

‘It’s more than I can say for you. Have you had a shave today?’

Bernie rubbed his chin. ‘No, I don’t think I have.’

‘Don’t say you’re going in for this awful stubble that everyone has now; it makes you look dirty.’

‘No, I am not about to grow a stubble!’ Bernie knew it was insignificant, it didn’t matter … but it riled him. So very much.

'I'll have that drink, Jacob,' he said. 'Shall we all go into the lounge; I have one or two things I need to say.'

'Bernie, no,' Emma whispered.

'Yes, Emma. I don't know about you, but I can't hold on to this any longer.' He stepped down into the lounge, crossed over to the dining area, and called through the door to the kitchen. 'Constance, would you come in here, please.'

'Coming,' Constance said, cheerily. Then, seeing Jacob holding the whisky decanter, 'Oh, we're having drinks, are we?' She looked at her watch. 'Yes, I suppose it is nearly lunchtime. I'll have a sherry, please, Jacob. Andrew, what would you like? Ginger ale?'

Bernie, sweating, began to have the feeling that he had strayed into a drawing-room comedy by Terence Rattigan or Noel Coward, the sort of thing he had once acted in with a Chigwell drama group.

'Yes, that'll do nicely. Thanks, Connie.' Andrew said, easing himself down into an armchair.

'Mum?'

'No, thank you, nothing for me.' She could hardly get the words out, let alone swallow a drink.

'Bernie?'

'Scotch. And water.' He crossed to the window, stood for a moment with his back to everyone. Behind him, partly muffled by the drumming in his ears, he heard Connie take her drink, give Andrew his, say something to Emma. Then close beside him, Jacob's voice, loud.

'Your scotch, Bernie.'

'Thanks,' he said, taking the crystal tumbler.

'You okay?' Jacob asked.

'Yes, I'm fine. Just … Sit down everybody, will you. Please.'

Jacob looked across at his mother, standing by the lounge door, as if poised for flight. 'Mum, come and sit by me,' he said, beckoning her to the long sofa. Only Constance remained standing.

'You, too, please, Constance,' Bernie said.

'Bernard, what is all this about? You are looking very serious. Has something bad happened?'

'Indeed, Constance, something has.' I couldn't have asked for a better lead-in line, Bernie thought.

'What?' Andrew leant forward on his stick.

'Has someone died?' Jacob asked.

'No.' Bernie looked startled. That's all we need, he thought.

'Oh well, that's a relief. It was beginning to feel like *Death in Paradise.*'

'What *are* you talking about, Jacob?'

'You know, Dad, the programme where there's been a murder on a tropical island, and the police guy out from England gathers all the suspects together and questions them.'

'No, never seen it.'

'No, Jacob, there's been no murder …' Bernie knew he sounded abrupt, but for heaven's sake, it was hard enough to say what he wanted to, without a diversion from Jacob.

'Oh, pleased to know that,' Jacob said.

'... but there have been other things … unpleasant things …' He knew the word was inadequate, but it was the best he could come up with that wouldn't get them asking questions before he had even got started. '... and it's time you all knew about them.' Four faces, with mixed expressions, were turned to him: Emma fearful, her body trembling; Jacob, puzzled – so Emma had said nothing; Constance anxious; Andrew ... well, he couldn't read Andrew; all three emotions were there, on Andrew's face, overlaid by what Bernie could only describe as scorn.

Jacob was the first to respond. 'Well then,' he said, 'tell us. The sooner we get the credits rolling on this episode the better.'

Andrew looked at him blankly; Constance's mouth twitched, in what could have been the beginning of a smile; she obviously watches the show, Bernie thought. Emma, reaching for Jacob's hand, said hoarsely, 'Yes, if you must.'

'I'm sorry, Emma.' He looked at her wistfully, wishing he'd not started down this road, 'but we have to.'

'I know,' she whispered. 'Tell them.'

'I wouldn't be doing it if I didn't think it absolutely necessary.' If he could back out now he would; he'd grab hold of Emma's hand, lift her off the sofa, whisk her away ... He'd had the chance to pull back there in the hall, when Jacob had spoken to him; even in the lounge he might still have called a halt, but no – he'd let a trivial thing like Andrew's comment on his unshaven face ...

'Oh, for heaven's sake, Bernie, whatever it is you have to say, get on with it.' Andrew, not looking at him, banged his stick down on the floor.

In all the wakeful hours last night Bernie had never for one moment considered how Andrew would react. A bad oversight, he said to himself. What's more, he should never have tackled it like this, as if he were on a stage, or summing up the evidence in a court of law. He should have taken Andrew aside, had it out 'man to man'; after thirty years of comradeship he owed him that much - perhaps if Constance hadn't interrupted them the evening before … It would have appealed to Andrew's better nature; the gentlemanly way, he would have called it. He had a fleeting image of himself and Andrew in eighteenth century dress wielding swords. It had seemed so straightforward, too, in the middle of the night – he had worked it all out, what he would say, how he would say it.

'Yes, please do, Bernard. We'd had more than enough of your theatricals.'

'Theatricals, Auntie Con? Oh, wow.'

'Shush,' Emma said.

'Unfortunately, Constance, this is not a scene in a play.' He had them all now, waiting for his next words. Somehow, though, he couldn't start: his heart was beating too fast; he knew alcohol was not the cure ... and he had to drive home ... but he felt he needed it. 'Fill my glass up, Jacob, will you. More water in it this time, please.' He held out the tumbler.

'Sure.' Jacob released Emma's hand and got up from the sofa, re-filled Bernie's glass and took it back to him.

Bernie took a long drink, put the tumbler down on the small table beside his chair.

'Thirty years ago …' He looked directly at Jacob: he daren't look at anyone else, '... when your father and I were at Cambridge, we used to visit a shop in one of the villages between Cambridge and Hertford. The village was Brockwood, and the shop was one of those wonderful places that sold just about everything you could think of, from Wellington boots to chewing gum; it had a bacon-slicer and a …'

'Like the one here,' Constance said, brightly.

'Yes, probably,' Bernie said, daring to take a glance at Andrew, head up, mouth turned down, basilisk eyes focused on the ceiling; the knuckles of the hand on his stick … white. 'As I was saying … a shop that sold everything, and also ran a Christmas Club for the …'

'Ah. For the kids, was it?' Jacob smiled. 'Oh, very nice.' No one else was smiling. 'Oh. Not so nice?'

'Oh yes, it was a very nice idea,' Bernie said, crossly. 'Throughout the year the people in the village deposited money with the shopkeeper, and come Christmas …'

'They had money to spend in the shop! Oh, great idea. Very enterprising.' Jacob was grinning.

Bernie glared at him; he's trying to prevent me from saying something, but I don't know what. A look passed between Jacob and his mother. Is he afraid I'll tell his father about us? Bernie forced his mouth into a fleeting smile. 'Yes, Jacob, it was a good idea, only this particular year …' Out of the corner of his eye Bernie could see that Jacob was about to interrupt again. 'It doesn't matter which year, Jacob.'

'Yes, all right.'

'This year, the one I have in mind, the Christmas Club money was stolen, and the shopkeeper and his wife were tied up and gagged.'

'Oh, how awful.' Constance said, her face contorted with disgust.

‘Yes, it was.’ Emma, her voice a bare whisper, was looking down at her hands.

‘Yeah, well, okay.’ Jacob said. ‘Well, not okay, obviously … but what’s it got to do with us? Bernie?’

Would Andrew now speak? Bernie waited. No, he would not. Bernie drew in a deep breath, then, letting it out slowly, word by word, he said, ‘It was your father, Jacob, who tied up the shopkeeper and stole the money.’

There, it was out; he’d said it.

No one spoke, no one moved; it was as if his words had put them all into a trance. Slowly Bernie turned his head: Emma – oh God, what had he done to her? – was still looking at her hands; Andrew’s eyes remained concentrated on the ceiling, his face totally inscrutable. Constance, after a sharp intake of breath, was frowning: she’s processing it all, Bernie thought. She can’t credit what I have just said; she doesn’t want to believe it either. And then Jacob: his eyes wide open, questioning, were focused on Bernie. How Bernie wished he could tell his best friend’s son that it was all a mistake, even a bad joke. He knew Jacob did not like his father, probably didn’t love him either, but he had, to a certain extent, respected him, even admired him, although he would never have said so, certainly not directly to Andrew, for the way he had made his way in the world, not asking for help from anyone. And now, in just a few words, Bernie had shattered Jacob’s illusion of his father as a man of probity.

He reached for his whisky; the tumbler was empty.

Very slowly, as if, Bernie thought, he’s trying not to disturb the charged air in the room, Jacob stood up, went over to the table and picked up the decanter; he crossed in front of his father, took the tumbler from Bernie's hand, refilled the glass … and threw the whisky in his face.

Whatever Bernie had expected, it wasn't this. He sprang back, his hands raised defensively.

Jacob's action served to release everyone else from their frozen state.

'I'll get a cloth,' Constance said – some of the liquid had splashed onto the armchair – springing up and dashing through the dining area into the kitchen; Emma, her face screwed up in agony, burst into tears; Andrew, face deathly pale, jaw set, bore down heavily on his stick and heaved himself up from the sofa. With his free hand he pushed aside Jacob's outstretched hand. Bernie moved to help him climb the two steps into the hall.

'I don't need your help either!' Breathing hard and using the handrail, Andrew pulled himself up the first step.

'Andrew, let me …' Constance, coming back with a J-cloth and disinfectant spray in her hand, ran across to him, put her free hand on his arm.

'No, leave me alone,' he said, shaking her off and mounting the top step.

'But …'

'No, Connie. Please.' He stomped his way across the hall to his office.

'Jesus, Uncle Bern, I'm sorry.' Jacob said.

'Why … why did you … do that?' Emma's words came out between her sobs.

'Mum, I'm sorry, I didn't mean to …' Swiftly he put his arm around her, his fingers resting on her shoulder.

'No,' she said, grabbing his hand, 'not you, darling. Bernie! What the hell did …'

'But you wanted … you said … We had to.'

'Yes, but not like that! It was so brutal, so …'

'Oh Mum, come on, there's no easy way to say something like that …' Jacob looked questioningly at Bernie, '... if it's true.'

'Oh, it's true.' Bernie said. 'I wish to God it weren't.'

'I'm sorry, Bernard …' Connie's voice was sharp; she said his name as if it was a curse. 'I don't for one moment believe you.' She was standing in the hall, J-cloth and disinfectant spray still in her hand. '... and I can't think why you could possibly want to invent such an accusation against your best – well, you say he is your best friend, but I …'

'Connie, dear.' Emma pulled her hand away from Jacob's hold and placed it tenderly on Constance's arm. 'It *is* true. I wish I could tell you it wasn't, but it is.'

'Are you part of this, Jacob?'

'No, Auntie Con. It's as much of a surprise to me … well, a shock, actually … as it is to you; although, I would have thought that you, being here, would know …'

'What would I know?'

'Well, whatever there was to know.' Jacob looked for help from his mother.

'You'd better tell them, Bernie, about the notebooks and …'

'Notebooks? *Andrew's* notebooks? The ones you took from his office?' Constance looked accusingly at Bernie. 'The ones Emma gave you?'

'Yes. The ones that Emma brought for me to see, so that we could update our stock by contacting some of Andrew's regular suppliers; but without bothering him, in hospital.'

'I see, but … I'm sorry, Bernard, but I can't make the connection between that … and the … the appalling words you uttered earlier.'

Deeply Bernie sighed. 'Come and sit down, Constance, and I'll tell you.' He leant forward, extended his hand to her.

'No,' she said briskly, waving the proffered hand away as if she found it offensive. 'I do not wish to *sit down.* You can tell me right here, in the doorway.'

'Very well.'

'You're a better man than me, Auntie Con,' Jacob said, 'I'm sitting down; I don't think I could take it, whatever it is, standing up, specially not with my bad foot.'

'Stop it, Jacob! This is not a joke!'

'Sorry, Mum. I know it's not. I will sit down though, if you don't mind; my foot *is* aching.'

'Oh dear, is it?' For a brief moment concern for Jacob overtook Constance's fury at Bernie.

'I'm fine, Auntie Con,' he said, lowering himself into an armchair. 'I can hear perfectly well from here. Go on, Bernie, tell us what's been going on. There's no need to shield me from anything; I know all about life in the raw, living in South Africa, as Mum will tell you.'

'Jacob, please stop; this is important. And now that Bernie has started all this …'

'I rather thought it was Dad who'd …'

'Shut up, Jacob. Your mother's right; this is important … and much as I regret it, you do need to know. And you, Constance.'

Briefly Bernie told them what he and Emma had found in the drawer in Andrew's office, *The Mercury* cuttings and the notebooks, and the inevitable conclusion they had drawn from all of it.

'Blackmail! Christ!' Jacob shook his head in disbelief. 'But …?'

'Let me finish,' Bernie said.

'You've heard the worst,' Emma said. It hurt her to see her boy so distressed. And Constance, too.

Jacob listened in silence as Bernie told them about the meeting with Garry and his sister, and finally the incident at *The Oaks*.

'Poor Andrew,' Constance said. 'He has suffered so much.'

'Connie!' Emma turned on her. 'He stole from those people! And he hurt them!'

'I know,' Constance said, 'but he would have had a good reason.'

'Oh yes, he'd have had a reason!' Jacob, up from his chair, pacing the room, was furious. 'He always had a reason, and it was always one that suited him.' He stopped pacing, stood still, glaring at everyone. 'Bastard!'

'Jacob dear …' Constance began to walk towards him. 'You can't possibly understand.'

'No?'

'No.' She stopped in front of him. 'You have never had to steal … so that your nearest and dearest can have the things in life they want or need.'

'Well, nor have you!' Jacob retorted, moving away from her.

'Oh, I have.' Constance, trembling, wrung the J-cloth in her hand.

'Connie?' Emma moved across the floor and touched her sister gently on the arm.

Constance swung round. 'Oh yes. You, of course, have no idea what it is like to go without. And as for you, Bernard, with your precious silver spoon in your mouth ...'

'Yes, all right, I had it easy, but ...' He had no idea what she was getting at, other than making him feel uncomfortable; nor, as he could see from her face, had Emma. What had not surprised him was Constance leaping to Andrew's defence. Maybe that was all it was; deflecting everyone else's disapprobation away from him, the man she – it was obvious to him now – the man she loved. He had always suspected it; now he was sure.

Gently, Jacob took the torn cloth from his aunt's hand, guided her to a chair and lowered her onto it.

'So, Constance,' Bernie said, looking down at her, 'what dreadful sin did you commit in your youth?' He had been unable to keep the sarcasm out of his voice; not that he cared.

'Oh Bernie, Connie'd never …'

'Yes, Bernard, it was a sin. Stealing is a sin, so is covetousness … and I was guilty of both, which is why I am the only one here who really understands Andrew. He stole to give Emma a better home and …'

'No, no, that's not right,' Bernie said. 'That wasn't the reason.'

'It was part of it,' Constance said. 'He needed to put money into the business so that he could provide a better home for Emma, just as I stole to feed you!'

'What? No!'

'Oh yes, my dear, I did. From the local shops … and department stores. Extra food, and toys, too. We had so very little. Our mother was incapable of looking after you … and our father … Well, he could always find another use for his money.'

'Oh, Connie … Why did you never say?'

'Would you have wanted to know?'

'Well … no. Not then, but … How old was I … when you were doing this?'

'About six, seven; I was thirteen. We all did it, all the girls in my class at school. For some of them it was just a bit of fun; you know, see what you could pinch before anyone noticed, but for me it was … it became, as things got more difficult at home, a necessity.'

'Oh, Connie, I know how much you looked after me when Mum was … and then when she died, but I had no idea …'

'No, and I wouldn't have said anything now, but for the fact that you were all so appalled at what Andrew had done, as if it was something quite beyond your ken, not at all the sort of thing that nice people living in Chigwell or Pengate would ever do; and certainly not boys who went to schools like Repton or Aldenham; but of course Andrew never went to that sort of school, did he? So, in a way, you might expect it of *him.*' She forced her features into a tight smile. 'So, there you are,' she said, looking up at Bernie.

'Yes,' he said, not quite knowing what to say, or think. Except that Connie's circumstances he could understand, even commend. Poor little Emma. And Connie, too. Behind the smile he had seen the held-back tears.

'And, of course,' Constance said, looking now at Emma, 'there's the blackmail. What a burden that must have been all these years … for both of you.'

'I knew nothing about it!'

'No, but it was that much money going out of the household every month …'

'I never missed anything; I wasn't aware of the blackmail, so how could I …?

'There was no blackmail.'

Andrew, leaning on his stick, was standing at the top of the stairs.

CHAPTER THIRTY-SEVEN

'What?' Emma spun round.

'Oh, my God,' Bernie said, under his breath.

'I'm sure you heard me, Emma, and you, Bernie, but I'll say it again: There. Was. No. Blackmail. Or, to put it another way, if you can't take in that simple sentence … I was *not* blackmailed, not by Freddie Gesson, nor anyone.'

'But … the money … the money that Garry had?'

'Oh yes, Garry.' He gave a faint, sarcastic laugh. 'Presumably you met him?' He was looking at Bernie now. 'I don't mean just that day at *The Oaks*. Very clever the way you contrived that, all being there at the same time. And so thoughtful, making sure I didn't really get hurt. Thank you for that; your work, was that, Emma?'

Confused by this turn of events, Emma could find no words with which to answer her husband. Instinctively she looked to Bernie for help.

'Oh, that's right, turn to your confederate for help. You've had a good time, haven't you, the pair of you, while I've been out of the way.'

'Dad, don't do this.' Jacob sprang up, and pushing his way past Emma - 'Sorry, Mum' - he ran up the stairs and took hold of his father's arm. 'Come and sit down.'

Andrew shook him off. 'No, thank you. I'd rather say what I have to from here.'

'I don't think that's a very good idea, Andrew; you obviously want to say quite a bit to us …' Gently Constance took hold of Andrew's arm and began to steer him into the lounge, ' … and you'll soon begin to get chilly if you stay out here.'

'Yes, yes, all right. Thank you, Connie. Bless you. I sometimes think you're the only one who really cares about me.'

'Oh no, dear, no. We *all* care about you. Don't we?' Constance beamed, first at Bernie and Emma, then at Jacob. Their faces were showing anything but care for Andrew: they looked hostile, troubled and perplexed.

'Yes, of course.' Bernie, his face now showing the appropriate amount of care, was the first to reply.

Emma, having suitably rearranged her face, managed, 'Of course we do, Connie.'

'Good,' Constance said. 'Jacob, bring over that high-backed chair. It will be more comfortable for your father.'

'Will do,' Jacob said.

'Put it just here, by the sofa.'

'Thank you, Jacob,' Andrew said, stiffly. He settled himself into the chair. 'And you, Connie.' He reached out and patted her hand.

Emma had watched in silence while this little pantomime – it was how she thought of it – was being enacted, but now, much as she wanted to run away from everything that was going on, she felt she had to speak. She wished Bernie would say something, but if he wasn't going to, for some reason she didn't comprehend, then she would have to: they couldn't continue in this polite drawing-room manner, not after what Andrew had said. If she didn't intervene now, Connie would be asking them if they'd like lunch here or in the dining-room!

'What did you mean, when you said there was no blackmail, when we both know …' she glanced at Bernie, '... that there was?'

'Precisely what I said. *I was not blackmailed!*'

'All right! Enough of this, Andrew.' Bernie's voice was harsh. 'You may not have been blackmailed …'

'I was not! How many more times do I … ?'

' … Okay! Blackmailed or not – we'll come to that later – *you* committed a serious criminal act … and you have been found out.' By rights, the man should have served a prison sentence! 'A bit late in the day, admittedly, and no consolation to those poor people in Brockwood …'

'That is where you are wrong.'

'Oh, you mean they enjoyed being robbed, and tied up and gagged! Andrew, you're a thief and a liar!'

'Yes, I am. I admit it. I should have admitted it years ago.'

'Well, why didn't you?'

'I didn't have the courage; I didn't want everything I had built up to come crashing down … and it would have done. And then what? I go to gaol, my wife hates me, my business partner throws me out …'

'I wouldn't have …'

'... my own accountancy business goes down the drain. Do you want me to go on? In a nutshell, Bernie, I had too much to lose.'

'Why,' asked Emma, quietly, 'did you do it in the first place?'

'Why do you think? I needed money.'

'But you had money; you had that money from Auntie Anna.'

Bernie's laugh was derisory. 'Oh, Emma, you don't still believe that, do you?'

'Well … I want to.'

'Good, because it was true. But not all of it. The original cheque, yes. That *was* from her. The rest of it came from … from what I did. There. Now you know.'

'So that parcel of land …?'

'There never was any land.'

'Andrew, dear …' Constance began to stroke Andrew's arm. 'why did you feel the need to do these terrible things?'

'Why? For Emma … and Bernie … and the business we had set up together.'

'There was plenty for the business.'

'Oh yes, plenty of your money; no shortage there. But how d'you think that made me feel? Poor old Andrew, born on a council estate, can't expect much capital from him; never mind, Rose and I have enough. If he just contributes his skill with numbers, that'll be enough.'

'Jesus, Andrew, do you really think I felt like that?'

'You may not have done, but I did! I had ambition, Bernie, and I wasn't going to let the fact that I had no money get in my way!'

'So you stole it.'

'I didn't look at it like that ...'

'Oh, for God's sake! What other way is there to look at it?'

'I saw it as a ... a sort of loan.'

'This gets better every minute,' Jacob said.

'A loan?' Bernie ran his hands through his hair. 'Jesus, Andrew, what kind of a man are you?'

'A man who does pay back a loan.'

'A man who ... Oh, my God, Jackie was right. You did.'

Andrew, his closed mouth set in a sardonic smile, nodded.

'Jackie? What's Jackie got to do with it?' Emma asked.

'She said ... We were trying to think of possible alternatives to blackmail, and she suggested that ... that Andrew might be the one who had ... sent the money ... to Freddie Gesson.'

If Bernie goes on tearing at his hair like that he going to pull it out, Emma thought; she had never really believed in that expression before, but now it was happening in front of her.

'Clever Jackie.' Andrew's smile was now real.

'You may have given it back but you should never have taken it in the first place. Should you?' Emma's eyes were blazing. 'I hate what you *did*, and I hate *you* for doing it!' With her face screwed up in agony she spat the words at him.

'But darling ... I did it for *you* ... for *us*, so that we could have ...'

‘You didn’t do it for *me*. You did it for yourself! All of it. Jacob’s posh school, this house, even your concern for the village shop! Just so that you could be the big man you never really were …’

‘Emma dear, that’s very harsh,’ Constance stretched out a hand to her sister.

‘No, Connie, it’s not. It’s the truth.’

‘Well, yes, Andrew did take the money …’

‘I’m not talking just about the money! Can’t you see, I’m talking about him! The person he is; the person who could do … !’ Her eyes almost blinded by tears, Emma threw herself at the patio doors, pushed them violently apart and rushed out into the garden.

‘Mum!’ Jacob sped after her. ‘Mum, come back. You’ll freeze out there.’ She was halfway across the lawn before he caught up with her.

Hearing him, Emma stopped running, and turning round buried her head in his chest.

‘Oh, Jacob …’ she sobbed.

‘Come back into the house.’

Over Jacob’s shoulder she could see Bernie and Constance, standing in the patio doorway. Much as she had wanted to throw herself into Bernie’s arms, she was relieved that he had not followed her; there was quite enough pain and anguish washing around already without adding the revelation of *their* relationship to the mix.

‘No I can’t, not yet.’

‘All right, then come into the summer house; it’ll still be warm in there.’

‘And there are blankets,’ Emma said, ‘I could stay there all night.’

‘Oh Mum, you won’t have to do that.’ He guided her across the lower lawn and opened the summerhouse door. ‘I was right, it *is* still warm; we shan’t need your blankets. Come on, sit down.’ He took hold of both her arms and gently seated on the padded bench. ‘There. All right?’

Emma looked up at him, smiled weakly. ‘Yes.’ she said. ‘No, of course I’m not. Oh, Jacob … what am I going to do?’

‘Well, that’s easy, Mum, you’re coming to South Africa with me.’

‘No no, I can’t! I can’t possibly do that.’

‘Why not?’

‘Well, because … I can’t run away. I've never run away. I wanted to, sometimes ... but I never did it.'

‘Well, now you can. And it’s not running away, it’s just … giving yourself a break from all that’s been going on.’

‘I don’t see how I can ever get away from it.’

‘You can’t now, but you will.’

Emma shook her head violently. ‘No, you don’t understand. All these years .. I’ve been living with a man I don’t know!’ Her body shook with sobs.

‘Mum … it’s all right. Shush now.’

Gradually her sobbing subsided; she sat up and wiped away her tears with the back of her hand.

‘Here.’ Jacob took a handkerchief out of his trouser pocket, handed it to Emma.

‘Ta,’ she said, and blew her nose. ‘Heavens!’ She looked down at the handkerchief. ‘A clean white hankie. You’ve obviously got someone doing your washing for you.’

‘Yes,’ Jacob said, ‘We ... I have.’

‘Who?’

‘Never mind that; I want to tell you something. About my life …’

Emma looked up at him. ‘You did, you said you’d given up farm ...’

‘No, not that. This is about *me*, me personally.’

This is where he tells me he’s gay. Emma took a deep breath. ‘Well, what?’ she said.

‘I have a partner.’

‘Oh. Good.’ It wasn’t much of an answer, she knew that, but it was the best she could manage until Jacob said more.

‘Someone I love very much.’

‘Oh, darling, I’m so pleased for you.’ Come on, tell me. ‘What is … your partner’s name?’

‘Naledi.’

‘Naledi? Oh, that’s …’ A man or a woman? ‘I don’t think I’ve come across that name before.’

‘It means a star. She’s African, she’s …’

‘Oh. Oh, I see.’ Emma wouldn’t have minded if Jacob had been gay, but now … a possible daughter-in-law. ‘Oh, darling, that’s wonderful!’ She hugged him, joyously.

‘Yes, it is.’ He laughed; relieved, she could see. ‘I think you’ll love my Naledi.’ Suddenly she understood; this is why Jacob had come home, not because of his father’s stroke, but to tell her his own news; she only had to look at his face as he said her name, Naledi, to know how much he cared for her.

'Oh, my darling, if she makes you happy, I love her already. Do you have a photograph of her?'

'Yes, lots of them,' He took out his phone, 'but before I show them to you I want to tell you something else.'

'Go on.' She had no qualms now; she knew that whatever it was it would be good. And God knows she needed good news. Painfully her thoughts were jolted back to the lounge … to Andrew and the robbery. Andrew: if Jacob wanted him to know, well, that was up to him. 'Tell me!'

Jacob's grin spread from ear to ear. 'We're having a baby.'

'Oh! Oh, Jacob!' Emma threw her arms around his neck. 'Darling, that's wonderful. Oh, that is so lovely.' She drew back, looked at him, her smile as wide as his.

'I'm so glad you're pleased.'

'What else would I be? I'm going to be a grandmother!' She leant over and kissed him. 'Now show me the pictures,' she said.

'Can anyone join in, or is this a private viewing?'

So engrossed were they both in the photographs – 'Oh, she's beautiful; she's tall, isn't she?' 'Yes, she is; in high heels, she's nearly up to me.' 'I love her beaded hair' – that they'd not heard the summerhouse door opening.

'Bernie!'

'Hi, Uncle Bern.'

'What are you looking at?'

‘It’s Jacob’s partner. Look,’ Emma took hold of the phone, turned the screen towards Bernie. ‘Isn’t she lovely? Her name’s Naledi.’

‘Gorgeous-looking woman. How’d you come to meet her?’

‘She’s a nurse; she works in the clinic, where I …’

‘Jacob’s not in farming anymore,’ Emma interposed quickly.

‘Fine.’ Bernie shrugged. ‘Whatever’s best for him.’

‘Thanks, Bernie.’

‘Listen … um … I hate to break this up, but I think you should both come back inside; there’s a few things I should still like to get clear.’

‘Oh no, not more. Please.’

‘I'm sorry, Emm, but I really would like to know when Andrew began paying back that money, and why.’

‘Does it matter?’Jacob asked. ‘Maybe he just had a sudden prick of conscience.’

‘The other thing I’d like to know is *why* he stopped paying? Was it because he knew the old man had died?’

‘Again, does it matter?’ Jacob asked.

‘Not really, I suppose. It’s just that …’ Bernie looked at Emma. ‘Shall I say?’

‘Yes,’ Emma said.

‘It’s just that … well, we know when Freddie Gesson died, and we know when the shop was put up for sale – it was all in *The Mercury* – and very soon after that your dad had his stroke … and we wondered, your mother and I, if there could be any connection between those events. That might sound a bit ridiculous to you, but …’

'No. Oh God, no. That makes *complete* sense.'

'It does?'

'Well yes. It's almost a textbook case. All that stress, the secrecy, keeping it from Mum, from you; then suddenly he's freed from it. People can keep going for years under the strain of work, then when they retire and they no longer have a reason to *be* stressed … they go to pieces.'

'All those headaches and that grumpiness,' Emma said, 'and not wanting to talk, and shutting himself away in his office; and the way he was on the day of Rose's funeral. I think you're right, Jacob.'

Bernie nodded. 'Yes, there is all that, but I have a feeling there's something else.'

'To which only Dad has the answer.'

'Yes. Come on, Emm, let's go inside.' Bernie took hold of her arm and pulled her up from the seat.

'Just one more thing before we go,' Jacob said.

'What, darling?'

'South Africa. You will come, won't you, Mum?'

'Yes, I'll come.'

'And you, Bernie? If you want to …'

'I'd love to, of course I would, but …' He looked questioningly at Emma. 'Maybe not yet.'

'No, best not right away,' she said. 'Oh, Bernie … to be away from it all, in the sunshine, with Jacob and Naledi and …'

'You will be; but now, we must get back.'

Slowly they walked across the lawn and stepped into the lounge, Emma first, then Jacob. Constance and Andrew, seated side by side on the sofa, looked up as they entered. Bernie, following, closed the door firmly behind him.

'We need to ask you a few questions, Andrew,' he said.

'Oh? Wha … what about?' He's nervous, Emma thought.

'The money you paid out over all those years. Where did it come from?'

'From my personal account, of course.'

'And you began paying it when?'

'Why do you need to know that? Does it matter?'

'It might. Please answer my question, Andrew.'

'No. I won't. Stop playing the barrister, Bernie; we're not in court.'

'No, but we well could be if you don't answer my questions here. Believe me, I have enough evidence to take this to a …'

You don't, Emma said to herself, but Andrew doesn't know that.

'To what … a tribunal of some sort?'

'Possibly, or … there are other avenues. Don't forget, Andrew, I do know the law.'

'Oh, I know you do.' He scoffed. 'I also know that you are quite a passable actor.'

Emma looked appealingly at Jacob. If these two go on sparring like this, we'll get nowhere, she hoped her look was saying to him.

'Dad, I think you should answer Bernie's question.'

'Do you?'

'Mm.'

'Well, funny that you should be the one to prompt me, Jacob; it was because of you that I began to pay that money back.' He paused, waiting for a response. When none came, he raised his eyebrows, looked fleetingly at Constance, then fixed his gaze on Emma and Bernie, 'Oh, does that not make you curious, you two great solvers of mysteries? Um?'

'Andrew dear, just tell us.' Constance patted his hand.

'Yes, go on, Dad, tell us.'

'I began paying back the money the year you were born.'

'Oh …'

'Did you not make that connection, Emma? I am surprised.'

'Just get on with it, 'Jacob said.

'I now had a son, a beautiful little boy. And when I looked at him, in the hospital a few days after he was born …'

'I am here, Dad, you can talk to me directly.'

'I prefer to do it this way.' Andrew said, glancing up at Jacob.

'Okay, if you want.' Jacob shrugged his shoulders and turned away. He's hurt, Emma thought. She so wanted to go over to him, but Andrew was speaking again; she would hear what he had to say first.

'When I looked at him,' Andrew said, 'I felt … I wished I'd not done ... what I did. At the time I had felt no guilt at all. I needed money, more than I had, to put into the business that Bernie and I had started. I didn't want to be the poor relation, the lame dog, I wanted to be an equal partner and to be that I needed to put in an equal share of money.'

'You didn't.'

'Easy for you to say that, Bernie; you *had* money, you'd always had money. *You* didn't know what it was like to want things, to strive for them.'

'Oh … Please, Andrew, spare us the violins!' Bernie turned away, disgusted.

'He did give the money back, Bernard.'

'Yes, Constance; thank you. And that brings me to my next question: when did you stop sending out those envelopes … and why?'

'Oh, Bernie, is this necessary?' Emma was finding this grilling uncomfortable.

'You said you wanted to know, Emma.'

'Yes, I know I did, but … could we do this later?'

'Oh, for God's sake, no!' Andrew barked. 'Let's get this *interrogation*' – the word came out with a snarl – 'over and done with. Now!'

'Are you sure, dear? You really shouldn't let yourself get so worked up.'

'No, I know I shouldn't, Connie. "Have another stroke, Andrew, and then that's you out of the way." '

'Nobody wants you out of the way, Andrew,' Bernie said. 'We just want to know the truth … and then we can all move on.'

'Oh yes, do let's move on!' Andrew said, his tone light and sarcastic. 'Let's decide what punishment this dreadful man shall have for the heinous crime he has committed.'

'Dad, stop this. Please. You're doing yourself no favours behaving like this.'

'Oh, *you're* sitting in judgment on me now, are you? My expensive, public school-educated son.'

'No, Dad, I'm not.' Thankfully Jacob is not rising to the bait, Emma thought. 'It's just that … Look, if there's anything else we ought to know I think you should tell us now.'

'What was the question? It was such a long time ago, I've forgotten.'

'When did you stop paying and …'

'Oh yes … and why. Well, that's easy. I read in the paper that the old man had died, and that the shop was up for sale. Therefore … no need for further payments. You do realise, don't you, that I paid back over the years … oh, must be ten times what I'd taken. They made a lot of money out of me, those people.'

'Oh, Andrew, how can you …?' Emma could feel her stomach knotting.

'Jesus! I can't believe you said that.' Jacob shuddered. 'You're like those guys who say slavery was a good thing ... because a few middle-class African-Americans now have a comfortable life-style! Oh God.' Jacob's face showed the disgust he felt. 'Any sympathy I might have begun to feel for you … Well, you've dealt with *that.*'

'Sorry, but you wanted the truth … and now you've got it.'

Jacob looked out of the window, Bernie, fists clenched, up at the ceiling; Emma fixed her eyes on Andrew's face, searching desperately for even just a tiny glimmer of remorse somewhere in his features. There was not one; he could have been a stone statue sitting there, for all the humanity he was showing. She felt cold inside; silently the tears began to roll down her cheeks. Not bothering nor caring to wipe them way, she slowly moved her eyes from Andrew to Constance, sitting beside him, looking down at his hand in hers.

Sensing Emma's gaze, she looked up. 'Shall I make us all a nice cup of tea?' she said, attempting a smile.

'Yes, do that,' Emma said, her voice hoarse, 'I'll come and help you.'

'I'll put the kettle on,' Jacob said, and he was out of the room before Constance could protest.

'Which only leaves you, Bernie,' Andrew said, sourly. 'Are you going to stay with the pariah? Or are you going to bolt, too?'

Emma, on her way to the kitchen, paused, stood still, waiting. She daren't look at Bernie. The silence stretched.

'Neither,' he said, his voice without expression. 'I'm going to lock the car; I've just remembered that I didn't do it.'

Without another glance at Andrew, nor even a flicker of his eyelids towards Emma, he walked out of the lounge.

He's leaving, she thought. In seconds she could be with him; they could *both* get into the car and drive way …

CHAPTER THIRTY-EIGHT

He had to get away. If he'd stayed God knows what he would have said, or done; he could see himself pulling Andrew to his feet, backing him against the wall and whacking him across the face.

As for Emma … if he'd gone into the kitchen to say goodbye, the way he was feeling he could have ended up lifting her off her feet and carrying her out to the car!

The van coming towards him honked its horn loudly and swerved. Christ! He'd been driving on the wrong side of the road! For how long? He had no idea. Probably just a few moments, but they could have been his last ones; luckily the van had been the only other vehicle on this stretch of road. Bernie pulled the car swiftly over to the left hand lane. Even though he was trembling now, he knew he must keep going, get himself home, then see if he could think logically through the mess that they were in, the mess that he, Bernie, had created by acting so stupidly, so hot-headedly. Why the hell had he gone back and made that scene? There were a dozen different ways he could have dealt with the situation … but no, he had blazed in like the hero in some third-rate film!

The Chigwell house was cold and empty; Jackie was at work and the central heating, off in the middle of the day, had not yet kicked in.

Bernie switched it on, full, and took a bottle of his favourite whisky and a tumbler into the lounge: he shouldn't really be drinking; he needed a clear head if he was to sort out what he should do next.

Oh, what the hell; he poured himself a good measure, screwed the cork back on the bottle, sat down on the sofa, and downed it in one.

So ... what now? Yes, okay, maybe they could manage for a while, he and Emma … because, the strange thing was – he reached for the bottle – Andrew did not appear to know that they had become lovers. How could he not have been aware? Was the man so self-confident – or so self-deluding? – that the idea of his wife, totally moulded into the woman he wanted her to be, could possibly be unfaithful to him, had never even crossed his mind?

'Bastards, both of us,' he said aloud, re-filling his glass.

He drank deeply, feeling strangely sober: there would be no more blundering in, as he'd done today. He would wait, until Emma was ready; let her go away first, with Jacob. Would he, Bernie, go ... to South Africa? No. No. That would mean more deceit; there had been enough of that.

When she came back, when Andrew was well again …

CHAPTER THIRTY-NINE

'Mu-um, kettle's on.'

'Coming.' Emma let go of the chair-back she had been holding on to and walked into the kitchen.

'Do you want your tea in here,' Constance asked, 'or will you be going back into the lounge?'

'Er … I don't know.' Emma wished she could be like her sister, calm and seemingly detached from the drama of the past few hours; Connie had always been like this in times of crisis, carrying out everyday tasks as if nothing untoward was going on around her. 'I'll stay here,' she said, almost collapsing onto the nearest chair: she suddenly felt unbelievably weak and tired; she doubted she could make it back to the lounge in one piece.

'Jacob tells me you're going to South Africa with him,' Constance said, brightly, looking round at him, lolling against the counter.

'Oh. Yes. Well, I'm thinking about it.' Had she said, definitely, that she would? So much had happened, it was hard to remember. She would like to go with him, but …

'You *must* go,' Constance said. She put Emma's mug of tea down in front of her. 'Even if it's just for a short time. I will look after Andrew for you.'

'For me? Do you think I care what happens to Andrew … after all he's done?'

'That's why you need to get away; so that you can see things in perspective.'

'Auntie Con's right, Mum. You're too close to everything here.' He stood upright, walked over to the table.

'I wish to God Bernie and I had never looked at those wretched notebooks. If he hadn't wanted the names of those stockists of …'

'Mum. Stop.' Jacob put his arms around Emma's shoulders; she leaned back against him. 'You're coming to South Africa with me. There's so much I want to show you … and guys there I want you to meet.'

'It must be a very healthy life, on a farm,' Constance said.

'Oh, it is.' Jacob squeezed his mother's shoulder, gave Constance a smile. So, as she thought, Connie doesn't know about Naledi, or Jacob's new job. Well, if he doesn't want to tell her … More deceit. Is this how it will be? It's going to be hard remembering who knows which lie. Clever Andrew, *conniving Andrew,* keeping his deceit going all these years!

'It can only do you good, Emma, going out there.'

'Yes, I expect it will.'

'And, if you wanted, Bernard could come out and …'

'Bernie?' Emma's heart did a flip. She didn't dare look at Constance.

' … although it will probably be good for both of you to be apart for a while.'

'Well …' Emma gave a faint laugh. 'I don't see why …'

'My dear girl, I do know what's been going on. I'm not a fool, you know.'

'I never thought you were, but …' They had always been so careful when Constance was around: no touching, no looks exchanged. 'I'm sorry, Connie, if it's upsetting you …'

'I'm surprised it didn't happen years ago; Bernard has always – what's the expression? It's rather coarse, but it says it all – had 'the hots' for you.'

'Auntie Con! I'm surprised at you.'

'Yes, well, we're all full of surprises, aren't we? I presume you knew, about your mother and …?' Jacob nodded. Constance turned back to Emma. 'So … you will go back with Jacob, Bernard will return to his business, and may or may not visit you in South Africa … and I will take care of Andrew.'

'That sounds like a very good plan, Auntie Con.'

'Thank you, Jacob. At times like this, you need a plan. I've always found that, even if you don't stick to it.'

'How you can sit there, Connie, talking about *plans* when I don't understand what's going on *now*! I mean … I had hoped that Andrew would at least show some remorse, some *regret* even, for what he'd done … But no, not a word! That horrendous thing he said about the shopkeeper *benefiting* from the break-in! As if we should all forget about the crime he'd committed, and pat him on the back for returning the money! You seem to understand him, Connie, so if you can, tell me what that was about, other than showing himself to be a vicious, nasty, uncaring man ...'

'I think he was trying to be kind,' Constance said.

'Kind!?'

'He was giving you a reason to leave him.'

'By being horrible about the people he'd robbed?'

'He doesn't want you to pity him.'

'He needn't worry there,' Jacob said.

'Pity him?' Emma said, scornfully. 'For what, for having to lie and cheat to get what he wanted?'

'You don't now, dear, but you might later, and he couldn't live with that. You know what a proud man he is.'

'Too proud to say he's sorry. If he is.'

'When I stole food for you, I didn't say sorry when I finally got caught; I didn't want anyone to see me as weak or pitiful. I needed to stay strong, in case … in case I had to do it again.'

'Oh, Connie …'

'That does make a sort of sense, Mum. I've seen that in my … on the farm, with workers who have stolen things. They're ashamed, but they don't want others to see it.'

'Yes,' Constance said, getting up. 'Enough of this recrimination, I must see to lunch.' She opened the fridge and took out a large plastic box. 'We'll start with soup; I've some lovely leek and potato that I made yesterday.'

'Oh, Connie, how can you think about …?'

'Because if I don't, no one else will, and we all need to keep ourselves properly nourished at a time like this.' She shut the fridge door. 'Especially Andrew. I must take him his tea.' She poured out a cup and took it through to the lounge.

‘I’ll see to the soup.’ Jacob walked over to the counter; he began to prise open the plastic box.

‘I couldn’t eat anything, not even soup,’ Emma said. ‘... and as for all of us sitting around the dining table …’

‘D’you want me to go and speak to Bernie, see if he wants to eat?’

‘Bernie’s gone. Didn’t you hear the car? I doubt if he’d want anything anyway; it’s only Connie who’ll want to eat. Cooking food that’s good for you and eating it has always been her way of dealing with things.’

‘It’s positive, Mum, and it serves a purpose … as will your coming to South Africa.’

‘I’m not sure, Jacob.’

‘Mum. You’re coming.’

‘I need to have a think first.’

‘You can think there, for as long as you want.’

‘Yes, I know that, love,’ she said, ‘but I still need a think here first. And I have to speak to Bernie … and much as I don’t want to, to your father.’

‘Don’t let yourself be swayed into staying here.’

‘I won’t.’ She smiled at him. ‘And you’re not going to start bossing me around either! I’ve had quite enough of that for one lifetime, thank you!’

‘Mum … as if I would.’ He began looking round for a pan big enough to hold the soup.

‘Good.’ She mouthed him a kiss. ‘Now I’m going to wrap myself up warm and go down to the allotment again.’

‘I’ll come with you.’

Emma shook her head. 'No. Thank you, darling, but no; I need to be on my own this time.' She smiled. 'Besides, you have the soup to see to.'

* * *

So, was that it? Done and dusted. End of.

Garry looked at the envelopes on the sofa and the banknotes on the table. They were his, all of them. No doubt about that. His, not Paula's, and not those guys who'd been in that Christmas Club all them years ago. He still hadn't counted all the money; he'd had that quick count with Paula that time, 'cept for what was in the two envelopes he'd stashed away in his jeans' pocket. He'd not shown them to those clowns in Islington either; well, they'd seen enough, and anyway, one envelope was much like another one ... wasn't it?

A cold shiver went through him: what if they *did* get the coppers onto him after all ... and *they* wanted to see the money! They wouldn't, no. Would they? Jesus, he was getting paranoid! Best thing he could do now was ... Spend it! Put it into *things*. Yeah, that's what he'd do, he'd take one of his mates and they'd go up West, and he'd buy ... No, he wouldn't take a mate, not even Baz. Who ever thought having money would be a problem. He knew one thing he wasn't going to do: he wasn't going to put it in a bank: Grandad wouldn't have liked that, his money going in a bank.

He reckoned Grandad would be having a smile to himself ... somewhere, wherever he was. And he'd be pleased with him ... 'cause he had done the right thing. He'd paid back that Raven guy, and he'd not hurt him none - Grandad wouldn't have liked that; he didn't like violence.

He collected all the notes together, in two piles, put rubber bands round them. Until he could spend them he had to keep them somewhere better than under the seat in his van; having to bring them into the flat every time he came home, in case the van got broken into here in the car park, was doing his head in. It had to be somewhere in the flat, somewhere they'd not be noticed.

He got up and walked into the kitchen. He opened the fridge and took out a beer. In the fridge? No, too obvious, and it had been done before, more than once; he'd seen it in films.

There was an empty Weetabix packet on the worktop. 'That should have gone in the recycling!' he could hear Paula saying. She was into all that stuff, in the shop and in her flat. 'All right, I'll do it,' he said aloud, grabbing hold of the box, starting to squash it flat, like she'd shown him. 'Bingo!' he said. 'Yes!' He took the box into the living room, stuffed all the notes and the envelopes into the waxy lining of the box, folded it over so the money wasn't showing, closed the cardboard top and put the box back in the cupboard next to the jar of Branston's and the packet of spaghetti hoops.

He took his beer back into the living room. He sat on the sofa and pulled back the tab. He emptied the can in one long, satisfying drink, wiped the froth off his mouth with the back of the hand and put the can down on the floor. He leant back on the sofa and shut his eyes. All them lovely twenties; and all of them his. He could light a fag with one if he wanted. Or light one just to see the flames; they was only paper. Oh, Jesus! He sat up straight. No! Them new plastic notes they was bringing in ... Oh, fuck! He was going to have to get rid of *his* notes sharpish. It was only fivers and tenners to begin with, and only a few of his were tenners ... but you can bet your life it won't be long before twenties go the same way. There was no keeping any of it: he had to start spending. Big time. Now. He leant back on the sofa again. Okay, where should he start? Wheels, yes; that would use up a good bit. But not just yet; give it a few months. So ... what else? What should he buy first?

* * *

Emma had no idea how long she had been sitting on Adam's rustic bench, but the winter sunshine had now faded.

She had been right to come; the allotment had always been a good place for thinking. Putting into practice the mindfulness exercises that Jacob had shown her, she had sat upright, gently breathing in and out. It had been an effort, concentrating only on the rhythm of her breathing, not allowing her mind to stray to the myriad of thoughts bombarding it.

Her heart rate slowed and her tense shoulder muscles relaxed; she began to feel calmer. Perhaps now she could think logically again. Jacob was right, she needed to get away … from Pengate, from Bernie, from Andrew; from all that had happened in the past couple of months … and before.

Would time and distance heal the wound that Andrew had inflicted upon her? She had loved him once, deeply, but what she felt now was both sadness – was this how his dream ended, being shunned by his wife and son? – and anger. Paying back that money had not really made things better: had Andrew seen it as the equivalent of serving a jail sentence? Should he still be punished for his crime? Emma shuddered at the thought of Andrew in gaol: no, she could never do that to him. Could she forgive him? Could she live with him again? And then there was Bernie: she did love him, but could she - did she want to? - start a new life with him? Throw away all those years that she and Andrew had had together. Could she do that? They were about to become grandparents, for goodness sake!

It wouldn't be easy but away from everything here, and with Jacob and Naledi's help, she began to feel that she might find the answers.

And in Pengate … Constance would take charge. As she had always done, to an extent that Emma had not fully appreciated until today.

As for anything else …

She hoped Garry Wade would use that money wisely; it had cost them all so much pain. She never did discover exactly how much it was; not that it mattered now, but he did have a right to know that his grandfather was not a blackmailer. Should they keep in touch with him? She had a feeling that Trev might. Would Trev go on working with Bernie?

‘Stop, Emma, stop,’ she said aloud, her fingers spread, keeping the questions at bay; she had thought enough, more than enough, for today.

‘Live in the moment, Mum,’ Jacob had said.

She brushed off the few leaves that had landed on her lap, stood up, relaxed her shoulders, took in one more deep breath and slowly let it out. A chilly wind began to skitter the dry leaves at her feet. She pulled her coat tighter around herself.

If she didn’t go back to the house soon Connie would begin to worry. Any minute now she would be sending Jacob down here to bring her home.

By the gate to the allotments there was a tiny clump of late snowdrops, half-covered in fallen oak leaves. The flower of hope, Connie called them. A line in a song came to her, about having ‘hope in your heart’ and not walking alone. Sentimental slosh, Andrew had called it; yes, well, she wasn’t going to worry too much about what Andrew thought, or said; not now. Emma found the words comforting and suddenly, like a ray of sunshine bursting through grey clouds, she could see a new life opening out in a way she had not thought possible in these past dark months: South Africa, Naledi, a grandchild: she might even be there when the baby was born!

She locked the gate and walked slowly up the lane.

* * *

‘She’ll be in the air now.’

‘Yes.’ Constance put the cup of tea down on the table beside Andrew’s chair.

‘Will she come back, do you think?’

‘She will,’ Constance said.

Andrew lifted the cup, put it back on the saucer. ‘I do love her, you know,’ he said.

‘And she loves you.’

‘Does she?’ He looked up at her; she was standing close to his chair.

Constance nodded. ‘Yes, she does, but ...’

He kept his eyes fixed on hers. ‘But if we are to make it work ... I shall have to change the way I ...’

‘Dear Andrew.’ She smiled at him. ‘We shall all have to change.’

‘All of us, Connie?’

‘Oh yes,’ she said. ‘Drink your tea before it gets cold.’

THE END

AUTHOR'S NOTE

When I read a novel I always want to know which places in the story are real and which are not, so, for those of you who also like to know, Pengate, Brockwood and Hewers Hill are fictional, as is *The Oaks.* There is, at the time of writing, no *That Music Place* in Almeida Street, Islington, but, in Upper Street, there is of course the *Kings Head,* a well-known pub and theatre, where I have spent many happy hours (and had plays produced by the legendary Sydney Golder). The play in the book is, however, fictional, and I have taken liberties with the food and the seating there, as I have with the café furniture at the hospital in Stevenage.

This book was, for the most part, written pre-Covid. It seems strange that in 2015, when the book is set, our everyday conduct was so different. I find myself wondering how Emma and Bernie and Andrew - and Garry. too - would behave if their story was happening now.